Black Kitten

by Melissa Sweeney

ISBN 978-1-7338679-2-4 (pbk)

ISBN 978-1-7338679-3-1 (eBook)

Chapter 1: Brooklyn Harbor

Vincenzo used the blunt side of his crowbar to bash in the head of the last Klansmen he had to deal with that day. He didn't know if he'd knocked out the last of the devil's teeth or he'd ripped his throat, but the bastard was choking on something.

He wiped the crowbar on the nearest shipping crate. Around them were wooden crates carrying everything from Ford cars to alcohol imported from Montreal. To better conceal them from the public, a half-dozen cargo ships were moored at the docks. Most had been emptied of contraband, but they still creaked and swayed in the New York Harbor, masking the noise of a bent crowbar.

The Klansman's hood fell off. "Stop," he pleaded. "Please."

Vincenzo whacked him good again.

"You weren't sorry when you were bad-mouthing us in the back of that bar." That was Luis, one of Vincenzo's acquaintances. He was standing by the other two Irishmen they'd walloped that evening. Even after being indoctrinated into the Family, Luis had yet to learn when to keep quiet. Vincenzo envied that. "Bet you feel really ashamed of yourself now. Bet you didn't think we were part of a gang."

The Klansman spat out blood. "You Pope-fucking wops are all the same, ruining this country with sin."

Vincenzo rolled his crowbar to its pointed side and smashed open the man's temple. His blood almost flecked his shoes.

Dominic sat the man upright. He was Vincenzo's other associate for the evening, one he'd known longer than Luis. Since Vincenzo had hauled these men into his car, Dominic hadn't spoken a word. He simply did what was expected of him and beat, tied up, kidnapped, and drove these disgraceful human beings to the docks under Vincenzo's orders. It helped that he was taller and more muscular than most Italian men, as Vincenzo was irritably short and Luis looked and acted like an eighteen-year-old when he'd just turned twenty-one.

Dominic rolled up his sleeves and checked his watch.

"I know," Vincenzo said, reading his mind.

"Eight minutes until three," he said anyway.

Vincenzo sized up the Klansman's injuries: a broken leg, a snapped pinkie, and a cracked eye socket.

He handed the crowbar to Luis, done with his work. "Dominic, help these men into the car. Luis, drive them to Bethany Hospital for the usual treatment."

"Pay for the treatments, sir?" Luis asked.

"All of it." He helped lug one of the now unconscious men into the trunk. "Drop them off saying you found them on the side of the road."

"Good Samaritan work. Got it, sir."

Despite the time warning, Vincenzo arrived at his next appointment fashionably late. It was at the other side of the docks, where factories spat out coal and imprisoned immigrant workers in their depths. The sea air was intoxicating, mixing with the smell of metal and sullying the view of Lady Liberty with ash.

As Dominic opened his car door, Vincenzo looked up at the factory. He'd grown up hearing horror stories about factory workers. His father would come home with scrapes that never healed and dirt that never washed out.

Vincenzo, age six, would implore that he help take off his father's work boots.

He'd get kicked for it.

Vincenzo, age twelve, demanded that he work in the factory alongside his father so he could also provide for their family.

He'd be beaten for it.

Vincenzo, now age twenty-three, was at odds appreciative of his father's work in the past and haunted that the work had wrecked him.

But it'd led them to the work they now shared. Vincenzo, a prominent figure in Brooklyn's strongest gang, and his father, just a few hairs above him in rank and power.

Just a few. His father wanted to forget that detail. Vincenzo held onto it like a prayer.

Dominic opened the steel door for him. On the first floor, immigrants worked shirtless to keep the cargo company going. They worked partly for the company, partly for Vincenzo's father, as he dealt with how much came and left through New York Harbor. Vincenzo had some control of it, if you could call such a percentage "his." He handled where the shipments travelled to. Speakeasies, privately-owned clubs, pansy bars. He made sure the drunks kept drinking and the cops butted out of the status quo.

Walking up to the second floor, Vincenzo took a breath before entering into his father's office.

Personally, he believed his father relished in stereotypes the way aristocrats relished in wines. He wore the suits, smoked the cigars. He greased his hair back with so much oil, you could smell it. He wanted someone to call him out for it, to utter, "He's in a gang, right?" and for him to blow smoke in their face and call them a slur. His dark office of filing cabinets and oil-lit lanterns told you exactly who he was, or what he aspired to be: a gangster boss, someone as feared as he was respected.

As if someone like him could be both.

Severo DiFiore closed the filing cabinet he was searching through. *"Where were you? I said to be here by three."*

Alone like this, his father only spoke in Italian. One would think he wanted to preserve the language. Vincenzo knew he did it to flaunt his ability to speak a language of which he had forty years of practice while Vincenzo had grown up speaking the English of New York.

"I was taking care of business at the docks," Vincenzo said, gesturing for Dominic to stay outside where it was safe.

His father pointed at the seat in front of his desk.

Vincenzo did as told and sat.

His father continued standing. *"What've you been doing this past week?* Nonna's *been worrying."*

A lie. *Nonna* hadn't complained a day in her life, even while having a man like Severo as her son.

Vincenzo said, *"I was working. This week's shipment has me over Harlem, Brooklyn, and Queens in the same day."*

"Then work faster and get home to her sooner. You're in charge of her now."

He didn't have the guts to point out how wrong he was, so he said, *"I can't be there all the time for her anymore. I'm working full-time. She's able to live at my house by herself."*

His father flung up his hand dismissively. *"I don't care what you do, just make it happen. Now, what's happening in Queens? How're the bars you're working at?"*

"Everything's running smoothly."

"And Brooklyn?"

"Fine."

"And Harlem?"

He dug his nails into the top of his hand. He wasn't ready for where this conversation was leading to. *"Fine."*

"And are you still dining at those sissy clubs?"

Vincenzo internalized his building rage into a misunderstanding. A misunderstanding they'd been arguing about for ten long years, ever since he started wearing trousers outside of the house because they felt nicer on him than dresses.

"Out of all the bars I run," he explained cooly, *"pansy clubs make the most money. People love them, especially in Harlem."* He knew he should've stopped there, but he couldn't resist selling his work. *"They're the most profitable when it comes to liquor sales. Rich clients love the atmosphere, and everyone who goes there wants to drink and have a good time."*

"With freaks," his father said. *"You know damn well why you enjoy going to those freak shows. It's not about the money. It's not about the Family. It's about getting a kick with faggots who dress like women. You must feel at home, 'ey, 'son'?"*

Vincenzo didn't know why he tried. Some people didn't get it, and most people wouldn't. He just wished that, if the ignorant refused to listen, they'd shut up and not bog down the Earth with noise. He guessed that was too much to ask.

Winning the final say, Severo handed Vincenzo documents stamped with his insignia. *"I want these jobs done by Friday. It'll keep you from loitering around those fucking bars for a goddamn week. Finally get you doing your job again."* He leaned over the table. *"You're not still seeing that cholo faggot, are you?"*

Vincenzo broke the skin over his scarred knuckles.

His father honed in on his son's nervous tic. *"You are, aren't you? Even after I told you not to."*

His heart beat fast. He knew he couldn't change him. Both Luis and Dominic had told him that. But it wasn't like he could rid himself of his presence. Family bonded him to this man who treated him as the shit on his shoes rather than his one and only son.

Though he probably thought differently on that last part.

Severo stood up with his hand raised, palm out, the way he'd ended so many arguments back at home. Vincenzo had learned to react quickly when he saw it, but it never became less shocking.

Vincenzo jolted backwards. His chair screeched out. He reached for the gun behind his back but prayed he didn't have to use it today. He already had blood on his hands.

His father snarled at him, the animal ready to come out. "You'd risk endangering the Family for someone like that? Your own mother, me? You'd risk it all for that harlot?"

"She's not a harlot," Vincenzo said back in English, "and you don't control who I see. Campo does."

"And Campo, what, agreed to this?"

"He did, so if you have anything to say, take it up with him. I'm sure he'd love to hear it."

That earned him a slap in the head, but he expected worse. Honestly, he never thought he'd be able to tell him off. He'd been practicing in front of his mirror for weeks.

He pulled up his slacks, salvaging what little dignity he had left. *"I have a meeting to attend to in Harlem. If we're done here, I need to head off."*

"Fuck you. You'll leave when I tell you to leave. If I catch you spending nights in that bar when you don't have to be there, I swear to God. Now, get out of my sight."

Vincenzo was already leaving. Tucking his coat close to his body, he shoved out of the door and almost caught his sleeve in the doorway.

Dominic jumped at how loudly the door slammed. "Did—"

Vincenzo stomped down the stairs. He'd learned to tame himself around his father, but since he'd found his place in the Family, that control had been dwindling. Nowadays, he could manage a half-hour per week around his father. Any more and he didn't know what he'd do, but he wouldn't be responsible for the property damage he'd cause.

He didn't allow himself to react until he and Dominic distanced themselves from the building and almost made it to the front gates.

Then, unable to hold back, he growled into a shout and punched the nearest wooden crate.

He knew he'd hurt himself when he didn't feel the initial bite of pain. The itch turned to numbness. Blood dripped between his injured knuckles.

Dominic took out a handkerchief.

Vincenzo turned it down. "He doesn't know anything about me. He doesn't get to suddenly care who I choose to be with."

Dominic didn't argue. "You said you had a meeting in Harlem. That's not true."

"It is."

He bit his lower lip. "Your father warned you about visiting that place."

That place, the seemingly worst place for someone to tarnish their Family name. As if prostitution and the bullying of businesses to make sure they bought your bootleg was something to be proud of. He hadn't even *met* her, yet he acted like he knew what she meant to Vincenzo.

Vincenzo got into the car. "Take me to the Black Kitten."

Chapter 2: Backstage Tequila

Sylvia sat backstage in the Black Kitten, finishing off her second tequila cocktail, visibly shaking.

Tonight was an okay night. A mood had hit her a few hours prior. After dry-heaving in the bathroom and drinking away her feelings, she started shivering about the infinite what-ifs that might occur in her melancholic life.

She swirled the last sip of her drink in her glass. She was staring into her vanity mirror. Smudges of makeup blemished the glass and blurred the self she wanted to see. Behind her was a brick wall from where the stage music reverberated. Unused pulleys, ropes, and curtains masked her from the other side of the Kitten. She couldn't wait to get back to it. To surround herself with life. To feel herself breathe again with the music and crowds. But first, she needed to get herself breathing without almost fainting.

She sighed into her hands. Nobody had to tell her how dangerous this was, being with a gangster like him, but God wanted to challenge her daily. Ever since she was a child, it'd been like this. Not that she complained. Knowing bad luck would forever trail her like a puppy was somewhat comforting, like she knew what she'd be getting into every day. She only wished He'd better equipped her for the aftermath. She wondered if Vincenzo ever felt like that.

High heels clicked up behind her. She saw the person in the mirror but turned so as not to be rude.

Laurence rounded his big hands around her cheeks. He was dressed up for tonight like she was, though he had a different motive and better taste. His wig was immaculate in golden waves, and with bolder eye makeup and jewelry to complement his dark skin, he looked like a Southern princess.

He made her face him. "I don't see it."

"See what?" she asked.

He angled the corners of her lips with his thumbs. "Ah, there's a smile. Now I don't have to worry about you drinking yourself to death back here."

"Can you stay like this for the rest of the night, marionetting me until I can smile on my own?"

"I don't think anyone can make you smile, love. You need to find something that makes you happy, or less sad, in your case." He took a seat beside her. "What's wrong?"

"Nothing in particular. I broke my nail this afternoon and cried for an hour."

"Oh, sweetheart." He played with her short wig, sprucing it up in ways she couldn't. "What's there to do?" He admired both of them in the mirror. "I can curl your wig. I can do your makeup like mine. I know how you love that. If nothing else, I can stay with you tonight, make sure you don't dip too far off the deep end."

"No, thank you. I'm good, really. I'm just tired. I didn't get much sleep last night."

Laurence clicked his tongue. "Well, if you want to hang out tomorrow, or sit on the phone and talk, we can do that as well.

Mitsuko and I are still planning that shopping trip into Manhattan. *Mitsuko!*"

Said woman came in and lounged against the door with her ankles crossed. She had one hand stuffed in her pants pocket, the other holding a glass of chilled milk, a palate cleanser between songs. "Laurence's paying for gas, I'm paying for his dessert. I said *one* dessert, sir," she pressed when Laurence whined. "You're more than welcome to come. In fact, I command you to."

"I know you've said no," Laurence said, "but we have room in her car, and we'd love for you to be there."

"I'll think about it," Sylvia said. "I'm feeling a lot better, really." She tried smiling on her own. "See?"

Laurence frowned at her attempt. "If you're not up to perform today, we can tweak your schedule. Like anyone out there cares what we do." He nodded towards the back door, to the floor of drunks hungry for a naked ankle.

"This isn't about a certain Mr. DiFiore, is it?" Mitsuko asked. "I swear, Sylvia, you shouldn't waste your time on someone like him. You deserve better."

"Here, here," Laurence said, toasting Sylvia's glass.

"I don't know," Sylvia said. "I *do* like him."

"Oh, I like him, too," Mitsuko said. "He's such a great guy. Let me name off all of his good traits." And she stared dead-eyed into Sylvia's soul.

"I don't trust him," Laurence said. "It's awful, what he does. All that killing and torturing."

"He doesn't really do that," Sylvia said. "He told me."

"I'm sure he's telling you the truth," Mitsuko said. "Just like how he doesn't kill any of us when he's ordered to."

"Mitsuko, don't say that!" Laurence put his hand to his mouth as he looked off to the side. To their left was a vanity table embellished with flowers and hand-written notes. It depicted young children of every shape and color, every group New York called to. Sylvia remembered their names and faces but had forgotten their laughs.

Laurence kissed Sylvia's head. "I don't want to see you getting hurt again, baby. Not again. You've dealt with too many men like that in the past."

"Men I've chased out of here with my knife," Mitsuko added.

"I know," she said. "Thank you for looking out for me. I promise I'll stay safe. He'll keep me safe."

A muffled *bang* pulsed through the backstage door. It sounded like a drunk slipping on his own weight, but the next voice she heard made her spill her glass and stand up quicker than Laurence.

Bobbie Martínez, the owner of the Black Kitten, came in with a cigarette in his mouth and his baggy eyes wide. "Raid," he said.

He always chose his words carefully—being short and blunt helped him run the best pansy bar in Harlem for over two decades—and that one word held everything that needed to be said. Sylvia had survived a dozen raids. Some people didn't.

The luckiest part: most of tonight's patrons weren't dressed up. They'd only be harassed by the officers and asked to leave the premises. Those like Sylvia and Laurence—ones who dressed up because they needed to and ones who dressed up for show respectively—were the targets of these raids. They were designed to burn down the one place a gay happiness could safely grow. And nobody cared about it but those who were burning.

Three officers had come to raid them. Sylvia didn't recognize them, but they all walked in like they belonged there. One even blocked the stairs, trapping them.

"Everyone, sit down," one of them said. "Get out your IDs."

"And lift up those dresses," another said, taking out his baton. "Better make sure your IDs match what's underneath, otherwise you're coming with us."

Sylvia hid behind the door. She knew how she lived was considered illegal, but what the police could do to pansies like them not only felt illegal but immoral and unjust. It certainly didn't make anyone in the bar feel like they had their best intentions at heart. It felt like they were bounty hunters.

One police officer, the one who hadn't taken his hand off of his belt, pointed at Sylvia. "You. Come here and show me your ID."

She stopped breathing. The patrons of the Black Kitten turned to see who'd been chosen as the first victim of the raid. Some whispered, others hid behind their tables. Laurence and Mitsuko were seething behind her like angered mothers, their hands refusing to let her go.

She tightened her shoulders, making herself appear smaller. "It's in the back."

"Well, then come over here," one officer said. "We'll be able to tell real quick if you're a real woman or not. The rest of you, up against the wall. Lift up those dresses for me. Yeah, just like that."

Laurence squeezed Sylvia's arm, showing her that he wasn't leaving her side. Mitsuko's glare felt sharper than the knives she kept hidden in her boot.

Exhaling through her pounding heartbeat, Sylvia stepped forwards.

Footsteps echoed down the stairs. Two sets, each paced and rhythmic. The officers thought nothing of it and continued their harassment. Regulars of the Black Kitten who knew the gaits hid themselves better.

Pushing aside the two officers like obstacles, Vincenzo DiFiore entered the Black Kitten out of breath and furious. He'd come in with Dominic, who stood as his bodyguard in case anyone thought Vincenzo wasn't a threat. Since he and Sylvia had become a "thing" a few months back, most police officers stopped coming to the bar. They knew what Vincenzo would do if he caught them hurting what he valued.

The cops must've been new, for they smirked like they were on his level. One even strode up to him. "The place's closed, pansy fucker. Go into the alley and fuck a dog while you wait."

Vincenzo didn't say anything. To anyone, he would've appeared bored, when inside he must've been burning alive. The look in his eyes told her that. That, and his knuckles were bleeding over the floorboards.

Bobbie ran behind the counter for his gun.

"Didn't you hear me?" the officer asked, now towering over Vincenzo. "Leave. Now."

She debated whether or not to run back into the back rooms and hide. With Vincenzo here, she knew her life was no longer in imminent danger, but she didn't want to see anyone get hurt.

"I said—"

Vincenzo whipped out his pistol, rammed it against the officer, and fired.

The bullet missed him by a centimeter and ricocheted into the wall. Dominic barreled into the second officer and knocked him down easily. Bobbie took out his gun and aimed for the last officer, but when Vincenzo had fired, the whole of the Black Kitten screamed and scattered, creating a perilous shooting range.

Vincenzo tackled the officer and straddled him. He pressed the barrel of his gun deep into his heart. "This's *my* bar," he said. "I *own* it. I *run* it. I can very well *sleep here* if I desire. You can't. Your commissioner can't. That goddamn chief of police can't so much as walk these streets with the parameters I've set in place."

"Y-you can't do this," the officer said. "You can't *shoot* at an officer, are you mad? I'll have you arrested, all of you."

"Try," Vincenzo dared. "Put a pair of cuffs on me, try to send me away. See what that damn Officer Wood says when you bring him the man who gives him his salary. I bet he'd unlock the cuffs himself and fire you on the spot. But don't take my word for it. After all, I'm just a pansy fucker, aren't I?"

When the officer began squirming, Vincenzo leaned over him so his eyes were level with his. "I am Vincenzo DiFiore, right-hand man to Mr. Campo d'Antonio III and sole proprietor of the Black Kitten. This's *my* bar and you have no authority sticking your three-inch cock through the door. So before I take you out in the lot and castrate you with a dirty razor, get the fuck out of my face and out of my bar." To solidify his speech, he fired two shots into the floorboards and spat in the cop's face.

That name—Campo—and the way Vincenzo addressed himself as part of his Family finally drove the officers out. It looked like they wanted to fight for their lawful harassment of the innocent, but the frazzled officer called them back upstairs and left.

Sylvia foolishly expected applause for Vincenzo's knightly efforts. He'd just saved them. He was their hero. But no. Those who hadn't run away whispered about him in the dimly lit corners of the bar, wary of his violent heart.

Laurence broke the silence and marched up to him. "What the *hell* is your problem?"

He was likely the only person who could speak to Vincenzo like that without taking a bullet. Dressed up, his confidence was boosted to astonishing levels.

Vincenzo fixed his collar and sleeves. "Did they touch anyone?"

His forwardness took Laurence aback. "No. They were about to interrogate Sylvia when you came in."

Vincenzo's eyes combed through the Kitten for Sylvia's.

She came to him with her hands folded in front of her. She couldn't look away from his bloody knuckles.

He hid them in his pocket. "You okay?"

She nodded. "Your hand."

She almost reached out to touch him. When she'd become more than an acquaintance, he'd asked her one thing: Don't ever touch him when he wasn't "prepared." She never asked what that meant because she understood. No physical intimacy in public. No signs that he liked someone the world saw as tainted.

It was the most romantic relationship she'd ever been in.

With the intruders gone, Vincenzo lowered his guard and took off his hat. Bobbie collected it and his overcoat, slimming him down and removing some of his armor. Dominic, now unneeded, fell into the shadows and awaited further orders.

"Can I get some alcohol to wash this with?" Vincenzo asked. He'd said it as a question, but everyone knew it as a demand, albeit a softer one than usual.

Bobbie picked a bottle from the shelf and poured it over the wound. The only indication that it hurt clenched into Vincenzo's jaw. Then he doused it out and let his skin heal.

"Girls, we're going to halt your performances for tonight," Bobbie said. "Take some time to relax. I'm going to make sure everyone's okay."

"Good luck with that," Mitsuko said under her breath.

As he dished out water with drops of alcohol in it, Sylvia turned to see Vincenzo waiting for her. He was standing near his favorite booth farthest away from the stage. With its dark curtains and low lights, it looked like a cave from where a predator would stalk its prey, nothing like the open tables throughout the basement.

She slipped in beside him. She never knew whether to keep her hands on the table or in her lap, which one made her look less nervous than she actually felt.

The stage musicians started up a jazz piece. Patrons walked around, too nervous to sit and too nervous to leave.

Vincenzo slouched in the velvet, unbothered by it all. He used his non-injured hand to light a cigarette from his pocket. The smoke wafted to the chandelier.

He always looked so nice to her, even with the way he was. Always clean-shaven, dressed to the nines in dark sweaters and shiny shoes. She wanted to run her hands through his black and curly hair, but she didn't want to make him uncomfortable. They hadn't kissed for days after their first date, and when he wanted to express his love, he did it behind doors or in the dark, a hidden love shared between them.

Sometimes, she dreamed of kissing him in public. Really push the boundaries set on them. The look he'd given her the day he confessed, the softness in his eyes, the licking of his lips, that stayed with her on the lonelier nights.

"So," she ventured, "what happened?"

He blew out his smoke. "I had a meeting with my father. It didn't go well."

"You said you have a weekly time limit for how long you can stomach being around him."

"I surpassed it."

She did the math in her head. "It's only Tuesday."

"Isn't that the way." He exhaled another lungful of smoke for five long seconds, then passed the cigarette to Sylvia. "Sorry, I only have one."

"That's alright." She shared it as quickly as possible. The filter had teeth marks in it.

"I'm sorry you had to see that," he told her.

"It's alright. I'll take gunshots over a raid. Just not both at the same time."

"It's sick what they can get away with. I'm going to have to talk with that police chief again. You'd think they'd listen after my first warning."

"Nevertheless, it's good to see you again. I haven't seen you in a few days."

"I've been busy. My father wanted to know about that, too, but in less so kind words."

"Did he say something hurtful?"

"Every word he spits out is hurtful to everyone but our Family. And even *then*," he tacked on but didn't add anything more.

"Not to be rude, but if I never met him, I wouldn't complain."

That finally got him to smile. When he'd first started courting her, she'd been unsure if he knew how to smile. Then, one day, he got her talking about her dreams, about moving to Manhattan and living peacefully as herself in a little house on the river. When she'd turned to ask him about his dreams, he'd been smiling. Perhaps he'd been laughing at her. Still, it was nice knowing he could find the happiness she was always searching for.

"I don't blame you for thinking badly about him. The way he talks about you, if he weren't my father..." He stopped before he said something he'd regret. "How've you been? How're your friends? They still hate me, it seems."

"They don't hate you."

He tossed his head back.

"'Tolerate' is a better word. They respect you, but their fear might be eclipsing their perception of you."

"It doesn't matter." He side-eyed her. "What do they say about me?"

"That you're a handsome, sophisticated gentleman who's taking care of me."

"I wish you wouldn't lie to me."

"I wish you'd believe me when I told you the truth."

He kept his eyes on the ceiling, overthinking her words to make them sound truer than they were.

It was a lie, of course, but putting out the notion that her friends liked him was best. It wouldn't help anyone if she said they feared him the way they feared a beast.

"Oh, I wanted to ask you," he said. "I'd meant to ask you this when I got here, but I didn't expect to see a wagon pulled up to the curb."

"What's wrong?"

"Nothing's wrong. I wanted to know if you'd like to dine at my place tonight."

Her lips parted. "Where?"

"My house," he said, like it was that easy to say. "Luis, his wife and daughter, and Dominic are going to be there, along with my grandmother. None of them will be a problem. Just don't pay any mind to Luis' wife. She's more a man than he is."

"But would that be okay?" she asked. "I don't want to impose."

"You're always welcome over." He leaned in, making their private conversation even more private. "My boss, Campo, he appreciates you. He's nothing like my father. He approves of our situation and says I can be with you if I'm ready to deal with how much of a target that'll make me. That's how it works with any woman or associate you become intimate with. If you don't want to come over..."

He moved back, hand slipping off the table.

After all the years of her being with men and having her heart broken by them time and again, she'd never met a family before. It felt too personal, even though they were lovers now. And to dinner, something she knew would mean a lot to him...

She held his hand, eager to feel his warmth again. "I'd be delighted to come. I only want to make a good first impression."

He warmed up her hand. "I've told my grandmother all about you. She loves you."

"Oh. I'm glad to hear that." The amount of love Vincenzo had for his grandmother—*Nonna*—showed in the stories he recounted. He actually had good things to say about her, memories untainted by trauma.

"You can come dressed as you are," he added, "unless you wish to change. We'll leave in about an hour. Is that alright with you?"

"Of course. Let me tell Bobbie and the others."

But as she went to tell Bobbie and the others, she saw them spying on her from across the lounge. They were pretending to get drinks when all of their attention was locked on her.

They looked at her the same way her mother had looked at her husband's funeral: terrified, a little misty-eyed, and unable to stop death from claiming their loved one.

Chapter 3: Dinner at Nonna's

Mitsuko had once told Sylvia that if a man asked you to meet his family, you needed to decide right then if you wanted to marry him or not. Meeting a person's loved ones, entering new territory with strangers who've heard everything about you. The quick once-over to see if you amounted to a suitable bride.

Sylvia almost puked in Vincenzo's expensive car.

He helped her in while Dominic buckled into the driver's seat. She'd kept on her womanly garments and tucked them underneath her rump as a nervous tic. Seeing herself reflected in the mirror, outside breaking so many rules, it made her dizzy, but what could she've done? See Vincenzo, in his home, meeting his *grandmother*, dressed like a stodgy gent? She walked to the Kitten every evening in a cardigan ripped from nervously stretching out the seams and pants too short for her long legs. That wouldn't do, for neither her standards nor his.

Vincenzo slid in beside her, staring at her with a question on his lips.

"Why, uh, why do you wish for me to come over again?" she asked to fill in the silence.

"I thought it was about time you met my family. My *nonna*, to be precise. Her real name is Enrica, but she likes when people call her '*Nonna*'. And Dominic and Luis are basically family with how much they're over. They live across the street from me. You know Dominic."

She waved at him through the mirror. He nodded back the same way. A man of few words.

"*Do* you *want* to come over?" Vincenzo then asked.

"I feel unfit. I don't want her to hate me."

"She won't, I promise. She's very, how should I say, *old-fashioned*, but I've explained everything to her, so she should understand. She also doesn't speak much English, so I'll do my best to translate."

"Does she know that I'm...?"

Dominic eyed her through the mirror, then pulled into the street, leaving his thoughts behind.

Vincenzo rapped his fingers on his thighs. "She knows as much as she can. She'll call you by your name. She'll call you a girl. She knows that much."

"Oh, that's good. Your family's good."

He snorted.

"Part of it is," she corrected. "It's still better than mine. I don't even think my father knew this side of me before he passed away. He just thought I liked dressing like a fool."

Vincenzo crossed his leg. "My offer to meet your mother still stands."

Sylvia's heart drained into her stomach. He'd asked this a few weeks ago on one of their dates, then, after learning about her childhood, every time family was brought up. To want to meet someone so wicked, she couldn't fathom it. It must've been that gangster blood in him that made him want to face his adversary head-on. "I'm afraid of what either of you will do once you meet."

"I wouldn't hurt her. Unless she spoke badly about us. Or you. Or got in my face. You said you haven't spoken to her in some time."

"She kicked me out at thirteen."

"Ten years, then." He faced the window, likely reminiscing about his childhood and contrasting it with hers.

She did the same, watching Harlem blur through her window. She felt it come back to her, that child's heart. A spot of rain had broken through the sky and dampened the streets black. She almost rolled down the window to air out her filling head.

It was true she didn't speak to her mother, but she did write her letters. About one a month, each a page long written in her finest handwriting. She'd seal each one with a kiss before tossing them into her alleyway garbage, never to be opened again.

She hoped things would be different with Vincenzo. She hoped to find a new type of love with him. One she wasn't frightened of.

He lived in a house completely different from what she'd envisioned. She should've known by his wealth that he lived extravagantly, but this defied her expectations.

Dominic pulled up to a pastel-colored grandmother's house. The lacy curtains and flowers in the window boxes, the gardening tools scattered across the front porch. There was a "welcome" sign hanging on the door knocker that looked handmade. Everything other than the three immaculate cars parked in the gated backyard showed off nothing but an elderly woman's Brooklyn mansion.

"Is this your grandmother's house?" she asked as they pulled in.

"It might as well be. I own it, but I'm never here, so she has free access to do what she pleases."

She heard *Nonna* before she saw *Nonna*. Her voice travelled through the house, down the stairs, then something thudded against the door, shutting it as Dominic went for the handle.

She was shorter than her grandson, with whiter hair and baggier eyes. She got around on a cane but used it more as a third leg, pushing herself forwards and crushing Vincenzo in a hug. Her wrinkled hands looked strong and worn and lovely as they massaged his back.

Vincenzo spoke to her in Italian and kissed her cheek, then said in English, "*Nonna*, this is Sylvia."

She interrupted him.

"I said I was bringing her. She's *Sylvia*, remember? My partner?"

She gave him a bizarre look, then squinted at Sylvia. "Oh!" she said, and embraced her as if she were her own granddaughter. Despite looking almost seventy, her strength was that of three Dominic's. "Sylvia, Sylvia. Welcome, hello! Vincenzo, he loves you. Every day with him."

"*Nonna*, please," Vincenzo said, and ushered everyone inside.

Winding up the wide staircase and nailed into the walls were dozens of photos and trinkets from the past. There were priceless Italian flower vases and porcelain dishes too high for Sylvia's nerves, and everything smelled like a mixture of mothballs and maple syrup, each one trying to mask the scent of the other. She did spot a few pictures of Vincenzo's family, but no baby pictures, strangely, none until he was about sixteen or seventeen, looking like a hooligan in street clothes too big for him.

"Sir!" Luis ran out of the parlor and took Vincenzo's hat and jacket. "Nice to see you again. And nice to see you, miss." He kissed Sylvia's cheek. "Good to have you for dinner."

Sylvia curtsied. She'd met this man twice in a rush of hellos and how-are-yous in the Black Kitten's back room. He was a bit flighty for her liking, but she appreciated someone so in love with being alive.

Sitting in the parlor sat a young woman swaddling an infant. She must've been Ana, Luis' wife. Sylvia had secretly overheard about their shotgun wedding last year through a conversation between Vincenzo and Dominic, though she didn't pry as hard as Mitsuko begged her to.

With this as their first introduction, Sylvia gave Ana a quiet nod in respect.

She didn't nod back.

"I'm Luis Gallo, ma'am, as I'm sure you remember, and this's my wife, Ana, and our little one, Sophie. We live just around the corner."

"It's nice to see you all."

Nonna spoke in Italian.

"*Nonna*, please," Vincenzo said again, and rolled his eyes to Sylvia. "She wants to know if she should make a bed for you upstairs. She can't take the stairs nowadays, so she has to stay down here."

Nonna retaliated.

"Your knees are weak, *Nonna*. I'm not arguing about this again."

Sylvia smiled at how lively his grandmother seemed compared to him, but she wondered if he still wanted her to spend the night. She never had, never thought she could. She had nothing comfortable to change into.

Nonna muttered to herself and went to check on the stove when she saw Vincenzo's hand. She asked him a question.

He hid the cuts in his pocket. "It's not a big deal."

It was to *Nonna*. Drawing her cane like a sword, she struck him in the back and yelled at him. While he did brace for the attack, he didn't raise his hand or shout at her. One good hit to his hand, however, and he bit his cheek to keep from yelping.

Sylvia couldn't stop herself. As everyone migrated to the kitchen and laughed at *Nonna's* anger, she confessed to everyone, "I wish to eat here more often."

"It does get a little wild here, I can tell you that," Luis said. "About once a week, we all come together and have dinner like a family. It'd be swell if you came along more often. I'm surprised it took this long for Vincenzo to invite you over. You've been an item for a few months now, right?"

"About, yes."

Vincenzo pulled out a seat for Sylvia, and she let go a relieved sigh when he chose the seat next to her and not one across the table.

Before she'd been kicked out, Sylvia's parents had cooked what they wanted and ate in separate rooms. When she did venture to eat, her mother would make note of how much food was on her plate. She'd transformed her hunger into a want, not a need. It made eating as an adult an arduous task. Now, whenever she ate out with Laurence and Mitsuko, she'd serve herself last, too afraid to speak up about what she wanted.

She couldn't do this at Vincenzo's house. After saying a prayer, they all served one another and passed plates teetering with food. Bruschetta, clams and pasta, asparagus, corn, seasoned potato wedges, bottles of Italian wine and squid with tentacles fried and curled. They asked her what she wanted and handed her mountains of food they expected her to eat. She kept passing everything over to Vincenzo without stopping the conveyor belt.

"Aren't you hungry?" Vincenzo asked, looking at her empty plate. He offered her a plate of bruschetta.

She picked an end piece. "Thank you."

"Don't be so closed off," Luis said. "You're family now. You get a cut of dinner."

"I have to apologize. I'm not used to this."

"What, dinner?"

She knew he was joking, but she left him unanswered. It felt rude, saying she wasn't accustomed to eating meals. She didn't want to damper the mood.

Luis wiped the globs of potato off of his face. "I'm sure you'll like this." He personally handed her a dish of casserole. "It has beef, sausage, peppers, noodles. It's super filling even after a few bites."

"Thank you." She filled up her plate. She didn't know what was ruder: not finishing all of it or pushing through and giving herself a stomachache. She paced herself with small sips of water.

She followed most of the table's conversations. Between *Nonna's* Italian and Vincenzo's, Dominic's, and Luis' atypical profession, she simply smiled and nodded while she ate. Vincenzo dined wholly on clams and pasta and saved the bread for Luis, who tore through it like main dishes. Dominic's plate consisted of meats, while Ana ate mostly vegetables. Sylvia made notes on how each man preferred his meal.

Not that she'd ever make dinner for them. When she found herself with a man, he'd pay for her food in exchange for her services. She'd never cooked for him like they were something more.

She grinned into her bite and hid it with her napkin. It was nice to dream.

"So, you two met at that bar over on Lenox Avenue in Harlem," Luis said. "You're a performer, aren't you?"

"I play the piano, yes."

"That's right. That's when you bought that grand piano for her, right, sir? He got three guys to heave it into her apartment. Crane and everything. He sectioned off the whole street for that operation. Dominic, you were there, right?"

"Busted my finger getting it placed," he said, bending said fat finger.

"That must've cost a penny or two. What was it? Five hundred, six?"

"Five-fifty," Vincenzo said, and the amount weighed down on Sylvia's neck. Back in May, she'd come home to a crane outside of her Sun-facing windows. She thought she was being evicted in the most dramatic of ways. To see Vincenzo guiding the crane into position, and with that grand piano. What had her neighbors thought? They vocally hated her, now they must've had more questions than vitriol for her and her expensive tastes.

"Do you like it, ma'am?" Luis asked her.

"I'm...grateful for it," she worded carefully. "I play it on my days off."

"I haven't been around the bar much, but if you can give me your schedule, I'd love to hear you perform. Vincenzo always goes on about the songs you play. He says you're a savant."

"I never said that," Vincenzo said, and Sylvia hoped he both had and hadn't said that, that he hadn't boasted about her too much, but that he had bragged a tad.

"Dominic said you were good," Luis went on. "You *and* your friends. Mitsuko and, what's his name, Laurence?"

Dominic recoiled at their names. To keep from engaging, he chewed the meat on his plate rather than the fat of the conversation.

"Yes, they're two of my best friends," Sylvia said. "Mitsuko often dances and Laurence is a phenomenal singer. We play almost every night, but nowadays, I'm taking more breaks to keep myself healthy."

"What do you mean?" Ana asked.

Her voice fluttered Sylvia's heart. She sounded like her mother, too judgmental for the conversation at hand.

She relaxed the muscles in her neck. "I've been working seven days a week for a long time, trying to keep myself financially safe. Since I met Vincenzo, I've been wanting to take a step back and focus on myself."

"And all you do is play piano?"

Vincenzo eyed Ana through his bangs.

"I do," Sylvia said.

"And you do this at your bar, or club? They're called pansy clubs, aren't they?"

"Sometimes."

"Ana—"

"So, why do you dress like a woman when you were born a man?"

Vincenzo slammed his glass onto the table and stood before the new mother. "If you're going to start this again, Ana, you can leave! In fact, get out. Get the fuck out of my house!"

Baby Sophie burst into whimpers and pulled on Ana's dress. Ana, keeping her pride, stood up and balanced the baby on her hip. She almost held Vincenzo's gaze before she ultimately chose to storm outside, heels clicking down the hall.

All the pep in Luis' face crumbled into his lap. "Oh, jeez, sir. I'm sorry. We did talk about it, just like you said. I thought she'd be good, or at least quiet."

"I specifically told her not to talk about it."

"I know, sir. I'm real sorry."

Sylvia set down her fork and tried to speak up for herself. For him, for his family. She had to impress them and show that she could handle being...

Whatever she was to Vincenzo.

Whatever she had the right to be.

Luis rubbed *Nonna's* shoulder and thanked her for the meal before jogging outside to find his wife. "I'll be right back!"

As *Nonna* and Dominic continued eating with the least amount of noise possible, Vincenzo turned to Sylvia. "Can you come with me?"

He said it in his question-demand way, not asking her so much as pleading that she listen.

They left upstairs, two steps at a time. She tried pinning which rooms were the bathrooms, closets, and bedrooms. She'd never been in a house so large. She mentally thanked him for not giving her a tour.

His bedroom had a fireplace, bathroom, and king-sized poster bed among antique furniture. It smelled like his usual cologne but stronger, more tangible on her tongue. A cross and a picture of *Nonna* watched over his bed, and an old-fashioned chamberstick sat at his bedside for extra light. On his writing desk was a signed baseball from his favorite team, the Brooklyn Dodgers, kept in a glass case. A dozen faded signatures marked the prized ball.

This, this better suited what Sylvia had in mind.

Vincenzo ran his hands through his hair as he paced to his windows. His room overlooked the harbor, silhouetting him in silver light.

When he caught her standing in the shadows, he motioned to his bed. "You can sit here."

Softer than a demand, but she sat regardless, her hands sinking into the plump comforter.

A shadow brushed between her legs and leapt onto the rug.

A kitten wagged its tail like a puppy as it meowed through a bundle of argyle socks. It was pure black aside from its white-tipped tail and the mark on its right cheek. Its eyes were like two full moons as it stared at Sylvia.

"Oh, sorry." Vincenzo tried and failed to catch the cat. "This's—"

"*Mezzanotte*," Sylvia said. She even said it with the preferred Italian accent. He'd told her this cat's name once, and she was sure to remember it. The way he said it was the same way he said "*Nonna*."

When he realized chasing her was not only fruitless but amusing to Sylvia, he gave up and let Mezzanotte destroy his socks. "Can I ask you something?"

"You may."

He went back to the window. "Are you sure you're ready for this type of life? I know I've asked you this before, but if you truly want this, life will only become more difficult for you. I've seen the way other men are with their wives and mistresses. It's not a good life."

"If I could be so brazen, I'd ask you the same thing. It seems my commitment to you is becoming a bother."

"You're not a bother."

"You don't have to lie. I've heard about this way of life in the newspaper. Gangsters with mistresses on top of wives. I believe they're called 'molls'. I don't mind becoming a moll."

Vincenzo's upper lip curled like a lemon peel. "That's not who I am. The Family might control everything I do, but they can't control how I feel, and that's not how I feel about you. You're—"

Whatever he was going to say caught on his tongue, and he pulled back and covered his mouth.

Sylvia fell back. She didn't mind being called such promiscuous words. Sweetheart became tramp, then whore, then worse when men found out what she looked like underneath her dress. It hurt. It destroyed her in her teens, mentally and physically scarring her, but she'd learned to deal with it because, in the end, that's all she'd ever be to most men. She was a fetish for them to hate or lust after. Both, if she was so terribly unlucky.

"Well," she said, "may I ask you...if I'm more than a friend to you?"

Vincenzo said, "I feel like we skipped being friends," and Sylvia didn't know why, but out of all the answers he could've given her, that was the one she wanted to hear least.

She went to touch him and bring him to bed, then brought her hand back and patted the bed instead.

He came to her, slowly but willingly. His weight leaned her into him like the Moon with its ocean.

"I said the wrong thing," he said. "I don't know how this works. This 'courting' business is...foreign to me. I feel like I should be working at the docks with my father and furthering myself in the business. Not this."

"Would you like me to lea—"

"That's not what I meant," he interrupted. "It's the opposite, really. If I could stay like this..." He placed his hand over hers. "With you, I'd stay in this room forever. Romance wasn't something I thought I wanted, but now I have it, and I don't want to ruin it with my inexperience."

"Did I change how you thought about love?"

"*Change* it? You beat it with a bat and left it in the streets, bleeding its heart out into the gutters. I'm ravaged because of you."

Sylvia kicked her heels together. "Neapolitan ice cream."

"Pardon?"

"Neapolitan ice cream is my favorite desert. I like eating bites with every flavor on the spoon."

"Oh. Did you want that tonight?"

"No. You said we skipped being friends. Let's step back and change that. My favorite food is Neapolitan ice cream. What's yours?"

"Clams, and pasta," he said, pausing between each food group. "Usually together, though I can eat them separately."

"With Parmesan?"

"Of course."

"Favorite animal?"

"Cats. I used to have this picture book of big cats that I toted around with me everywhere I went. You?"

"Little animals. Gerbils and squirrels. Spiders and rabbits."

He gave her a look. "One of those things is different from the rest."

"I think they're cute, especially tarantulas."

"Good Lord."

She smiled, and as it tugged on her cheeks, it didn't feel as forced as usual. Maybe it was because she was looking at Vincenzo's own smile and seeing how he was desperately trying to hide it.

"Then, let's see, how about *least* favorite thing to listen to on the radio," he asked.

"Oh, when the dreary men talk about politics. I haven't the time for them. Coolidge is a fine man, but a forty-minute conversation about the upcoming election is just too much when one is preparing for sleep."

"I understand. Mine are the advertisements. They make a baseball game run for three hours long, sometimes four. I've timed it. I hate it."

"They're powerful, aren't they? They tease you with what you might want and showcase all the good it'll bring you. Suddenly, I think I really do need that new dish soap."

Vincenzo smirked and brought himself closer. Their hips were now touching. "Favorite color?"

"White."

"Black. Favorite season?"

"Summer."

"Winter." He moved closer, lips breathing on her ear. "Favorite part of a man?"

She tried to give an answer, but she was grasping. She couldn't think. "Well, it depends on a variety of factors. A pretty face is always good."

He hummed against her skin, a laugh, barely audible.

"Then there are, uh, more personal aspects. Shameful ones."

"And those are?"

"J-just look in a mirror." She crossed her legs, but it made things worse. "You have all of them."

"Do I now?"

She tilted her head back, silently begging for more. "And you?" she breathed. "Favorite part of a woman?"

"Hmm, what's there to say?" He tasted her throat. "Like you said, there're factors that play into it."

"I'm guessing the neck is one of them?"

"I was guessing it was one for you." His teeth grazed her skin. "Was I right?"

She felt herself melting into him. How had he guessed it right? She hadn't gone into her bedroom fantasies with him. She thought it would turn him off.

"I suppose face is what comes to mind first," he said, "but a woman's legs tempt me so. Yours are so long, they go all the way up." A shy hand traced up her thigh. "Sometimes, I wonder where they end."

She lost control of her lower half and parted her legs. "Is there anything else tempting you tonight?"

He pulled back and stared at her lips, then her eyes. Then he conceded to his desires and kissed her.

His kisses always came with a price. He'd grimace at first, then glance around the room before committing the act. Sylvia couldn't fault him for this, but a trepidation did creep in every time they found a moment together. She guessed it never really went away, that fear of opening yourself up to someone and wondering if they'd end things halfway through because of what they found.

He didn't. Working with her movements, he backed her into bed, pressing his lips to hers. The kiss turned into a wider, more passionate one that opened Sylvia's mouth and sunk her into the sheets with love. Her brain fogged over in dreamy, sweet emotions before she felt and heard Vincenzo moan into her mouth. At that, she snapped to attention and imprinted that rare sound into her brain for later.

Vincenzo broke off to catch his breath, and Sylvia looked up to him examining her like so many others did, unsure of what move to make next.

Trying to help, she reached between his legs and went to touch his warm spot.

He jumped back and smacked into his bedpost.

"Sorry." She pulled her dress back over her knees. "I know. Your limits. I forgot. I'm sorry."

He covered the place where she'd touched him. She'd learned months ago that his arms and hands were okay, but places like his face, neck, chest, and unspeakable parts turned to pressure points on her fingertips.

To her surprise, he came back to her, albeit with less drive to bed her and more barriers she could no longer cross.

Her short-lived confidence burned away with shame.

"It's not because of you," he promised. "It's me. I thought I'd be okay with it by now. 'It' meaning being with someone, not, well, you know."

"We don't have to rush things. Some men are never ready for it, and that's okay. I'm just happy being wanted."

"How dismal."

She shrugged it off. "Should we go back downstairs?"

"I'd rather not." He fell into his bed's indent.

She copied and sat beside him. She followed his bed canopy's folds and curves all the way down as if they were waterfalls stilled for this one moment of peace.

"Sylvia."

"Yes?"

The bed shifted. "Do you...like being with me?"

"I do."

"Then may I ask you a rather offensive question?"

A heavy air settled around the bed. He hadn't prodded her about the question one would have about being with someone like her, but his hesitance, his fear. She felt that, every time. She knew why men acted this way around her. She'd hoped Vincenzo would never feel compelled to ask her such things.

She braced herself for the worst. If he asked something rude, she'd muster up the resolve to tell him off. She'd promised her friends she wouldn't be mistreated again.

He pulled on his sweater collar. "If I didn't have the luxuries I've been able to acquire, if I weren't so powerful, would you still want to be with me?"

Her mind drew the blankest of blanks. The answer was so overt to her. What she struggled with was why he felt compelled to ask her. Surely they'd been together long enough that their relationship forwent that of a prostitute and her enquirer.

She said, "If you had nothing but the clothes on your back and a titleless name, if you treated me with the same respect you do now, I'd be forever smitten by you."

Vincenzo gave her his full attention, cheek squished against the blanket in puzzlement. "Really."

"Truly."

"You're lying."

"I wouldn't lie about that," she said, and meant it.

He stared at her for a three-count, then nodded to himself, reaffirming something that he always knew. Then he kissed her and stole away her held breath.

Chapter 4: Fatherhood

Vincenzo woke up alone and confused. Confused because he was alone, since the last thing he remembered was watching Sylvia sleep at two in the morning and wondering when he'd garner up the courage to ask her to move in with him. Now she was gone, like she hadn't been there in the first place.

With the worst possibilities tearing into his mind, he checked the bathroom, then his balcony overlooking New York Bay. The air was thick with haze and hid the Statue of Liberty from view. He almost kicked down his door when he saw Mezzanotte sleeping against the frame and Sylvia's letter by his bedside.

He'd learned about Sylvia's love for letter-writing after their second date. After driving her home and walking her to her doorway, he'd found a letter in his pocket. Instead of saying her true feelings, she'd often write them down and tuck them away in pockets or underneath drinks. His heart always jumped when he discovered a new letter.

With his heart recovering, he unfolded his new letter.

Beloved—

I wanted to thank you so much for such a wonderful evening yesterday. I slept soundly for the first time in months, and it was from you resting by my side. Like a husband, someone beloved. (See above.)

Last night—you and I, I'm reliving those moments in my mind, dreaming about your lips on mine and the way you held me. Your love is different from any type of love I've felt with another man. I'm beginning to feel overcome by you. How did you put it? Ravaged. What a violent word for what we share.

I want you to know that I had a difficult time leaving your bed this morning. Your relaxed, sleeping face is a sight to behold. Alas, I need to be elsewhere. Mitsuko and Laurence had wanted me to go into Manhattan with them today. I hope I didn't wake you. Your grandmother has given me some bread and tea. I don't think she understood me, but please give her my regards for last night's meal. You have a beautiful family here. I'm humbled to think I'm now a part of it.

Good morning, my love.
Sylvia

Vincenzo read the note three more times, hearing her voice, making sure he didn't smudge the wet ink. Then he placed it in his bedside drawer along with all the others.

He flopped back into bed and covered his eyes. Every decision he'd made last night came back to him. What had he done with her? He remembered kissing her, hovering over her like some lech. He'd *kissed* her *neck multiple* times. He hadn't even asked her permission first. He'd be sure to ask that from now on. It was what she would've wanted.

He hiked up his legs. He was so destructively in love with her. Everything she said unapologetically broke his heart and bonded it back together in sappy love. She was so delicate, yet so put together, like she could live through anything, even him, and come out on the other side unscathed. He couldn't see himself with anyone other than her. He prayed that she felt the same way.

Scooting Mezzanotte out of the way, he walked downstairs and found *Nonna* reading the newspaper in the parlor. She'd made herself tea and had his breakfast ready for him on the kitchen table.

He snuck up to her armchair and kissed her cheek. *"Good morning,"* he said in Italian.

"Good morning, my little bean. How're you feeling? All better?"

"I am. I'm sorry for excusing myself and not coming back down to say goodnight. I was heated."

"That's okay, but don't let all that food go to waste. Take some for your lunch and dinner, and bring some to your friends. Sylvia was up at five this morning. It's too early!"

"*Why were* you *up at five?*" He picked up his plate and joined her in the parlor. "*Sylvia said you made her breakfast.*"

"*I did. She barely ate anything last night. I wanted to make sure she was fed.*"

"*Do you like her?*"

When she didn't speak up, he said, "*So you don't like her.*"

"*I wouldn't say that. She's a proper young lady with good manners. A little shyer than I imagined, and taller.*"

"*I suppose.*"

"*Spanish?*"

"*Italian and Spanish share a lot of commonalities, Nonna. She picks up on Italian words easily.*"

"*It's just that it would be better, is all, among other things,*" she added, but smiled into her tea. "*I can tell how much you like her. Is she kind?*"

"*Kinder than she should be.*"

"*That's good. I'm glad you finally found somebody. I was worried you'd be alone forever.*"

"*Well, you don't have to worry about that now. At least for the foreseeable future.*"

"*Speaking of futures, now's the time to start thinking about marriage.*"

He pulled his cup from his lips. "*What?*"

The candlestick phone in the kitchen rang. When *Nonna* sat up to get it, Vincenzo held up his hand and went to answer it himself. He hated hearing her grunt as she used both hands to lift herself onto her cane. She deserved to relax on these mornings.

He picked up to something crashing on the other line. He heard a baby's cries and someone struggling to live before he got a sense of who was calling.

"Luis," he said, calming the irritation in his tone.

"Vincenzo!" he yowled. "Is your *nonna* there? Is she free?"

"We're eating, so no."

"Aw, jeez, sir. Can I come over for a moment? Sophie's crying like a, well, baby, and I don't know what to do. I've tried changing, burping, feeding, rocking, singing, and nothing, *nothing* is working. It's been like this for hours. I'm tired, and Ana left to see her friends."

"That doesn't sound like my problem. We're eating breakfast. Can't it wait?"

"Well, you see, sir, *Nonna's* always so good with her. Two seconds is all it takes and she's out like a lamb. Would you mind if I bring her—"

"No."

"It'd only be a minute."

"No. We're eating. You're her father, aren't you? Surely you can—"

"Nobody's ready for parenthood, sir! I'm not used to it yet. *Nonna* knows that best."

"Who's on the phone?" Nonna asked. "Is it Luis?"

"It is."

"Trouble with the baby?"

"Ye—How did you know?"

"Because it's the early morning and his wife's car is conveniently absent from their driveway." She set down her tea. *"Tell him to come over."*

—✧—

He arrived two minutes after Vincenzo hung up the phone. His pits were stained black and his eyes were pleading that someone baby his baby.

Sophie's screams were sirens that instantly gave Vincenzo a headache. She had food spilled on her frilly pink dress, which also gave him a headache, and he hoped she wouldn't stain anything in his home.

Luis collapsed into a pile of exhausted bones on the couch. *"I don't know how you women do this, ma'am."*

"It's not as hard as it looks." Nonna took her away from him and jumped her on her knee. *"She ate?"*

"Yes, ma'am."

"Pooped?"

"No, ma'am. Not yet."

"I see. Alright, little one, it's okay." She rocked the baby all the way into the kitchen, singing nonsense to her that felt oddly reminiscent to Vincenzo.

"Since when does my *nonna* know how to baby your child?" he asked Luis.

"For a while now. Sorry for barging in like this, sir. When she gets like this, when I can't control her, I usually bring her here."

"And this's a regular occurrence?"

"Kind of. You're normally not home at this hour, but *Nonna* told me that if I ever needed help with parenting that I can come here. She works magic on that child, sir, truly."

"I'm not sure how I feel about that."

"It's only until I get a better handle on her. It's hard, keeping her happy, making sure she's growing up right." He had the audacity to kick up his feet to the coffee table. Vincenzo slapped them down.

"Ow."

"You'll scuff up the grain." He sighed. "Would you like anything to drink?"

"Is it too early for scotch?"

"It is," he said, and went to pour two glasses for them in the kitchen. He had to plug his ears as Sophie continued crying, albeit in less screeches and more so in hiccupping sobs.

When he came back, he handed Luis his glass. "You're leaving after she calms down."

"Yes, sir." He took a shot and exhaled loudly. "I hope Ana didn't knock you too hard last night. We talked a lot about it after dinner, about what to say and not to say around Sylvia. She doesn't get it, so I asked her to keep her opinions to herself until she's willing to accept it."

"I appreciate that."

"It's...hard to tell her why it's okay sometimes, though, you know? I wanted to ask you about that."

"About what?"

He tensed up and, to combat his sudden nervousness, laughed. "Not that I have a problem with it, sir. We all got something different about us."

"Luis."

"I just want to talk about it, is all. Every time someone tries to ask you about it, you shut them down. We gotta learn, don't we? Who better to ask than you? We're friends, aren't we?"

"We are?" was his immediate response, and the change in Luis' face—the hurt, he noted—made him think that maybe he wasn't friends with Luis, but he valued him enough to know that he wanted to see him happy.

He faked a smile. "Kidding."

"Oh. Don't scare me like that, sir. I'm working on three hours of sleep here. But we are, aren't we? We're friends? Friends talk to one another about their relationships. They're companions, buddies."

Vincenzo couldn't see himself as a "buddy" to anyone, but he also didn't see himself with a lover or a kitten. He said, "What I have with Sylvia is what you have with Ana. There's nothing more to it. Plus, I don't have to explain how she sees herself to anybody. She doesn't either, so I don't want to hear you asking her these types of questions."

"Oh, no, sir. I get that part. What I'm worried about is her, you know? She's a good gal—not much of a talker. Ana, you know, she can handle herself, but can Sylvia? Is she okay being a gangster's gal?"

"She is." He sipped his coffee. "Turns out she doesn't care one way or the other how this'll end up, so nobody has to worry about that."

"What do you mean?"

"She told me last night that she doesn't care how I feel about her, so long as she's appreciated by somebody. It seems like she's perfectly content with a man who doesn't beat her."

"Oh. I didn't get that impression from her at all."

"She keeps up appearances in front of others. It's her defense mechanism, I believe. She's dealt with a lot of terrible things in her past, and it's made her strong, strong enough to be with me and this business."

"Got it. That clears things up a bit."

Feeling the waters settle, *Nonna* came back into the parlor with Sophie whimpering instead of flailing. She placed her in Luis' lap and pushed the curls from her eyes. *"Be gentle with her, darling, and talk to her when she's feeling restless."*

"Got it. Thank you, ma'am."

She smiled, then brought in a plate of cookies and left to clean the kitchen. Luis scoffed them down with the same fervor he had last night and let Sophie lick the icing off of his finger.

Vincenzo didn't get children. He didn't get the crying, the puking, the smells, the wetness, yet whenever he interacted with Sophie, she never smiled at him. Not once. Even when he pulled funny faces at her in private. Maybe God really didn't want him to be a father. It wasn't something he craved, as the thought of child-bearing was nauseating to him, but he wouldn't have minded showing up his father in fatherhood.

When Luis caught him staring, he lifted Sophie towards him. "Do you want to hold her? She's calmed down some. She can get more Dad Time."

Vincenzo gaped at her like some prized jewel covered in poison.

Guessing his answer, Luis handed her off.

Vincenzo buckled. He kept from dropping her, but her head, unable to support the weight, flopped back. He cradled her the right way before Luis lunged.

"You've held her before, right?" Luis asked, worried.

Vincenzo hyperfocused on keeping the baby from dying. He knew these creatures were malleable, but in their mothers' arms, they looked more secure, less threatened. "Why's she moving so much? Is that normal?"

"Yeah. Sir, is this your first time holding a baby?"

"I didn't know they felt so warm."

"They're human, after all." He played with her socks. "Do you ever see yourself having kids? I haven't seen you interested in anyone before Sylvia. I thought you were against it."

"I don't think I'd be able to have children with her."

Luis looked up at him and deconstructed that thought for too long. "Right," he then said. "Of course. Does, uh, Sylvia ever want children?"

"I just said—"

"Hey, you can always adopt! One of Ana's friends from church adopted a boy from Connecticut. Is that something that's on the table?"

"Don't place your baby-having habits on me. They're too messy, and Sylvia...probably wouldn't want one, though I'd have to ask her."

"And if she does?"

"Then I'll do whatever she wants," he said automatically, then added, "It'd take some time. We'd probably hire a nanny."

"Ah, maybe that's best. I always wondered if me and Ana should've waited, but I didn't have a choice when I found out she was four months pregnant, you know?"

"Sylvia and I won't ever have that problem."

Luis laughed heartily, and Vincenzo realized he'd been waiting for that and finally relaxed with him as "buddies" would.

They mingled for a half hour, eating breakfast and talking about nothing. Mezzanotte came down after finally waking up, then saw that the baby was here and darted back upstairs. She and Vincenzo didn't have a lot in common, but they did share their fixation/fear of small humans and how they worked.

At around ten, Sophie decided that she was too cranky to stay a minute longer and wailed for a nap.

"Yeah, she didn't get much sleep last night," Luis said. "I'll head out now. Thanks for having me over, sir."

"I didn't invite you over, but sure. Next time, come without the child."

"No way! You gotta learn how to be a daddy."

"Ew."

Instead of hugging or kissing him goodbye, Luis made Sophie wave at him before she yanked her hand away. "Talk to you soon."

He didn't know what to say to that, so he repeated the phrase and gave him a single wave. Then, after making sure *Nonna* was sitting down and resting, he went upstairs to one of his spare bedrooms and tried imagining a nursery. Just a silly look around, constructing the placement of the crib—or cribs—and thinking how it would've been better to keep the baby in his room, so he and Sylvia knew it was safe at all times.

When he started envisioning the color scheme and where he could buy rainbow wallpaper, he physically walked himself out of the room. What was he doing? He had a meeting to attend to in two hours. Why was he wasting time?

As he got ready for the day, he wondered why he thought thinking about his future was considered a waste of time.

Chapter 5: Letting Loose

Sylvia set aside her drink as she sniffed up another line of cocaine. She was behind the Kitten's bar, enjoying one of Vincenzo's many imported luxuries. He sometimes dabbled in this affair—not as often as alcohol—but enough that he could deliver ten grams a week to the Kitten without any problems from the authorities.

He hadn't introduced her to this unladylike behavior. Just like with cigarettes and alcohol, she'd been using far longer than he'd been selling. Men in her past had gotten her hooked when she was sixteen, though she was certain her mother was a user when Sylvia was but a little girl. It'd always been around her, ready to make her forget about life for a blurry night.

She threw back her head as her brain tingled with new feelings.

"Okay, I think that's enough." Mitsuko, the responsible adult for the evening, dusted the remaining powder into a glass. "Be drunk, fine. Be high, alright. Not both at the same time. You need to get home tonight."

Mitsuko, *she* had nothing to worry about. During the Great War, she'd been sent to France to help in the war effort. She was a Japanese military nurse, and a magnificent one at that, ready to help when asked. When the War ended, she applied for American citizenship and nearly drank herself to death on cheap liquor.

"I have nothing to live for," she'd said. *"What's the point of it all?"*

That's when Bobbie had stepped in. Feeling sorry for her, he'd offered her a half-hour on stage and let her keep the tips she earned. After finding her calling, she sobered up with Bobbie's help and never touched a bottle again. She always wore this beautiful wedding ring on her left hand. Everyone knew she rejected the idea of marriage—she preferred women like Laurence preferred men. Sylvia guessed she was married to her sobriety.

"I haven't had that much," Sylvia lied.

"I believe you." Mitsuko kicked her feet towards the floor. A few men tried to catch their attention from across the bar. She threw an ice cube at them and made them scatter.

"Be nice. You're so cold-hearted."

"On the contrary. I'm marvellously agreeable when it comes to rationale." She pushed back the drink Sylvia was trying to grab. "Stop meeting with Vincenzo. I'll pay out whatever he's paying you. I'll buy you a piano. I'll buy you three."

"I don't want pianos. I want *him*. He makes me *so* happy." She hugged herself. "It's nice to feel loved."

"Love's been scientifically proven to worsen your health. The ramifications are astounding. They call it 'love sickness'. And not that you're doing this, but if I'd come to America looking for someone to fix me, I'd be in worse shape than when I was dragging men out of trenches."

"I'm not expecting him to 'fix' me. Being with him *makes* me happy. And if I'm happy, I won't be sad, right?"

"You need to learn how to be happy without a man's help."

"I'm still learning how to be happy *period*."

"Name off some things that make you happy. Things, not people."

She thought on it, twirling the ends of her sideburns. "Ice cream."

"Good."

"Calligraphy."

"A great pastime."

"And piano, I think. I'm good at it and I like making songs. Does that count?"

"It absolutely does."

Laurence, who was singing a jazz piece on stage, ended his performance by kissing a man he'd chosen to duet with from the audience. The man gladly reciprocated and gave the onlookers another reason to clamor with applause.

They were notably lively tonight, the audience. No wonder Sylvia was in such a pleasant mood. Some of them kept their bowler hats over their eyes so they wouldn't get recognized, but many of them were singing along, keeping the bar's energy at its peak.

After finally wiggling himself free, Laurence beelined for the bar and poured himself a glass. His mood dribbled from jovial to apathetic until his glass was full and his spirits were empty. "I want cake."

"We don't have any," Mitsuko said. "The transformation is coming along poorly, just so you know."

"What transformation?" Sylvia asked.

"The one where we convert you into a pure, unmarried woman who isn't being courted by a rabid dog."

"It's not working, huh?" Laurence asked. "You know, nothing we say can ever convince you. Is the sex that good?"

"Laurence, not helping," Mitsuko said.

"Please, I just had a time on stage. Let me indulge in a fantasy."

Sylvia's face went redder than the cherry pattern on Laurence's dress. "We haven't slept together yet, you two, my goodness. I'm not even sure he's interested in that kind of relationship."

"Interesting," Mitsuko said. "I'll catalogue that in my growing book of 'The Unsolvable Mysteries of Vincenzo DiFiore'. In such a book includes chapters on the weird way he wears his jacket and how his outfits consist of nothing but black."

"He protects me."

"You're not protected, you're in danger!" Laurence said with a good slap to the table. "I knew a girl who once fooled around with a gangster. He bought her jewelry and clothes and purses, then he gets the boot, killed in the dead of night, and then they came after *her*, demanding that she pay them back. I never saw her again. I don't want that to happen to you, Sylvia. But gracious, if he wasn't so handsome! You have lousy taste."

Bobbie, who was a ways down the counter, filled out a dinner order for a couple and sent them away. Then he took out a cigarette and joined his friends. "Sylvia, are you good to perform tonight?"

"Of course." She sprang up like a rabbit and shook out her hair, accidentally tilting her wig out of its pins. Laurence fixed it for her before she left.

"I think I took too much."

"You got that right," Mitsuko said.

She left them be. They didn't get it. She knew what she had with Vincenzo was reckless, but she wasn't like them.

She couldn't be content with being alone or teasing men on stage and having the ability to walk away. She wanted to be in love with love and have it wake her up and fuel her day, to prove that she could enjoy herself with someone and not dread every minute of it.

Why was it wrong to want that from a man she wanted to marry?

"Marry." She must've really been tipsy tonight.

As she pictured herself in a wedding dress, she accidentally bumped into a table and spilled over a glass. She apologized to no one and tried to scoop up the drink before someone absorbed it with a napkin.

She looked up. The person wasn't a someone. Perhaps still a stranger by definition, but she'd know that mustache anywhere. "Dominic?"

It was. It was Dominic, Vincenzo's bodyguard friend, alone with a copious amount of strawberry daiquiris. Pieces of his greased-back hair were sticking up and he had red rings around his eyes. He was either plastered or drugged. Somehow, Sylvia couldn't imagine either. Were bodyguards allowed to drink?

He gave her a nod. "Evening."

She couldn't remember ever speaking to him without Vincenzo present. In truth, she couldn't recall hearing his *voice* until present. Not only a man of few words, but a man of many wonders. He should've had a chapter in Mitsuko's book. "Good evening. Is Vincenzo here?"

"Uhh...no?"

The way he slurred his words told Sylvia that he'd not only lost Vincenzo, but he also didn't know what bar he was currently drinking at.

"So, why are you here tonight?" she asked. "Not that you need a reason. Just curious."

"I don't need a reason, right? A man shouldn't be judged for where he drinks. I could walk in here and enjoy the music and nothing else. No big deal."

"I agree, I think. Like I said, I'm only curious. I didn't know you drank."

He said something that Sylvia zoned out on, but she came back to, "I'm not drunk. I mean, I'm not supposed to drink here. I'm not supposed to *idle*. It's frowned upon in the Family."

"I'm sorry to hear that. I love to idle here, especially when I was a...I don't like the word 'spinster', but 'bachelor' doesn't fit any better, does it? When I wasn't with Vincenzo, I often came here to pursue my options, if you know what I mean."

"That's not right," he mumbled, then, as if not realizing what he'd said, stammered, "Wait—shit, don't tell Vincenzo I said that. He'll tell Campo. He'll tell everyone, then I'll...I'll..."

Fear dripped down his face. He was actually worried about what would happen if Vincenzo tattled on him for drinking at the bar to which they supplied alcohol.

"It's okay," she told him. "I won't tell him. Now, what don't you think is right?"

"Nothing. I didn't mean it. I'm not thinking right tonight. Drank too much."

She smiled through the hurt. "Do you like what the Kitten stands for?"

"I know I shouldn't," he said.

"And why's that?"

He looked to Laurence and Mitsuko. "Your friends, they're good people."

"I believe so."

"Even if they're different," he clarified, "even when they dress like that, they're still good people."

"I hope so. I'd hate to learn what actually makes them bad people." She called over the waiter to fill up Dominic's drink. "Do you think it's gross?"

"The daiquiri? No, it's my favorite."

"No, us. Me. People who dress up and act differently than what's expected of us."

He held his elbows. "I'm not sure. Vincenzo would want me to say no."

"I'm not asking what Vincenzo would want. I'm asking *you*. What do *you* think?"

He covered his mouth. "I'm not sure. I'm lost."

"Lost on what?"

"Well, you and the, uh, black man, for instance. Are you the same? Is he a man or a woman?"

"He's a man who dresses like a woman. *I'm* a woman."

"Oh." His eyes grew heavy, thinking through the drunkness. "And the other one? The Asian woman?"

"She's Japanese. She enjoys the company of women and likes dressing masculine."

He covered his eyes. "This's indecent of me."

"No, it's not. I don't mind answering these questions. They aren't secrets we're trying to keep."

"One more question, then." He scooted up his chair, leaning over the table with a new passion. "The way all of you act, is that okay with you? Do you ever feel ashamed of yourselves for what you do? I only ask because I…wouldn't forgive myself if I acted like this."

"Well, it depends on how you look at it. Technically, drinking daiquiris is illegal. Your work profession that keeps the Kitten operational is illegal. This bar existing in the first place is most certainly illegal to a lot of people. Yet despite all the disapproval, they still exist. People will continue drinking and they'll continue being curious about the same-sex despite all these laws preventing us from doing so. It's in our nature to experiment with fun." She patted his back. "I'm glad you're here."

"But this isn't me. Vincenzo won't like what I'm doing."

"And what are you doing? Politely questioning us? It's okay to question things you're unfamiliar with so you can make better, informed decisions later on. Do you want to ask me anything else? I'm in a particularly chatty mood tonight."

"No. Not right now. I've asked too many questions, and my head hurts. I'll just keep watching."

"And that's okay, too. It's okay to watch the game before you choose to play."

He rubbed his pounding head. "I don't get the analogy."

To be honest, neither did she. She didn't even know what she was talking about. Why was Dominic here? He should've been dancing with everyone else. The show was about to start, didn't he know.

She left him to stew in his thoughts and jumped on stage for her piano. Upon seeing her open the hood, the crowd greeted her with applause.

Laurence amplified their cheers once he came back on stage. The lights caught on his sequins and let him sparkle like the Sun. Mitsuko gained support from regulars who loved being ignored by her. One woman screeched when she handed her her empty milk glass. Mitsuko's wink sent her into hysterics.

Sylvia started with uplifting songs she heard on the radio. The music flowed through her, coming to her hands naturally without the use of a music sheet. Laurence sang along like a holy angel while Mitsuko thrashed her body like a rag doll to the melody. The crowds hollered for their favorite artistically-inclined kitten.

After the third song in the lineup, Sylvia noticed Dominic still at his table, staring up at them. He seemed transfixed by their performance, like he wanted to leave but couldn't. He almost stood up to join in the clapping when Laurence started an unexpected strip tease that caught him off guard. He lifted up his dress and showed everyone his lacy garter belt. Dominic tripped out of the bar with a hand over his eyes.

Feeding off the Kitten's energy, Sylvia stood up to play the piano before leaving it entirely. She flounced about, then turned and walked the stage again. She posed with Mitsuko, kicked her heels, and the crowd hooted and cheered for *her*. Somewhere into the chorus, she lost all control of her body and launched her wig into the rafters. From either surprise or reverence, the crowd lost their minds with her.

Dare she say it, but she was having fun. She was *enjoying* herself. Would she have preferred if she found this high without substances? Yes, but she took what she could get. She couldn't let these highs slip away easily.

Like there, right there. Between those kissing in the booths and drinking away the night, she saw Vincenzo trying to disappear without a goodbye.

"Vincenzo!"

He was making his way towards the stairs, but he was having trouble passing through everyone. Boxed in, he found it easier to just push his way through. It appeared that he didn't want to push the women, and he didn't touch most of the men. The way he acted seemed infectious, like he didn't want to touch anyone until he reached the night air outside.

"Vincenzo!" She left the stage and waved at him. "When did you get here? Come join us!"

He walked between two dancers without looking back.

Sylvia reached out and took his hand.

He whipped around, looking disgusted, petrified. She'd broken his rule. She'd touched him without warning.

Nonetheless, she held firm. "Did something happen? Is something wrong?"

"Let me go."

Desperation, then. She hadn't heard that from him before, that ache. "Vincenzo, wait. Talk to me. What's wrong?"

"Please—" He tried to pry her hands off of him as if she were a stranger. She'd never seen him so distressed yet so unwilling to voice his problems. His hands were clammy.

As he finally ripped her off, her heel twisted wrong and she fell backwards. The person behind her had thankfully moved, so she didn't fall on them, but she ended up cracking her head on the floor and her vision burst into stars.

She stared up at the blotting-out ceiling. People crowded in the corners of her vision and asked what was wrong. She didn't care about that as much as she cared for the person panicking above her.

He was sweating, cheeks flushed and jaw clenched in anguish. His breathing picked up with every new person he found staring at him.

Unable to be seen any longer, Vincenzo pushed aside two lovers and dashed up the stairs, leaving himself unexplained and the Kitten deadly silent.

61

Chapter 6: Alleyway Conversation

Vincenzo escaped from the bar gripping his chest. He tried to breathe but couldn't. He tried to calm down but couldn't. Where had Dominic parked the car? He'd left, hadn't he? He'd run out quicker than Vincenzo had.

He'd been to parties bigger than that, ones louder with more guns in guests' handbags and cocaine in their breast pockets. Why was today so different? What'd he done wrong?

The crowds. They were bad today, blocking his view of the exit with bodies and noise. Whenever he felt trapped at normal parties, he'd excuse himself to a balcony or run to his car to "grab something he forgot." He tried to control this side of himself in public, but tonight, it'd overtaken him.

He pressed his sweat-stained back against the brick wall. *Sylvia.* He'd abandoned her. She'd fallen and he was too much of a coward to go back and make sure she was okay. "Claustrophobia," they were calling it. What kind of man used that as an excuse? A fear of being trapped? What if she'd gotten a concussion? What if she was bleeding?

He grasped at his chest, at the corset he wore to bind his chest. He was outside. He could breathe freely here. Just thirty more seconds, then he'd go back and fix everything.

The door to the Black Kitten squeaked opened.

Vincenzo gasped and took out his gun.

Sylvia stopped in her tracks, and he stared into her pleading eyes, shoulders shaking from the night's cold.

He lowered his gun. "I'm sorry."

"What happened?" she asked. "You ran out like someone was targeting you. Are you okay?"

He couldn't look at her. He didn't feel worthy. It was one of the first times he'd seen her without her wig. Normally cropped in a bob, it was now a bloom of brown curls that framed her face too well. She looked too beautiful for him to stare.

He pulled on his turtleneck. "Are you hurt?"

"No, just confused."

"Everything's fine."

"But are *you*?"

He shut his eyes to find a lie, to say that he was fine, just angry or impatient at the world he hated, but the more he dug inwards, the more trapped he felt. "Yes," he said. "You can go back inside. I'll be in shortly."

"But—"

Two rickety cars sputtered up to the Black Kitten. Bullet holes indented the doors and bumpers. When the driver noticed Vincenzo, the cars shut down and the back doors opened.

Hannigan and his men pulled up thirty feet from them. His group befouled the streets of Manhattan, slumming through Irish neighborhoods with guns out and moods murderous. Sometimes, they drove past Campo's establishments to make fun of his triumphs. Why they'd decided to target the Kitten tonight, Vincenzo wouldn't know. Perhaps his luck was that bad.

He hid his gun behind him. "Sylvia, go back inside. Now."
She didn't move.

"*Sylvia.*"

She wouldn't, or couldn't. She saw them, no doubt: Hannigan's own guns. Pistols, Vincenzo got. Every man should've carried one in this city. But Tommy guns? Not even Campo dealt with those. What could be done with one Tommy gun could be done with handguns and good men. Hannigan had never worked with either.

"DiFiore," Hannigan said, keeping his eyes on Sylvia. "I thought I heard you getting fucked in this alleyway. Did we interrupt something?"

Two of the men snickered, pretending to know what they were making fun of.

Vincenzo counted his odds. He could shoot at least three of them before worrying about himself, but he had Sylvia with him. For the rest of his life, he'd have her with him.

Hannigan gestured to Sylvia. "So, is this your new gal I've been hearing about?"

Vincenzo broke eye contact with Hannigan to side-eye Sylvia. She's turned to stone, piecing together who these men in heavy accents were to Vincenzo. He'd mentioned them before, this gang they pitifully called a "rival," but he hadn't expected her to meet them. He thought he'd never allow it.

Swallowing, Vincenzo asked, "Why're you here? You found some time to kill, evidently, but you're not coming into one of the most high-paying bars looking for a good time with men and women who have standards."

"We wanted to see you. We heard you've been spending your nights here doing whatever the hell you wops do in those cellars. We had bets on what ugly broad you managed to nab for yourself, but this sight is even better." He held out his hand. "Let's bring her over. Let's see who this new gal is."

Vincenzo shackled his hand onto Sylvia's wrist.

"Oh, getting protective now, are we? About time, you emotionless dog. What's your name, miss?"

Sylvia went to speak, then looked away. "Sylvia, sir."

Half of the men laughed.

"What a pretty name," Hannigan said. "That garish makeup doesn't do you any favors, though. You might need to ask those fairies downstairs how to do it better."

Sylvia, either stupidly or smartly, said nothing. Nothing she could've said would've saved her from their plans.

Hannigan stepped up into her space. His car's headlights cast his dirty shadow all over her.

Vincenzo's finger hovered over the trigger. If she caught his nonverbal cues, he could have her back in the Kitten and have half of these men dead on the asphalt by the time he needed to worry about getting shot.

Something moved between the parked cars. Vincenzo looked for a fraction of a second to make sure he wasn't being ambushed more than he already was.

Dominic came up behind Hannigan. He had his gun raised and was calculating if and when to shoot.

At least he had backup now, but two against six—three against six, if he counted Sylvia, though he wouldn't let that happen—still wasn't enough.

A new car drove up the street. It came in steadily so as not to cause suspicion. When Vincenzo read the license plate, he took his chance and pulled Sylvia close to him.

Dominic aimed for Hannigan's head just as the car door opened. There were five men in the car, including Luis, giving them the numbers to finally be at odds with Hannigan.

One of the people who jumped out was a plump man in a three-piece suit. He'd just put out his cigarette as a wall of smoke announced his entrance. He wasn't armed, and he didn't have to be. Every one of his men had their guns trained on Hannigan.

"Good evening, gentlemen," Campo d'Antonio said, his tone smooth. "I'm happy to see you. Did you fancy a time at my establishment? I must apologize, but I don't allow in any patrons who threaten my men. Might I suggest the Viola Tavern in Manhattan? They give out free drinks to any man who performs on stage. I'm sure you'd be wonderful at it."

Hannigan frowned. He tried to remain as cool and collected as Campo, but the difference in gang leaders was almost laughable.

"Whatever you choose for tonight," Campo said, "I'm going to ask that you leave as gracefully as you came. I'd also like to hear an apology for whatever troubles you've given my Vincenzo and his company here, though I can't expect such anomalies like guilt to be practiced in your group." He grinned. "So please, if you can, kindly fuck off."

The sound of firecrackers sent Vincenzo up against Sylvia. He used his body as a shield, crushing her so he'd receive a bullet instead of her.

The ear-ringing spray lasted ten seconds, ten seconds of screaming and cursing and tires screeching into Harlem. Ten seconds of Sylvia crying into his ears. Vincenzo, staring into her chest, held her and prayed that he'd hear her heartbeat come tomorrow morning.

When the gunfire ceased, he saw neither Hannigan nor any of his gang members around. He saw no bodies, none that Hannigan had left behind. His gang had either fled through the back entrance or over the curb. It left Luis hopping on his feet and Dominic rubbing his sweaty neck.

Campo fixed his tie like his appearance was his biggest concern. "That was exciting."

Vincenzo wished he could be an ounce of the man Campo was. He was in control of all of them. Luis and Dominic, Vincenzo, his father. He was the titular leader of the d'Antonio Gang of Brooklyn. He was Campo, the world's best gangster boss, at least according to Vincenzo.

"I am very sorry about that, you two," Campo said. "Are you alright?" He air-kissed Sylvia's shocked face. "I'm sorry you had to see that, but I'm happy you're still here. You *are* okay, aren't you?"

Sylvia, jaw dropped, looked to where Hannigan's men had been standing a minute prior. "I'm...not dead."

"Not that I can tell, no. I heard he'd been circling this neighborhood for a few hours. I believe they were looking for someone, so I thought it'd be wise to pop in and investigate the matter. I knew Vincenzo would be preoccupied keeping this bar clean and running. I was worried when I saw he'd been cornered."

Luis could no longer bear keeping quiet and ran up to Vincenzo. "That scared me right, sir! I've never been involved in a shootout like that before. I was up the street tending to a bookkeeping deal when Campo drove up and gave me this gun!"

"Hopefully, they don't come around again," Campo said. "It'd be best if we relocate for the time being. It's too dark to be out unprepared. Vincenzo, my boy, are you alright?"

Realizing he was being spoken to, Vincenzo stuttered, "Y-yes, sir. Thank you. I apologize. I didn't have enough time to get out, and with her with me..." His heart was pounding between his breasts. Knowing his boss had just witnessed him fail was making him lose his train of thought. "This's, uhm, Sylvia Belmonte, sir, the girl I told you about. Sylvia, this's Campo d'Antonio III."

"It's a pleasure to finally meet you, Ms. Belmonte. I now know what you were talking about, Vincenzo. She *is* very beautiful."

Vincenzo couldn't recall ever going on about Sylvia's outer beauty to him, but he nodded. "I'm sorry for the trouble I've caused."

"It's alright. I know that when you're in love, your brain tends to blur what's right and what's wrong. Best to keep your feelings hidden when it's like that. Our world doesn't do well with love."

Vincenzo nodded automatically, not thinking about what he was agreeing to. Dominic bit his lip and turned to the car.

Luis checked on both of his friends. "Sir, do you wish for us to give chase?"

"We shouldn't let them limp away too soon."

As Luis and the rest of the gang members got back into their car, Campo smiled at Vincenzo the way Vincenzo wished his father would. "This's the first time I get to meet your lucky lady friend, and it seems I've made a rather explosive impression. Do accept my apology, Ms. Belmonte, for this rather rude and unserviceable impression you must have about me. I simply wish to keep my men happy and alive."

"It's...quite alright, sir," she said. "That's all we can hope for."

He laughed a deep belly laugh. "True enough. As a token of my apology, let me offer you a personal invitation to my birthday party next month. There will be three-course meals and entertainment all throughout the night. You'll be one of my special guests if you do decide to join us. I heard I have a reputation when it comes to hosting marvellous parties."

She gave a quick bow. "It'd be an honor, sir, thank you."

"Fantastic! It'll be nice to meet you on less chaotic terms." He got in his car and waved at them through the window. "I'll leave you two alone to sort yourselves out, then. Be safe, Vincenzo."

After waiting for the car to drive down the street, Sylvia collapsed into heavy breathing. "Oh, my goodness," she wheezed. "That was awful—that was the worst, I thought—"

Vincenzo latched onto her until his nails broke into her skin. "Why the *fuck* didn't you run away when I told you to?"

She winced at his tone. Dominic, who was locking his gun, looked up in alarm.

The anger from his inability to protect her rose his voice into a shout. "When we're met with a threat like that and I tell you to go, you go. You don't think it over. You don't freeze. You could've been hurt or worse. You could've been taken away from me and I wouldn't have been able to protect you!"

She tried backing away from him. "Don't yell. I did my—"

"I'll yell as loud as I want until it gets through your head! You can't act like that in those situations. Just because you don't value your life doesn't mean you can throw yourself out in the *fucking* trash, do you understand me?"

"Vincenzo." Dominic went to mediate, then balled his hands into fists.

"What? Where the hell were you, anyway? Why did you wait five fucking minutes to—"

Sylvia was pulling harder and harder away from him, twisting her body to get him off.

Her eyes, once wide in fear, were now filled with tears. "I...I don't..." She covered her mouth in a sob. "I'm sorry."

Vincenzo blinked. Her tears simmered the blood in his ears so that he could hear himself think. He was in an alley, with Dominic, holding her wrist so tightly, he felt her pulse beat on his thumb.

He looked at the wrist he was holding. Beneath her glove was a faded yet deep, handmade scar. It followed her blue veins down to a beauty mark on her forearm. It was an old wound she often hid with her gloves, but because of his grip, he saw it.

Taking advantage of his stupor, Sylvia yanked herself free and started walking away.

"Wait." A thousand apologies followed him around the corner. *"You don't value your life."* Who was he to accuse her of that? He knew what she'd lived through, he was just scared of losing her and finding himself without a reason to become better. And he'd just insulted the very person he aspired to be: gracious, kind, forgiving beyond their means.

He expected her to run back into the bar, but she didn't. Walking straight past the entrance, she broke into a sprint and ran down the street, her short heels tapping down the sidewalk.

Bobbie, Laurence, and Mitsuko stopped Vincenzo from pursuing her. They came out of the bar glaring at him. Mitsuko had one of her knives out. Laurence had his hands on his hips. They looked more intimidating than usual.

"What?" he asked, but Bobbie, grabbing him by the arm, walked him down the stairs.

"What're you doing?" he asked.

"Showing you something you need to see," he said, and shut off all the lights to the Black Kitten.

Chapter 7: The Kitten's Memorial

"Due to a physical altercation that was beyond our means of control," Bobbie announced, "the Black Kitten will be closed for the remainder of the evening. I ask that everyone please leave and relocate yourselves until tomorrow afternoon, when we'll be opening back up at our usual time. Thank you for understanding."

He received some backlash, but after seeing Vincenzo again, the crowds began finishing their drinks and trickling up the stairs. Laurence and Mitsuko walked alongside him like trained bodyguards. Dominic followed them in without a word. Some bodyguard he was. It was like they thought Vincenzo wouldn't hurt them for treating him like this. He had a reputation to uphold that couldn't be sullied by those who society pitted beneath him.

But it was because of the crowds that he let himself be led in. They were still watching him and wondering why he, a gangster, was letting himself be handled so rudely. His heart hadn't stopped pounding.

Bobbie brought them backstage. Without Sylvia, the space felt oddly empty.

"Why am I here?" Vincenzo asked.

Mitsuko answered for him. Cornering him, she winded back her small arm, stood on her tiptoes, and slapped him straight across the face.

She had the strength of a man. She'd been sent to Europe to work as a military nurse during the Great War. Perhaps seeing men die in her tent had hardened her dexterity into something fearless. That blazing look in her eyes gave him that impression. She was ready to fight him and win.

"You do not," she said, "ever, *ever* yell at a woman like that, you worthless piece of shit with a pistol. If I ever, *ever* hear you scream at her like that again, if she ever gets caught in another goddamn *shootout* because of you, I'll make sure you never speak to her again and that you're banned from every pansy club in New York, got it?"

Insults and threats came to him at once, some he regretted even thinking about, but he couldn't act with her hand on him. He shoved her back, and she let go, but she held his gaze, something he guessed he'd have to battle more ardently from now on.

Bobbie lit a cigarette near the mirrors. Dominic finally looked ready to act like he was expected to, but Laurence prevented him from doing so. Hand on his wrist, this feminine man kept him back, saying, "Oh, no, you're staying right here." And Dominic froze, spellbound.

Vincenzo did what he could and fixed his ruffled clothes. "Don't ever touch me like that again."

"Oh, you're one to talk, asshole."

"Now, then," Bobbie said. "Mr. DiFiore, I do appreciate the work you do for the Black Kitten and I understand what you have to do to get by. You live a hard life, just like the rest of us do."

"But you can't do this to us!" Laurence said. "That was gun-fire outside, wasn't it? Some car came up and started shooting!"

"And you said Sylvia doesn't value her life," Mitsuko said. "How dare you tell her that? You know nothing about what she's lived through."

"I know—"

"Did you hit her?"

He wanted to ask, *Who do you think I am?* but he couldn't imagine how lowly she thought of him. He said, "I didn't."

"Bullshit."

"I *didn't*."

"You're lying."

"I grabbed her wrist," he confessed. "Same as what he's doing to him." He pointed at Laurence and Dominic. "And I was about to apologize when she ran away. Now I need to go find her—"

"Oh, you're not leaving," Mitsuko said. "Not until we're done with you."

"You don't have the right to talk to me like this."

"And you haven't the right to be anywhere near the angel that is Sylvia if you yell at her, you fucking piece of shit—"

"Okay," Bobbie said. "Okay, Mitsuko, Laurence, I can handle this. Go outside. Make sure everyone gets out. Then, if you can, go check on Sylvia. I don't want her doing anything she might regret. It looked like she was running home. You can check for her there."

Laurence huffed and dropped Dominic's hand like it was rotted. Mitsuko stalked Vincenzo in a half-circle before leaving with him, making sure to slam the door on her way out.

Vincenzo swallowed his pride from being handled in front of his own subordinate. "I'll pay for any damages done to the Black Kitten and the cars outside. And I'll lessen my time here. I shouldn't be here so often."

"I don't care about that right now," Bobbie said. "Vincenzo, are you in love with Sylvia?"

With everything he'd just done to defend her, the question felt like Mitsuko's slap to his face. "Why do you ask me that?"

"Because *I* love her. I love every single person who enters this bar. This place means the world to me."

"I understand that perfectly."

"No, you don't. If you did, you wouldn't have said what you said to her."

His discomfort made him spit out, "She was in danger. Hannigan, he cornered—"

"She chased you after you ignored her."

"I didn't ignore her, I needed to leave."

Bobbie turned away to a vanity mirror adorned with pictures, bouquets of flowers, and notes. Vincenzo always guessed it to be Laurence's table. Certain pictures had lipstick kisses on them and hearts surrounding the person's head.

"I don't," Bobbie started with, "*ever*, want to see Sylvia the way I saw her when she first came to my club. She was dirty and sick. She had a cough that wouldn't let up. I bought her so much medicine because no doctor would take someone like her from someone like me. Mitsuko took time off to nurse her. Laurence let her sleep at his place until we found her a place to stay. For four months, she had no desire to eat or bathe or…"

He wiped something from his eyes. "Don't ever say that she doesn't value her life. She's worked too hard and loved too much to hear that from her own lover's mouth."

A knife twisted into Vincenzo's heart and stayed there, handle protruding between his ribs for someone else to wound him. "I know. I'm sorry."

"I'm not the one who has to hear the apology." He addressed the vanity table. "Has Sylvia told you who this table belongs to?"

"She has not."

He picked up a framed photograph with care. It appeared the oldest out of the pictures, the corners bent from being taken out of its frame too many times. It was of a black man with styled hair and a bright smile. "It's a memorial. Every soul here has either gone missing due to gang violence or was murdered without justice."

Vincenzo reevaluated the faces staring down at him. Many of them—almost three-fourths of them—were either black like Laurence or had tanner skin like Sylvia and Bobbie. Like him.

He tried recognizing them. It disgusted him, but as he took in these friends and lovers, he forced himself to remember a face or body type, to see if he'd ended a life too short by mistake. He was all too familiar about the prejudices they faced. The police encouraged it. Nobody spoke out against it. And gang members were often the catalysts of such hate. They killed girly men or manly women who disrupted the norm. Vincenzo actively discouraged it and thought Campo knew better than to attack the innocent, but what if...

"Please understand where we're coming from," Bobbie said. "The Black Kitten is more than a bar where we can drink and have sex. It's a place for us to feel accepted. We can be our true selves here without the fear of being killed. I thank you for your services, but we can't have any more of us found dead or beaten in the streets. If you really love Sylvia, try to give her the best life you can. And if that means leaving the picture, I highly suggest you take that to heart."

Vincenzo folded his hands in front of him, then realized he was picking up a tic from Sylvia and hid them in his pockets instead. He'd just found Sylvia, she who listened to his problems and never belittled his thoughts. He wanted to be with her forever, but if his lifestyle and attitude were making her unhappy...

He'd say he'd take being her husband over being a gangster, but leaving the gang meant leaving in a casket, and he knew he and she weren't destined for the same afterlife.

"Can I ask you a rather blunt question, Mr. DiFiore?" Bobbie asked. "How do you see yourself? Do you see yourself as one of us? Do you see yourself as a pansy?"

Vincenzo went rigid, then cleared his throat at the silence. He knew the correct answer, but nobody else needed to know. It was his business, his life. But he needed this silence to end, to push the conversation away from him. "Not...not necessarily. It's...well—"

"Because she's a woman, just as he's a man"—he gestured to Dominic, who was still frozen from Laurence's touch—"and you're a man, and I'm...now...a man."

That pause Vincenzo heard too often in his head filled his lungs with water. "What?"

He shrugged, though a restlessness kept him fiddling with his cigarette. "Surely Sylvia has told you. I'm no longer hiding it from those who ask."

"Hiding—" Vincenzo backed away. "What do you mean? What are you insinuating?"

"That I'm a man," he clarified, "though I haven't always felt that way. When I found out that this was an option, it changed my opinion on everything. I did hide my past from the people I met, from the men I dated, but after years of running the Kitten, I decided I didn't want to hide anymore, even if it cost me my life.

"So I'm not going to let this sanctuary become a bullet-hole-ridden, destitute hub for gangsters who can't keep us safe, or cringe whenever they see us," he added to both Vincenzo and Dominic, who'd stepped back a full foot. "It means too much to me."

Vincenzo held his head. Sylvia, he understood. It didn't take much time for him to hear her story and to know that he still liked her for her. But this revelation, with Dominic standing here and listening to everything...

He clamped a hand over his mouth. He'd been certain no other man could possibly know the pain and self-discovery that came with labeling yourself anew, yet here he was, talking with one whom he'd known for months. He even passed. How lucky some people were.

Bobbie took another long drag from his cigarette. "I'm going to start cleaning. I'm guessing everything was left a mess. Have a nice night, gentlemen. You can see yourselves out."

When he left, Vincenzo walked up to the vanity table to give himself more room to breathe. The mark Mitsuko had left on him was as red as the memorial roses.

He took a seat in front of the vanity, arms slack in front of him. He always hated his reflection, but now he wasn't only

seeing himself. He saw the faces of the dead, these young people with love letters alongside eulogies.

He sat there for an hour before he and Dominic left to go
home. Neither man spoke to one another, but both of them
desperately wished the other had.

Chapter 8: 1 A.M. Ice Cream Visit

Sylvia opened her second tub of ice cream for the night. Neapolitan, the good brand they sold downstairs at the Harvest Market. They only had one freezer that couldn't hold that much ice cream, but with a talking-to from Vincenzo, they now had two freezers, one filled entirely with Sylvia's favorite coping mechanism.

She'd stopped crying yesterday, two days after the shooting. When she'd called out from work, Bobbie had understood; even *he* still sounded rattled from that night.

How had it spiraled into Vincenzo yelling at her? He'd always been so kind to her. She really thought he wasn't like other men.

Something had scared him at the Black Kitten, something he didn't want her to know. It'd almost cost them their lives. If Campo hadn't saved them from Hannigan, where would they be? Would she be here, sitting alone in her living room, eating ice cream against the radiator?

She rubbed her hands over the heated metal. She could've been eating at her dinner table, but the floor was much more inviting. With the warmth and the occasional car passing by from the window, she could've slept here knowing the world was still turning while she dreamed.

Her apartment was small compared to Vincenzo's home, and had less decor and memories on the walls than his. The only two things of worth were her bedroom radio and her piano. She'd purchased the radio all on her own after working for months at the Black Kitten, her big purchase after earning her apartment key. When she'd hooked it up, she, Laurence, and Mitsuko had spent hours listening to dramas and eating ice cream together. It helped her get to sleep when she had nobody to sleep next to.

And her piano. Her lovely, incredibly grand piano, shiny and black with lace draped over the music rack. It was the one present from Vincenzo she'd never be proud enough to accept. It took up her entire living room and outclassed everything she owned. Of course, she'd always wanted a piano. When she played it, she thought of Vincenzo: dark, a little hard to get to know, a beautiful voice.

She wondered if she should've prodded him as she'd done, or if she should've respected his boundaries and let whatever had been tormenting him fester. Had he not liked the noise? Had Hannigan ordered him to come outside? She wished she was closer to him. So much of his life needed to be kept in secrecy, but she dreamed of them sitting together and him divulging everything to her.

Standing up with her tub of ice cream, she sat down at her piano and drifted her fingers over the keys. She'd written two songs about Vincenzo, one about their first kiss and one about the shootout. Each song had a different tone, but they harmonized well with one another.

She didn't want to end things with him. His sympathy, his acceptance, she liked those parts of him. And she loved his touches, shyer in public, more adventurous in private. She *liked* him, in the most honest of ways.

Was it because of *her*?

It made sense. Laurence, Mitsuko, and Bobbie had taught her not to think like that. *"None of this is your fault." "You're not to blame for his actions."* But how could she not put part of the blame on herself? When her friends had come to check up on her, she'd been sobbing into her pillows about what a poor lover she was. With their encouragement, they'd convinced her that she was a good person.

They'd also told her that Vincenzo was a horrible criminal and that she should break up with him that week.

She didn't want to feel like this anymore. She didn't want to feel guilty for liking what she liked and then feeling terrible about it and crying. She wanted a romance. She deserved one, didn't she?

She shut away her piano. She'd never get one. God had made that clear the moment she'd woken up from a dream of being a little girl and realized she'd woken up too soon.

Someone knocked on her front door. It was a light rap, but at one in the morning, Sylvia questioned which one of her neighbors wanted to speak with her. "Speak," a generous term for their complaints. They always had it out for her, whether she left her windows open or she walked too loudly. Her existence triggered something hostile in them.

She tried ignoring whoever they were and threw out her empty tub. Laurence and Mitsuko wouldn't have come over this late, and Vincenzo, on the rare nights he'd visit, always announced himself beforehand.

But the knocking didn't stop. It grew louder and more forceful, scaring her.

She listened attentively now, hoping to hear footsteps leave down the street.

The person stopped, but she didn't hear them leave. They were waiting there, plotting.

Then the door cracked and splintered at the weight of a man's heavy foot.

She covered her mouth. The knocking ramped up. More pieces of her door broke apart from how badly this person wanted to enter her home.

She forced herself to move. She wouldn't stand by and risk the worst happening again.

She ran into her bedroom and fumbled for the revolver in her nightstand. Another gift from Vincenzo. When he'd gifted this to her, she'd locked it away and hadn't touched it since.

The knocking stopped.

She stood with her back to her bedroom door. If the person had left, then she would never know who'd wanted to intimidate her. If they'd entered...

She stepped outside and aimed for the door.

A silhouette of a man stood at the top of her stairwell. He was tall, taller than her, and muscular, with a bowler hat covering his face.

Her finger wouldn't close around the trigger. She wouldn't believe it. She thought it might've been a mistake, a foolish thought after discovering an intruder in your own home. But she was a foolish girl, and she couldn't justify hurting someone without giving them a chance to explain themselves.

He ran at her, and she screamed. He had something in his hand and tried to hit her with it, but she grabbed his arm and pushed him into the wall, jumping her telephone from its holder. Afraid of what he'd grab next, she shoved him down the stairs and almost fell herself.

The intruder toppled to the landing and a gunshot fired, filling her house with the sound of death.

The bullet lodged somewhere into the wall. It hadn't been fired from her gun, but from the man's, which he'd dropped upon falling. The blunder spooked him enough to abandon whatever mission he'd set out to complete. He crawled down the rest of the steps, picked up his gun, and ran outside through the now broken doorway.

When her neighbors' lights didn't turn on, Sylvia, shaking, went back to her phone and reconnected it on the table. Her legs were numb. Her heart felt dead and sickened by fear, like it'd never return to its natural hue. Anyone could've come in now and finished what the intruder had intended. She was defenseless.

She stared at her telephone. The police wouldn't come. If they did, they'd harass her. Her neighbors would gossip about it tomorrow. She'd get in trouble.

She dialed the only number she knew that could help her.

She waited. Long, torturous rings rang through her ear and out to the kitchen.

Twenty seconds came and went, and he didn't answer.

She hung up and tried again.

Again, he didn't answer.

Teeth chattering with fright, she dialed his number one last time and waited.

And waited.

And waited.

The phone clicked.

"Hello?"

She hiccupped. He sounded so much colder than usual. *"Hello?"*

"Uhm—" She covered her mouth. Where was her voice?

Vincenzo, too tired to play this game, clicked his tongue and hung up.

"Wait." She dialed him for a fourth time. Now she was hurt, hurt about disrupting him, hurt about feeling hurt. She'd just been attacked, why did she feel so guilty about this?

He picked up again. "Who the hell keeps calling this number?"

"I-it's me," she said. "Uh, Sylvia. I'm sorry. For calling. It's late. Um." She cleared her throat. "I just. Someone just. Broke into my apartment. He came up the stairs and I retrieved your gun, but I couldn't shoot. For whatever reason, I just couldn't do it. Then I pushed him down the stairs and he left, but he shot a hole in my wall and now the door won't close, and I don't know what to do because now he can come back and—"

She sighed into tears. "I'm scared," she confessed. "Vincenzo, I'm really scared."

He stayed so silent on the other line, she was afraid he'd hung up on her again. The only sound she heard was his tempered breathing tickling her ears.

"Vincenzo?" she asked.

"Are you hurt?"

God, he sounded so angry with her. She shouldn't have called. She was only upsetting him now. "I'm not."

"Do you still have the gun?"

"I do."

"Ammo?"

She checked. "I have some."

"Okay." He moved something on his end. "Turn on all the lights and lock yourself in your room. Keep the gun on you at all times. After I hang up, call the police. I'll be there in an hour."

"But it takes almost two hours—"

He hung up before she finished speaking.

—◇—

The cops never arrived. They never did for her. Rarely, they came to settle down the neighbors yelling at her, but either they knew about her involvement with Vincenzo or her neighbors had told them she was a liar who'd never call them for a real emergency. They were lovely folk, her neighbors.

At around two thirty, she started getting ready for bed. It felt natural. Nobody would come for her. She'd already messed up that week by not listening to Vincenzo. This was her punishment: trying to get to sleep knowing someone on the streets wanted her dead.

A car screeched to a stop outside of her apartment. It sounded like it hit something to stop, like the curb or a pedestrian.

She covered herself with her blankets. She'd dressed for bed in nothing but a pale pink slip. Should she have gotten ready? She wasn't wearing any makeup. He wouldn't like that.

Before the person came in, she picked up her gun and went to unlock her bedroom door.

The second she unlocked it, the door forced itself open.

Vincenzo almost walked into her chest, then lurched backwards and looked up at her. His hands latched to her forearms the same way he'd done after the shootout, though he didn't look as angry. He looked horrified. "Did he hurt you?" he panted. "Are you hurt? Are you—"

"I'm fine," she said.

He grit his teeth at her answer, then looked at his hands and detached himself. In the limited light, she saw he was a bit untidy. His hair wasn't combed out and his collar was uneven. She wondered who this breathless man was and who looked worse to whom.

She held herself. "Um—"

"What did he look like? Who was he? Which way did he go? Did he have a car?"

She stuttered on her own words before biting her tongue. She had been perfectly calm up until seeing him, but now with him in her home, clearly angry with her...

She teared up. "I-I don't know. I'm sorry."

He stepped back. A million thoughts filled the space between them. "Do you have any, like, bags?" he asked. "Any suitcases or heavy bags?"

"I...think I have a few." She pointed to her bed. "Underneath."

He walked in and squatted beside it. He looked to her but not *at* her. "May I?"

She nodded, and he tossed aside crumpled up letters and socks to reveal her duffel bags. They were from her youth when she needed to move from place to place, never knowing where she'd be sleeping for the night. They had dust on them.

He pushed back his hair. "You're coming to live with me. You're not living in a fucking slum where things like this can happen to you at night. You'll take what you need for the next few days, then I'll come down with a few cars and bring down the rest. Is that alright?"

When she didn't move, he picked up a bag and lifted it to her vision. His eyes, she couldn't read them anymore. He looked like a different person.

"Okay," she said, and started packing up her things. She picked out her favorite dresses and gloves. She chose between her favorite heels. Would bringing two pairs seem vain?

"Is this really okay?" he asked again.

"It is."

"I won't force you to go if you don't want to. I just think it'd be safer if—"

"You want me to go, so I'll go. It's fine."

"But—"

She lingered near her underwear drawer, unsure if he wanted to see her bloomers, and he took the hint and said, "I'll, uh, be outside, then," and left.

She wanted to pace herself. This felt like every other time she'd been kicked out of a house she felt safe in. Not as heart-wrenching, but still not great. And she knew her neighborhood wasn't safe, and it'd been her dream to move in with a man. Now, though, she wanted to go to bed and be unconscious for nine, twelve hours so she didn't have to live through this pain.

After gathering what she could, she let a few tears fall before buttoning up a trench coat and closing her bedroom door.

Vincenzo helped her into the car. He kept looking down the dark street, scanning for movement. He didn't say anything to her.

As they drove, she shielded her eyes against the window's cold glass. Her self-hatred was more paramount than ever. If she hadn't had a telephone, she'd be dead in her apartment and her body wouldn't have been found for days because nobody would've come looking for her.

Vincenzo talked to himself until they reached Manhattan. How this happened, who this man was. He'd apparently broken into Dominic's home before coming here because he'd refused to pick up his phone, but he hadn't found him and thus left by himself. He kept asking if she was cold or hungry—if all of this was *okay* with her—but she only shook her head or nodded to whatever he wanted. She wasn't in a position to make demands.

When they reached his home, he took both of her bags in one arm. She tried to be helpful and open the door for him, but he had the keys, so she stepped back, trying to make herself disappear.

"*Nonna's* still asleep," he whispered.

"I'll be quiet," she promised, but her ankle hit the doorway and she almost collapsed into Vincenzo. She avoided breathing too loudly after that.

The fire in his fireplace had reduced to embers. She saw the indent in his bed from where he'd been sleeping a few hours prior. His kitten, Mezzanotte, was fast asleep on his pillow. She scampered underneath the bed when they came in.

Sylvia's feelings sunk her onto the edge of the bed. She was his lover. Why did she feel so unwelcome in his own room? He still hadn't looked at her. Probably because she wasn't wearing any makeup. She must've looked dreadful.

She tightened her coat around herself. "I'm sorry I made a mess of tonight. I should've been able to handle it myself, but

I was too scared to move and ruined everything again. I can sleep downstairs tonight. That way, I won't bother you any more than I already have."

Vincenzo sighed.

Sylvia didn't know why. Hearing her failures spoken aloud actually helped. She was a nuisance who took up too much space. For all she'd done, she should've slept outside.

He came over to her. In the strangest of turns, she expected him to hit her. Too accustomed to her previous loves, when something violent occurred, at the end of the day, she expected to take her lover's pains across the cheek. Her expectations allowed her to think of no other outcome.

Vincenzo lifted her face by her jaw so that the two of them finally saw eye to eye.

His face was painted with sorrow. His brow, furrowed. His lips, tight enough to leave wrinkles. His soft thumbs traced the corners of her nude lips. If she'd been wearing lipstick, he would've smudged it.

"Sylvia," he said. "I am so, *so* sorry for everything you've endured this week. I'm sorry for yelling at you, for the things I said. I'm sorry for hurting you, and I'm sorry this attack happened, as I'm sure it came from Hannigan or one of his men. You didn't deserve it and showed tremendous bravery on your part. I know I shouldn't expect forgiveness, but..."

He leaned down and kissed her forehead, then the corner of her eye, lapping up a tear that'd crystallized into a diamond. "I'm so glad you're still here."

Her sadness swelled into something far greater than she could bear. To counterbalance it, she held him back.

"You're such a strong and patient and wonderfully loving girl. I'm sorry I insinuated anything else about you or your life. It was completely out of line."

She remembered what he'd said, but after seeing the shooting and hearing him yell at her, it'd all hardened into one painful memory.

She laced her fingers with his. "I forgive you. And I'm sorry, too, for not listening."

"Don't," he said. "You shouldn't have to apologize for anything. I should've been more articulate. When I saw Hannigan pull up, all I thought about was you getting hurt and I lost my senses, but that doesn't excuse my behavior towards you. I'll do better next time, I swear."

"That's alright. I forgive you all the same."

His smile was painful. "Why? Why do that?"

"Because I've been with men who've said they're sorry, and I've been with *you*, who actually feels remorse and wants to change." Giving him time to back away, she slowly lifted her hands to his face. When he didn't pull away, she cupped his cheeks the same way he'd done to her. "Such a pretty face can't go to waste with unspoken apologies."

Vincenzo took her hands, fondling them slightly before the whole situation made him pull back. He settled on his side of the bed with red ears.

Sylvia did the same. It wasn't the first time she'd shared a bed with him, but tonight felt like she was sleeping *with* him, or the idea of him.

She let herself breathe as she watched the fire dance in its own ashes. Her self-degradation was still with her—it'd always be—but it helped hearing that Vincenzo didn't absolutely hate her enough to kick her out.

Making sure he knew that, she asked, "May I tell you something?"

"You may."

"I know I've mentioned this before, but my psyche is very poor. You say my strength is something you admire, but I'm not strong. I often feel like a terrible person. I'm lonely and needy and see the worst in everything, *especially* in myself. I try to fake it when I'm with you, but I'm having trouble keeping up that persona. I just want you to know that in case I start falling."

His side of the bed remained still and quiet. The logs popped with sap and startled her.

He shifted his weight to hug her middle. "I'm sorry you feel the need to tell me that, like you thought I might've glossed over such a big part of your life. But I've always known. I don't think I would've fallen in love with you if I hadn't. You're so open and transparent with your feelings. Even when you laugh or joke, I know there's a chance of you falling into darkness. To be quite honest, I like that you're so sincere with it. I wish I could be like that." He kissed her neck. "You inspire me."

She blinked back a sob aching to be let go. "I didn't think I'd ever inspire anyone before."

"Why not?"

"Because of my psyche, I guess."

He breathed against the exposed part of her back.

"What?"

He didn't answer at first, then said, "I want to make you happy. I thought giving you presents would do the trick, but I've come to the conclusion that I need to go about it another way."

"It's not that I don't enjoy your gifts. You're very generous with me. Sometimes, I don't think I deserve it. Sometimes, it feels like too much."

"I only do it because I feel like that's all I can do. I'm so paranoid when it comes to romance. I'm inexperienced and hate being touched. I feel like a failure. My wealth is all I have."

She turned to face him properly. He'd bundled up the blankets around his face for protection.

"If you teach me to be more confident, I'll teach you how to be romantic. In a year, you'll be making love to me while I profess how wonderfully talented I am."

One of his hands slipped out of the blankets to cover his mouth. "Let's, uh, start that another day. Not tonight. Just give me the do's and don't's of how you want to be treated."

Her heart returned to a healthier shade of pink. "Well, no yelling, for starters. I was a bit miffed when you yelled at me. I get upset when men raise their voices."

"I won't do it again."

"Even when I yell at you?"

He held her hand. "Even if you're a thousand yards away from me in a field of flowers, I shan't ever raise my voice to you."

"Well, for *that*," she said teasingly, "if you had handpicked flowers for me and were calling me over, I wouldn't mind you shouting my name."

"And why are we *both* in a field of flowers?"

"A picnic," she decided. "Just the two of us. In Italy."

"Italy's a fascist wasteland at the moment. Let's bring it over to Spain."

"Or France."

"France, it is."

As much as she would've liked to have fallen asleep with that image in mind, something else needed to be said.

"Vincenzo, one more thing. When you ran out of the Kitten in such a hurry, what happened? Did something frighten you? Was it the noise? The excitement? Do you not like when we're that loud?"

After finding a comfortable way to hold her hand, he asked, "If I tell you, will you promise not to tell your friends?"

Was this something more than she had speculated? Was he involved in gang business? Well, more gang business than usual? Had he been threatened to leave the bar against his will?

She nodded, waiting for the real answer.

"I have this...*condition*," he said, "among others. If I'm in a closed space and can't see the exits, I panic. I lose my breath and can't think rationally. I'd needed to leave, and when you stopped me, I couldn't think of a way to tell you, so I ran, and I'm sorry."

"So you have claustrophobia?"

From underneath the bed, Mezzanotte poked out her curious head. Just a peek, with her ears up. She met Sylvia's eyes.

"You know the term?" Vincenzo asked.

"I do, but I didn't know such a thing scared you."

"It doesn't *scare* me," he said, but he didn't have another word to describe it. She didn't suffer from it personally—throw her into a locked room filled with as many people as possible and she'd be content—but she now understood why some parties might've been too much for him. She hoped Campo's party wouldn't be as extravagant as he'd implied.

"I'll keep that in mind from now on. If it ever becomes too strenuous, please tell me and I'll help however I can. I can take you outside or sit with you until the feeling passes. Or you can go out alone, if that's better. Which is better?"

He blinked at her, then hid his red face into her neck and hugged her tightly.

She smiled. "What? Tell me what you're feeling. If you like that I'm so open with you, reciprocate it."

"I just love you," he said. "I really, really, *really* love you."

That, that sent her off dizzily into her dreams.

Chapter 9: Adjustments

Vincenzo didn't know if "husbandy" was a word, but when he woke up and wanted to surprise Sylvia with bacon and oatmeal in bed, he felt "husbandy."

"Husbandy" when he caught himself daydreaming about her. "Husbandy" when he added extra sugar into her oatmeal because he knew her fondness of sweets. They were an act of atonement for all the heartache he'd put her through. No longer would pianos or places to stay be enough. Now, he needed to change the way he behaved. He needed to become a husband through "husbandy" manners.

But new concerns *did* come with her living with him. He discovered that he was not a great cook or even a decent one. He burned her bacon and added so much milk to her oatmeal that it turned to cereal. He ended up munching on fruit as *Nonna* took over.

Nonna herself seemed...okay with the transition. He'd told her about the break-in and that Sylvia would be living with him from now on.

"In the same bed?"

"Yes, Nonna, *in the same bed."*

"And you're not married? No, my little bean, only if you're married."

"We can't get married, Nonna."

"Yes, you can!"

He concocted a lie that Sylvia was actually sleeping in one of the guest rooms, but *Nonna* was forbidden from taking the stairs, so she'd never know. She probably did know—she wasn't stupid—but she needed to keep up her modesty in her own home.

And while sharing a room with Sylvia was lovely in theory, it hadn't worked out as well as he'd hoped. For one, she slept in nothing but a slip, a thin, lacy one-piece that hardly hid her knees. When he'd woken up and seen it'd rolled up past her upper thighs, he'd almost collapsed. He was right. Her legs went all the way up.

His second concern was her feminine needs and how they were in stark contrast with his. He knew how forwards she was. Not "forwards," per se, but "more open" than he was. Her kisses left him breathless, her hands begged to touch more. It was all very titillating for him. His parents weren't affectionate and romance novels could only provide him with so much.

She dealt with stress very differently than he did. When stressed, he'd work and work and not come home until two, then pick up more work and stay out until the Sun set. If it became too much, he'd hit. He'd hit someone or something at the harbor and regret it the next day. He didn't know how else to manage his feelings. He certainly wasn't used to Sylvia's way.

He'd found out later that morning. While attempting a go at lunch, he found a Mezzanotte hole in one of his socks and went to change it. He couldn't walk around his own home looking disheveled. Not with his lover upstairs.

Sylvia had politely informed him that due to her hectic night prior, she was going to retire for a nap. He battled between walking around sockless or disturbing her, but when he'd decided, he was already at the door. And he'd be quiet, of course. He wouldn't wake her.

When he entered, he found her not only fully awake but atop the covers instead of under, and instead of her legs crossed and knees tight, they were spread open, her hand lost deep between her shivering, sweaty thighs.

As she let out a soft moan, she noticed Vincenzo gaping at her.

He ran. He bolted down the hall and locked himself in the guest bathroom. Back against the door, he covered his face in shameful exhilaration. Of course she did things like that. Society told him they didn't. Church told them it was a sin. He himself hated the act, but he didn't judge those who did it.

He just couldn't believe that she felt so comfortable to do *that*. Right in his own bed. It'd only been a day. It was like they were married, though married couples should've been able to take care of one another's needs.

He couldn't wipe the smile off of his face. *"Like they were married."*

——◇——

That afternoon, he called up Luis and Dominic to help move in the rest of Sylvia's belongings. She said her refrigerator and rugs wouldn't blend well with *Nonna's* interior decorating and therefore wouldn't be worth transferring.

"Don't talk like that," he told her. "You can bring in as much as you want. This's your house now, too."

While he could get ready in ten minutes, Sylvia needed more time, so he gave her her space and started cleaning the first floor. He put away the glass coasters and rearranged the couch pillows. He went to dust off the lamp when he discovered a note on the end table. It was addressed to him in perfect handwriting.

He unfolded the letter.

Vincenzo—

I'm terribly sorry for my unladylike behavior you bore witness to this morning. I thought I'd locked the door, but it seems I'm not well-equipped with living with someone quite yet.

I hope you can forgive me and erase such an awful sight from your memory. From now on, I'll keep such indulgent acts locked away in the privacy of a bathroom.

My apologies—
Sylvia

Vincenzo puffed out his cheeks. Why did she apologize for every little thing? She apologized for being herself, for the clothes she wore, for wearing too much makeup, for not wearing enough. His mother was the same way. Why did they take the blame for everything they did?

He knew why. It was the climate of the culture, something instilled. He still hated it, but he couldn't tell them to simply be stronger. It was like telling him to be more open with his emotions. It was a learning experience that varied from person to person.

High heels tapped down the stairs. He hid away the note and pretended to be busy.

"I'm sorry I took so long," Sylvia said.

He held his hands as he stared out the window. The knuckle he was scratching turned redder than Sylvia's cheeks.

Knowing she wouldn't mention it aloud, he cleared the air by saying, "I don't mind if you do that sort of...relaxing upstairs."

"I shouldn't be doing it at all."

"No, you should. I mean, you can. Honestly, it's something I should be able to do for you. Being your, well, you know."

"My person."

Person. He sat on that, how he was failing her as her suitor, her "person." If he was following the norms expected of him, they should've had a child by now. Would it be in poor taste to ask her her opinion about bringing up a child? After what he just saw? Whatever her psyche told her, she'd be a great mother.

"You don't have to, you know," Sylvia said, "do that."

"I know. It's not you," he added.

"I know." She flattened out her dress. "Something in your childhood?"

"Yes," he said, and ended it there. He'd tell her when he was ready, which would be on his deathbed. And even then, to actually speak on how he grew up wasn't a conversation he ever wanted to have with anyone.

Anyone but her.

In time.

——✧——

Dominic and Luis came by around noon time. They took two cars to make sure they had enough room for everything. Vincenzo wanted three, but Sylvia had gotten nervous when he recommended a moving company to move out her piano.

"I don't want to be a bother," she said.

"Don't be so down on yourself," Luis said as he drove. "You're the princess today. Ask for anything you want."

She took Vincenzo's hand. "I believe I have everything I want right here."

"He doesn't count, you lovebird!"

They hauled out her dresser, her kitchen supplies, her food—it worried him how little she had—and more of her personal knickknacks. He never knew how much powder a woman needed. Her makeup alone took up an entire box. He and Sylvia hoisted it together into the backseat.

Because he wasn't much of a handyman and Sylvia was melancholic, he had Dominic and Luis take care of the rest. If he disregarded Luis' occasional whine of protest, he was a fine worker, but Dominic was the picture-perfect candidate for this. He was heavily built and did everything asked of him.

It was why Vincenzo had wanted to bring him to Sylvia's house during the intrusion. He would've likely found the man if he'd come.

"Where were you last night?"

Dominic, who was on the floor disassembling Sylvia's writing desk, looked up with a hammer in his hand. He placed it down. "Pardon?"

"Last night. I'd tried to find you, but you weren't home. Where were you?"

"Oh." He went to pick up the hammer, then forgot what he wanted to do with it and scratched his upper lip. "Nowhere special."

"Where were you?"

He didn't say.

"Dominic—"

"I was meeting a friend," he said. "A professor I had in college."

Vincenzo cocked a brow. He himself had dropped out of middle school to focus on earning money for his family. He knew Luis had finished high school and was planning great things for baby Sophie, but what about Dominic?

"I went to a private catholic school in Connecticut," he said, reading Vincenzo's mind. "He wanted to meet up yesterday, so I drove to his lake house and slept over. That's all."

Luis called for Dominic's help outside, and Dominic almost ran out of the room to escape Vincenzo's simple question.

Vincenzo watched him go. The belief that he'd driven six hours to actively make time for someone in his personal life didn't sit right with him.

Dominic didn't have friends.

To celebrate Sylvia moving in, they all went to the Black Kitten for drinks. Vincenzo picked up the tab, but he put a limit on how much Luis and Dominic drank. Luis because he'd just turned twenty-one and was still too juvenile to drink, and Dominic...

It wasn't that his story was outrageous. It was that, since Vincenzo had brought it up, he hadn't made eye contact with him. He hadn't spoken up or thanked him for giving him free drinks. He kept playing with his facial hair, hiding his mouth.

"Do you think...?" Sylvia poised. They were at Vincenzo's booth about to eat dinner. He'd ordered her a slice of chocolate cake, but after bringing up Dominic's oddities, she hadn't touched it.

"I don't think so," he said. "He wouldn't."

"I don't think so either. The man who'd broken into my house was bigger, larger, I think."

"But you didn't see his face."

She shook her head.

"Whatever it is, I'll confront him about it tonight. He shouldn't be lying to me, even if it's about something trivial."

"I'm sure the truth is nothing too important."

Across the bar, Luis, who'd retrieved his one allotted drink for the night, tried making room beside Dominic at his lonely table for one. He pointed at the card tables and the stage, offering ways to brighten him up. It surprised Vincenzo how little Luis minded the Black Kitten. It'd taken Vincenzo a week to let his guard down around so many strangers, then a full month to casually share a drink with Bobbie. This was Luis' second time here.

The doors leading to the backstage opened to Laurence and Mitsuko. They were partway dressed for the night. Laurence still had his pants on and Mitsuko wasn't wearing any jewelry. They maneuvered around the tables and made a beeline for Vincenzo and Sylvia.

Vincenzo went to excuse himself, but Mitsuko slammed her foot into his cushion, boxing him in.

"What's going on?" Laurence asked. "Just a few days ago you were crying about this man, now you're drinking and eating like nothing happened."

"Ah, I was going to tell you tonight," Sylvia said. "Let's talk in the back. It's quite a long story."

"No, tell us now."

"I want to hear how shitty this man's apology was," Mitsuko added. Like Vincenzo had guessed, that glare of hers hadn't faltered.

Sylvia lied about the story's length and glossed over most of what'd gone down. She didn't go into her anxieties about love or her dreadful self-image. He guessed those talks were reserved for him, or they already knew and he was that late to the party.

When she finished, Mitsuko dropped her foot, stared at them, then snatched out the blade hidden in her boot. "You're *living* with him?"

"In the same *bed*?"

"You *moved* in?"

"And didn't *tell* us?"

"I was going to make a phone call this morning," Sylvia said, "but things got ahead of me. Then Vincenzo wanted to help me move out, then he suggested that we come here to celebrate.”

“*Celebrate?*” Laurence asked. “He made you homeless!”

“That’s a rather dark way of interpreting this,” Vincenzo said.

“Oh, hush!” He stomped away before Vincenzo actually got mad. “Mitsuko, come here. I need to sing. And get drunk. And *not* in that order.”

But Mitsuko didn’t move. She stood over their table with her hands in her knickerbocker pockets. She didn’t look as pissed off as normal. She looked confused and unhappy, like the sight of him was *that* troubling.

“What?” Vincenzo dared to ask.

“I don’t get you,” she said.

“You’re not obliged to.”

“Well, for curiosity’s sake, and because I’m one of Sylvia’s best friends, I am.” She started to turn away, then pointed at him. “We’re going to have a chat later. In private. I need to settle something that’s been bouncing around in my mind.”

When she left, Sylvia folded her hands on the table. “She’s rather disagreeable tonight.”

“You don’t even know. After the shootout, she slapped me.”

She gasped. “She did *not*. Vincenzo, you’re lying.”

“I’m not. She seems set on killing me.”

“*That*, she might be.”

The Black Kitten’s lights dimmed, introducing tonight’s performers. Mitsuko danced to a lone saxophone while Laurence helped the mood by shaking his rear and even coming down to mingle with his people, a queen amongst her peasants. He snaked between the tables in search of a fool.

It came in the form of Dominic. Stealing him away from Luis, Laurence heaved him up on stage for a dance. All the protest Dominic should've had about it melted into his spaghetti arms, and he stood like a frightened deer in the middle of the stage. Served him right, hiding the truth from Vincenzo. Maybe this would teach him not to keep secrets.

To help him better relax, Laurence snuck up behind Dominic and slapped his behind so hard, he yelped. His drunk face reddened in a mix of fear, bewilderment, animosity, and something Vincenzo couldn't place. He'd never seen such a rush of emotions cross his face before, like the slap had short-circuited his brain. Laurence, smugly pleased with himself, shrugged off whatever he was feeling and continued dancing.

Sylvia hooked around the curtain to watch. Her foot was tapping to the beat.

"You can go," Vincenzo told her. "I'll stay here."

"You know, with permission, any member of the audience can come up and dance with us. If you want…" She gave him a wink before setting off to her piano.

He liked to think he wasn't chained to her by the collar, but as his toes curled from being alone, he moved his seat to keep her in sight.

Capturing him like she'd done months ago, Sylvia played her piano with utter perfection. She sat up regally and created music with her eyes closed. He knew she did that to better connect to the music, but it was also a subtle jab at everyone who might've thought she wasn't as talented as she was. If people weren't pieces of shit, she would've had a magnificent job playing for a rich baron in Manhattan.

He walked towards the stage. He wanted to be closer to her. He wanted to be redesigned by her with new ambitions stemming from her and everything she needed.

He took one full step onto the stage. For a dazzling second, he was taller than everyone else, noticed regulars who noticed him. He was a performer at a pansy bar. He was part of the community.

Taking it all at once, he sat back down and stayed at ground level for the remainder of the night.

Chapter 10: A Boss' Birthday

She never thought she'd live past twenty three. She also never thought she'd attend a gangster boss' birthday party through her lover's invite.

As she got ready for the night, she had trouble believing that both were happening at the same time.

Campo's party was a mere four hours away and she'd just started getting ready. She couldn't help it. One program on the radio turned to three, then she wanted to learn how to cook an Italian dinner from *Nonna*. Shockingly to her, *Nonna* didn't hate her enough to shoo her out, but she kept reminding her to, "Go now, the party, be ready," so Sylvia could only assume that she wanted her thrown out by week's end.

She hid in the bathroom, specifically the bathtub, pruning in a two-hour bath. Which dress would draw the least amount of attention? Which wig looked the plainest? They wouldn't want to see her tangled mess of curls. Could she dye her blue one? It'd take some time, but...

"Sylvia?"

She blew out bubbles, then lifted her mouth above the lukewarm water. "Yes?"

"You okay?" Vincenzo asked through the door.

"Yes, just relaxing. I'll be out in a minute."

"That's fine. Take your time. I have something waiting for you when you come out. It's laid out on the bed."

"Oh, okay. Thank you," she said, and masturbated off her nerves to the image of Vincenzo strewn out across their bed, bow tied around his naked body. What a surprise that'd be.

After she dried off and wrapped herself in a bathrobe, she came out to find him gone, and in his place was a dress.

If it could be called that. It could've been a painting, fabric dripping off the bed, something preserved in art. Off-white in color, the piece shimmered in beads and thin layers of lace all the way to the floor. The design matched her chosen clutch for the night. It'd complement her heels. It was perfect, too much so for her.

Mezzanotte, who must've known an expensive dress when she saw one, stood guarding it a foot away. Ever since Sylvia had moved in, this little one had been staring her down. Now her stare had some attitude to it. Her claws extended into the comforter.

"Please, I'm trying," Sylvia reckoned with her. "I can't help that he does these things for me, but I know he loves you very much. You likely receive more presents than I do."

Mezzanotte slow-blinked at her.

"Please don't be mad. I'm doing all I can." To show her, she gave her her hand.

The cat chuffed and scampered underneath the bed. The dress had been won, but her friendship—tolerance—would have to be earned another day.

Sylvia sat beside the dress. She knew what this party would mean to him. He'd want her to look elegant and confident.

She positioned herself at her vanity, forced herself to look in the mirror, and started primping. She needed to like herself before she worried about anyone liking *her*. Most people wouldn't like her, but that shouldn't have mattered if she felt confident enough to date a gangster who earned more money in a week than she made in six months.

After doing her best with her makeup, she picked up the dress by its waist. An off-white evening gown. Had he meant for it to look like a wedding dress? It felt rich, like him.

She expected to hate it, but when she wiggled into its tight fit, she saw a new girl in her mirror. She was tall and slim. Her legs even looked good, and that was a feat most dresses couldn't pull off.

Was this what confidence was, dressing in a pricey dress and not ripping it off the moment it touched you? If so, how many dresses did she need to buy to keep this going? Did she need to sleep in them?

Someone knocked on the door.

She ended the twirl she was giving to the mirror. "Yes?"

"Just wanted to know how far along you were."

"Oh, yes." She closed her powder compacts and ran to the door. He must've been waiting for her to finish. What was she doing, wasting all this time? This was *his* room.

She opened the door. "I'm sorry—"

Vincenzo went to say something back, but he, as well as she, lost their words.

He was wearing an ironed three-piece suit with a pair of new shoes and a gold watch. He wore his hair back and smelled of cologne and wet sex. His face was clean shaven, dark eyes uncovered by his bangs. He always looked magnificent to her, but *this* Vincenzo left her enchanted.

He retracted his hand and looked her up and down, catching the sparkles of her dress and the extra makeup she'd placed around her eyes.

Unable to hold herself back, she took his hands and pulled him into the bedroom. He came willingly. She wondered what he wouldn't do under her command. This dress held an authority she wasn't used to.

She pressed him against the door. His smile told her this was okay. To make sure, she caressed his face and watched for any protest.

His head fell into her palm like a cat to its owner's hand.

Biting her lip, she leaned down and stole a kiss.

She stole many kisses. Many kisses stopped being kisses and became explorations of his mouth, a daring maneuver she was quite proud of. She hadn't done this before, kiss him first. He rewarded her bravery by moaning into her. He wrapped his arms around her and pulled her in. She almost touched his rear before she stopped herself and held his face instead.

"Sir!"

Vincenzo clicked his tongue against Sylvia's.

"Sir, you ready up there?" Luis called from downstairs.

"Yes," he groaned, and went to wipe the spit from his lips.

"Oh." Sylvia snuck in and dabbed away a splotch of lipstick.

"We have to be careful tonight," he said. "No good doing this at Campo's. Some of the men there hate their wives as much as they hate Hannigan."

"They'll be jealous, then?"

"Immensely." He kissed her cheek, then her neck. "You look beautiful. I want you to know I bought this dress before you moved in, so I haven't broken my promise. I was just trying to find a time to give it to you. I hope you like it."

"I do." She giggled at his kisses. "Who should be careful of whom tonight?"

He smiled into her skin. "Don't tempt me."

"No promises."

Dominic, Luis, and Ana were ready and waiting downstairs. Ana had on a red dress that matched the rose on Luis' lapel. Dominic wore a brown suit with his hat already on. Luis bounced on his heels. Dominic kept the hat over his eyes.

"Are we ready?" Ana asked.

"We are," Vincenzo said, and kissed *Nonna* on her forehead. *"We'll be home by midnight. Please don't wait for us."*

Nonna had Sophie in her arms, the babysitter for the night. She waved her little hand. "Bye-bye. Have fun. Wear fun masks."

Sylvia guessed that was a translation error and said her goodbyes.

The night brought with it a cool autumn air. Dead leaves danced down the road as Dominic drove past. When they passed a park Sylvia hadn't known existed, she went to ask Vincenzo if they could visit sometime.

His knee was jumping against his hand. His eyes, while looking out the window, were unfocused, cloudy with thought.

"Vincenzo?"

He moved his head towards her, but his eyes lingered outside.

"You okay?"

He nodded.

"Talk to me."

"My father and mother are going to be at this party. I don't want you meeting them."

"Would it be better if you didn't introduce me to them? Maybe only to your mother?"

Dominic looked at her in the mirror, then shook his head and turned down a street towards the water.

"Whatever you tell my mother will get funneled back to my father. He's under the belief I broke up with you. Once he finds out you're living with me, he's going to be furious. He might even blow up at this party. Then Campo will be disappointed, he'll never invite me to another party again. It'll all be over."

"Should I not have come?"

"No, it's not your fault, but if anyone says anything to you, just smile and look at me. I can handle them—most of them are beneath me in rank—and who knows, maybe some of them might not know about you and the Kitten, so then you'll be—"

She held the hand over his knee. She waited for him to flinch or push away, but he didn't. He was prepared for her to hold him.

"It'll be okay," she said. "Everything will be fine. We'll stay clear of them and stay with our friends. That way, we'll have strength in numbers, and nobody will bother us."

"But—"

"We'll be okay. If it becomes too much, we'll leave."

"But I always leave Campo's parties. He has hundreds of guests. I can't leave this one. He's turning fifty."

"He'll understand. I'll give him a talking-to."

"Sure, he'll allow that." He rubbed a hand down his face. "Thank you. I needed to vent."

"Of course. I pride myself on being able to talk down a terrible situation. It helps with my anxiety."

"I'm glad you pride yourself on something."

"Vincenzo, I was making a joke. I freeze up when I'm tense, you know that."

"Oh." He smiled even more. "I'm glad you like to joke."

"And what does that mean? I can be, what's the word, a jokester."

"You're usually so stoic. Do you mind if I, say, try to joke with you more often?"

She half-smirked in confusion. "Sure? You can crack your best knock-knock jokes at me."

Dominic snorted, then hushed up when Vincenzo gave him a look.

Based on how Vincenzo talked about Campo, Sylvia expected grandeur. She'd seen mansions on coastlines and magazine clippings of English manors. She'd dreamed of royal life as much as any little girl had.

Campo lived more majestically than that.

His home was a four-story mansion on the curve of Grassy Bay. His lawn and driveway stretched out and let them bask in his gardens. Immaculate, they were, with no flower out of place.

Black cars were parked around an angelic fountain, where Italian men escorted their partners out of the back seats. Many of them had chauffeurs who would stay outside for the night. She couldn't imagine how expensive they cost.

The house itself was lit with electricity. Silhouettes of rich folk walked by the windows while others dined on the balconies. The smells of dinner, the gold embellishments. It was a fantasy book she'd fallen asleep to, lost in its pages with fairies tempting her into their world. Like she wouldn't eat a slice of cake or two.

As Dominic parked the car, Vincenzo pressed his back into the seat.

"Hey, it'll be okay," she told him. It was nice not having to worry about herself tonight. She'd imagined herself shaking in the corner of some hall, holding back her stomach while her brain told her she didn't belong. Now, instead of falling into despair, she had the chance to save someone from their own darkness. If she was smart, she would've taken her own advice.

"This's gonna be great!" Luis said. He helped his wife out of their car, then shook Dominic's shoulders. "Are we ready, lads? Ready to party the night away?"

"Calm down," Vincenzo said, but he was on his tiptoes now, tallying how many people he needed to walk between.

Sylvia noticed some of the men they were passing were wearing eccentric eye masks. Some were gold, others blue and purple. Flowers popped out behind their ears and glittery eyes. How odd of them. Didn't they know whose party this was?

They stood in a line to gain entry into Campo's mansion. Two butlers handed something to each person as they entered.

"Which color are you going to choose?" Luis asked. "I'm picking red to match Ana's dress. Dominic?"

"I'll take whatever they give me," he said.

"Vincenzo? Sylvia?"

"Had we needed to pick something out in advance?" Sylvia asked.

"Oh, right," Vincenzo said. "Campo likes to host masquerade balls for his parties."

The butlers came into view. In their hands were plates of those colorful masks. Their ribbons cascaded off the plates like rainbows.

"It's an Italian thing," he continued. "They're exclusive parties where guests wear elaborate costumes and masks. Campo doesn't go all out with the gaudy outfits, but the masks—" He selected a turquoise mask, Sylvia a gold one. "He likes the masks. Thinks they're fun."

The hall welcomed them with jazz, gossip, and cigarette smoke. The foyer and dining hall had been furnished to the brim with taste. Red drapes hung over the windows. Chandeliers and sconces lit up an already bright house with warmth. Each main door had at least one bodyguard, server, or maid, all wearing masks. They doted on the guests with tranquil smiles.

"Is this okay?" she asked Vincenzo, noting the size of the crowds.

"For right now, yeah. Here, do you want me to tie on your mask?"

She stared at her choice and how bold it looked, then at Vincenzo's and how he hadn't put it on yet.

They traded quickly.

"We messed up," she said.

"I always pick the wrong one. I have no blue in my suit."

"And I hate gold—"

"*Vincenzo.*"

Even though it wasn't Campo's voice, Sylvia imagined Campo calling to him. Or Luis. Or even Dominic. She didn't know any other man who'd address him so casually.

A man and woman came up to greet them. The man, middle-aged with salt-and-pepper hair, was dressed as handsomely as Vincenzo. The woman was meek, her brown hair pinned with a golden flower that matched her dress. They walked arm in arm like a couple, but the woman's disheartened face and the man's dominating presence made them look like prisoners of one another's company than lovers at a party.

Vincenzo squeezed Sylvia's hand, and she was brought back into that alleyway. The fear of losing her. The feeling of being trapped. He was scared, and cornered.

The man spoke in Italian to Vincenzo, then asked him a violent question. Spit hit the ground as he spoke.

Vincenzo glared at him with his head down. He must've wanted to scream a thousand insults. She saw that much in him. He'd said many of these men were beneath him in rank, but this man looked different. They looked almost like equals, a fact that infuriated both of them.

Without blowing up, Vincenzo answered the man with a simple, mellow, *"Sì."*

Which sent the man off. He growled, actually growled, an animal dressed in a suit. Hands went to their belts. Sylvia caught the gleam of a gun and went to run, then felt herself turn in a half-circle. She spun away from whatever brawl was about to take place.

Vincenzo led her into a dead-end far from the foyer. Here, away from the crowds, he kicked the wall hard enough to leave a dent and cursed the man he'd almost killed.

"Was that—"

"My parents," he panted. "I didn't know they were going to—I mean, I did. They always come early to these things." He ripped off his mask and pinched his nose. *"Fuck me."*

"Hey—"

"You're not a 'sick' person. We're not sick. *He's* the sick one."

Sylvia knew of Severo. She hadn't planned on ever meeting him, he who broke her lover's heart every time he opened his mouth. It was why she never wanted to see her mother again. Their life-draining energies had no business being a part of their lives. She was lucky. She had the choice to cut her out completely. Vincenzo had to see Severo every other day, reopening himself to beatings and slurs that were seen as normal.

She rubbed his shoulder. "To Hell with it, then. Let's leave. You don't have to deal with him tonight. We can take the car, drive out to the water. You can tell Campo that your grandmother fell, I'm sure he won't be mad at that. He'll understand why you have to go, and we'll leave."

He was still looking away, fearing who'd see them, so Sylvia ended it with, "It's your choice."

And that little phrase, whatever he took from it, lifted him back up to normal. His eyes returned to their natural light. "Okay," he said, his head clearing. "Okay. I have to, uh, say hello to Campo first. Wish him a happy birthday."

"Let's go find him."

"Just...give me a moment, alright? I feel like if I see my father again, I'll strangle him."

"Alright." She stood beside him against the wall, hiding their handholding from nosy guests.

He tried regaining his breath in slow intakes. "Thank you."

"Of course."

"I mean it. Your understanding and acceptance of me is...unfathomable at times, but I appreciate that you put up with me."

"I like to think that I don't put up with anyone but myself. I *chose* to be here. I *chose* to be with you. I *choose* not to listen to your father and his opinions about me, though I do care about how it affects you. Because I love you and want to see you at your best. That's what confidence is, right?"

She wondered if he believed her. How could one not care about people's opinions of you? At what point did you forget them and continue on with those who admired you rather than ridiculed you?

"I wish I could be as open as you are," he said.

"Drinking helps," she said bluntly. "Is he serving alcohol here?"

He smiled and tied his mask back on. "Is a gangster serving alcohol at his own party? There's probably some in the ball-room. I'll get you one drink, then we'll run."

"Just *one* drink?" she teased, and left with him, hand in hand.

Chapter 11: Taking a Gamble

If Italy stopped being a dictatorship for one summer, he'd like to take Sylvia to the Vatican and christen her as a saint. He'd pay whatever it cost, beg for however long. It wouldn't take much on God's part to bless her into more of a saint than she already was, given her work tonight.

The thing was, this was all *because* of her. And that wasn't a bad thing. If his father had disrespected him in front of his associates, he would've scoffed, mentally called him a fucker, and left for the buffet in search of a drink.

But to hear him call Sylvia a whore he'd lowered his standards to pursue, he almost shot the bastard. Shot him twice in the head and once in the heart, then, if he hadn't been tackled by Campo's men, he would've proceeded to cut him up with a knife he'd steal from a passing plate of cheese and crackers.

"You're all sick, you know that?"

To say, "Yes," to him without fearing the consequences. God, the rush. It stroked his fragile ego to think he'd finally silence the fuck who almost programmed him to be as low as he was.

Bless Sylvia for reminding him that he was the better man.

They trekked around the opposite side of the house to avoid bumping into Severo again. Vincenzo had needed a full symphony to calm down. His bloodlust drained the more time he spent with her, and parading around this mansion with masquerade masks on whilst avoiding his father...

"Like cops and robbers, aren't we?" Sylvia asked.

If not a saint, perhaps a mind reader. "We better not be the coppers in this scenario."

"I wouldn't want to be the robber."

"Well, you did rob me of my heart."

He didn't know how that could've sounded stupider, but Sylvia sucking in her red lips to keep from laughing definitely stabbed the very heart she'd stolen. He was glad his mask was covering most of his face.

They circled back to a lounge where nobody was really lounging. Guests stood and clinked their glasses together, gossiping the night away with faceless strangers. They crossed paths with a butler carrying Campari with lemon wedges. Vincenzo called for two glasses and gave one to Sylvia.

"He can just carry alcohol like this?" she asked.

"No copper's going to squeal on us tonight. He's paying off most of New York to keep quiet. The rest are too scared to say anything."

"My." She took a sip. "These men are truly something else. I feel so out of place."

"Don't be. You're outshining every woman here."

"I wouldn't say that at all."

"Why not? What happened to that charming confidence of yours?"

"Like the Moon, it waxes and wanes. One moment I feel like the tallest person in the room, the next I want to hide and pretend I don't exist. I feel daring, dressed like this outside of the Black Kitten, but I'm definitely noticing how...different I look, compared to these women."

"Different how?" he questioned. "You're outshining everyone here."

"Well, aren't you the romantic tonight."

"Like you said, it waxes and wanes."

They walked down a hall overlooking the water. Across from the windows was an on-going card game beneath a life-sized portrait of Campo's niece, Gabriella. They had a game of rummy going, and among the men, holding one-third of the deck, was a sweating Luis.

"How unfortunate," Sylvia said as they gravitated towards him.

"Fifteen minutes into the party and he's already down."

"Is he that unlucky?"

Luis shakily placed down a two on his neighbor's set, but two turns later, that same neighbor ended the game and scooped up his winnings.

"*Damn* it!" He slapped his cards on the table. "One more go, just one more."

"He's just lousy at cards," Vincenzo said.

"I wish I could've helped him."

His ears piqued. "Are you a gambler?"

"I do enjoy playing, yes."

"I didn't know that. Are you good?"

"Well, I wouldn't say that."

"Oh, sir!" Luis waved them over. "Where'd you run off to? Don't tell me you were off with your date, 'ey?"

Vincenzo motioned him out of his seat, then gave it to Sylvia and took the seat beside her. He wanted to call her bluff.

He hadn't seen her play cards before. It didn't seem like her scene.

"Good evening, Mr. DiFiore," the dealer said. "Is the lady playing tonight, or are you playing together?"

"That's up to her, but it'd be best if—"

As the dealer dealt out the cards, Sylvia quickly hid her hand against her chest. "I wouldn't mind playing against you, dear."

Luis whistled. "What a card, miss. Knock him dead!"

Vincenzo instinctively went to explain the game to her, as he'd never seen a woman confidently play against a table full of men, but before he could reorder his own cards, she fanned out a trio of queens.

A man at the table oohed. Another muttered something Vincenzo thankfully didn't hear.

"Look at that, Vinny," one of the men said. "You got yourself a card, haven't you?"

"It's still early," one man was quick to point out, and started his turn.

Not giving him the time of day, Sylvia played like a professional against amateurs. She devoured all the aces. The tens had no chance. Her points racked up as the men's looks turned from admiration to befuddlement to even anger.

Vincenzo didn't know how she did it, but she somehow predicted each one of his turns. She'd give him this look that'd break his heart, then pick the right card at the right time and destroy his potential winning blow.

With nearly ten cards in his hand and the deck almost gone, Vincenzo fell back with a laugh. "Well, darn."

"You have to bring this gal around more often," one man said to Vincenzo.

"I never knew she was this good," he confessed. "How'd you get like this?"

"Oh, you know," she said, and ended the game by placing the final queen on Vincenzo's set.

Even though he lost, he smiled at her triumph. If he'd known about her love for gambling, he would've played cards with her at the Kitten. How many dates could they've gone on with her having fun and him praising her? They didn't have to play for money, either. Seeing her happy would've been enough.

"Lucky girl," the dealer said, and dealt out her winnings.

Sylvia stared at the two ten-dollar bills being shoved her way. Campo must've visited the bank that night. They were crisp and smelled like him.

"Is this all for me?" she asked.

Two of the men grumbled incoherently.

Vincenzo took the bills for himself and helped Sylvia up. "Let's go get you another drink. Excuse us, gentlemen."

"I'll take the next hand!" Luis said. "Let me take her seat. It's the lucky seat."

Vincenzo didn't have many favorite places to be, but Campo's balconies were certainly contenders. He'd discovered them years back during another congested party. While beautifully orchestrated, they consisted of too many men and women he was expected to indulge. He'd escaped here one night to catch his breath, then kept coming back with excuses to smoke or clear his head.

He led her to a balcony overlooking the water. The Moon hung above their heads and sparkled the bay with stars. Down by the water's edge sang river frogs and night bugs, dueting the jazz music inside.

Sylvia leaned over the railing with her eyes closed. "It's so nice out tonight."

"It is." He popped open his breast pocket and returned the two bills to her. "I didn't like the way they kept looking at you. If they saw you taking their money, it might've set them off."

"They did seem a bit odd."

"They're shitty men with shittier morals."

"I thought you got along well with them."

"You have to be nice to men like that. It's the only way to get up in the world. So, how'd you learn to play so well?"

"I count cards."

He laughed. "Seriously?"

"I used to watch games on my breaks at the Black Kitten. After so many years, you get bored playing by the rules. You want to branch out into riskier games." She dropped her head onto his. "Do you still want to leave?"

"Hm." His lips were inches away from her temple. "I'm not sure. If my father stays out of my way, I'll be fine. Certain party atmospheres I can deal with. Like—" He went to catch himself but couldn't. "Take the Black Kitten, for example. If it's not too busy, I do enjoy having a drink there."

"You do?"

His heart picked up a little. "You know, these parties are fun and all, but the Kitten brings with it an atmosphere that's...different. The people are different, the tastes rawer."

"Rawer?"

The truth fizzled back into his heart. He *could* tell her. It was his choice, but he chose to keep that secret away from her. Just a few more months and he'd tell her the real reason he enjoyed the Black Kitten. Once he was ready. "I just like it, is all. Sometimes, I wish I was there rather than here, with no obligations or work to do, but *you're* here, so I can breathe easier."

She nestled her head against him like a baby bird. "*Vincenzo*," she purred. "My love, you're making me swoon tonight."

He hoped so. He didn't know why he was trying so hard to capture her heart when she'd already captured his. It must've been because of his father and what he'd said to him, but he didn't want that to be the case. He didn't want his actions to dictate how he lived.

He licked his lips and leaned over to kiss her. He didn't *have* to do anything tonight. Like Sylvia had said, he had choices. He could stay like this for hours and only worry about her running out of breath. Hopefully, to warn him, she'd give a little tug on his hair or bite his lower lip.

He opened her mouth with his.

"Ah."

He pulled back.

"There he is, though he seems busy. Let's leave them be."

He covered his mouth. He'd left the balcony doors open a crack, and in the crack, Campo d'Antonio was watching them with a crowd.

"S-sir." He smoothed out his hair and blazer. "I apologize. I didn't know you were—Did you need anything?"

Campo came out with his entourage, a mix of men and women wearing black masks. They watched them like crows.

"Good evening, you two," he said. "It's nice to see you again, Ms. Belmonte. How're you finding yourself?"

"Oh, it's, uh, wonderful, sir. Thank you again for inviting me."

"You're welcome every year."

Vincenzo wiped his lips and took out a small box from his back pocket. It was a watch he'd found in Manhattan with his initials carved into the gold. "Happy birthday, sir. This's from me and Sylvia. Here's to another fifty more years."

"Just fifty?" He air-kissed his cheek and gave the box to one of his acquaintances to hold. "Thank you, my boy. Have you found your seats yet? I want you sitting next to me this evening. You're his anchor for tonight, Ms. Belmonte. Make sure he doesn't leave early."

"Oh." She nodded hesitantly. "Of course, sir, although," she added, "although, I have been feeling a bit faint, so—"

"Is everything alright?" he asked, genuinely concerned about her lie. "If you're feeling unwell, please, by all means, don't push yourself to stay here. I'm sure Vincenzo would be cross with me if I made you stay."

"I'm sure he wouldn't, but thank you. I just don't want you to think ill of me if we, say, suddenly disappeared without notice. Vincenzo wanted a chance to say happy birthday to you if and when we leave."

"How considerate." He took a drag from his cigarette. "If you do stay, Vincenzo, I'd like to hear your voice before the main courses arrive."

Vincenzo choked on his collecting spit. Was he serious? Had he heard about his argument with his father? Was this punishment for acting out, or for showing public affection with Sylvia? And which was worse: getting caught acting childish or coquettish?

"Uh, right," he said, "sure. Not a problem, sir."

"Marvellous! Now, I have another question for you. Have you happened to see any of my grandchildren tonight? I'm looking for my lovely Gabriella, but she's nowhere to be found."

A door slammed somewhere downstairs, followed by a shriek of a young child.

"Ah!" He pulled up his trousers and left for the doors. His crowd followed. "I always say that if you can't hear a child, you're in danger. Anyway, I'm glad to see both of you again. Dinner's in one hour, so make sure you find your seats! I can't wait to hear your performance, Vincenzo!"

He said more, but Vincenzo tuned him out. *"Hear your performance?"* Now? In front of Sylvia? He wasn't ready. He'd hadn't practiced in weeks. She'd only laugh at him again.

When they were alone, Sylvia asked, "You okay?"

He shook his head and downed the remainder of his drink.

Sensing that he needed it, she offered him her glass.

He finished that, too.

"You need more," she guessed.

"I have about ten minutes to get as drunk as God will phys-ically allow me, and even then, you know, I can keep going."

"Good thing we're at a lawless party. Let's go find our seats before I lose you."

"And even then," he reminded her.

"And even then," she said, and hooked her arm around his as they re-entered the party.

Chapter 12: Mother

She entered the banquet hall, drinking heavily, worrying even more so. This room had the most amount of people in it, packed into tables and around serving maids. They all looked happy as they dined on hors d'oeuvres. Vincenzo was the only one pulling sickly faces as he drank.

"Hear your performance." Was he going to play a song for Campo? Write a sonnet for him? A speech? Why was he so nervous about it? Had he practiced it well?

She tried steering him away from the denser parts of the crowds and closer to the windows. A live orchestra was performing here on an elevated part of the floor. The piano mirrored the one in her apartment, although someone had kept up with this one's waxing and made it look even more expensive.

"How grand," she said. "Vincenzo, look."

He did, then picked up a new glass and chugged it down.

She tried a different approach. "Do you know where our seats are?"

"Uh, yeah. Let me—"

"There you are!"

Vincenzo groaned. They'd just found their place cards when two drunk men sauntered up to them.

"Campo was out and about looking for you," one of them said.

"You're up next, aren't you?"

Vincenzo pinched the top of his hand. She wished she knew what was upsetting him so she could help. She had to save him somehow.

Unable to say no, Vincenzo made sure Sylvia had a drink and a plate of bruschetta before leaving with them. "Sylvia, go find Luis or Dominic. You can stay with them until I come back. Or you can stay out in the hall. That's it. Go out and—" But his voice was drowned out by the crowds, and he was taken away from her, leaving her alone in this strange world.

She folded her napkin over her lap. Each chair had two glasses and three plates of food, some half-eaten, some not. Who would she be sitting next to? A mayor? A prince? She wouldn't discredit it.

"Are you sitting here?"

Ana, who must've had an agenda on avoiding her husband for the night, stood alone behind her.

"I am," Sylvia said.

So she sat, and Sylvia almost sighed. She looked like she had a lot on her mind and Sylvia didn't think she had it in her to hear it.

"Where did Vincenzo go?" she asked.

"I'm not sure. I think he went to speak to Campo."

"That makes sense." She chose her glass. "Is this the first party he's ever taken you to?"

"Is it that easy to tell?"

"Quite." She drank the tiniest sip. "You know, women at this status need to keep their guards up in order to benefit from society."

"I beg your pardon?" Sylvia asked.

She swirled the drink in her hand. "These men see us as our man's finer tastes in life, like handbags or large houses. Our job is to cut those people down with clever words and pretty eyes, to never back down from their rude remarks to show we can handle whatever they throw at us. It's what you need to do, if you're pretending on being a woman. I don't feel like you're doing a good job at it."

Sylvia caught her reflection in one of the glasses meant for her. She picked it up, admiring a face she didn't usually hate but didn't necessarily like. She saw herself just like this, like a stranger looking into a mirror. The person she saw might've been her, but if she were to wake up and find herself in a different body with a different face, she wouldn't have complained. She used to think if that ever happened, she'd hoped for a prettier face and a slimmer body so that blending in would be easier.

She finally looked Ana in the eyes. She had on lovely makeup. "Not to be so forwards, but do you like me?"

"No," she said, "I don't particularly like you."

"May I ask why?"

"Do you need a reason?"

"I don't, but if I could shed some light on anything you might be confused about, I'd like to help."

She set down her glass. "I know this might be difficult for you to understand, but this party is neither the time nor place to discuss such topics. Keep it at those speakeasies you work at. But to answer part of your question, I care about how I'm seen in the presence of my husband, and now that includes you, so any advice I can give you to fit in is beneficial to me."

Sylvia didn't know what she was expecting. It hurt knowing she wanted to prove her wrong and couldn't. To change a hateful mind on an idea which had never been contested before. It must've been because of the alcohol. It made her brash.

"He's over there, by the way," Ana said, "in case you wanted to catch the show."

Vincenzo had found himself in the middle of the stage. He was at a microphone, fiddling with the cuffs of his dress shirt. Upon his arrival, the guests quieted down until Sylvia only heard herself breathing.

She scooted out of her chair. He wanted her absent from this. Maybe it was a commemorative speech meant only for Campo's men, or maybe he was embarrassed by a birthday speech he'd written for him. She left for the nearest door.

The trumpets led him in. Then the piano, performed by a beautiful dark-skinned woman, and then a guitar of all things. It didn't fit the motif of any jazz song she knew, but it did fit an Italian one.

When he started singing, guests drew their attention away from their meals to watch the spectacle for themselves. Men turned in their chairs, women covered their mouths. Sylvia had made it to the door before her knees weakened at the love song.

She assumed. Somewhere, Campo and his wife would be swooning. His high notes conjured a sense of intimacy that was new to her. His Italian was dominant yet smooth, powerful yet loving. He sang most of it with his eyes closed, letting her take in every part of him. Even the tiniest things like his open mouth, she'd never seen him speak—sing—so openly before. Why hadn't he wanted her to see this? Because she'd fall to her knees and do unspeakable things to him? Honestly, very likely, but shame on him for not wanting her to experience this.

When he finally opened his eyes, he looked at their table and saw only Ana, and his microphone slipped. He began searching the tables, bouncing between businessmen and lawyers as he sang, trying to find someone he wanted.

As he saw Sylvia standing above everyone else, that fear he was feeling vanished, and he smiled. His voice grew, as well as his confidence, and his voice reverberated off the walls and into Sylvia so strongly that her jaw quivered. At the final lines, he reached out to her, all the while keeping eye contact with the only person in the room who mattered to him.

The crowd applauded. A holler was thrown out by the drunker lot. Vincenzo gave a polite bow.

Sylvia took several long blinks to remember where she was, then hobbled back to her seat. She used the tablecloth to better hide herself and her shaking hands. She wished she was drunker than this. She didn't know what to do with these new Italian words now implanted into her brain. They sounded romantic.

Vincenzo found her just as Luis ran up and said, "That was great, sir! Better than last year. What a bold choice."

"It was per Campo's request. I haven't practiced in weeks."

"It's one of his favorites," Ana said.

"Even worse." He wrapped his arm around Sylvia. "Did you like it?"

Despite everything in her mind telling her not to, she scooted away from him and pressed a hand between her thighs.

"Hm?"

"I..." She lowered her voice so nobody at the table heard her. "I haven't allowed myself to imagine you singing an Italian opera in my presence."

"Not really an opera, but I did take singing lessons at my church when I was younger. Campo, he likes it. Thinks that, if I wasn't working for him, I could pick it up as a profession. What's wrong?"

She bit her lip. "The excitement might've gotten ahead of me."

His brain spun in circles before he saw what she was hiding between her legs. *"Oh."*

"Make it go *away*," she whispered, hiding her laughter against his neck. "What an impression to give to your friends."

"W-what should I do?" Luckily, he was laughing as well and doing a poorer job of hiding his embarrassment. "What makes things like that go away?"

"I don't know. Take my mind off it. Make me think of anything other than your..." She couldn't finish. She needed to calm down in order to be invited to more of these parties.

"Well, what's there to say? The weather?"

"Anything, darling, please. All I can think about is you and your co—"

"Okay," he said, interrupting her. "Uh, Mezzanotte, then. She's a Bombay, I believe. She likes hiding socks underneath my bed. In truth, I hide my best ones in a locked drawer and let her have her favorites."

"Vincenzo, how is you taking care of a kitten who pilfers socks going to fix this? It's only making it worse."

"T-then, how about, uh..."

"Talk about nonsense, you utter buffoon."

He smirked. "I'm not one to talk nonsense."

"Goodness, that is so much like you."

Luis tapped the table. "I can't wait for Campo's cake, sir. It smells so good. Did you see it? I peeked my head into the kitchen and saw it myself."

"I haven't really had the time," Vincenzo said, still leaning into Sylvia's body. "Sylvia, dear, do you need to go use the—"

"The bathroom, yes," she said. "Can you direct me to the nearest one?"

"Of course."

But before they could run off and do unspeakable acts alone, the laughter of a child much too young to be at this party skipped through the crowd.

Luis, delighted, waved into the crowd. "Gabriella!"

A little girl ran around the tables with a fiddle in her hands. Behind her, two women and three men acting as her bodyguards accompanied her.

"Ah, there she is!" Luis said. "*La mia Gabriella*! You look wonderful!"

Gabriella twirled her dress. "*Ciao,* everyone! That means 'hello' or 'goodbye' in Italian. Grandpa said to greet everyone with that tonight."

"You are so smart." Luis lifted her up and kissed her cheek. Her bodyguards kept a close eye on how high he lifted her.

"This's Gabriella d'Antonio," Vincenzo said. "She's Campo's granddaughter, and this's Gia and Elena, his two daughters."

The two women curtsied.

"And little Gabriella here knows how to play the violin," Luis said, "or should I say the *fiddle*."

Gabriella giggled. "My momma taught me how to play in elementary school, and the violin and fiddle are sister strings, so it's really easy to play."

"And so terribly Irish," Vincenzo said, and Campo's daughters laughed.

Sylvia looked for the joke. Was it because they didn't favor Irish traditions? If so, why was she allowed to have the instrument in the house?

"This's gonna be so funny," Luis said. "In truth, sir, I thought you were gonna sing some Flannigan jig to get the ball rolling."

"Like I'd know any," he said, and touched Sylvia's arm. "Every year, we try to get a jab at Campo for fun. Last year, we got him after he scored a deal with a Mexican brewery on the border."

"We had to pay so much for that damaged bridge," Luis said.

"Are you planning on pranking him tonight?" Sylvia asked.

"Yeah!" Gabriella exploded. "I'm gonna play the song I've been practicing!"

"We have to get her set up for dinner now. If you'll excuse us," Gia said, and spoke to her daughter in Italian before toting her off.

Sylvia tugged on Vincenzo. "What's going on? Should I prepare for anything, well, illegal?"

"No. Just clap along to the beat."

"Won't his security intervene?"

"Oh, no. They're the reason we're allowed to do this. They want to get him as badly as we do."

The crowd launched into a cheer, and Gabriella waved at them from the stage. Campo clapped the loudest for her, yelling cute Italian phrases Sylvia needed to learn. She noticed that the men behind him had on conniving smiles as they clapped.

"Everyone," Gia announced, "our lovely *angelo* Gabriella has a song she wishes to perform for her *nonno* on his fiftieth birthday."

A low applause. Sylvia clapped softly, waiting to see if she needed to duck in cover or scream.

"Now, without further ado, please enjoy *a song by our little angel.*"

Bursting with anticipation, Gabriella readied her bow, wedged her fiddle into her neck, and played.

It definitely wasn't an Italian song. It didn't start off slow and didn't sound very traditional. The abruptness startled her and most of the guests, but it set off every man in the room like wind-up toys. Vincenzo and the rest of them got up and clapped to the rhythm of the fiddle, stomping their feet like they were trained in Irish dance. Those in on the joke sang to the piece in terrible Irish accents.

The rush of culture mixed with so many people moving, Sylvia hadn't noticed the chefs bring in a three-tier cake from the kitchen. The layers of green, white, and orange might've irked Campo if not for the ridiculous amount of leprechauns and rainbows sticking out from the frosting.

As Campo was taken by his cake, Vincenzo and a few others delivered the finishing blow: a bag of green confetti. It exploded over his balding head like a pollinating flower, and through the singing and clapping, he burst into a belly laugh he couldn't control. Taking his knife, he sliced through his rival's flag colors with the vitality of a true gangster boss.

Vincenzo, who'd been so composed around his peers, snorted back his laughter as he gathered leftover confetti and rained it over his head. It was like a child had been hiding behind those heavy-set eyes. Sylvia clapped louder when she saw it, encouraging him to break out of his shell.

Seeing the woman next to him took all the joy she had and murdered it.

She was sitting near Campo, looking to see how much laughter was appropriate. She wore a grey dress. Her hair was lighter now and her mask was black and feathery, but Sylvia had memorized her facial features before she was too afraid to meet her eyes.

Had she'd known Sylvia would be here? No, she'd changed both her first and last name. She wouldn't have known. Sylvia had *wanted* to tell her—she'd written about it in so many letters. So, why was she looking at her now? Why was she standing up and coming towards her, eyebrow arched in the way that meant she was angry at what Sylvia had done?

Sylvia stood up and almost knocked over a plate in a butler's hand. She couldn't say sorry. Or say anything. She didn't want to get hurt, to have her mother yell at her and wake up the neighbors with how deviant she was.

She ran. The night was a dream she wasn't meant to finish. Reality had come to rip away her dress and pearls and wake her up from this fantasy.

She passed Dominic, who was trying to ignore three women who were obviously flirting with him. She covered her face in case she looked ugly.

"Sylvia?"

She burst through the double doors into a patio of cushioned seats and open umbrella stands. She thought it'd never end, this ocean of dining bodies, until she tripped down a set of steps and reached the back lawn.

Too disoriented to think, she ran east, opposite of the front lawn where they'd parked. How stupid. Her mind was splintering on her heels. But she kept on her path with her dress hiked up. She had to keep going until she could no longer run.

Her escape ended at Grassy Bay, where toads were croaking between cattails. They helped mute the sound of the fairytale party behind her, but she could no longer play pretend. Her mother had come to take her from her happily ever after.

From the lawn, her old name was said.

She fell. She gripped the sides of her cheeks until her mask fell into the sand. Did she have to turn around? Could she have stayed still, helpless prey against a stalking predator?

Her mother, Clara, almost out of breath as she was, took out a fan from her purse and fanned herself. "What on God's Earth are you doing here? This's a *private* party, and look at how you're dressed. What is wrong with you?"

Sylvia squeezed the wrist that had the memories of her mother carved into it. It'd been years. It still burned with pain.

"Come with me," her mother said. "You need to leave. Now."

Her voice squeaked. Her legs betrayed her when she tried to stand.

"Now," her mother seethed, and freed her from the wet sand. She forced her up the steps like a child against the will of her mother.

"Why..."

"Shut *up*," her mother snapped, and Sylvia did, obedient as ever and ready to follow wherever this woman would take her.

A sparkle caught her eye. On her bony wrist, her mother was wearing a silver bracelet studded with what had to be fake diamonds.

Growing up, they weren't penniless, but her mother had forbidden her from buying anything "luxurious." This included jewelry, ice cream, toys of any kind, extra clothes even though hers were stained, books. Always meant to feel like her existence was a burden to her loved ones. Yet here this woman was, wearing a dress that looked too good on her at a party pulled straight out of Alice's Wonderland.

Sylvia pulled away.

Her mother whipped around. "Come here."

"I'm not leaving with you. I was invited here, personally, by Campo, so—"

"No, you weren't. You..." Her expression darkened. "Are you some sort of escort here? To some man? Is that what you're still doing? Acting like a whore and selling yourself to perverts for cash?"

There she was. That villainous tone. Her natural state. Sylvia added another level of protection to her voice. "No. I mean, yes, I'm with a man, but we're together as—"

"I knew it. You haven't changed." She wiped off the hand that'd held her. "You're disgusting. Back when you were living with us, you brought those filthy men into my house. They stole from my purse. They kept us up. We were laughing stocks of the whole neighborhood."

"But I've apologized for that," Sylvia said. "I was thirteen. You—" She teared up. "You should've been more responsible for me."

"What?"

The truth slipped out. "You never cared about me, ever. You always thought I was a terrible person growing up. What kind of mother hates a child that's suffering so much?"

"You never suffered."

Sylvia's heart, the one she'd tried to mend from years of abuse, shattered.

"You wanted sympathy and attention and did everything you could to get it, including throwing away your life to dress as a woman. Now look at you. Just a prostitute living for shameless men. It's embarrassing."

She covered her mouth to keep from vomiting up pieces of her heart. All those letters she'd written to her and thrown away, the nightmares, the scars. She'd accumulated so much hurt from her, yet *she* was the one expected to apologize.

Her brain, once submissive and resigned, which had grown into her mannerisms quite well, clicked. Dormant gears began to creak and turn. She was standing now, over the woman who'd almost taken her life, and saw herself bigger than her and her efforts.

This woman, she wasn't her mother. She was a person who'd given birth to her. The rest had been tossed into a river, sealed inside a picnic basket meant to be abandoned.

"You are the worst," Sylvia said, "most hate-filled, most vile woman I've ever had the displeasure of knowing. You've taken your privileges of marriage and love and child-bearing for granted, none of which you ever deserved, and I don't ever, *ever* want to see or think about you again."

She went to leave and be done with her for good, but Clara grabbed her wrist and went to strike her for speaking out.

Sylvia stepped back and blocked it. Taking her hand, she then shoved her back and knocked her down. The force knocked herself down as well, but the shock from the cold sand unclouded her brain to better see who this woman was.

"How *dare* you," Clara said.

"Oh, yes, how *dare* I," Sylvia said. "I should've said that years ago."

"You—"

"I'm not afraid of you!" she yelled at her. "I'm done brooding over how you feel about me. So go on, yes, say whatever you please. Tell me I'm the worst decision you've ever made. Blame me for all of your shortcomings. I've heard it all before, and it means *nothing* to me now!"

"But—"

"No!" she shouted. "*I* am talking! Do *not* talk over me!"

Running up from the garden footpaths, Vincenzo, her angel with his hair out of place, surveyed the situation from above. "Sylvia," he panted, and ran around Clara to help her up.

"Who's this?" Clara demanded.

Vincenzo ignored her and held Sylvia's hands. "Baby, what's wrong? Dominic said you were crying."

She went to say that she was fine, better than most nights she'd lived with this person, then saw her hands shaking and swallowed dryly from saying so much at once.

Clara cleaned off her dress. "Sir, I'm not sure if you're aware, but this man is not a woman. He's lying to you."

Vincenzo scowled, likely smelling the sulfur on her. "The only woman I fail to see here is you, for one wouldn't dare speak to another woman like this."

"But he's not—" She sighed. "Sir, I'll have to ask you to leave me and this man alone for a moment. I need to speak to him privately."

"And who are you?"

"I'm Clara Benítez, sir. I'm sure Mr. d'Antonio has told you about me. I'm his personal hair stylist in Queens."

Vincenzo dropped his head with a calculating stare, then his eyes widened. "Is this...your mother?"

"I am," Clara said, somehow proudly.

Sylvia glanced between them. She'd told him about her—she must've said her name once or twice—but with their differing makeup styles and height, it was hard to tell the family resemblance.

His eyes unfocused into the sand as he reached behind him for his gun. He didn't stall like he had with his father in the foyer. His aim on Clara's face was deadly accurate.

Clara screamed and covered her face, but it didn't affect him. He held his arm out, eyes trained down the barrel of the gun. "You're the bitch who hurt Sylvia."

"What?"

He cocked his gun and cornered her against the stone wall. "Give me a reason not to shoot you right now, and make it good."

"What? Why?"

"Because thirteen years of abusing your child and kicking her out because she was different is everything God put you on this Earth not to do, and I shouldn't have to tell you that in order for you to get it. A reason. Now."

"But I haven't *done* anything to h—"

He fired into the stone and made her cower. Sylvia watched the tears fall from her cheeks and wondered if she should've felt bad. She did, somewhat, but she also had no qualms with letting Vincenzo continue.

"You can't do this!" Clara said. "Campo would—"

"Campo would not give less of a *fuck* if I dragged you into the bay by your hair and drowned you, so I suggest you give me one reason to spare you before I paint this beach with your blood."

"Why are you attacking me for this?"

"Because I'm this woman's husband and, unlike her, I don't have the self-control not to murder you for all the things you've done. Now—"

"*Vincenzo!*"

Vincenzo lowered his gun. His father burst into view and wobbled down the steps. Visible sweat was bleeding through his suit as he yelled at them in Italian. He screamed something at Sylvia. She heard at least two curses about her and her promiscuity.

"Fuck." Vincenzo grabbed Sylvia. "We need to leave. Are you ready?"

She nodded and ran away with him. She glanced down at Clara, now sobbing and begging Severo to help her. She'd never seen her so pitiable. She hated how little she cared for that and how that wasn't the alcohol talking. Ten years of unresolved anger, all pushed out in thirty seconds and unable to be taken back.

Good. She wouldn't have taken back a single thing, except maybe not falling down. She was still learning how to stand up for herself.

She dazed out until she heard the car door slam behind her. Vincenzo battled between closing his door and starting the car at the same time. "Fuck, fuck, fuck."

"Where're we going?" she asked.

"Away. I'm taking you home."

"No." She knew herself too well. Even with Vincenzo, going back home to a dark room and trying to sleep would've left her nauseous. And she didn't know if he'd stay with her. He'd fired a shot during Campo's party. He was going to be reprimanded for tonight.

Upon hearing her refusal, Vincenzo paused and waited to hear what she wanted to do.

She took off her wig. "Take me to get absolutely fucking wasted."

Chapter 13: Date Night

Brooklyn had fewer good speakeasies to dine at than Harlem, but if you looked hard enough, you too could find yourself in a basement of drunken, feathery rule breakers too drunk to stay straight.

Yet despite it being a Thursday night, Brooklyn was astir with noise. Horse-drawn carriages carried couples to their midnight destinations. A theater was advertising *Metropolis* for a cool twenty-five cents. Vincenzo had gone to see it with *Nonna* back in spring. Those "robots" scared the daylights out of him. He wondered if Sylvia would enjoy it, or if she'd ever been to the theater before.

"Where is it that you wanted to go?" he asked her while he drove. "Knowing *Nonna*, she's probably asleep by now, and I don't have any obligations until tomorrow evening."

"I wish to drink, no more, no less."

He took his eyes off the road to make sure she was okay. She was curled up in the passenger seat like a cat. The underneath of her eyes were red, but she hadn't sobbed once, not even after yelling at her mother.

"That sounded too harsh, didn't it?" she asked. "I'm feeling strange tonight, Vincenzo. I apologize for my rudeness."

"That's—"

"Actually," she said, "I'm *not* sorry. Why should I apologize for feeling how I feel? Men don't apologize nearly as much for their feelings, yet women are expected to not only apologize but accept everything all the time. I'm sick of it."

"I don't suppose you have to apologize for that," he said. "You were brave tonight, going against that woman. I caught a bit of what you yelled at her. It was nice to hear that side of you."

"That's why I want to drink. We've earned it after withstanding our parents."

He nodded. He couldn't imagine how cathartic it must've felt. To scream at your abuser about all the pain they'd inflicted on you, and to walk away like that. If that'd been him with his father, boy, he'd be in trouble. Or dead. He liked thinking his father wasn't ruthless enough to actually kill him.

"I know a bar down here," he said. "It's called the Viola Tavern. I supply them alcohol every now and again. Do you want to go there?"

"Vincenzo, you can take me to a derelict shack without a roof and I'd be happy."

The Viola Tavern was a typical speakeasy that you needed to enter in through the back. When the bouncer opened the door, Vincenzo pushed through the non-intimidating man and blocked Sylvia from taking in his stench. It looked like he wanted to say something. He was wise to keep it to himself.

"Not a friend, I take it," she whispered.

"Oh, he's a shit. He hates black people, refuses them service. One day, I got into a fight with him about it. He used to be the manager of this place, now he's the bouncer who works for me." He puffed out his chest. "I showed him, didn't I?"

She wrapped her arms around him. "My, look at my strong, handsome man, fighting for the freedom of his people."

"'*His people*', huh?"

"Yes. I heard those laws affect Sicilian men, don't they? Because you have tanner skin?"

"Oh." He entered the main floor. "Yeah, I suppose."

The Viola Tavern had a different feeling from the Kitten that always made him feel more claustrophobic than usual. It was smaller with less welcoming talent performing on stage. A lone trumpeter sat in the corner with his hat out for tips. Nobody acknowledged him as they drank alone at their candlelit tables. The bartender was dozing off near the sink.

"How, uh," Sylvia said, "well, dreadful."

"It's a shit place for my fine liquors. I send my best to the Kitten. This place gets the leftovers."

"I much prefer the Kitten."

"We'll leave in a jiffy. Just watch this. I think it's the most fascinating thing." He checked who was working in the back and found his man. "Watch."

The little man behind the counter, who was taking the orders of two kissing women, didn't notice Vincenzo until he called for him. At the sound of his voice, he stiffened and almost dropped the glass he was cleaning to the floor. "E-evening, sir."

"Two scotch highballs and a gin Rickey," he said coldly, and the man, almost flustered by being demanded of so cruelly, left like a dog to make his drinks. He kept stealing glances at Vincenzo when he thought he wasn't looking. It was the funniest thing. Vincenzo hadn't even threatened him to make him act this way.

When he obtained the drinks, he sat Sylvia down at a booth in the far corner. "Isn't that something? Poor kid's scared to death of me."

"Scared?" Sylvia questioned.

"Yeah, didn't you see him? I've never said much to him, just drink orders and questions about the bar, but he trembles like a leaf every time I talk to him."

Sylvia put a hand to her mouth as she stared at him.

"What?"

"Sweetheart, you're at a pansy bar."

"Yes, I'm aware."

"And men at pansy bars, what do they enjoy? Do they enjoy the company of men or—"

"That's a trick question," he said with confidence. He'd learned a thing or two from frequenting these bars. "Many of the men actually have a plethora of female friends. They don't have the male companionship I have with Luis and Dominic, they're like Laurence, who has you and Mitsuko."

That didn't sway her. "Yes, but men like that like *handsome* men, and what are you?"

"...Italian."

"No, darling, you're *handsome*. You're one of the most handsome men I've ever met, so when you visit these places dressed like this, you turn the heads of several men seeking the company of other *men*."

Vincenzo looked at her, looked at her some more, took a sip from his glass, then said, "You're wrong."

"That man was blushing."

"But he always blushes, that's just what he does."

"So he blushes whenever you're here?"

"Well..." He turned.

The bartender gasped, waved, then ran into the back.

"No," he said.

"Vincenzo, I've been in bars longer than you have. I know the signs."

"But...*how*?"

"Well, some men don't enjoy the pleasures of a woman—"

"No, no, I know that, but I'm not like that. I don't like men."

"It doesn't matter if you do, dear, you still attract their attention. They're all around you, you know. They don't have to look like Laurence to be different." She pointed at two shady men sitting in the corner. While he couldn't see their faces, he saw that one was bald and the other was a large man wearing a hat. "Those two could be having a romantic date together, yet they look as regular as you and I."

As if able to hear them, the two men got up at the same time and left through one of the back doors.

"Right," Vincenzo said, feeling slightly warm. "I should say something to the poor kid. I don't want him getting the wrong idea."

"Hm," Sylvia said, and drank her drink in silence.

He tried to make conversation after that about Campo's party and how dull this bar was compared to the Kitten, but she seemed bored by him all of a sudden. All he got was a, "Hm," or a, "Quite." She was slouching in her hand. She *sighed*. Was this another one of her upsets? Was her Moon waning?

She got properly drunk like she'd wanted to, and after two cocktails, both of them left with their arms slung around the other. The night was meshing together. His father and Sylvia's mother had combined into a monster they needed to flee from. His blurry vision made that challenging.

"We should wait until I sober up before I get behind the wheel," he said.

"I agree. Agreeable. Your sight is rather poor tonight."

"What does that mean?"

She shrugged, unsure of herself.

Outside the Viola Tavern was a residential area with grocery stores on the corners and pockets of parks between the condensed housing. Down near one of *Nonna's* favorite churches was McKinley Park. Vincenzo liked it because he could wait on the park steps and watch the birds. He didn't feel like he belonged in church. He'd rather listen to the sermons outside, fingers threading the cross around his neck.

"Where're we going?" Sylvia asked.

"Where do you want to go? Wanna go home? Go hit up another bar?"

"No." She stopped. "Here." She tugged him into the middle of the road. They had to dodge a car and skip over the trolley tracks to make it over unscathed. "A romantic date in the park. Take me."

As if he had a choice. Though he thought it cliché, he decided to humor her if it meant finding out why she was acting so strangely. He'd seen her drunk. This wasn't just her drunk.

They followed a path down to the center of the park. Vincenzo glanced down the pathways and found they were alone. He relaxed a bit. "So, what's wrong?"

"Nothin'."

"Do you want to go home? Are you tired? Are you upset?"

"*No*," she moaned. "How many bars do you own?"

"I don't really 'own' any. I keep them in check. I provide them with alcohol."

"But you own them! You do. Don't lie. How many Laurences and cute bartender boys are at these bars? I'd like to meet them. I'd like to meet these boys."

The slow realization dawned over his eyes. "You're *jealous.*"

She didn't say no. She didn't say anything. Just pouted, face scrunched up like a child.

Since meeting her, Vincenzo had seen her as a goddess, someone who'd survived through so much and became this untouchable force of healing energy. She hated no one, forgave everyone for everything. But since hearing her fight back against her mother, this vision of her was cracking. Now, she was less of an untouchable goddess and more of a reachable, flawed girl he couldn't help but fall in love with all over again.

He smiled. "You're *jealous,* aren't you? You're jealous that someone was flirting with me."

"And so what if I am? Is that a bad thing? I can be jealous. We're together, aren't we?"

"Yes, but I'm surprised you got jealous over someone so insignificant."

"Because I've never seen someone fawn over you before. It's only ever been me." She crossed her arms. "Let me fawn over you more."

"Don't you?"

"No. I feel like I'm not allowed to. You flinch or shy away, and then I feel like I'm taking advantage of you."

"Taking advantage of me?"

"*Yeah,*" she whined. "I feel guilty for liking you so extremely. I don't wanna feel that way anymore, but I don't wanna feel like what I'm feeling is bad."

"I-it's not," he stuttered, not sure why she was explaining this to him in a public park. "It's completely valid."

"It is. You know, I'm a sensual person. I'm a woman in tune with my feelings. I...I..."

To settle her, he brought her behind a thick tree. She was shivering through her coat.

"I don't want to feel ashamed of it any longer," she whispered.

"I know," he said.

"I love you very much, and I don't have money to buy you this and this." She lifted up her pearls, her dress. "All I can give you is my heart. I want to love you." She blushed. "I want to make love to you, to show you that I care."

Now, he was burning hot. His brain, heart, and drink were fighting against him. He saw quick visions of her in bed, with him, naked and doing...

He mentally blocked that out and hugged her. "I'm sorry you felt ashamed of that because of my failures."

"But they're not failures! Neither of us are failures. We have to keep telling ourselves that."

"I know." He leaned up and kissed her cheek, trying to make up for his drawbacks. He thought he'd done a spectacular job tonight. Him kissing her in his room? Their time on the balcony? Him playing off of her excitement after he'd sung to her? It amazed him that most people expected more, and that he was in the minority with his feelings.

But as much as she shouldn't have felt ashamed, he couldn't open up to her sexually. As much as she begged for it, making love with her was something he could never do.

Though. Hands were an option, and tongues. And, as he thought further, other objects could become his substitute, and it shouldn't have mattered what it was, so long as she climbed that mountain with him.

He double-checked that they were alone, then dropped his virgin hands to her bottom.

She inhaled into his hair, leaning over and holding him.

"You shouldn't have to get jealous over me," he whispered. "You're the only girl I want to be with."

"Oh." Reciprocating his touches, she squeezed the roundness of his bottom, lifting him up to her height.

He gasped. Her individual fingers, touching his...

It wasn't arousing, he didn't think, but his heart, it was beating so hard, filling him with feelings.

"Is this too much?" she asked.

If she'd asked him yesterday, he would've said yes. He hated his body, but he couldn't tell her that. Men didn't hate their bodies the same way women did. It didn't happen.

But it did for him, very often.

Sylvia didn't make him hate it as much.

"It's not too much," he told her.

She smiled. "From abstinence to touching your woman in public. How indecent."

"Quite the extreme, isn't it?"

"Nothing I'm against."

"Do you want me to go further?"

"If you did that, I don't know what I'd do."

He kissed her long, exposed neck until it turned red. "Tell me what you'd do."

She moaned and spread open her legs against the bark of the tree. He watched the focus drain from her eyes. "I...I don't know. Tell me what you want and I'll do anything, *anything.*"

His thoughts scrambled. Was everything on the table? What was *off* the table? What was on his?

As he debated telling her what he was thinking, a car pulled up near the park. Its lights illuminated them to the world like a spotlight.

Vincenzo strained his eyes. Near the front steps of the park, four men came into view. Their hats and coats veiled their identities, but he would've recognized their silhouettes a street away.

"Shit."

Hannigan, with his motley crew of Irishmen, closed in around them. He didn't see any of those stupid Tommy Guns they loved, but he did see a baseball bat.

"There you are," Hannigan called out to them. "Why is it that every time we catch word of you sneaking around New York, you're with this little tramp getting it on in public? Don't you feel ashamed?"

Sylvia tensed up at Hannigan's accent, then looked down at the gun in Vincenzo's pants.

He weighed his options: firing, causing a massive panic with somebody getting killed, or trying to talk with a man whose opinion didn't matter, who'd hate them regardless of what they said.

A year ago, he would've fired. He wouldn't have had a problem with finally ending this bastard's life. He'd held back with Sylvia's mother. He'd been close, but he'd promised himself that he'd never kill anyone in front of Sylvia. He couldn't do that to her.

So, they ran. Backwards through the park and between the trees like children playing tag. They were faster than Hannigan's crew, as Hannigan cursed and ran back to his car to give a delayed chase.

"Get them!" he yelled.

"Where do we go?" Sylvia asked, easily keeping up with Vincenzo in heels.

"Home," he said. "It takes about twenty minutes to get there by foot."

"But won't he come after us? Won't he attack your home? Everyone, they're still at Campo's party."

"If this were anyone else, I'd worry. This's just a pack of dogs that need a distraction. They won't have the balls to attack us at *Nonna's*."

"I believe you. My anxiety says otherwise."

"Well, tell your anxiety to quit it. Hear that? No firing. This's just a scare tactic." They left the park and swung into an alleyway where a car couldn't chase them.

"Do you do this often?" she asked.

"In a car, yeah."

"A little tiring."

"A bit."

She splashed into a puddle. "Am I a bad person for liking this?"

"Which part?"

"The part where we're running away from violent men through Brooklyn at night."

"Oh, silly me." He held open a chunk of fence for her to slip through. "I thought you were talking about the two of us fondling one another passionately in the middle of a park."

"Oh, that, too." She laughed, then kept laughing, wheezing as the two of them ran for their lives in the middle of the night. He couldn't help himself and laughed right along.

157

Chapter 14: Testing It Out

When they got home, *Nonna* was asleep with a book in her lap and baby Sophie was starfished in her crib. Vincenzo made sure to kiss his grandmother goodnight and check to see that Sophie was breathing before shutting her bedroom door.

He came back to the foyer and said to Sylvia, "Let me call Campo and tell him what happened."

She glanced into the kitchen. The grandfather clock said it was almost one in the morning. They'd run nonstop from the park to get here, but with how much adrenaline he had in his body, he figured neither of them would be going to bed any time soon. "Could I possibly make something to eat? I didn't eat much today."

"Of course."

"Would *Nonna* be cross? Did she make any dinner tonight?"

"I told her we'd be eating at the party. Ask me if you need help finding anything."

He caught himself smiling at her as she left. Seeing her at both her most ordinary and most elegant, what was better than that?

He knew, at least for her, what would be better. She'd stated it several times, her wants. He'd been trying to find a way around them all night.

He rang for Campo's home. This night had slapped him silly. He needed to come back to his senses.

Someone picked up. "Hello?"

Vincenzo furrowed his brow. *"Hello?"* he asked in Italian. *"Why're you using Campo's personal phone?"*

His father hung up.

Feeling the anger foaming in his stomach, he rang for the number again, finger jabbing into the rotary. What was he doing, picking up Campo's private line? Was the party still going on?

He picked up again. *"If you call—"*

"I need to speak to Campo."

"Why?"

"Because Hannigan found me again. After the party, I left to go get drinks at the Viola Tavern, and his men surrounded us and chased us away. They knew where I was going to be when I hadn't mentioned it to anyone."

Severo thought on this, making Vincenzo listen to the whistle in his dying lungs. Then he asked, *"What of it?"*

"What—This's the second time this happened. He jumped me at the Black Kitten—"

"It seems like they have a problem with you keeping in touch with those faggots you fancy at those bars."

Vincenzo gave the receiver a look. Even with his life in danger, he was still on this. What was it with old men and their fascinations with another man's romance? *"What does that have to do with anything?"*

"I've mentioned this to Campo multiple times, and he agrees that you spend too much time there. You're becoming more of a target the more you parade this fetish around on a leash. If this continues and you start placing the Family in danger, you'll pay for it. I'll make sure of it."

"But—"

"Now shut up and don't call back. And don't go out with that pansy nigger again."

And he hung up.

Comebacks and criticisms came seconds too late. Even if his father had been right and he should've been stepping back from the bars, he needed to be with Sylvia for his own mental sake. After years of questioning, she'd been the only one to understand him. He couldn't have that with any other girl. Why couldn't his father see that?

"Vincenzo, when you have a moment," Sylvia said, and ducked her head back into the kitchen.

He did have a moment to spare, but he took several more on the couch, refocusing on who mattered most.

During his very short phone call, Sylvia had wrecked his kitchen. Already, soup and vegetable slices stained the counters. She'd left the fridge open for easy access, but she also had every cabinet door open. He couldn't judge—he never cooked for himself—but something about her destruction was admirable and also concerning.

"I was on the phone for no more than two minutes," he said. "Is this how you cook?"

She set down her ladle. "It's usually worse."

He looked over her shoulder to see what monstrosity she was cooking. "What're you—"

The flirty insult he'd planned slipped away. The smells, salty like home, and the bag of clams, still fresh from being caught that week. He was brought back to his childhood. That feeling of safety, however strong it already was, grew thicker around him.

"You're making clams and pasta?" he asked.

"Uh, yes. I think. It's *Nonna's* recipe. She tried to teach it to me this afternoon, but I don't know. I have garlic, and I notice she bought fresh Parmesan yesterday." She read the clams' label. "I'll get better at this. I'm not used to cooking for two."

Every time Vincenzo came home from work, whether he was thirteen or twenty-three, he was met with *Nonna* cooking. It was his one constant in life, something he knew would never change. To see Sylvia trying her best to replicate that feeling, even though she was trying to boil the pasta and the clams in the same pot...

He hugged her from behind, burying his head into her back. He'd once called her his wife, but she was much more than that. She knew what made him happy at his worst and over the Moon at his best. She was his angel, his soulmate.

He took her hand and led her upstairs.

"Oh my," she said. "Where're we going?"

He led her into their room and closed the door.

"Now, what's this?" she asked, smiling.

"Hm?" He kissed her, then again, backing her into the bed until he was straddling her. Mezzanotte, who was sleeping on his pillow, got up to see if she needed to run.

"Did something click?" she asked.

"I'm not sure." He parted her bangs to better see her. "I've been thinking over what you said to me in the park. About wanting to, you know, make love."

"Oh." She tried closing her legs. "You don't have to. You don't have to force yourself."

"I know. It's just, I've been so afraid of this side of me, I never trusted myself to be intimate with another person before. It's true that I'm not as...forwards as you, but that doesn't mean I'm..." He searched for the right words. It was hard to describe an idea so twisted in your head. It was like chopping away vines. "I'd like to try, to be more open, with you. I'd like to experiment."

Sylvia touched her chest, holding her breath at what he said.

"Because I want to," he confirmed. "Not because I feel pressured to. I feel comfortable enough to try things with you." He laughed at himself. "It sounds silly, but I feel safe with you."

"How is that in any way silly?"

"I don't know. It doesn't feel manly."

"Feeling safe with a woman?"

"I guess." He pinned her down and kissed her. Mezzanotte wagged her tail at his movement. He wished cats weren't so observant.

"Vincenzo."

He stopped. "What's wrong?"

"I just want to ask, since you're experimenting..."

His heart skipped.

"May I touch you?"

His body did what it knew best and locked up, protecting him from any outside threats. He knew this would've come up eventually, but he wasn't ready to tell her the truth yet. Cruelly, he thought it would've slipped out by now. His family would've taken her aside or she would've brushed against his pant legs and thought, *"Oh."* "Oh, you're different." "Oh, you're just like me."

Then he'd have to go into why he hid so much from her. Why it was such a big deal in the first place. Why he'd been so, *so* scared to tell her the truth. Because she'd think him a liar. Or a girl. Or someone faking it for attention, just like his parents thought, even though he'd told them time and time again that it wasn't a big deal when he *knew* it was. But he *knew* nobody would understand it, so he hid away the truth and kept everything to himself.

Then he remembered who was underneath him: his stability who accepted every part of him.

He gave her a small, small nod, barely registering as consent, and braced for the worst.

Working with his pace, Sylvia slowly wiggled her arms free, reached up and over his head, and wrapped her arms around him.

Her fingers curled in and out of his hair, messing up the gel and recreating his natural look. There wasn't enough room for him to do the same, so he hovered above her, watching her watch him. He'd never made so much eye contact with a person for so long, even with her. He felt himself go hot, everywhere.

"Okay," she said, and dropped her hands. "Thank you. I've wanted to fix that for forever."

"Huh?"

"Your hair. I love it slicked back, but I love this look even more."

"But don't you want to, well, touch anywhere else?"

She looked down at his crotch. "No."

"Don't lie."

"I'm not. While I *would* enjoy touching you there, you don't want me to, right? I can see it on your face, and it's not as if I need that part of you to feel loved."

"But you do."

"I'm just an incredibly horny girl, Vincenzo, and my hands are perfectly adequate in relieving me. I want you to do whatever you feel comfortable doing, and if that's fondling me behind the tree one minute and shaking to touch me the next, I don't mind. I'll wait. I do like thinking about the possibilities, though," she added. "That can't be helped. You're far too handsome for me not to fantasize about it."

He almost fainted. His body was so rigid, and then to hear that? Here he thought he should've been doing so much more. Now, not only was she not expecting anything, she understood why he couldn't go any farther than this.

Well, partly. Whenever he was ready to finally tell her, he knew he'd be okay.

He dropped his forehead against hers. She cooled him down. "Thank you."

"Of course. This's about you experimenting with what you're okay with, and I'm okay with it all."

He kissed her lips.

"And nothing is mandatory."

He dipped down to her neck.

She moaned. "Unless you're okay with it. Neck-kissing is lovely."

"It is?"

"Oh, *yes*—" She moaned and broke away from him.

"You okay?"

"Uh..."

Hearing her hesitating, he pulled back and made sure she was alright.

She was, but that wasn't the problem. Hiding her face, she used her free hand to cover the spot between her thighs. "I got excited again," she said.

He kept himself from looking down. For his sake and hers. Did he have to do anything? Should he try? Did he want to?

Kind of.

Just a bit. A taste, even, to say he'd tried it.

She peeked at him through her fingers.

"Do you want me to relieve you?"

"Only if you want to."

He looked up.

"Only if you want to."

He breathed into her neck, taking in the perfume hidden in her soft skin. It'd be okay. It was only them, alone, and his father wasn't even a phone call away because he'd told him not to call again.

But why couldn't she take over? He knew men were supposed to initiate things in the bedroom, but he didn't mind a woman handling the reins every once in a while.

Stealing one last kiss from her, Vincenzo slipped off the bed and found himself on his knees like a squire about to be knighted by his queen.

She tightened her knees.

"Sorry." He backed up. "Is this too much? Is it—"

"No, it's okay. I just didn't want you seeing anything that might...alarm you." She parted her legs. "This okay?"

"Yeah," he said, but his mouth had gone dry. He'd read novels about romance and studied poetry describing nights between lovers. Watching Sylvia's hand disappear underneath her dress, he didn't feel at all prepared. He felt weak, weak for her.

He worked quickly. For a daft moment, he didn't know how to take off her stockings. He thought her slip had some type of button on it like a pair of pants. He didn't know she wore so many layers.

And he didn't know what to expect. This part of the body he'd agonized over for years, it looked average by his standards. Dare he say it, but he was a bit jealous. It *was* different than what he'd thought—definitely hairier, and bigger—but it was as soft and pink as his and, as she bit her lower lip, just as sensitive, it seemed.

He played with her using his hand. He'd seen this in artwork and knew it happened often, but he hadn't imagined himself doing this with anyone before. Certainly not on his knees, pumping her up and down and maneuvering his weight so as not to make it awkward.

Whatever motion he'd decided on doing, it was doing more for her than it was for him. Upon the first touch, Sylvia grabbed the sheets and melted into pleasure. Her legs spread open and lifted up her dress, giving him more room to work with. "Oh, *Vincenzo*."

Dumbly, he nodded like she was asking him a question. He was concentrating so hard on pleasing her, he didn't realize where he was in the process until it was very prominently in front of him.

He licked his lips before pleasing her in a new way.

He didn't know how women—or men, he considered—did this well, or at all romantically. It felt too thick in his mouth and too hard in his hand. He wanted to ask if he was doing anything wrong, but her begging that he, "Keep going," because he was, "So good," how could he disobey her? He thought kissing was enough. This opened so many new doors.

Too many doors. Between his legs, a damp warmth was beginning to spread. He covered it with one hand, but the tightness of his pants did him no favors. He hoped it'd go away or that it'd magically make him cum and get it over with. He had a job to do here and it was distracting him.

With his confidence rising, he looked up to see if she was still enjoying herself.

Gasping on the love leaking from her lips, Sylvia clawed into his hair and pushed him even deeper.

He gagged. Mezzanotte meowed and scratched his thigh. Was this better? Worse? Was she close?

She tightened her knees around him and moaned. Every time he pulled back to breathe, her hips bucked for him to come back.

This was it. He knew it. All the writings he'd studied. The illustrations. She was close. So he worked faster, sloppier, guiding her to the top of her mountain.

If you were to ask him, he didn't know why he kept her in his mouth when she came. Maybe because it was their first time and he didn't want to disrespect her by pulling back. He also might've wanted to taste it. He was experimenting, after all. He couldn't say he hated the taste if he'd never tried it.

He did spit it out afterwards. He had to make sure none of it stayed inside him, as he couldn't contextualize it in a healthy way yet. Maybe later, when he had a few more tastes of her.

After cumming, Sylvia rightfully collapsed, arms shaking to keep herself vertical. Mezzanotte, intrigued, jumped onto her thigh and sniffed her.

"Did I do okay?" Vincenzo asked, trying to push his cat away.

Without the words to answer him, Sylvia took him by the jaw and kissed him. Even when he'd done such a dirty act. She must've been hungry.

A knocking came from downstairs.

The strength of the knocking alone indicated that something was wrong, but Sylvia slamming her knees together reaffirmed that concern. "That's him," she whispered. "The same knocking. The man who broke into my apartment."

It surprised him how quickly his arousal turned to bloodlust. Heart icing over, he jumped to his feet and wrenched open his bedside drawer.

Sylvia, still in a daze, reacted slowly as he handed her his gun.

"Use it," he whispered, "if you need to."

"Alright," she said, and hid her exposed body underneath the covers.

Vincenzo tiptoed down the stairs, arming himself with a knife from the kitchen counter. How dare someone take this away from him? How much longer would he have to fight to be with her?

It'd always be this way. Nobody understood them, people who'd been shaped outside of the ideal mold. But he wouldn't stop fighting. He wouldn't stop visiting the Black Kitten or kissing his lover. That was *his* world, and nobody was taking it away from him.

Just as he expected another knock, Vincenzo said a prayer and went to open the door.

The knocking stopped. Someone walked down the stairs, bored with waiting. The threat gone, or delayed.

He eyed the windows by the door. The right one gave him the best view of the street, but he would have to part the curtain.

He tried, and caught sight of a man standing in the dark. He wore a trench coat and a black bowler hat.

He was the fucking man from the Viola Tavern. The one who'd been sitting with the other man. Of course. Vincenzo hadn't made the connection because of the cursed alcohol, but now, it was coming together. All he needed left was his face. Then he'd kill him.

As he went to part more of the curtain, the window cracked and shattered in his face.

Glass exploded around him. Pieces spread across the carpet like snow. Something bashed into his arm and rolled near the coffee table, but when he aimed his knife at it, expecting to find a person, he was met with a rock, a jagged boulder the size of his head that would've knocked him out or killed him if the aim had been right.

A car skidded away. The footsteps were gone. Their mission, whatever it could've been, was complete.

Vincenzo took large gasps of air to calm himself down. The night was infiltrating his home and making him shiver. It had to have been that, the night air. One-fourth of his window was gone and exposing himself to darkness.

He had to move. If he got to his car, he could apprehend whoever was doing this to them and end it all.

But he couldn't. His feet wouldn't budge. Sylvia, upstairs. *Nonna...*

A door opened behind him.

Nonna reached out her candlestick. Her glasses were skewed on her innocent face.

"Close the door," he whispered.

She did as told.

He stared at the massive boulder by his foot. When people cursed him out or shot at him and his men, he stayed strong. People attacked him for a slew of reasons, all of which he could deflect.

This rock felt more sinister than all those times put together. Never before had someone actually attacked his home at night. He felt taken advantage of by a stranger, "stranger" because he hadn't seen this muscular man by Hannigan's side. And he didn't know who'd thrown the boulder. Until he saw his face, he had no idea who or how many people wanted him dead.

Acting as the man he was, Vincenzo fixed the problem the only way he knew how. Since he wasn't a handyman, he mended the hole by lifting the coffee table onto its side and leaning it against the pane. To be safe, he did the same with the other window. He didn't have another coffee table that long, but a barrier was still a barrier. It protected you from the evils outside.

With the front of the house secured, he double-checked that the back doors were locked and that the windows were firmly shut. He also turned off the stove—it was a lost cause, the pasta had been overcooked—before he went back to *Nonna.*

She was behind the door, hand covering her light. *"Is everything alright?"*

"Yes."

"Was it a break-in?"

"Yes, but they're gone now." He kissed the top of her forehead. *"Love you."*

"I love you, too."

Sylvia had learned from her ways and stayed locked inside of their bedroom. He had to announce himself before she unlocked it. She had his gun in her hand.

"Did you get him?" she asked.

"No." He flopped into bed.

"What happened?"

"They tried to break in."

"Do you think this's because of me?"

"I think it's because of both of us."

"Jealousy is a deadly sin, isn't it?"

"I'm sure that's it."

"It must be, isn't it? I don't want to think of any other reason."

He caressed her face with his clean hand. He wouldn't let anyone hurt her, even if the world had other motives to end their lives.

"Oh, God, the pasta." She bolted upright. "I'll make you a plate, if it's ready."

"Don't. I took it off the stove. Just stay here, please."

She curled his bangs around his ear. "It'll be okay."

He closed his eyes. It could've been. With the world quieting down, he dreamed of a cottage the two of them owned, with a dog and a kid they'd adopt off the streets. He was okay in both worlds.

As they snuggled together in the real world, her kissing his fingers one by one before moving to his lips, he was reminded of what he had, what he needed to protect: both her and himself, and what they'd created together.

If this could be their new normal, how happy he would be.

Chapter 15: A Question to be Asked

"Wait." Mitsuko unfolded her napkin and reread her notes. "So you went to a rich and powerful gangster's birthday party *after* you saw him shoot at a gang he's in contention with. Then you ran into your mother whom you haven't seen in ten years and finally stood up to her for all the pain she's caused you. And Vincenzo almost shot her, but it's—"

"It wasn't a big deal," Sylvia repeated.

"Right. Sure. So then, after drinking yourself rotten, you got to second base with him in some park, which was *then* cut short because the gang who shot at you found you, so you fled home to have sex—"

"A pleasure night," Sylvia corrected.

"Pardon me, a '*pleasure night*' with him, only for *that* to be cut short because the *same* man who broke into *your* home tried breaking into *Vincenzo's* home by throwing a *boulder* through his *window*, and he didn't even *get* the guy."

Sylvia read over Mitsuko's handwriting. "Also, we cuddled for the rest of the night."

"Oh, right. And...they...cuddled...all...night." With the last of her information scrawled onto her napkin notes, Mitsuko balled up her paper and tossed it at Sylvia's face.

"Hey."

"Your life sounds fake, Sylvia Belmonte, and very unsafe."

She unfolded the napkin on her knee. They were all sitting together, she, her, and Laurence, at the Black Kitten's bar. Mitsuko and Sylvia were sitting as patrons on their break while Laurence served them behind the counter. It was Halloween, or the Saturday before it, and most of the guests were dressed for the spooky weekend. Even the jazz musicians were in on the themed night. It got them a free plate of bruschetta and a fun night with friends.

Sylvia was wearing a typical flapper look with more feathers and sparkles than usual. Laurence was in a nice white suit, but with the flowers sticking out of his hair and lapel, he looked more like a flowerpot than a well-dressed bartender. Mitsuko, in her opinion, had on the strongest outfit—a full American soldier uniform, complete with a pointed bayonet. She'd said she wanted a French uniform since she was more familiar with it, but she couldn't find one in time. Bobbie had on an orange tie with his black suit. It was the most he could do.

Vincenzo, sadly, couldn't attend. He was currently in Canada on a weekend-long business trip, finalizing some type of contract on Campo's behalf. Luis and Dominic were now her chauffeurs to and from the Kitten. Dominic *had* refused, but Luis had convinced him to loosen up. He hadn't dressed up—he was moping in a booth across the bar, deep into his fourth glass of strawberry daiquiri—but Luis had. A tail, a pair of cat ears, and painted-on whiskers and he looked like a buzzed black cat.

"So, after all of this, you're still choosing to be with him?" Mitsuko asked. "I was in the Great War, you know. I dealt with bloodthirsty men who wanted to murder because they could. I dealt with women who had to end men's lives because they were bleeding too much from the inside." She toyed with the ring on her finger. "I know when to fight my battles, and I know when my help isn't needed. I want to make sure that this's something you really, *really* want, enough that you're willing to fight for it forever."

Sylvia recalled the night she'd spent with Vincenzo: him listening to her in the park, him standing up for her against Clara. They'd played cards together, drank happily together. He'd given her the most of his physical love he could offer, all for her sake.

"Because I'm this woman's husband."

He'd said that so matter-of-factly, that throwaway line, but she'd bundled it close to her heart, keeping it as warm as it made her feel.

She dunked one of the ice cubes in her drink with her straw. "I know you're worried about me. It's because you've seen me in abusive relationships and don't want to see me going down that same path. I know Vincenzo is a very influential man with a wealth of fortune that gets him into trouble, but I think I've made it clear that I love him and want to stay with him so long as he treats me well, which he has for many months. He asks me how I feel and changes his attitudes dependent on *me*, and we've both grown with each other's help, so I don't wish to justify this any more than I already have. I love him, and I want to be with him, and if you still think it's a bad idea, I don't know what else to tell you."

Mitsuko's eyebrows raised.

Laurence, who was looking towards Dominic and Luis, came back to their conversation and said, "*Wow.*"

"Indeed." Mitsuko dropped her head into her hand and stared at her.

Sylvia stared back. She felt in her heart that she could persuade Laurence. He'd had suitors, one-night stands, long-term "lovers," though he hated the term. To her knowledge, Mitsuko hadn't been with anyone. She wore a wedding ring, but she was sure she hadn't actually fallen in love. Her heart was too full of friends and duties.

"I'm sorry you don't like him," Sylvia said, trying a new approach. "If one of you had fallen in love with a gangster boy or gangster girl, I, too, would have my reservations."

Laurence looked away, back to Vincenzo's friends.

"But I'm happy now, I think, and I don't want that taken away from me. I'll fight for that 'til the end."

Mitsuko sipped on her favorite drink of choice: milk. Her eyes stayed on Sylvia. "Let me ask you the most important question a girl like you needs to answer: If he proposed to you tomorrow, would you marry him? Would you spend the rest of your life like this, forever tied to him by the red thread of fate?"

Not even thinking over the answer, she said, "Even though it's impossible and that the world won't allow it, even though our parents wouldn't approve, yes. Indefinitely."

Mitsuko sighed through her nose, defeated in her valiant efforts, then roared into a snarl and chugged her milk. "Then I want to meet him. I demand to."

"You already have, sweetheart."

"No. I want to meet him with you, with Laurence, with those two little thugs he's always with that Laurence hasn't taken his eyes off of. Yes, Laurence, I noticed. You're not sly."

"Huh?"

"And add that grandmother into the mix. I want a full conference. Favorite food, favorite music, how many men he's killed, how he feels about you when you're in the room, when you're out. If you're marrying him, I need to know everything about him in case this goes south."

"We might be able to do that. Oh." She reached into her dress and pulled out two envelopes.

"Nice hickey, by the way," Mitsuko said. "I saw that the second you came in."

"Thank you." She dispensed out the gifts. "These are from Vincenzo. He said they're Halloween presents."

"Is it laced with anything?" Mitsuko ripped hers open with her bayonet. Laurence used his painted nails.

"I'm not sure, but by the girth of the notes..."

Mitsuko took out ten one-dollar bills.

"It felt like cash."

"What on Earth?" Laurence said, licking his fingers to count his individual bills.

Mitsuko held one up to the light. "Is he paying us to keep quiet?"

"I don't believe so. He told me they were Halloween gifts. I don't think he knows what the holiday means. I think this's the first time he's had companions to share it with."

"Ugh, why's he so insufferable?" Mitsuko folded up the envelope and stuffed it into one of her military pockets. "Where is he, anyway? I should thank him. Maybe he'll forget that I slapped him that one time."

"He's in Canada on a week-long business trip. He'll be back Monday."

"Is that why those two are here?" Laurence asked, looking at Dominic and Luis.

"Laurence, please," Mitsuko said. "I can't handle both of you like this."

"What?" he asked.

"What's wrong, dear?" Sylvia asked. "You've been spacing out. What're you thinking about?"

"The better question is '*who*'," Mitsuko corrected.

"*No one*," Laurence said defensively.

Sylvia turned in her stool and tried seeking out Laurence's fixation.

Laurence physically took her face and positioned her back into their tight circle. "Please, spare me."

"Of what?"

"You wouldn't know this because you've been off snogging with your dearest," Mitsuko said, "but Laurence has been having a crisis of conscience."

"No, I haven't," he said. "Stop telling people that."

"But you are."

"Can someone please tell me what's going on?" Sylvia asked.

"Nothing's *happening*," Laurence said. "Look, back when you told us you and Vincenzo were living together, I might've drunk too much. I thought it might've been funny to bring someone up on stage, you know, we do that often, and I happened to see Dominic."

"And he reacted," Mitsuko said.

"I saw that," Sylvia said. "You slapped him."

"I touched his *rear end*. I forgot I even did it, but when I did, instead of being mad or disgusted with me, he was..."

"...Turned on."

"No, *no*," he said. "He was *not*. Stop saying that. He was...well, embarrassed, clearly."

"I'd be, too," Sylvia said.

"Don't say that. I'm trudging through enough guilt. So then, after the number, I went to change my shoes, and he came into the back room with me. He was stuttering and fiddling with his hands. I didn't know he had that type of side to him. Finally, he asked me not to touch him like that again, which I apologized for and said I wouldn't, but the way he said it, it's been on my mind. It's like he wanted to say more to me."

"And now he's pining," Mitsuko said.

"I'm not!" he almost shouted, then hushed up by looking Dominic's way. "He's just odd. He's never acted this way before."

"So, basically, I'm struggling with a lot," Mitsuko said. "Forget my shitty apartment complex upping my rent this month and my father's birthday that's coming up that I'm debating on writing to him about, *this's* what I need to focus on. Two queers falling in love with monsters."

"Not in love," Laurence said. "Falling into *curiosity*. And they aren't monsters, we just went through this. They're normal men."

"So do you like him?" Sylvia asked.

"What? No. This's all I know about him: He's quiet, a bit shy, and when we perform, he seems entranced by us. What more is there to work with? It's like he's...he's..."

"He's scared to open up," Sylvia said. "It seems like he's interested in you. Why not give it a chance?"

"Because he's a scary gangster who'll probably gut me like a trout if I tell him that I like him—"

"Aha!" Sylvia said. "So you *do* like him."

He choked on his words. "Well...well, yes, okay, in a purely physical sense, I, someone who enjoys the company of men, may or may not find a tall, muscular, conventionally attractive man handsome. There. Happy?"

"Not really," Mitsuko said.

"Not asking you. However, seeing as he's a man who works for a gang that kills people—"

"A man who also works for a very tolerant and kind-hearted man who cares for us—"

"I simply must put these feelings aside and find another suitor to cater to my interests. I've done it plenty of times before, I'll do it again. Plus, we don't even know if he's funny like me. I can't risk that sort of humiliation now."

Sylvia scrunched up her nose. She hated when he acted like this. "A woman shouldn't waste her chances on love."

"Contrary to what most of the men here think, I'm not a woman."

"Oh, you know what I mean. You'll never know unless you ask. Why don't you go up and talk to him? You can apologize again and make it a conversation piece."

Laurence was already shaking his head. "Off the table. It's too awkward. He's this big man and I'm..." He gestured to his flowers. "*This*. And he seemed really upset about what I did, so I'm keeping my distance."

"Let me help, then. I can talk to him for you."

"No."

"Yes," Mitsuko said.

"Mitsuko, not helping. Sylvia, no, please—" He went for her hand. He missed. "He doesn't like people like us. He'll only hate me more. *Sylvia*."

"Alright," she said, "I won't say anything, I promise. I'll just make sure he isn't drinking himself to death. He looks sad."

"Because he's being forced to spend his weekend at a pansy bar *when he isn't a pansy*."

Not believing him, Sylvia left for Dominic and Luis.

"Good luck," Mitsuko said.

To her, Vincenzo was now her family, and she thought he saw Laurence and Mitsuko as acquaintances at best. But her with Dominic and Luis? Were they her friends? Acquaintances? If she and Vincenzo ever split up, would she find herself hanging out with them? Would she catch up on Luis' growing child or Dominic's…

She didn't know. His family? Was he close to them? Did he have a secret wife or child? Did he have any wants or goals?

She interrupted them mid-conversation. Luis was patting Dominic's back while Dominic was scribbling on a napkin. He hid whatever he was doodling when she neared.

"Hiya," Luis said. "Like my tail? Ana said it was too frivolous, but how could I not? You look great."

"Thank you. I didn't mean to interrupt you. I was just wondering if everything was alright."

Dominic slid his drink closer to him, away from her.

Luis read the mood, then faked a smile. "We're peachy. So, uh, do you want me to buy you a drink? Do your friends want anything?"

"No, thank you," she said. "It's just that, over there, all of us were talking. It seems like there's something wrong with Laurence."

Dominic drank.

"Oh, no. What's wrong?" Luis asked. "I know he's kind of, well, you know, he kisses others and…" He ended that thought. "Anything we can help with?"

"I don't think so. I can't recall what happened, but it sounds like he did something to Dominic that's troubling him."

Dominic finally came to attention. "Why's *he* upset? He didn't do anything."

"Uh, you know, I'm sure it was nothing, nothing at all," Luis said. "Don't worry about it, all water under the bridge. Now, I don't know about you two, but I'm starving—"

"What's he been saying?" Dominic asked.

"He wished to apologize, but he doesn't think you like him." She lowered her voice. Was she breaking her promise? She wanted to build bridges. Loving, connecting bridges. "You know, he seems quite...Hurting your feelings wasn't what he intended to do." She tried looking at him properly. He was leaning away from her. "This's just me asking now, as I'm his friend and I care for him."

"Uh, Sylvia—"

"But do you have any interest—any at all—in pursuing him?"

Since he was such a clamshell, she noticed the smallest changes in his character. The moment she asked her question, fear bled through his bloodshot eyes. His chair squeaked back and his shoulders tightened. Luis lost his fake smile.

Maybe it was genetic, these Italian boys who needed to hide their feelings until you were blunt enough to confront them about it. Vincenzo did his best, but when a drink entered you, it broke you down until you either cried or hit something.

She backpedalled. She felt like she'd stepped on a landmine. "I don't mean to insult you, if you consider such a question an insult. You don't have to answer me. You can forget I even asked."

The more she spoke, the more Dominic cracked. He stood up, knees banging into the table and jumping Luis in the process. The stairs were across the bar, too far away to reach, so he took the next closest route: through the backstage.

"Dom, wait!" Luis tripped over his tail and chased him. Sylvia followed.

"Dominic, wait a moment!" she said in vain.

Laurence and Mitsuko watched them go, Mitsuko watching Sylvia, Laurence, hurt, watching Dominic.

"It's okay," she mouthed at them, and followed Dominic into the back room. He'd shut the door behind him but forgot to lock it.

Both she and Luis gave the man his space. He was catching his breath at one of the vanity tables, exhausted from running.

"Hey, Dom, what's the problem?" Luis said lightly. "It's okay. We can just leave. Everything's fine."

"No, it's not!"

Sylvia flinched. Dominic had never raised his voice before. He turned to her. "Who told you?"

"What?" she asked. "Nobody told me anything."

"No, I saw you. You were talking to him right before you came over. Who said what?"

She stepped back, scared of this new man coming into focus.

"Hey, you know, it's not a big deal," Luis said. "Let's get some fresh air and—" He touched Dominic's arm. Dominic swatted him away.

"Dominic, please listen," Sylvia said. "I didn't mean to make you upset. Laurence, Mitsuko, and I were talking about what happened that night. I know he likes you, or is at least interested in you. He doesn't pursue anyone because he's afraid of commitment. I wanted to ask your opinion on his behalf. If you're uninterested, that's fine. He'll leave you be. It'll be okay."

"You—" He dug into his hair and pulled, messing up the hair that always looked short of perfect. "Why're you doing this?"

"I just wanted you two to be happy."

"How?" he yelled. "How on *Earth* can this make either of us happy and not totally fuck us over?"

Sylvia covered her mouth in shock.

"Okay." Luis physically stepped in-between them. "Okay, this's getting a little heated."

Dominic walked around him. "I'm not like you or Vincenzo who has the luxury of coming here. I'm not allowed to be seen liking any of this."

Whatever he was getting at, Sylvia nodded. "Alright. I didn't mean to hurt your feelings. When people enter the Black Kitten, they usually want to express themselves in some way." She reevaluated this man who she'd known for some time. "I didn't know you were in hiding."

He stepped back. "I'm not in hiding."

"Yeah, he's not," Luis said. "Dom, come on. Let's leave."

His breathing ramped up. "I know I spend too much time here, alright? I know I shouldn't have done what I did on stage. It was wrong, but you mentioning it to everyone is only going to make things worse."

Sylvia backed up into the door. What was going on? Was Dominic truly someone like her or Laurence or Mitsuko? If so, why was he yelling at *her* about it?

She couldn't imagine not living as her true self, but she knew its power. She knew that, aside from most Kitten patrons, people were disgusted by fairies and their magical hearts. Some people didn't have the magic. Some people had so much of it, they needed to cloak its brightness to save themselves. She'd let herself shine and got beaten for it.

"Okay," she said, the guilt finally reaching her. "I won't mention this to anyone, ever. I swear."

"It doesn't matter," he said dismissively. "Everyone in this God forsaken building's going to know eventually, and then I'm done. Through. I'll be dead by next week." His neck muscles throbbed as he tried holding back his hate. "This's how all you people act. You have your way with innocent men and then spoil their lives by blabbing about it to your friends. It's like a virus."

"What?"

"*You*, you people. You're all so..." He sighed. "I'm not reliving this. I'm not going to be tainted by this lifestyle again."

Luis, speechless, turned to Sylvia with an apology forming on his lips.

From being yelled at, Sylvia, before, would've cried. She would've curled up in a corner and apologized for speaking up when she hadn't been spoken to. Now, either from Vincenzo not being present or from her spending so much time with him, she didn't back down. Her heart beat more from anger than humiliation.

She put her hands on her hips. "Now, see here."

The two men looked up.

"Firstly, I do apologize for bringing this up so suddenly. I can see that you're not comfortable with the topic and I will not bring it up again with you or anyone else. *However,*

I will not allow you to yell at me like this and insinuate that what I and many of my friends do is considered 'tainted' by your standards. That is unfair to everyone here—including you."

At his inclusion, he inhaled.

"So do *not* yell at me because I asked you a question you didn't have to answer, and if you need anyone to talk to about this, maybe don't yell at one of the only women here who would've been willing to listen to what you were going through."

"You—" He went to lean against a vanity table, but his hand slipped. "You don't know what you're talking about."

"You're right, she doesn't," Luis said. "Dom, breathe. Just *breathe*. You're fine."

"But I'm not," he said. "She knows, he knows, they all—"

Before he finished, the door to the backstage opened. Mitsuko and Laurence had arrived. Mitsuko had her bayonet at her side. Laurence looked ready to cry.

A moment of silence passed. Luis lowered his raised hands. Dominic shuddered.

Then he cursed and stormed out of the Kitten. He took five large steps, arms pumping, and slipped into the alley through the back door.

"Dom, wait!" Luis called out.

Laurence pushed back the curtain to watch him go. He opened his mouth to call for him but held back and went to Sylvia instead. "What did you say to him?"

"Nothing."

"Bull."

Luis opened the door seconds after Dominic had closed it, but after hearing a car start up and tires squeak against the pavement, he moaned and hopped on his heels impatiently. "Dang it!"

"What is going on?" Laurence asked. "You said you weren't going to intrude."

"I didn't..." Her heart swelled in her throat. "I didn't mean to hurt him. I just wanted both of you to be happy."

"But he can't," Luis said. "I, uh, I gotta go get him. I have to make sure he's safe. Whenever he gets like this, he gets bad."

"O-okay," Sylvia said.

"...And I might not come back tonight," he said.

"Oh." With her ride tethered to him, she opened her vanity table and fished out her purse. "Is that okay? Mitsuko? Laurence?"

"Go where you have to go," Mitsuko said, keeping her arms crossed, looking perturbed.

Laurence, hand bunching up the parted curtain, kept his thoughts and attention on the closed door.

They left after Sylvia apologized to Bobbie for skipping out halfway through her shift. He'd wanted an explanation. She'd pointed to Luis furiously rubbing off his whiskers with a cup of water.

She wasn't drunk enough to handle this. She didn't know what she could've done better. All she saw was Dominic's face and how disgusted he'd looked at her. Most people looked at her like that for how she dressed, not for what she thought.

And she hadn't *known*. She hadn't known Dominic was in hiding. Who would've? Why go to a pansy bar so often when you secretly despised the patrons for who they kissed? Why yell at her for asking?

She got into Luis' car with these questions. Who was she to demand such information from a man she didn't even know that well? There was a good chance they'd never be friends after this, so why did it hurt so much?

After buckling herself in, Sylvia leaned into the car seat and sobbed.

"Oh, no, baby, don't do that now." Luis gave her his handkerchief. "Come on. It's nothing bad."

"But it is," she cried. "I made him so angry. I shouldn't have asked. It was so rude of me."

"No, no." He started the car and drove off. "Dominic, he's...He's a turbulent guy, he is. Good one day, a disaster the next. The last few weeks have been hard for him. I guess I can fill you in, seeing as he basically told you, but he's, you know, he's funny like that."

"So you've known?"

"Yeah." He scratched his nose. "Feels weird finally bringing it up, but a couple months after knowing him, we were driving into Manhattan and he told me. Told me he hadn't told anyone yet but trusted me to keep it secret. And by God, I kept that promise for three whole years. Never even told my wife about it.

"But this's important. Vincenzo can't know. Nobody can. He was right. Us guys can't be funny like how Vincenzo is with you. He's the boss' favorite, so he's a little untouchable when it comes to certain requirements, but Dominic's lower on the totem pole. He has to keep what he likes tight-lipped, otherwise he might go missing or get hurt. We can't have that happening to our guy."

"I understand." She wiped her eyes. "I'm a terrible person."

"No, don't go off saying that. You sound just like him when he gets into his moods. You were right. He shouldn't have blown up on you. It was a question that he could've said no to and that would've been that. But since that whole fiasco with Laurence, he's been a little high-strung. He thinks everyone knows his secret because he's coming here so often with Vincenzo."

"But doesn't he like Laurence? Is it because of the color of his skin, or the bar? Us?"

"You're a smart girl. You know that he wouldn't be getting this emotional over a man he hated."

Knowing that, she felt even worse. He'd *wanted* to be with Laurence, for so long, but not only was he expected to sway from it, he was expected to denounce the very man he was. To be safe.

She took off her shoes and hid her wet face in her knees. She needed to take baby steps to stand up for herself, but, like everything in her life, it'd backfired and left her hating herself even more.

She wondered if Dominic felt the same way.

Chapter 16: Winter Blues

Nobody was killed on his business trip, so it was already going better than planned.

In truth, he detested these outings. They offered him a reasonable vacation and he was grateful for the opportunities to sightsee around Canada, but give him thirty gallons of alcohol to distribute across New York City's pansy bars and he'd be happier, more fulfilled. These trips? They felt demeaning, almost. Like a joke. He didn't even have his friends to keep him company.

At least it was over. Now Campo had a new line of alcohol from Montreal to Brooklyn for $240 less than what the seller had offered him. With Campo's signatures and scripts to read, Vincenzo had become a perfectly alright negotiator.

But he didn't know why he'd asked him to do this. Campo could make grown men cower and strangers cry at the sight of him entering their establishment. Vincenzo was getting there, but he couldn't do it without Dominic to back him up or Luis to drive him there. All he had was this driver Campo had provided him.

Mr. DuPont. Not even an Italian, with his blond-white hair and fair skin. Not that it mattered, but he knew Campo preferred his men Sicilian-born and rarely worked with any other type.

He was a decent man, Mr. DuPont. He was ten minutes early to every appointment and always had time to point out historic buildings on their rides.

"I do like to be punctual," Mr. DuPont said as he drove. "My daughter, on the other hand, well, she'll be late for her own funeral."

"That so," Vincenzo said, admiring the snowy scenery passing by. He had another ten miles of small talk to withstand before they reached the train station. So far, he'd learned about the man's life in France, his wife whom he adored, and his daughter, Émeline.

"She lives back home as a public relation worker. She's like a guide for tourists, and a very good one. I needed to leave due to work, but I send her money every month. Campo's been a very kind man, you know this, and he offered her a job here, but she didn't want to leave France."

"That so."

"Lovely, she is. Émeline DuPont."

This old man was nearing his fifties, so Vincenzo didn't want to be contentious with him. Plus, he was a friend of Campo's, but he could only handle so much. He pressed, "Sir, while this Émeline sounds like a wonderful girl, I already have a suitor."

"Oh!" he exclaimed. "Sir, I didn't mean it in that regard! I've heard you have a lucky little, uh, *individual* in your mitts. Campo's told me all about her."

Vincenzo strained his smile. Back in the summer, he'd politely asked Campo to refrain from speaking about Sylvia to strangers. Not that he was ashamed of her, but after these attacks, he needed to be careful about information leaking about his personal life.

"I just love her," Mr. DuPont said. "Ever since her poor mother became ill, she's been such a sullen girl. How I want her to come over and find a man."

Vincenzo noticed his wedding ring. He selfishly noticed most people's rings, but instead of keeping it on his finger, he wore it on a silver necklace close to his heart.

"You seem to have a loving family," Vincenzo said.

"Thank you. Whenever I see a young man out without a little thing at his side, I worry about how unhappy he must feel."

"What a dismal feeling that must be."

"Isn't it?"

Vincenzo sighed. He knew he should've ignored this veering conversation, but he'd gotten hooked. "What I would give to have what other men can."

"I beg your pardon?"

"Marriage," he said. "To marry someone. I'd like to have that one day with her."

"Ah." Mr. DuPont fixed his white driving gloves. "Perhaps I've said too much."

"You haven't," he lied. "If I had my way, I would've married her this year. This world, or the men who run it, have other plans for my happiness."

"My apologies, sir. Forget I said anything. I was just making conversation."

"You're fine." He itched his hand. "Not to be so rude, Mr. DuPont, but if I had the feeling that Campo set you up for this..."

"Oh, no, sir! It's nothing like that. He's just worried about you, like a father is with his son."

His smile came back. "That's what I thought."

He laughed abruptly. "It seems you caught me. Before you came here, Mr. d'Antonio might've called me to bring this up with you. He's curious, how can you blame him? He wants to see you happy with this Sylvia person."

"You can tell Campo that, while I appreciate his concern, until the world changes, my spouse and I will be content as we are."

"But will *she*?" he asked. "You work in a business that can shape laws into your favor. Can't you rewrite some documents here and there to finalize the marriage process?"

"I—" The thought came, then went. "Perhaps," he then said. "I'll have to think about it."

"I hope it happens. How I love weddings."

As he half-listened to Mr. DuPont talk about his wife and daughter, Vincenzo created a world where his unattainable was now possible. Campo had altered his birth certificate, why couldn't he doctor one for Sylvia? If he did that, if they got married remotely on some island without his father present...

As they neared the station, he admired his ringless hand. Could he ask Sylvia for her hand in marriage? Could it happen? Did she *want* to be married? He'd changed so much of his life for her, but he never dwelled on the question for too long. It depressed him.

He hid his hand in his jacket. No use fretting over that now. He had too much work to do. He had to clean up the house, make it suitable for a bride, a wife. And he needed to become a better man to *be* her husband. He was doing well, but there was always room to improve. That'd take months to accomplish, maybe years.

And if he came up with any other reasons to prolong the proposal, he'd add them to the list.

—◇—

He returned to Brooklyn later that afternoon. Gone was the October warmth. Within days, autumn had settled within the bare trees of his cul-de-sac. The grass was dying and the Sun was being blocked by a wall of clouds. It wasn't as cold as Canada, but he couldn't wait for winter to come. He'd met Sylvia during spring. Spending winter with her? His birthday? *Christmas*? He couldn't wait.

He drove himself home. After calling Dominic three times, he couldn't get a hold of him, and despite being more powerful than Luis, he knew that Saturday was Ana's birthday. His business trip gave him a convenient excuse to miss it, but he didn't want to pull Luis away from that. And he couldn't dare ask Campo or *Nonna* to pick him up, and Sylvia didn't have a car.

So, when he saw a stranger's car parked in his front lawn, it gave him pause. A black Bentley with cracks in the windows and wheels too dirty to be owned by any of his men.

Then he saw Luis sulking on the front steps.

He exited his car with his luggage. "Luis."

"Oh!" He slicked back his hair and helped him with his bags. "Thank God. I thought you were coming later tonight."

"I just got home. Why—"

"Okay. First, uh, before you come in—"

He tried to walk through him.

He stopped him. "B-before you come in, know that I did everything to calm things down. That's what I do, I'm a calm fella, and that's what I tried to do."

He shoved him a bit too hard and opened the door.

Nonna was cooking a hearty meal in the kitchen and rooted him back home. The table had been set, but with the amount of plates out, she couldn't have been cooking for just him, her, and Sylvia.

Something thudded upstairs. Mezzanotte ears perked up from behind the curtains.

"Welcome back, my little bean," Nonna said. "Did you have fun? Did you eat? I'm making pasta and steak, and I have a pizza in the oven. I thought everyone could have a little of something, but I don't know what your friends eat. Can you translate?"

"What friends?" he asked more to Luis than to his grandmother. By the door, he saw two pairs of unfamiliar men's shoes.

"Well—"

"Move it, we got a cold one here."

Hurried, slippered footsteps rushed down the stairs, and around the corner came Mitsuko. She was carrying a foot-long bag into the kitchen and walked around Vincenzo like he wasn't the owner of this house. "Why are we lollygagging? We have work that needs to be done. Luis, what's the damage?"

"Nothing new on my end," he said. "He's still not answering the door, and I won't take your advice and break a window, ma'am. I got a level of trust with him I need to protect."

"Coward. And don't call me *'ma'am'*. Only certain girls can call me that." She dropped the bag into one of the boiling pots *Nonna* was tending to. *Nonna* didn't seem that fazed by the behavior, or that a stranger, at least to her, was parading around her home quite rudely.

"Why're you here?" Vincenzo demanded. "I didn't invite you in."

"Is this really your home? I love your interior decorating skills. It reminds me of my grandmother." She bowed to *Nonna*, who smiled and bowed back, then took out her hot bag with oven mitts. "Bag of rice," she said when she caught Vincenzo staring. "It works well to calm a girl down."

"I wish I could bring one over to Dominic," Luis said. "I knocked and knocked, but he's not answering. It's been two days. And I *know* he's not dead because his fireplace was going last night and I heard his gramophone change artists from the steps."

"What's wrong with—" Vincenzo stopped. "No, what's going on *here*? Where's Sylvia?"

"We invited ourselves over after Laurence received a disturbing call from Sylvia yesterday night." She started up the stairs. Vincenzo followed. "She kept saying how she was a terrible human being who had no right enjoying any of the gifts she's been provided with. It's a slip in her personality. You haven't seen much of this side of her, but when it gets to 'calling-her-friends-at-midnight-crying' bad, that's when we're called in."

"Why is she upset?"

"A whole story that I'm not allowed to talk about. Just know that some words may or may not have been exchanged at the Kitten between Sylvia and Dominic that may or may not have sent Sylvia into thinking she's a monster and Dominic into his house out of fear." She opened his bedroom door. "Happy Halloween. Welcome to the nightmare."

Sylvia was in bed, propped up by six pillows with tea in her hands and a wrap over her forehead. Around her were empty beer bottles and a carton of half-finished ice cream with the spoon sticking out of the vanilla. Laurence, out of his womanly garments, sat next to her, touching her forehead like a doting mother.

Her red eyes, rubbed of makeup and tears, looked at him pathetically. Then she burst into tears and hid her head in Laurence's shoulder.

"What's wrong with her?" Vincenzo asked.

Mitsuko draped the bag of rice over Sylvia's buried feet. "It got bad."

"Terrible, sir," added Luis. "She's been like this all weekend."

"And why didn't anyone tell me?" Figuring he wasn't going to get a decent answer from any of them, he sat beside Sylvia and touched her head. He knew her Moon waxed and waned, but he didn't understand why they were tiptoeing around the problem. It couldn't have been too dire—he didn't read that kind of atmosphere—but this was *his* room. *His* home. Where was his agency with these people, and why couldn't he yell at them?

He touched the blankets. "Sylvia, baby, tell me what's going on."

"I *can't*," she said, muffled. "I found something out about Dominic that he didn't want me to know. Now he's upset with me and I'm a bad person."

"And what was it that you found out?"

"I can't tell you. Oh, I'm such a fool," she cried.

"Stop saying that," Laurence said. "You're a beautiful, young woman, so stop putting yourself down because of dramatic nonsense. Why don't we go out for that walk, or listen to a nice tune?"

She covered her face and, like a turtle, wiggled into her blankets and hid herself from the world.

Vincenzo ran through every month of every year he'd known Dominic. He lost all communication with his family in Connecticut. He liked painting. He did what he was told. He owned two cars.

He was going to lose his mind. What had Sylvia found out? It couldn't have been a part of their gangster business because it was affecting her and her friends. Had he said something about the way they lived? Was he finally fed up with this life-style? Did he actually hate what the Black Kitten stood for?

He better not of. If that was true, he'd kill him.

"Alright, then." He leaned down and kissed what he believed to be Sylvia's head. "I'm going to buy you more ice cream. What else do you need?"

"Nothing."

"Then cookies. Can you two take care of her for the time being?"

"We've been doing it for years, I'm sure we can manage," Mitsuko said.

"We'll be fine," Laurence said in a kinder way.

"Thank you. Before I leave, I'm going to help *Nonna* cook, being that she's cooking for six."

"Are we invited to dinner?" Mitsuko asked sarcastically.

"Why wouldn't you be?"

They all looked at one another, and Vincenzo slowly realized how foreign the question sounded in his mouth. A few months ago, he would've forbidden them from entering his home. Now, even though they'd technically broken in like vagrants, he wouldn't have let them leave without first offering them some food.

"I'll take milk, then," Mitsuko said.

"And I'll take a glass of water with lemon, if I can," Laurence said.

"And Luis?" Vincenzo asked, but he was looking out the side windows to Dominic's house, hopping on his heels. It was a tic that came out when he was losing control of a situation.

Chapter 17: Experimenting

Sylvia considered hiding underneath the covers until next year before restarting her life.

Well, she *was* living. If Vincenzo begged, she took baths. She ate under *Nonna's* orders. She took walks with her friends. And she'd stopped bursting into tears whenever she saw Dominic's unlit home.

From what Vincenzo had told her, Dominic had started working again a week after the incident. He met up with Luis on occasion and worked on simple missions before hiding away in his house. Sylvia wouldn't have known. She wouldn't ask—or call, God forbid—and ruin even more of him.

She couldn't take the guilt. How much of his life had she shattered? These men with their appearances and their masculinity. Dominic hadn't been killed like he'd thought, but if his attraction slipped out to Hannigan, she'd freely die along with him in regret.

This lifestyle was easier to live with at the Black Kitten. Not many important people openly flaunted it in public. If they did, they disguised themselves or pretended they knew nothing about sex. Dominic, Luis, Vincenzo, they had *so* much to lose. She revered Vincenzo's determination to keep this up with her, but Dominic, did he have the fortitude to uphold such a beautiful burden?

Sylvia sighed for the third time that hour.

Mitsuko, who was eating lunch with her in the Kitten's back room, said, "Why not apologize to him if you're so broken up about it?"

"Because he hasn't come here in a month. He didn't come to *Thanksgiving*, Mitsuko. He celebrated it *alone*. I can't call him or knock on his door to apologize now. He hates me, it's final."

Mitsuko crossed her legs so she had more lap on which to eat her sandwich. "Seems like he wants to stay upset."

"Don't say that. Nobody wishes to stay unhappy. I just didn't know he was hiding it, you know, or that he was even interested in the first place."

"So why're you so distraught? You did nothing wrong."

"Yes, I did. I shouldn't have confronted him about it. It wasn't my place."

"And it wasn't his place to snap at you and make you feel like the devil for asking him a stupid question, so drop it. And your question turned out to be right, by the way, so if he doesn't want to talk about it, then fine. But if you're an unmarried man who constantly hangs out at a *pansy* bar, don't be surprised when *pansies* start wondering if they could pursue you. Seems like he needs someone to push him into the pool."

Sylvia picked at the crumbs of her sandwich. "I don't want to push anyone into any pool. They should jump in for themselves."

"Guess it works for different people." She napkined her lips. "How about this: About twenty minutes ago, Vincenzo came in."

"What?" She didn't know he was coming in today. "Why didn't you tell me?"

"Because I wanted you to eat something. I now have both you and Laurence to worry about and I can't have you skipping meals and him thinking that pursuing Dominic is actually a good idea."

"Oh, pick a side, Mitsuko. Do you want us to fall in love or not?" She threw away her trash. "I'm going to talk to Vincenzo about this."

"Good luck, soldier."

The Black Kitten had thinned out since she'd left for dinner. It was a Wednesday, and it'd snowed the night prior, so not many brave souls had risked walking or driving in the streets. Only a handful of regulars were passed out in their usual tables, candles half out, plates licked clean.

And only two people were at the bar: Luis and, by some means aiming to make Sylvia feel more terrible, Dominic. They were both on their second or third glass, their cheeks reddened a wasted pink.

Unable to make eye contact with them, Sylvia beelined for Vincenzo's booth. A month of silence just for him to come back. Was everything fine? Were things worse?

Vincenzo made space for her. "Evening."

"Evening. Did you know Dominic's here?"

"I did. Luis forced him and me to come out as a sort of friendly alliance. This was supposed to be a fun night, but I don't think it's going to happen."

"Oh, Vincenzo, tell him he can leave. He shouldn't be here if he doesn't want to."

"Luis said he didn't want him decomposing in his home this winter, but I don't think drinking will make things any better."

"What kind of drunk is he?"

"Emotional."

"Oh, dear." She motioned to drink his drink.

He obliged, then stared across the bar to his friends. "Sylvia, can I ask you a question?"

Her nervous heart fluttered.

"Is Dominic a pansy?"

"No."

He looked at her.

"He's not," she pressed. "I'd know, and he isn't."

He dropped his head in his hand, watching her.

She kept her face straight, but her lower lip was trembling.

"That's his secret, isn't it?" he asked. "It's why he's in hiding. It's why he clams up whenever he's here. He likes men."

"That's not true."

"You don't have to lie to me. I know better than most not to take that information lightly."

She gripped where her heart was. "Vincenzo, you mustn't say anything, and he mustn't know I told—"

"You didn't tell me, so you don't have to worry." He slouched. "Took some time to crack that, huh? To say I never knew. I consider him my...accomplice."

"Friend."

He nodded at the right word. "And nothing. Never knew a thing."

"He's suffering."

"Then we should help him. I've always wondered who these men are to me. They work for me, and I value their work ethic, but when I saw him so broken up about this, it hit me. They're my friends. I want to see them happy. And I want to give Dominic the chance so many of us don't get." He went for his pocket. "May I show you something?"

"You may."

He took out a piece of paper and unfolded it on the table. On it, he'd written, crossed out, and arrowed a whole letter of information. She knew his handwriting was atrocious, words slanted and smashed together, but she wondered what language he'd written this in.

"I set aside time to really think over the possibility of their relationship. Dominic is a strong man, very forceful, a real man's man. But he's *shy*. He doesn't speak unless spoken to, even when he's not working. He's quiet, subservient. Laurence is the exact opposite of that. He's determined and passionate. He speaks his mind and doesn't let anybody tell him otherwise. I feel like you and I are quite similar. We're not obtrusive, we mind our own business. But opposites attract, do they not?"

She nodded, though she was trying to find where on his paper he was reading this from.

"I don't think Dominic's strong enough to bring this up with Laurence by himself, and I believe Laurence is too headstrong to make the first move, but if we were to, say, give them a *push*..."

"You're planning on playing cupid with our friends?"

"...Yes."

She tried to read his notes one last time, then laughed. "You're funny."

"Is that a compliment?"

"I'd hope so."

"Good. I spent a few hours making this. It's been helping me postpone my conversation with Campo about those break-ins."

"You haven't told him yet?"

He added an arrow to his notes. "Bit of a hypocrite, am I not? I think Dominic should come out and admit his feelings, yet I can't talk to my own boss about a somewhat serious issue."

"It's a threat on our lives."

"I know. I plan on telling him at the start of December. I'm just...nervous, that he might think I'm a coward, like how my father thinks of me." From his pocket, he took out a packet of white powder she knew too well. "Wanna relax?"

She tipped their glass at the packet. "Absolutely."

An hour passed and neither side of the bar met up. Luis and Dominic drank and whispered in secret. Laurence, finally in his stage clothes, sang and performed for his patrons. Mitsuko did as well, though her spark was dimmer; she didn't flail or jump off the stage to make the girls in the audience swoon.

Sylvia, after shaming herself for a month, drank happily. She shared Campari and vodka cocktails with Vincenzo and mixed their final sips with his cocaine. She preferred alcohol, but if given the chance, she had no issue mixing different levels of fun to make a night more enjoyable.

With every glass of Campari, Vincenzo built upon his notes. They drew upon Dominic's mysterious past and his future with Laurence. They made a life for Mitsuko and her fictitious wife, for Luis and his wife. When they ran out of space, they used napkins.

"Mitsuko would have a dog," Vincenzo said. "I won't argue this."

"She wouldn't have a pet to begin with."

"Yes, she would. She'd love dogs. A husky."

"Husky?"

"Or a, what's the word, a St. Bernard. She'd have that."

"No. I refuse!"

"Oh, please—" He stumbled out of his seat with his half-finished glass. "I'm gonna go ask her. Where is she?"

"Dancing."

"*Dancing*. Her dancing is so...*provocative*, don't you think?"

"That's what she goes for."

"I can...I can do th..." He held his head, eyes going in two different directions.

Taking his hand, Sylvia helped him to the main floor. She didn't quite know who was playing at the moment. Laurence, right? Was she supposed to be playing tonight? She stopped at an empty table to think about it. Vincenzo kept going towards the stage.

Laurence lifted his yellow dress and earned a soft clap from the audience. He was the perfect performer. Even while he was going through this emotional time, he kept everyone engaged. He danced and sang for hours and never complained because he liked it. Sometimes, Sylvia couldn't play piano on account of multiple internal problems. But Laurence outdid himself every night and his fans ate it up.

Sylvia craned her neck to see if Dominic was enjoying the show.

He had his back to them, his forehead on the table.

The Black Kitten quieted down. Confused whispers broke out, each one catching her dizzying attention.

A new singer introduced themselves to the stage. Their steps were uncoordinated like they were plodding through water to get there. They got there, though, and held the microphone with both hands. Laurence backed off to give them room. Mitsuko turned at the sudden intermission.

Had Sylvia taken more than cocaine? Surely this wasn't Vincenzo, standing tall, or tilted, rather, at the microphone. Centered with the lights on him, he looked like he belonged. With the performers. With them.

He adjusted the microphone to his height, then waited for the trumpets to lead him in before he opened his mouth.

Sylvia became teary-eyed. She'd heard him sing at Campo's party, but *this* voice, it had a mission. It had no filter, no volume control. He held his heart during the choruses and walked with the microphone during the verses. And he was smiling through it all.

Smiling just as blissfully, Sylvia bobbed her head to his voice. What had she meant to do today? It felt important.

Shrugging it off, she skipped up the steps and met with her talented love.

Vincenzo clapped for her arrival. She knew the song he was singing now—"Baby Face" by Jan Garber. It was begging for a piano accompaniment, so she gave it to him, heightening the great piece to a perfect one.

Her fingers danced over the keys like an uncontained child. At the chorus, Vincenzo lay across the body of the piano and kicked his legs up. Sylvia licked her lips at him, and he strolled over and sang behind her, his hips grinding into her lower back.

She moaned with his vibrato. He sang to his baby, his sweet baby, the one that sent him to Heaven every time he saw her. She hoped it was about her. It could've been about his cat. Or *Nonna.*

After the song ended, Vincenzo lifted her up and spun her around the mic. Their feet were too silly to dance, but that didn't stop them. Legs were kicked, dresses were raised, and kisses were given in front of everyone. The crowd certainly didn't mind; Sylvia guessed they weren't cheering for the song.

She finally exited off the stage after Vincenzo got to humping her piano like a cat in heat. She needed a break, but he didn't. He sang every song from his inventory. Some lyrics were changed to Italian mid-chorus. Luis sang along where he could.

Sylvia let herself swoon until a sinking feeling hit her. She'd been having so much fun. What had her brain wanted her to remember?

She covered her mouth. *Dominic.* Her apology. How had she forgotten? She'd only drunk two glasses, right?

Zigzagging between the tables, she returned to where she'd seen him last.

He was gone. He wasn't on the floor like how Luis was, cuddling his empty glass. He'd vanished yet again.

Vincenzo broke off into another song that almost distracted her, but she remained focused and scoured the booths.

She interrupted a kissing couple, a man monologuing about his youth. She excused herself and carried on. She couldn't let him disappear again.

She covered her mouth and tripped backwards. In a booth for two, Laurence and Dominic were keeping each other company.

She ducked behind a table. They were sitting shoulder to shoulder, dining on a plate of crackers. Dominic had his head low as he discussed something in secret. They must've been talking for some time. The candle on their table was half out.

"That's awful, what you lived through," she heard Laurence say, quietly.

"It ruined me," Dominic said even quieter. "It's why I hate this scene. It's why I can't open up to anyone, ever. It'll kill me."

"But you're not ruined. You're still here and doing fine."

"But it's walking on eggshells. It's travelling eighty miles to New Haven for a quick time just to drive back home feeling humiliated that you've stooped so low. I don't want to live like that any longer."

"You don't have to here."

"I told you, I can't—"

"I meant here, with me," He placed his hand over his. "You don't have to hide anything from me."

Dominic pressed his drink to his lips, considering the temptation.

Laurence leaned in, giving him time to back out if he wanted. They were at a circle booth. If either of them desired, both of them had a way out.

Dominic looked down at Laurence's lips. Sylvia knew he was looking for that, a way out. To not give in to what his heart had been groveling for. She'd found that love with Vincenzo and hoped every little girl and boy like her could one day have what she'd been blessed with.

Melting under the weight of Laurence, Dominic sighed, wrapped his limp arms around him, and let himself be carefully kissed.

Sylvia teared up again. What an emotional drunk the two of them were. And all of this because of her.

This sad scene before her. This was all her fault. He must've hated her for pressuring him into this. What a terrible, bad friend she was.

Pulling on her pearls, she left her very secret hiding space. "Dominic."

They pulled apart. Dominic's lips were smeared with burgundy.

"I'm sorry I did this to you. I shouldn't have asked you such a personal question. You have every right to keep this part of you a secret so nobody ever has to know."

Dominic and Laurence looked at each other, then back at Sylvia.

"I hope everything works out for you in the end. I do very much love you and support your need to keep this secret." She looked at Laurence's hand slowly wringing its way back into Dominic's hair. "Less so than Laurence, it seems."

Dominic sucked in his lips. "Thank you," he said. "I forgive you."

"He does," Laurence promised. "Sylvia, darling, uh, go out and find Mitsuko. I think she has something for you to do."

"Okay." Feeling herself fall, she collapsed into a nearby booth. Thank goodness he didn't loathe her anymore. Maybe she'd finally get to sleep tonight. She wondered why he was talking with Laurence. She thought they disliked one another.

Before she lost herself to her dreams, she heard the jazz song slip into an instrumental piece. Someone fiddled with the mic, and Vincenzo said proudly, "You're all invited to my Christmas party! All of you, at *Nonna's*. She makes the best cod."

Had Christmas come so soon? She'd lost track of the time.

It'd be her first Christmas with a lover.

She couldn't wait for it to pass.

Chapter 18: Mitsuko's Rescue Mission

Mitsuko couldn't believe many things in life, but the scene unfolding before her was quite unimaginable.

From Sylvia exposing herself in her booth as she slept. To Laurence kissing Dominic in the booth next door. To Vincenzo singing *I'm Nobody's Baby* to his crowd of six. Almost everyone had left after to his erotic performance, and it wasn't because it was bad. In reality, he sang the song better than the woman who recorded it, and he had the skill that most people would kill for. It was just that it was two in the morning and people had places to be tomorrow.

Had he been drugged? Should she have checked his drink like she had been with her friends? She almost didn't want to intervene. He looked too happy to be himself on stage.

But whatever had slipped through his mind, she'd seen enough. One more song and Sylvia would be naked on the ground and Dominic and Laurence would need to be hosed down.

She went to Bobbie first, the only sober man standing. "What are we going to do about this?"

He shook his head. "Did you know Vincenzo could sing?"

"Did you know that Laurence's soulmate would be a gangster boy with a mustache?"

Across the bar, Laurence moaned into Dominic's hairy upper lip and pinned him down.

Mitsuko gagged. Do it upstairs in the attic, where Bobbie had a few extra mattresses stored up there for this specific reason. She had to listen to these noises through her apartment walls. Now she had to deal with it at work?

"Okay," she said. "Here, I'll...I'll sandwich them in the back of my car and drive them home. I don't trust any of them getting behind the wheel like this."

"And I have to clean up." He looked at the mess Vincenzo had made on stage. He'd somehow ripped off the curtain and was kicking it to the beat of the song.

From the shadows, two men got up and walked towards the stage. With their black coats on and bowler hats hiding their shadowy faces, Mitsuko hadn't registered them as people. They looked like monsters.

When they reached for something in their coats, Mitsuko lunged for an empty bottle and ran up on stage. It was just her and her friends here, there wasn't anyone to protect them. Nobody but her.

To assert her dominance, she flung herself around Vincenzo and pulled him back like they were friends. "Hey, Vinny, your wife's getting a little *loose* back there. Think it's time you bring her in for the night, otherwise these two handsome men are gonna swipe her from you."

Vincenzo tried focusing on her face, then on the hand on his shoulder. Before he put two and two together, she grabbed his wrist and placed herself between him and the men. They definitely looked like they had weapons on them, but whether or not they had knives or guns would make her rethink how much Vincenzo meant to her.

The two men stopped, hands dropping to their sides.

She played up her act, slurring her words and swinging her bottle, trying to remember how to act drunk. "Did you handsome gents wanna come up and have a little fun? I can find a nice little thing to play with. You can watch."

"Having a little too much fun, are we?" one of the men asked Vincenzo, completely ignoring her. His subordinate looked behind them at Dominic and Laurence. They'd successfully uncoupled, but while Laurence was fixing his top, Dominic had recognized the two men and pretended he hadn't. He hid his face from an obvious threat.

Mitsuko cleared her throat. "Come on, boys, come up on stage. We'll get another round going. Boys, boys!" She got the musicians' attention. "What do you like the most? Something slow and sultry? Something big and powerful?" She swayed her hips, inching closer to them. "I'll take the lead, if that's what you're into."

"Lady, I don't know how much English you know, but we don't need any of the crude services you offer."

Her nose twitched. She hadn't taught herself English just to be downplayed by assholes who spit-shined their own shoes. She tightened her grip around her bottle. "Then you should keep searching for a pansy bar to root in tonight, being that none of us here actually speak a language you two would ever understand."

The men snarled and took their first step up the stage stairs, but Mitsuko blocked them with her body. "If either of you actually wanna indulge in the sweet comforts of a pansy bar and suck a fat cock or fuck a wet girl's pussy for thirty seconds, I'm sure we can find someone desperate enough to fuck you. Now, if you can just tell me what sex position you're more well-versed in and what kind of leather you prefer to cum in, we can start this night off right."

They reacted how most men would after hearing a woman speak that vulgarly. Articulating it into words—being direct about how you wanted it—and suddenly you were a disgusting whore who needed to be calmed down for your own desires.

"This place is filthy." The larger man spat on the ground and exited up the stairs.

"Tell Vincenzo that we're watching him, *little thing*," the other said. "More intently than ever."

She went to curse them out and tell them that she wasn't their delivery boy but held back. She hadn't seen their real weapons.

She watched them go until they disappeared around the corner. Bobbie, who'd taken out his gun from behind the counter, followed them up the steps.

Keeping alert, she dropped her bottle and went to pick up Vincenzo.

He was asleep standing up, spit dripping onto his shoes.

"Ugh, come on." She hooked an arm around his waist. She really hated how much she loved Sylvia. "Come on, you dumb whore. Find your feet."

"Huh?"

"We're leaving. Everyone!" she shouted. "Wake up. Stop being drunk. We're going home."

"Am I driving?" Luis asked.

"Hell no." She picked up Sylvia by her arm and got her standing. Laurence was up and ready to leave. Dominic was staring at the staircase, waiting for the men to return.

"Who were they?" she asked him.

"Men," he slurred. "Bad men. They work with Severo."

She didn't know what a "Severo" was, but she reckoned a serpentine-like man was someone to be avoided.

With her entourage of drunks, Mitsuko led her friends through the back doors and piled them into her car. She sat Vincenzo in the passenger seat and everyone else in the back. She didn't know why, but she felt protective over him tonight, like those men would eat him alive if she wasn't careful.

She drove chaotically to the main road. She saw neither Bobbie nor Severo's men anywhere. Hopefully, they'd disappeared as quickly as they appeared, leaving Bobbie to lock up his Kitten safely. She hoped nothing bad would happen to him alone, but she knew keeping these idiots down there would've only made things worse.

"Where're we going?" Sylvia asked, leaning over to pet Mitsuko's head.

"I'm driving you home. You lot lost your drinking privileges for tonight."

"What about my car?" Vincenzo asked.

"Relax, you own three. I'm sure it'll be there when you come back."

"I'm sorry," Dominic said. "I don't usually get like this."

"I'm sure Laurence didn't mind it."

"Hey, I-I'm not drunk," Laurence said. "I can hear you. I'll remember this."

"Good, because I have some questions about you and your revelations tonight."

"On your grave."

"Bite me."

Laurence's house was only a few blocks down from the Kitten. To her relief, he and his new man didn't kiss each other goodbye. They acted like strangers as neither of them wished the other goodnight or even looked at one another as they separated.

But as Mitsuko said her goodbye and drove off, Dominic said, "Wait. Can you drop me off with him?"

"And why would I do that?" she asked.

"I need to make sure he gets home safe."

"He's already home."

He strained his brain for a reason to stay. "But the stairs. He might trip."

"I don't think I can do that, for I don't think either of you would forgive me if I did."

"But..." Like a dog, he stuck his head out the window and watched the clustered group of apartments fade into New York.

"Window up," she ordered, and he complied with a tiny pout.

She stared at his grumpy face through the mirror. What a baby. "Dominic, why're you doing this to yourself? Don't you think you'd be happier pursuing someone else? Vincenzo's already in a pinch when it comes to what he has with Sylvia, and Sylvia, when she's dolled up, has a good enough time passing, but Laurence is different. You know that. He's a black man who dresses like a woman for fun. You better not take that lightly if you decide to go through with this."

Dominic rolled his thumbs in circles. His babyish face had gone harder, more serious. She thought it was sensible advice, as he wasn't that plastered and could've taken what she was saying and applied it to this newly budding relationship.

He said, "I'm not stupid."

"I never said you were."

"Yes, you did. Look, I know this's a bad idea. I know I'm better off dead than doing this, but you don't get to choose how I ruin my life."

"And how is it ruined? By being with him?"

"No, by—" He gestured to himself. "*This.* Everything is wrong with me, from the way I act, to the way I think, to the way I feel. I wish I was strong enough to say no to this, but...I don't...*care* anymore," he forced out, trying to convince himself it was true. "I'm tired of caring about what people think of me. If I'm going to ruin my life, let it be by my choice, not the choice of someone who hasn't bothered to get to know me."

"That's my man!" Luis said too loudly.

She clicked her tongue. She hadn't meant to invoke guilt about his choices. She wanted to make sure he knew that involving yourself with the same sex or someone who society disliked—both, in his case—was going to be hard and that you should prepare for the worst.

It sounded like he thought that what he wanted with Laurence was both his choice and the wrong one. She'd have to talk with him about that, and to Laurence. Make sure her friends weren't engraving their tombstones too early.

She changed the subject. "So, since you're drunk enough to debate with me, how do you feel about our Laurence?"

"I'm not drunk."

"Lovely. So? Your thoughts?"

He hid his face. "No comment."

"That tells me everything I need to know." She turned off of Park Ave. "By the way, his favorite drink is rum, his favorite flower's lavender, and he loves jazz records, Earl Hines particularly. He's his favorite singer."

"Noted," he grumbled.

She must've gotten drunk off the atmosphere. She thought she hated these gangsters. Maybe she only liked them if they were drunk and helpless. Then they could owe her favors.

It brought her back to France, dealing with stupid men and love-crazed women. Things were easier, then. She was less connected with people. Until she'd entered Merchant Hospital and found *her*. She'd drive with her through the countryside, with Émeline, her blond hair catching the summer air as she laughed away the worries of war...

She hit the brakes and skidded onto the sidewalk. Vincenzo's head was thrown forwards, Sylvia's nose smushed into the seat.

She clutched her throat, trying to breathe in her car's fumes. That woman didn't normally invade her headspace like that. She could control it better, meditate her into the back of her head until she was a dream. If she couldn't shake her out, she'd stay at home with the lights off, contemplating all the wrong she'd done in her life until she went crazy.

She slapped her cheeks. She needed to snap out of it. Worrying about that woman was less important than taking care of the loved ones she still had.

She wondered if she really believed that.

Trusting that Dominic and Luis could walk up the steps to their homes without dying, she let them struggle to open their front doors by themselves and pulled into Vincenzo's driveway.

The wind on this side of New York was especially freezing tonight, and there was this oppressive chill in the air that had her hair standing on edge. She hadn't felt this way when she'd come up to comfort Sylvia into not hating herself. As she helped her out of the car, she scanned the street for any idling cars or human figures. She saw neither.

"Do you have your house keys?" she asked Vincenzo.

He tried fishing them out, then stopped what he was doing. "I don't feel good."

"Because you got plowed silly and writhed on stage for almost two hours."

"I wanna sleep here tonight." Sylvia got down on her hands and knees and started crawling into the bushes. "I'm sleeping outside."

"Sylvia, no." She pulled her back. "Your stockings, Sylvia. Your dress. Vincenzo, help me—"

Vincenzo staggered up the steps, leaned over the railing, and vomited into the snowy hedge.

She was surprised to see him hurl so unceremoniously. As if he couldn't be any more pathetic in front of two women. He got a splotch of it on his shirt.

"Give me your house key," she said.

He wiped his mouth and threw them. She had to jump to catch them.

"Asshole," she muttered, and corralled them inside.

"Quiet," Vincenzo said. "*Nonna's* sleeping. We'll wake her."

"Oh, right. That means 'grandma', Mitsuko."

"Thank you, Sylvia." She guided them upstairs. That black cat was sleeping in the center of the bed. She hissed and hid before Mitsuko closed the door.

Sylvia face-planted into her preferred indent of the bed while Vincenzo tried his best to tuck himself in. He kept making sure Sylvia had more of the blankets.

Mitsuko looked over her friends' sleepy states, then pulled out the blankets from underneath them and tucked them in.

"Thank you," Vincenzo said.

"If you remember anything about tonight, don't bring this up again."

He sniffed through a clogged nose. She was afraid he'd start crying—maybe he was an emotional drinker like all of them were—but he said soberly, "I'm sorry about this. I just wanted to have fun for once, but I screwed up everything like usual."

She said nothing. She'd helped him to bed, she wasn't going to mother him.

"I know...I know you hate me, that you wouldn't have done this if I wasn't tied to Sylvia like this." He rolled over and caressed Sylvia's cheek. "I know I cause nothing but trouble for you and the Black Kitten, but I still appreciate what you do for me."

"I wasn't going to let you die. I'm not a monster."

"I am," he said, "a monster."

"I wouldn't discount it. Who were those two men who were trying to get at you, anyway? More monsters?"

"Who?"

"The bowler-hat men."

He squinted. "I don't remember seeing any bowlers. When was this?"

Not caring to argue, Mitsuko turned and gave him a low bow. "Goodnight, Vincenzo."

Sleep stirred up his final, "G'night."

With intent to give them back, she took his house keys and made sure to relock his door. She didn't want the poor grandmother to get up and take care of her adult grandson's drunken mistakes, and if either of those two drunkards came down the stairs, they wouldn't make it back up.

She kept her back to the street as she tested out the right key door. The house had a vintage door handle and lock that made putting the key in difficult.

A twig cracked behind her. The cold wind, blowing through the bushes around her.

She swiftly kicked up her boot and gripped the handle of her hidden switchblade. Not now. Not at night. What kind of fucker attacked a woman alone and at night?

Someone who wanted her more than dead.

She stopped moving. Through the door window, she saw two men standing across the street near a parked car, waiting for her.

"Fuck," she whispered, and reopened the door as fast as she could. Time worked against her as she fought to relock the door. Then, with her nightmares twisting into reality, she took one of the kitchen chairs and wedged it underneath the handle. She did the same with the back door and checked that every first-floor window was firmly locked. Why did he have so many windows in this stupid place, so many access points? She never let go of her knife.

Back upstairs, the cat was sleeping on Sylvia, Sylvia was open-mouth snoring, and Vincenzo was staring at both of them, silent.

"Move over," Mitsuko whispered.

"Huh?"

"I'm sleeping here tonight. I'm not getting followed to my house by monsters."

"Who're these monsters?"

"Ain't that the question we'd all like answered." She uncovered a handmade quilt stuffed inside their shared closet and crawled into bed next to Sylvia. "Goodnight, Vincenzo."

"...Goodnight," he whispered, and passed out seconds later.

Chapter 19: Frantic Phone Call

Sylvia knew before she opened her eyes that she was sleeping in a bathtub.

It happened, just as snow fell in winter and rabbits left their burrows in spring. When she found herself destructively drunk, she somehow awoke in a tub, nestled in her coat and usually with a headache. The headache was there now, and from how sick she felt, she knew she was about to pay for last night's festivities.

She hoped. All she remembered was Vincenzo singing.

And Mitsuko. Lots and lots of Mitsuko.

Taking her time, she eased herself out of Vincenzo's porcelain tub. At least she'd gotten home. Had he driven her back? They always drank together. One wouldn't have drunk without the other.

She didn't want to open her eyes and think, but her missing memories made her ponder. She remembered looking out a cold window, wanting to roll it down but stopping herself because someone had told her to keep the windows up.

She took her time to freshen up at the sink, splashing her face with ice-cold water and scrubbing away her day-old makeup. After trying to fix her bangs in the mirror, she patted off her dress, folded her coat/blanket into the hamper, and opened the door.

Vincenzo was fast asleep in bed. Mezzanotte, who was hidden underneath a quilt, turned to blink at her.

And Mitsuko, who seemed the most awake out of the four of them, got up slowly so she didn't wake the other two. She yawned as she patted the floor for her socks. "Morning."

"Good morning," Sylvia said. "Mitsuko, darling, why are you sleeping with Vincenzo?"

"Because, despite my denial, I actually do have a heart. Sometimes." She scratched underneath Mezzanotte's chin, and Mezzanotte let her, as if Mezzanotte was the type of cat to do that and that Mitsuko was the type of girl to sleep in a man's bed.

Sylvia rubbed down her cuticles. Something inside her was heating up. She loved Mitsuko and knew she wouldn't try anything with Vincenzo, but still. Goodness, seeing her and him in the same bed. And for Mezzanotte to be so friendly with her. Sylvia had yet to pet her.

"But I know," Mitsuko said, and slipped off the bed. "I know that look. Like I'd ever."

"Oh." She shrank back. She'd been holding her breath.

"Don't say sorry. Don't you dare. You're essentially married to this man. Of course you'd be jealous of another woman sleeping in his bed." She slapped where she assumed was his leg. "Good thing my type has tits."

He moaned and rolled over.

"There he is. So, Sylvia, you fell asleep in the bathtub again. Congrats."

"You say that like it's a natural occurrence."

"It is when you drink five or so glasses of vodka and I have to drive you and all of our friends back to their respective homes."

"So you drove us home?"

"I did." She got up and freshened up in the bathroom. "You and Vincenzo gave us a wonderful performance that would've made God blush. Do you remember?"

"Not at all."

"Is that Mitsuko?" Vincenzo asked groggily. "God, my head."

"And then, right before I was about to depart to my abode, I decided it was much too dangerous for I, a petite *'little thing'*, to be out on the streets alone, so I slept here for the night."

"Why is she talking so loudly?" Vincenzo asked. His eyes had yet to open.

"She's talking normally, sweetheart, but I understand. Do you want anything to eat?"

"I don't know." His body relaxed back into the blankets, and he snored once before his eyes went as wide as Mezzanotte's. "Wait, *what?*"

Mitsuko came out running her wet hands through her hair as a makeshift brush. "Morning. Again."

He cursed and covered his chest like an embarrassed lady. "Why're *you* here?"

"Should I repeat myself? Look, I'm going to make some breakfast. When you two come back to life, meet me downstairs."

Once she left, Vincenzo covered his face. "How embarrassing."

"She said she spent the night. It's alright. You know these…circumstances don't faze her as much as they faze most girls."

"But it fazes *me*. I'm still nervous about you seeing me in my…" He looked underneath the blankets. "*Undergarments*," he whispered.

She laughed and kissed him good morning.

——✧——

Mitsuko helped *Nonna* make porridge, bacon, eggs, and toast for breakfast. They talked mostly in English, but Mitsuko was polite enough not to say anything when *Nonna* muttered and sang to herself in Italian.

It surprised Sylvia how skilled Mitsuko was at making a confident meal, but then she felt bad. She was a strong girl who could not only reject the joys of alcohol but also mother her friends when they needed it. Of course she could make a beautiful breakfast when they were staving off their hangovers.

Vincenzo, having no business in the kitchen, started a fire in the lounge while Sylvia made herself a cup of tea and sat close to that fire, feet tucked underneath her. The drink helped clear her head. She now remembered Vincenzo singing, and her playing her piano. Had Dominic also been there? She couldn't remember if she'd apologized to him for making him feel so uncomfortable. She hoped she had.

The lounge telephone rang, and even though she was the closest one to it, she didn't answer. Since living with Vincenzo, she kept away from the phone. She had nightmares about picking up to Vincenzo's father or scary gangsters demanding something from her. She gladly let Vincenzo answer.

"DiFiore residence, Mr. DiFiore speaking. Yes, this is he." He twirled the wire with his free hand. "Uh, yes. She's right here," he said, and handed the receiver to Sylvia.

"Who is it?" she asked.

"Laurence."

She took the phone hesitantly. Laurence never called unless it was urgent. He kept his questions to himself until they reconvened at the Black Kitten. Had she forgotten her schedule? No, Mitsuko would've reminded her.

She dropped her voice. "Hello?"

"Sylvia!" he almost shouted. "God, I thought I was talking to Vincenzo's father. I almost, almost...It doesn't matter. Sylvia, sweetheart, I think I'm fucked."

At hearing the swear, Vincenzo turned to make sure their conversation was friendly. Then he kept tending to the fire, guessing the call wasn't meant for him.

Sylvia cupped the receiver close to her ear. "Talk to me."

"Alright, first: Do you remember anything about what I did last night?"

"Sorry, I can't remember most of what *I* did last night."

"Well, I do, and I, well..." He settled into the bed or couch he was sitting on. "You will not speak of this to Vincenzo or Mitsuko or anyone else so long as you live, do you swear?"

"I swear. For real this time."

"Okay," he said. "Um, okay. I...I think I kissed Dominic last night. I remember going up to him and talking a lot with him, and then after, I...I kissed him."

"That's great," she said.

"*Great*? No, it's *awful*! Bad! Not a great thing at all!" He lowered his voice. "He's a *gangster*, Sylvia. He lives off of dirty money. He's in those shootouts that nearly cost him his life. It's not safe."

"That may be true, but do you like him?"

"You keep going on about 'liking' someone. How can I? It's not as safe as the songs make it out to be. We come from two different worlds, worlds that will never be compatible."

"But are *you two* compatible?"

He groaned. "Is this confession now? Should I come out of the pews and confess that I may like him, that I may want to get to know more about him and am thus tormented by him and his coyness about opening up to us? He's not there, is he?"

"He is not."

"Oh, thank god."

"Mitsuko is, though. She's making breakfast. She allegedly slept over."

"Oh."

"Would you like to come over as well?"

"What? God, no. At least, not right now. My emotions are out of control, and I'm still recovering from last night. Sylvia, do you think I should talk to him, or should I act like I don't remember what happened?"

"I think you'll do right by at least talking to him. Was he friendly when you two last spoke?"

"...Yes," he said. "Very."

"Then you should try. You'll do a better job at opening him up than any of us can."

"Okay. Vincenzo mentioned a Christmas party during one of his final songs. I might be keen on coming over then, if it's still on, and if, uh, Dominic is coming. Not that I wouldn't come if he isn't coming."

"I'm not sure. I'd have to ask."

"Don't do it now. Another time. Tell Mitsuko and the other one that I said hello."

"He has a name."

"And we will do right by not speaking about them any more than we should. I'll see you at the Black Kitten tonight, won't I?"

"If I can fight off this sickness."

"Drink tea and eat small meals." He cleared his throat. "Can I...Do you have his number? I know he lives close by. I feel like calling him would be better than talking to him face to face. If he hangs up on me, I'll know that what happened between us was a one-time thing and end things there."

"Of course, dear," she said, and relayed his telephone number to him with Vincenzo's help.

"Thank you again," he said, "for listening to me ramble."

"It's not ramble, it's love. You're falling in love."

"Oh, don't say that! Spare me, please. Can you imagine me, bringing him to dinner to meet my family, going out to the theater, together..." He trailed off. "Uh, anyway."

"Good luck, Laurence," she said.

"I'll need it," he said, and hung up.

"What was that about?"

Sylvia started and turned to see Mitsuko hovering over her shoulder. "Nothing."

She didn't budge. "He's doing it, isn't he? The reckless man."

"I'm sure I don't know what you mean."

"I'm sure you don't, because you were asleep in a booth when it was all going down."

"What was going down?" Vincenzo asked.

"Hush," Mitsuko said. "Girls are talking."

"Do you approve?" Sylvia asked her.

"I approve of neither of you falling for men."

"So you prefer us falling for women?"

"Of cour—"

"Okay," Vincenzo said, throwing a log into the fire. "*Nonna* might not know English, but I don't want this type of conversation permeating through her understanding."

"What?" *Nonna* asked.

"Nothing, *Nonna*," he said.

"I gave him his number," Sylvia told Mitsuko. "I hope that was alright."

"Wonderful. Maybe they'll be on speaking terms before the Christmas party."

"You're having a Christmas party?" Vincenzo asked. "When? I can order extra drinks to the Kitten."

"That'd be fruitless, being that the party's happening here."

"What?"

"Last night. *'My grandmother makes the best cod'* or something along those lines. You invited all of us over, and I'm keeping you to that promise. I love Christmas."

Vincenzo plopped beside Sylvia. "Another gap in memories, huh?"

"Yes. Pick a weekday, preferably. And we need to get presents. What shall we get Dominic and Laurence? A box of chocolates?"

"Engagement rings?" Vincenzo asked, smirking.

"Don't tease them, they're in delicate parts of their lives," Sylvia said. "Can you picture them sending us rings and flowers and silly gifts like that?"

"They're not silly." Vincenzo placed his hands on his lower back and stretched. "Let's plan for the thirteenth of December. It's in-between two business trips I have and it's not too far away from Christmas Eve."

"I'm fine with that," Mitsuko said. "Laurence's parents are coming down next week, and Lord knows I'm not speaking to my parents on a holiday they don't believe in."

"Now I can finally start decorating this place. I've been putting it off because of work. Sylvia, is that alright with you?"

"It is," she lied, because as they were making these holiday plans, Vincenzo had gained this jovial smile to him. He looked around the room, biting his lower lip, his migraine washing away at the thought of decorating for Christmas.

"We have everything upstairs in the attic. We need to buy a tree. It's a bit too chilly to put up the outside decorations. Maybe we'll wait until this afternoon. Mitsuko, would you like to help?"

"Alas, putting up tacky Christmas ornaments in thirty-degree weather is not how I want to spend my day off." She looked to Sylvia. "Do you—"

"Then Sylvia can help with the interior decorating," Vincenzo said. "You and *Nonna* can collaborate. I'm sure she'll let you take over some of the artistic design. *Nonna*."

She peeked around the corner.

"Do you want to get the Christmas tree this week?"

"Oh, yes, yes!" she said. *"I can't wait!"*

Sylvia...understood it. Why people loved this holiday, why they decorated their lives for the changing of the year. She supposed they liked sitting at a table with their family and talking about how many presents they'd buy for each other with all the money they'd saved up for the special day. That's what she thought, anyway.

She wondered if she'd had any Christmases like that. The earliest one she recalled, her father had been yelling so loudly at Clara, the police had been called. The next year, he'd passed away, and that seasonal sadness had stayed with her for every Christmas since.

Mitsuko said her farewells after eating two men's worth of breakfasts and stealing a pastry for the road. She crept carefully to her car like someone was watching her—there was, it was Sylvia. She kept looking down the street and sped off like someone might've been chasing her.

With the idea of Christmas now in the air, Vincenzo had switched moods. He went on ecstatically about how he'd arranged the Christmas ornaments. He re-dressed in a light grey sweater, pilly and striped and nowhere near his normal black attire. He was even smiling, and he hadn't drunk a drop of   alcohol.

From the attic, he handed Sylvia small boxes that rapidly became larger and heavier ones filled with holiday trinkets. Half of the attic consisted of holiday-themed boxes, with reindeer for the front lawn and Christmas lights for the outer deck and railings. He promised he'd set those up, as it was too cold for her to leave the house.

Some of *Nonna's* ornaments she liked, though many of them she didn't get. The fake presents wrapped underneath the Christmas tree for "festive flare," the glass Santa Claus dolls set on the staircase. She must've had a hundred of them dressed in jolly, pointed hats. Weren't they tripping hazards?

Sylvia went along decorating the house as best she could. She knew what everything was and where everything went—as per *Nonna's* guidelines—but her smile was gone. The spirit radiating between these two family members, she couldn't replicate it if she tried. And she *did* try. For him. She'd never seen him so happy and she didn't want to be the one to put a damper on the mood like always.

After trying to make a centerpiece work on the kitchen table and failing, she retired upstairs. She kept her steps light and didn't creak any floorboards. She simply disappeared and nestled into bed.

She clenched her teeth to keep from crying. Why was she like this? One night of fun and she was back to her old self, dragging those she loved into the misery she couldn't keep away. It shouldn't have mattered if she hated Christmas, she should've felt happy for Vincenzo and this holiday that meant so much to him. All she was doing was making things about herself.

The door creaked open. Sylvia, mouth covered by her pillow, looked up.

Mezzanotte stared up at her with those wide, golden eyes, ears up in case she needed to run. She must've wanted Sylvia gone so she could enjoy her afternoon nap alone.

Sylvia pouted and gave the cat her back. This was her bed, too. They needed to learn how to share.

Mezzanotte jumped onto the bed and pawed her side. Sylvia went to shoo her away when a warmth touched her heart.

The little kitten crawled on top of her and made cautious bread on her hip. Then she yawned and lay out across Sylvia's chest.

Sylvia cried at the cat's acceptance for three straight minutes before the two of them drifted off into a needed nap.

Chapter 20: Fifth Avenue

Picking out a Christmas tree from their local fire station was almost as perfect as he'd imagined. There was snow on the ground, but it wasn't snowing, so driving wasn't death-defying. And the tree itself, freshly cut from the Adirondacks with a striking scent that sent him to his very first Christmas of making cookies and ornaments with *Nonna*. And he'd only vaguely threatened the tree seller to give him a bigger discount than advertised.

It was just...*Sylvia.*

He hated how he was. Something he must've said or done had tripped her back into her darkness. He did his best to lift her spirits—he even gave her the final say on which tree they'd buy—but every attempt seemed to make her bluer. Her mid-day naps became morning, afternoon, and evening naps. She stopped eating meals and turned to nibbling throughout the day.

His mother, she had these mood swings during the holiday. Cooped up in the house, his father not coming home until the morning, she was left alone with ten-year-old Vincenzo, staring into her cold cup of tea in silence.

When he caught Sylvia doing the same thing in the lounge, he knew he had to act.

First, he played music that reminded him of Christmas. He swathed her in blankets and made her hot cocoa with more marshmallows in it than cocoa.

She turned down the music, shrugged off the blankets, and drank two sips of cocoa before placing it in the fridge.

He tried being spontaneous. When he had the music playing low, he danced in the kitchen and even shook his rear to the beat. When Sylvia entered the room, he, face flushed, took her in close and danced with her.

She gave him a confused smile, thanked him for the dance, then went about her day without mentioning it again.

After four days of silent begging, Vincenzo laid down his final card.

He ambushed her after her second bath. She'd drawn them out and made his room smell like flowers. She was in the recliner now, wearing pink slippers and a matching bathrobe. Mezzanotte was sitting with her, albeit on top of the recliner instead of in her lap. He was glad they'd gotten closer.

"I just finished in the tub," she explained.

"Hm," he hummed, and came to her.

After losing her personal bubble, she cocked her brow. "Hi?"

He smiled seductively and straddled her.

She tightened her core. "What's this?"

"Nothing." He nipped her ear.

She whimpered and tried parting her legs.

"Do you want more?" he whispered.

"Yes, please."

He'd learned from her lessons and kissed, nipped, and licked her like a hungry lover. Their groins were touching. Heat was radiating between them and their mouths. He used the most of his body to please her, though he always preferred a good handhold to this. His libido was almost dry. Hers was probably overflowing.

He pulled back and ran a hand through her hair. "Why're you so sad? What can I fix for you?"

"Oh. Nothing. I'm fine. It'll pass."

He pulled down her bathrobe and outlined her collarbone with his tongue.

She moaned. "W-what about you? You're never like this."

"I suppose at certain times of the month, I want to indulge you. And if anything's bothering you and this's the only way to get you to open up..." He bit her neck. "I suppose I don't have a choice, do I?"

She dropped her arm over her eyes. "I don't want you to be mad at me."

"Sylvia, nothing you can say will ever make me mad—"

"I hate Christmas."

He lifted his head.

"I don't have pleasant memories of it. Clara would yell at me, and my father had passed away around this time, and when I was without a home, winter was especially hard on me. It makes me sad knowing I can't be as happy as you are right now. I feel like I'm bogging down the experience for you."

Her words crushed him and the joy that'd been coursing through him all week. Many of his Christmases had their problems—fights, political disagreements. The first time he'd come home wearing boy clothes was during Christmas Eve. He'd been nearly beaten to death by his father while his mother watched and *Nonna* tried her best to make it stop.

And all this time, Sylvia had been putting on a brave face and bearing that kind of familial pain alone.

He tucked her hair behind her ear. "You don't have to decorate anymore."

"I don't mind it." She pursed her lips. "That's a lie. I *wish* I liked it, but I don't. And I know that I would've liked it if Clara hadn't ruined it."

"Shh." He pecked her lips, rocking the recliner. Mezzanotte, having enough, jumped off.

"I'm too sad a girl," she said.

"As if that would dissuade me from you, though, if you want your memories changed, I think I can help."

"It's a fantasy."

"I disagree. I hadn't thought to love anyone before you, yet here I am and I've never been happier."

Sylvia covered her mouth with the tips of her fingers. "You charm me so."

"Let's make new Christmas memories together. We'll make a holiday so grand, it'll erase all the wicked ones from memory."

"How would we go about doing that?"

"I have some ideas." He went to get up, but Sylvia grabbed his wrists and kept him on her.

"Stay here," she said, "if you want to finish what you started."

He settled back into place with a smirk. "I guess I'm not one to leave things half-finished." He kissed her again. "Disrobe, please."

——✧——

It took a few phone calls and some persuasion with Mitsuko, but Vincenzo finally found a day in which all of their friends were free, and their trip into Manhattan was set.

"Is it fun?" Sylvia asked as he drove. "This 34th Street Christmas village?"

"It is," Vincenzo said as he drove. They were all in the car, him, her, Luis, baby Sophie, and Dominic. Ana hadn't been invited and *Nonna* was having breakfast with her church friends. He was thankful Mitsuko had her own car to pick up Laurence in Harlem, otherwise his claustrophobia would've acted up.

"Oh, it is, ma'am!" Luis added. "The trees are decorated Christmas-like and everyone's selling little trinkets on the streets, and when you shop, it's phenomenal. There's so much to buy, or barter for, if you know your way around a deal."

"You have to be there to experience it," Vincenzo summarized.

"What's your favorite, sir?" Luis asked.

"I couldn't pick a favorite, but the chocolate stores are nice."

"Well, I guess I know what I'm getting you for Christmas."

"We're here to buy presents, right?" Sylvia asked.

"It's tradition. Every year, *Nonna* and I go down to Fifth Avenue and buy our Christmas presents for the year. Since my, uh, *circle* has grown this year, I thought it'd be fitting for all of us to go in together and buy our presents."

Sylvia fished out her purse and played with the beads lining the edge. "I'm not sure if I have a lot to buy fancy presents for everyone."

"Oh, don't worry about that." He reached over and pushed down her purse. "I'll give you all the spending money you need."

"Are you sure?"

"Of course. I do it with *Nonna*, though she insists I shouldn't."

"Perks of being with Vincenzo," Luis said. "I have to get Ana a new purse, and my mother needs a new perfume she likes. Maybe I'll get you an early present, my little girlie." He nuzzled Sophie. "Vincenzo, what do you really want?"

"Surprise me."

"You always say that. Sylvia?"

"Anything's fine, but please, don't buy me anything expensive. I mean it."

"I can manage that. Dominic—"

From the mirror, Vincenzo watched as Dominic made no attempt to mingle with any of them. Since taking off, he hadn't stopped staring out the window, a hand over his mouth.

"Ah," Luis said. "Well, uh, I'll surprise you, too. Get you...a new hat."

He used his own hat to cover more of his face.

Vincenzo scowled. Why had he come if he wasn't interested in hanging out with them in the first place? He'd spent days orchestrating this trip.

He kept the thought to himself. He knew this was better than him staying cooped up inside all winter. He just needed to find a way to make everyone comfortable again.

34th Street and Fifth Avenue were aglow in warm light and giant Christmas ornaments. The smell of chestnuts and pine sprinkled the air like glitter, and people were ringing bells through a cacophony of honking horns and neighing horses.

He parked close to the festivities and helped Sylvia out of the car.

"How magical," she awed, taking it in.

"Well, this *is* your new Christmas memory," he said. "It should be perfect. Now, where do you want to go first? What do you want to see?"

"I haven't a clue where to begin. Let's walk and see."

They broke into the main drag where horses were pulling carriages of sightseeing families. On the sidewalk, men in red suits sold Christmas cards for five cents a piece and small toys for fifty. Luis sprinted to the first one he saw and let Sophie pick out her favorites.

Vincenzo watched Sylvia for the same sparkle in her brown eyes. She kept her head up as she admired the luminescent light posts and the growing city before her. He couldn't wait to show her the candy stores and fashion streets, to let her pick out anything she wanted. Perhaps she'd find solace at St. Patrick's Cathedral. Maybe they'd cuddle together in a carriage ride around town. Honestly, he'd take her anywhere if she'd only ask.

"Hey!"

Mitsuko, dressed as manly as she dressed at the Kitten, and Laurence, dressed as a man yet still owning his feminine charms, called out to them across the green. They were quite a pair, coming at them with so much determination and confidence. People parted for them like they were off somewhere important.

Sylvia met them halfway. "I'm glad you made it," she said, hugging them both.

"I needed to finish Christmas shopping," Mitsuko said, and nodded to Vincenzo and his friends. Laurence waved. Luis waved back.

Dominic looked at his reflection in the storefronts.

"G-glad to see you lot out of that bar," Luis said, filling in the silence. "Now I can actually see you."

"Don't look too closely, I have a migraine from traversing down here," Mitsuko said. "Laurence was adamant on telling me where to go."

"I come down here often, so I know where to go," he said.

"You come here often?" Vincenzo asked. "For Christmas?"

"Oh, yeah. Every year. My parents actually live on 42nd Street near the library. Mitsuko had us on a path that would've led us to Grand Central."

"I was avoiding *traffic*. It's different coming from Brooklyn when you're coming down from—" She rolled her eyes with a smile and elbowed Laurence. "That aside, hello. Where are we going first?"

"Let's stop by this chocolate store," Vincenzo said, pointing at a small store between two larger ones. "I want to show it to Sylvia. They're fine with all types of people, too, so none of us need to worry."

"Then lead the way."

The store was layered in pounds and pounds of chocolate. Lining the walls, in barrels for five cents a bar. At the front counter was every assortment of chocolate and piece of candy you could ask for: Hershey, Lindt, Turkish Delight. Tootsie Rolls in logs and a pick-and-choose box where you could handpick five pieces for ten cents.

He had the best memories of this place. He'd loot as many pieces as his pockets could carry; it was the only "good reason" to wear dresses with pockets, his father had thought. He'd laughed when Vincenzo showed him how much he could leave with and patted him on the back with pride. His mother hadn't approved, but she never stopped them from stealing.

Now, he wanted to buy his friends all the chocolate in the world and then some. He asked which candies Luis favored, which flavor of chocolate Laurence liked most. With their backs turned, he scooped up five bundles of each and bought them merrily.

"What're you doing?" Laurence had asked.

"Stocking stuffers," he explained, and asked the shop owner for two of the Hershey bars Dominic was eyeing.

"I better get some, too," Mitsuko said. "You still owe me."

"I didn't peg you as someone who liked chocolate."

"I'm a human being, you oaf."

"Well, what do you want, then?"

"This." She pointed to a brand known for its spicy aftertaste. He bought three as she tore open the packaging with her teeth.

"Can I buy you anything?" he then asked Sylvia.

She looked through the counter glass, then at a single Hershey bar. "If this isn't too much."

"Not at all," he said, and bought four.

They hit up a record store next. This store was much larger and gave each of them a wider range to explore by themselves. Sylvia went off and roamed through the older records.

Mitsuko checked out the phonographs in front. Luis stayed outside to haggle for roasted chestnuts.

Dominic stayed close, but whenever he and Laurence drifted into the same aisle, Dominic decided that he needed to find a record across the store, away from the man he'd recently kissed.

Vincenzo met up with Laurence in the Louis Armstrong section. They studied the same records, reading which songs were on certain albums. When he tried pinpointing which records Laurence liked best, Laurence sighed and dropped his head. "What am I doing wrong?"

"Excuse me?"

"About *him.* I don't know how to go about talking to him anymore. I called him, and we talked for a while before I asked him about what he thought about us, and he ended the call. I wish I could comprehend him. I mean, which one does he like best? Armstrong? Hines? Ellington?"

Vincenzo examined the records before looking over and examining the man who had their back to them. He had his arms crossed, elbows tight to his person.

"I...don't know," he whispered. "He's a quiet fellow, and I hadn't known about his, uhm, wishes, so I don't know how he works internally."

"I wish I could—" Laurence squeezed the air in front of him. "*Break* him out of that damn shell he's in. He has his reasons for keeping to himself, but that's not how this works. He's a pansy, just like I am, just like Mitsuko is."

Vincenzo made sure nobody was listening to them.

"It's not right for people like us to let our flames dim in the presence of others who want to be there for them. I mean, how did you deal with it? Coming out and saying how you really felt about who you were?"

"How do you mean?"

"I mean how you're like Sylvia, and how you—"

He didn't know if he had anything more to say, but he didn't leave it to chance. Gripping his arm, Vincenzo jerked Laurence down and held him until he almost broke through his jacket into his skin.

"Ow!" he said, but then the realization that he'd said something wrong dawned over him. "Wait." He crouched down. Vincenzo was so rigid, he couldn't pull back. "Was that...Did you not...?" He looked to Sylvia a mile away at the counters. "Does she *not* know?"

When Vincenzo didn't answer, Laurence gawked at him and tried freeing his arm. "She doesn't *know*? Are you serious?"

Vincenzo couldn't take these whispers any longer and walked him out of the store. To make sure he didn't bump into Luis, he brought him all the way down the street. The contrast of the cold air from the warm heat in the stores made him shiver. He liked thinking that's what he was shivering from.

His world was shifting, turning his stomach so he'd vomit. His mind tried to divert him to different paths. *"He really meant this." "He truly meant that."* That he hadn't insinuated that the secret Vincenzo had been keeping was so easily obtainable, a man he hadn't even spoken to directly before had figured it out. Someone must've squealed. Someone was telling his friends. He'd be shunned again. Found out. Ridiculed.

He brought Laurence to the green and hid him behind a leafless tree. "How the *fuck* do you know?"

"Because I'm observant and pick up on verbal clues, but hell, Vincenzo, I didn't know it was a *secret*. You're a gangster who goes to pansy bars. How was I supposed to know you were keeping it hidden?"

"You weren't. Nobody's supposed to…" Suddenly, Dominic's actions made perfect sense to him. His world was breaking down and he had no problem watching it burn with him waiting it out in a goddamn volcano.

"Vincenzo." His voice went softer, the way that reminded him of *Nonna* when she was younger. "You should tell her. You and her are basically the same, just the reverse. She'd be the most sympathetic to how you feel."

"Because I can't, alright? Laurence, listen to me. You can't tell her the truth. She can't know because—"

"Okay."

"—I don't want her to—" He stopped.

"Okay," he repeated. "Fine. I'll take it to my grave. I think you *should* tell her, but if you're not ready, that's fine. I haven't told Mitsuko or Sylvia some of my deepest secrets, and I know some people simply can't tell other people. I'm just saying that if you're going to dedicate your life to her, it might save you some anxiety down the road if you mention it to her now. It's not like she'd think it distasteful. You might even become closer—"

"I'm not talking about this," Vincenzo said, declaring the conversation over. "If I catch wind of you talking about this with her or anyone at the Kitten—"

"Oh, don't be so dramatic. To my grave, like I said."

"I'm serious."

"As am I. Like I said, we're here for you. I'm just sorry I asked you so densely without knowing it was a secret. Seems like that's a trend in your lot." He looked down at Vincenzo's hand still on him. "Now, may I go buy Dominic his Christmas present, or do you plan on threatening me again?"

He didn't answer that last part and let him go, flexing his fingers to work the blood back into his digits.

Laurence tipped his hat, flicked his scarf, and left back to the record store. "You gangsters and your secret-keeping, my word."

Vincenzo thwacked his head against the tree. He hadn't gotten that angry in so long. How easy it was to revert back. How easy it'd been for Laurence to accept himself both inside and outside of the Kitten. Vincenzo accepted how he lived, but if anyone "caught" him or found out what he was doing, he'd not make it.

Like he'd ever tell Sylvia that truth. He'd die with his sex decaying inside of him. And *that* was a promise he'd never break.

Chapter 21: Christmas Party

She kept herself cheerful and charming leading up to Christmas. She had no clue how to uproot herself from this hole she was digging, but she'd once read that women needed to keep smiling in order to uplift their spirits.

That was days ago. Her cheeks were beginning to hurt.

She'd neglected to tell Vincenzo this, but it'd been during winter that she'd tried to end her life. She'd failed, thankfully, but ever since that night, her winters had become cursed with dread. It seemed that, to contrast her lover's happiness, this time of the year set out to bury her in sadness.

She pretended to be engaging for Vincenzo's sake. In just a few days, he and *Nonna* had repurposed their living quarters into a winter wonderland. She thought the Santa Clauses outside were enough, but the fake snow on their tree almost made her laugh. Vincenzo delicately layering each branch in flour made her wonder how this boy got into the business of breaking the law for money.

He'd also officially moved Sylvia out of her apartment. They donated the last pieces of furniture she had no more use for—her dining table, her old bed—and, after months of procrastinating, they finally brought in her grand piano. His back doors were wide enough to heave in the heavy instrument through the gardens. He decorated it with pine cones and fake ivy.

She saw that child in him all week with how he treated her and *Nonna*, with how feverishly he called their friends to set up their upcoming Christmas party. Luis and Ana would bring the pasta. Mitsuko would drive Laurence over with the desserts—Mitsuko with brownies, Laurence with a cake he'd bake—and Bobbie, who was shy to attend, would come with a sausage platter his parents often made during the holidays.

Dominic declined the invitation.

"What do you mean you're not feeling well?" Vincenzo asked over the phone. "Do you need to go to the hospital?"

"It's nothing serious, but it'd be best if I stayed home tonight. I'm sorry. Tell everyone I said Merry Christmas."

When he hung up, Vincenzo looked like he'd been slapped through the phone. Sylvia had been beside him, listening and wondering if he'd have the heart to accept.

"I don't get it," he said. "He hasn't been sick a day in his life."

"I don't believe he's sick at all," Sylvia said.

He scowled. "If he wants to ignore Laurence until they part ways, fine, but how's he to do that? They're both mutual friends of ours now. He can't escape him forever."

"You're very much in love with their love."

"I am. He deserves happiness. When we went Christmas shopping, Laurence told me that they'd spoken privately over the phone. To know he has any interest in that sort of thing is such a start for him. He's never done that before. If this is his one chance to be happy, why not take it?"

"Did it take you a while to gain the confidence to court me?"

"Their courting and ours is very different. When I made my advance, I didn't know anything about you, including your past. All I knew was that you played piano and that you were beautiful. When I found out…"

"When you found out?" she urged.

"I wanted to learn more about you," he said. "I felt like we'd work out."

"So do you think they'll work out?"

"For our sake, I hope so. I don't think I can stand the rest of our lives stuck in-between two men too prideful to admit they like each other."

"Well, whatever they choose, I hope it feels safe," Sylvia said, and covered her wrists with her sleeves.

——◇——

"Merry Christmas!"

Luis, arms open, embraced Sylvia in a snowy hug and kissed her cheek. Then he did the same with Vincenzo and *Nonna*, squeezing them while trying not to drop any of his Christmas presents. Ana came in holding Sophie, which optioned her out for not hugging anyone. She gave them all one small nod, though.

"I can't believe you got bullied into throwing a Christmas party, sir," Luis said. "Not that you'd decline. It looks lovely, these decorations. Is anyone else here?"

"Not yet."

"Mitsuko said she'd be 'fashionably late'," Sylvia said. "I told her to be here by six. She said, 'We'll see'."

251

"Sounds like something she'd say," Luis said.

"And Dominic isn't coming," Vincenzo said. "He said he's sick."

"What?" Luis looked across the street. Dominic's lights were off, his house blending into the black waves of Upper Bay. "Maybe I'll pop in after dinner and bring him some soup, or a kick in the rear. He should be here with us."

Outside, as if right on time, two cars pulled up into Vincenzo's driveway, and Mitsuko and Laurence left out of one car, Bobbie out the other.

"We didn't forget where you lived," Mitsuko yelled from the driveway. "We just wanted to make an entrance."

"Ha, I believe it!" Luis said. "Merry Christmas, everyone. Bring it in!"

Vincenzo helped take coats and presents as he greeted everyone in the doorway. Luis hugged, Ana nodded. Laurence was dressed as himself, wearing a green sweater and long khaki pants. Mitsuko wore a Santa Claus hat and her usual knickerbockers that sent Ana's upper lip into her nose. Bobbie was dressed in a three-piece suit that looked ironed for the occasion. Each one had a handful of presents alongside their chosen meal.

"Thanks for inviting a bunch of fairies to your Christmas party. It feels strangely ideal." Mitsuko kicked off her shoes and entered his home like she owned it. The bell on her hat jingled with each step. "Where's the tree? Do you do Christmas trees?"

"Make yourself at home," Vincenzo said sarcastically.

"Gladly." She went down one hall, then came back and went the other way. "Why do you have multiple living rooms?"

"You should be walking straight into it—"

"Oh, found it."

Laurence gave Vincenzo his jacket. "She seems acclimated."

"She thinks she lives here."

"She does the same thing at my house." He leaned into the foyer, sneaking glances up the stairwell. "Is...anyone else here?"

"This's everyone."

"Oh." He looked down at his handful of presents. One was noticeably bigger than the rest. "Okay."

As everyone followed Vincenzo inside, Sylvia asked, "Have you heard back from him?"

"God, no. He hardly looked at me when we were shopping. Why should I care, anyway? It was just a drunken mistake, don't you think? Nothing to write home about, nothing to fret over."

"I'm sorry."

"Don't be. I'm perfectly content." He dropped Dominic's present near the door. "There. Out of mind."

Nonna had taken up every inch of the kitchen to cook dinner. She made the first floor smell like a real Christmas, rich in flavors that blended with the candles lit around the house.

"Merry Christmas!" she said in English, and took everyone in her arms.

Luis dumped their gifts by the tree. "We should've bought more."

"We have plenty," Ana said.

"We bought about five per person, but we didn't know what to get, or what any of you are into." He looked down at Mitsuko's pants, then laughed at nothing. "Well, you know, do you buy boy things or girl things? There're only so many cards you can buy for someone when you don't know."

"You didn't have to buy us anything," Sylvia said.

"I just didn't want to hurt anyone's feelings, so we went for some generally neutral presents, like glassware and candles and—"

"You're ruining the surprises," Ana said, hitting his arm. She seemed in a good mood. From questioning her sex to now wanting to keep her Christmas presents a surprise, she seemed to have turned over a new leaf.

"No, by all means, ruin the surprise," Mitsuko said. "I want to know what you thought to get us. For one, I like knives and cats."

"Shoot! I knew it! Get a girl a knife and a new feline, what was I thinking."

Sylvia laughed. Vincenzo had kept his promise: This was by far the best Christmas she'd had. No yelling, no arguments. Everyone was genuinely excited to be here with their loved ones. The tree shimmered, the food smelled divine. She was almost able to let her guard down and enjoy herself without feeling like she was bringing down the party.

They had a sort of "early dinner" that consisted entirely of hors d'oeuvres: crackers with melted cheese, cooked broccoli, tiny plates of cookies dipped in cream. They kept coming, and Sylvia wondered how *Nonna* did it all. She didn't look tired, though it was past her usual bedtime.

Everyone split into two groups to continue talking. Sylvia stayed in the kitchen with Mitsuko, *Nonna*, and Ana and her child. Vincenzo relocated to the lounge with Luis, Laurence, and Bobbie. They lit cigarettes over wine, drowning the house in smoke, and spoke about the news while *Nonna* and Ana caught up with gossip.

The way they knew how much cheese and spice to add to everything made Sylvia envious. Her parents had prohibited her from cooking by herself and, when she was homeless, she couldn't afford to buy anything like spices or fancy vegetables when buying a roll of bread would suffice. All she knew was how to mix drinks.

She hovered over a large pot of pasta, watching the bubbles pop.

"I made this," Ana explained. "It took about three hours to make."

"What impressive dedication. I couldn't make a dish look as wonderful as this."

"I can try, if I have that sort of time to spend on food," Mitsuko said. She was sitting rather unladylike on a kitchen stool with one leg hiked up to her chin. "I can make delicious scrambled eggs."

"Quite," Ana said. "So, do *you* know how to cook?" she asked Sylvia.

"Not well. Before I was kicked out, my mother never let me cook by myself, so I never had the chance to learn."

Ana swallowed at that. "How unfortunate. Why were you kicked out?"

"Bold," Mitsuko said.

"She's allowed to ask," Sylvia said. "My mother found out I was dressing like a girl and threw me out, so I had to make do with what I had." She smiled warmly. "This spread smells lovely. I'm surprised it only took three hours to make. If I cooked this, it would've taken me six or seven, and it wouldn't have been nearly as tasty. How did you make it?"

"Pasta alle vongole?"

"If that's what it's called. I thought it was clams and pasta."

"It...is, but in Italian." She sucked in her red lips, debating on whether or not to tell Sylvia something so obscenely mundane that Sylvia didn't care that much about it in the first place. She was only trying to be nice. "This's a family recipe, so I can't give you every step, but regular clams and pasta is easy to make." She spoke to *Nonna* in Italian, then took her place at the stove.

Her teachings were that of a strict nun's, and that was a compliment Sylvia hadn't meant to make. She didn't listen to Sylvia when she asked questions, she didn't explain herself, but she didn't hit her, so she probably thought she was doing well.

"Thank you for this," Sylvia said for the third time that lesson.

"It's fine." She scratched her ear. "If you're going to act like a woman, you should learn how to cook."

Sylvia looked into the sitting room. Vincenzo was enjoying something Luis had said. He hadn't heard.

Mitsuko dropped her leg and dug daggers into Ana's back.

"Why do you say that?" Sylvia asked.

She stirred the pasta. "Was that not right?"

"Did it sound right?"

She sighed. "Look, I don't know what's right and what's wrong to say around you people. I'm trying my best."

"Well, saying, 'You people,' sure isn't helping." Mitsuko's chair screeched out, but Sylvia held out her arm.

Ana waited for a better explanation, her arms squeezing her child.

"I'm a woman," Sylvia explained very clearly. "My mind, my spirit, my feelings, all of them are women."

"And if you don't like it," Mitsuko said, "then it doesn't matter to how you live your perfectly ordinary and dull life, *you cheeky whore.*"

"Mitsuko." She hoped Ana didn't know Japanese to translate that last part. She and Mitsuko had traded Japanese insults for Spanish ones. "Ana, I'm happy you're trying to understand, but certain phrases sound very hurtful. If you have any questions about how to address us, we can teach you. But I just want to learn how to make pasta tonight. I don't want to fight."

"And if you don't want to teach her right, I can," Mitsuko said, "and that doesn't come from me being a girl, it comes from growing up in a house with three cousins, four grandparents, and two neglectful parents who never bothered to cook for us."

Ana put the pot on low. She kept clearing her throat. "Wait ten minutes and the clams should be ready."

"Thank you," Sylvia said, and took Mitsuko by the arm back to Vincenzo.

"What an asshole," Mitsuko whispered.

"At times," Sylvia replied, "though I'm glad she's trying to understand us."

"Don't bother with her. An ass doesn't stop being an ass, they just stop talking around you. Keep that in mind the next time you try to change one's mind."

The men made room for them in the lounge. Mitsuko perched on the armrest next to Laurence, and Sylvia, feeling uneasy, sat right next to Vincenzo, their thighs touching.

From whatever they'd been saying, Vincenzo was lively. He massaged her thigh in front of everyone while he talked business with Bobbie.

She bit her inner lip. She couldn't focus on the conversation. His cold fingers, squeezing her warm thigh. It took all of her willpower not to dip down and kiss him.

She pressed her head into the back of the couch. Calm down, be polite. Distract yourself.

As she contemplated playing piano for everyone, she looked up to Laurence, who was sitting closest to the Christmas tree. He had his eyes on Dominic's house. His fireplace was going.

When the conversation lulled and the men took drags from their cigarettes, Sylvia asked, "Did Dominic say why he wasn't feeling well?"

At the name drop, Laurence straightened.

"I didn't pry," Vincenzo said. "He didn't sound enthused about leaving the house."

"He hasn't been at the Kitten, either," Bobbie said, "excluding the night you all got properly smashed there."

"I wish he were here," Luis said. "I should go over and bring him some cake."

Laurence rubbed his pant legs up and down as if to restart a fire, then said, "I..." He tried again. "Let me go. Over there. I want to check up on him, make sure...None of his presents are here. I should bring those over for him, at least." He sat up as he spoke to put on his jacket and shoes. "I'll be right back," he said, and left without another word.

Sylvia gave it a heartbeat of thought before she—all of them—skirted to the window like hungry flies. Mitsuko spied on them through the Christmas tree, Bobbie pretended to watch the Moon. Luis made himself the most suspicious, launching himself over the couch to get the best view of Laurence's heroic efforts.

He was plodding through the snow to get to Dominic's door. Dominic had yet to shovel his walkway and made Laurence's journey more formidable.

"He's got some valor, hasn't he?" Luis said. "When Dom gets like this, I try to give him his space until he comes out of hiding."

"Does he do this often?" Sylvia asked. "Is this a very Dominic thing to do?"

"Not for work," Vincenzo said, "but for personal issues, he tends to be a little...reactive. He can torture information out of a man for hours and say nothing about it the next day, but if he, say, gets in a fight with his family from whom he's estranged, he tends to shut down emotionally."

"He does know he's invited, doesn't he?" she asked. "We can be his family for the holidays."

"He might not feel like he belongs," Bobbie said.

"How do you mean?"

"I just feel like that's the case," he said, and took a drag from his cigarette. "I know the feeling."

Grabbing hold of the icy railing, Laurence heaved himself up to Dominic's front door and knocked.

Twenty seconds passed. The wind howled through the fireplace and tossed Laurence's scarf.

He knocked again, said something at the door. He squinted at the window, knocked a second time with more strength.

The lights remained off.

He stepped back and waited, took another step back and waited. After waiting in the snow for thirty whole seconds, he bundled up his coat and left.

Sylvia sighed. She didn't know him that well, but she could've if he opened up. She'd almost pushed through to Ana, she couldn't have imagined what she could've had with him.

The steps must've been icier than they looked. When Laurence touched the railing, he slipped on the first step and fell in an almost comedic way, legs kicked out in front of him, mouth gasped in a surprised "O."

The door opened to Dominic in slippers and a bathrobe, his hair unstyled for the first time since Sylvia had met him. He hadn't shaved in days and had a little stubble growing around his chiseled jaw.

He helped Laurence up with both hands. He asked him questions and gestured to the new rip in his wet pants. They traded off polite back and forth almost like strangers, laughing nervously and looking away, until Dominic went for his door.

Laurence grabbed his hand and said something that made him stop.

They spoke to another, Dominic wiped his mouth, and the two went into his home, together.

"Hey!" Luis said. "What're they doing? I can't see any-thing."

"Very, very bold of him on this holy night," Mitsuko said.

Vincenzo leaned forwards, fingers pressing into his lips. He squinted as if to see through the walls.

But to all of their relief, they came back after fifteen minutes. Only Vincenzo had stayed by the window for the full time, waiting. Everyone else ate hors d'oeuvres until he announced that they were coming back.

Laurence was holding a half-dozen presents while Dominic carried the other half. Dominic had changed into semi-casual attire and had run a comb through his hair. It didn't have any product in it, though, so it still retained a somewhat youthful curl.

Everyone pretended to act as nonchalant as possible when they came in.

Everyone but Luis.

"There's my boy!" He jumped up and hugged Dominic. "Got over your cold pretty quick, yeah? What timing."

"Laurence was...very persuasive," he forced out. He looked at Vincenzo with hurt in his eyes. "I'm sorry I came late."

"I'm just glad you came. Merry Christmas."

"Merry Christmas!" Luis echoed. "Dom, you have to try Laurence's cake, and Ana's clams and pasta is perfect. She and Sylvia collaborated on it."

Dominic nodded, then looked over at Sylvia. His gaze was dubious—it wasn't as clear as happiness or anger, but it was something close to the surface. Something that needed to be said.

As everyone sat for dinner, Sylvia's chest hurt. What was wrong now? Was he still angry at her? Was this about the Fifth Avenue trip? That hadn't even been her idea.

She couldn't eat. While everything looked wonderful, her nervousness had eaten away her hope and left her with a stomach ache. When the conversation allowed it, she excused herself to the bathroom to hide. She kept the door open in case anyone else needed the space, but she needed to calm down first. He'd probably thought she had food on her dress or that she'd done her hair differently, which she had. She'd used a new shampoo.

She took a breath. If she didn't feel settled come ten tonight, she'd mention something to him. Maybe she needed to give him a sober apology or a taste of her pasta.

Someone knocked on the door frame and made her jump.

Dominic seemed just as startled. He took up the entire doorway with his hands behind his back, so she couldn't slip out without apologizing. But she didn't know how to apologize, and she didn't want to slip away. She wanted to know what was wrong.

"I..." He looked down the hall, then at the floor between them. "I didn't know if you were done in here."

"I just finished up."

"Oh." He dropped his hands. He was holding an envelope.

He rubbed down the ink bleeding through the paper, then opened his mouth and bit the corners of his lips to find his voice, but he couldn't. It was lost.

Giving up, he handed her the letter addressed to her. "If you can read this by tonight," he said, "please." And he left.

Chapter 22: Feeling Safe

Sylvia stared at Dominic's letter, waiting for his footsteps to fade into the living room, before gripping the bathroom counter behind her and panicking.

It was such a thick envelope, three or four pages, at least. He'd written a thesis for her, someone who, by her account, he still disliked very much. How much hatred must've been inked on these papers.

She peeked down the hall to make sure he'd truly left before slipping out towards the foyer. Everyone was now in the lounge and she didn't know if she'd be able to hold a conversation with such information weighing her down.

Was this a favorable letter? A hateful one? *"If you can read this by tonight."* How on Earth would she find the time to read it tonight without people seeing? And why the time limit? What would happen if she didn't read it by midnight? Would she be gunned down? Put on a list?

She found Vincenzo fussing with the garland on the front table.

"Oh, Sylvia," he said. "Can you tell me if this looks right? I can't be certain if it's centered."

"Not right now. Look." She handed him the letter. "Dominic just gave this to me. He said he wanted me to read it by tonight."

Vincenzo took the envelope like it was laced with something. "Dominic doesn't write letters."

"I know. I'm scared of what's inside."

"He's so dramatic. Do you want me to read it instead?"

"Let's read it together. He never said you couldn't read it."

"Let's hope that's the case, because I can't take him going dormant for another week," he said, and pulled out the first page.

To Sylvia—

I want to address this first and foremost: I'm not a forward man.
I've never been. I find it difficult to express myself and hate being accepted by people like you. I find that kind of endorsement unacceptable.

I don't mean to sound rude. I know we share similar paths. I just can't be caught straying off the path people expect me to take. I'm not like you or your friends. I can't be caught again.

Here's the truth:
During my final year of college, I was sent to prison for sodomy.

His name was Thomas. We met in one of my art classes. I get why you people congregate at the Black Kitten. It feels safe, and welcoming. That's what I found with him.

We had a sort of connection—we knew the other was different, as if each of us had signs pointing to our shameful hearts. Sometimes, I dreamt of marrying him, as if a world like that could ever exist. It was foolhardy that I pursued him for two years. I know that now.

One night, he climbed into my bed and held me. He was solemn—he kept apologizing for nothing. I didn't understand his sentiment. I thought he was apologizing for loving me.

Later that evening, my door was unlocked from the outside, and the two of us were arrested for sleeping together.

He testified against me. To save himself, he said I'd taken advantage of him due to me being two years his senior and that he was too afraid to leave me in fear of being expelled. He explained our nights together in detail. He exposed every secret I told him to a room of strangers. I was mortified. I felt ripped open, the feeling of hollowness remaining with me to this day. For two hours, I watched as my world disintegrated through my fingers and washed away in the coming tide.

When it was my turn to testify, I went up to the podium and wept.

He graduated from Yale with honors while I endured five years of hard labor in prison. Supposedly, his parents had found out about us and did everything they could to make sure he'd be spared the humiliation of being with me. I have not spoken to him since that trial. I don't know how much of that was true.

When I was free, my life had become irreparable. My family had disowned me and I'd been expelled from Yale.

After struggling to find work, I moved from Connecticut to New York in hopes of starting from scratch. I found that path with Campo. He expunged my past from my records and never mentioned it to anyone. He gave me a chance to restart.

Then Vincenzo brought me to the Black Kitten, and my world was shattered all over again.

This's why I can't be like you. I can't boast about my love for the same sex without feeling the shame and guilt cutting me up inside. I want to feel normal again, and that means dousing out these feelings until they're extinguished for good.

But I don't think I can hide from Laurence any longer.

I hope you can understand where I'm coming from. I apologize for stooping so low as to write to you about my feelings, and I'm sorry for everything I said to you at the Black Kitten. It was unkind and unfair. When you finish reading this, please come find me. I think I'll be too afraid to come to you.

Best regards—
Dominic Scordato

Vincenzo leaned back and sighed, "Fuck."

Tears formed in the corners of Sylvia's eyes. His story was a tale she'd heard countless times at the Black Kitten. Of betrayal, of the humiliation they shouldered being their true selves in public. She'd had many close calls with being arrested, and Laurence had been jailed once for dressing femininely. He'd served six months, though his time had been lax after he'd romanced the officer in charge of him.

"Oh, Vincenzo." She lay her head against his. "What shall we do?"

"I don't know. I never knew about this. I hadn't pinned him as..." He read over the middle of the letter. "We should, uh, support him."

"Agreed."

"Nothing but encouragement."

"And nothing out of the ordinary. We need to tell him he's loved without being forthright since he—"

The wooden floorboards creaked loudly behind them, announcing Dominic into the hall.

He bowed. "Excuse me. Luis was asking if Sylvia could play for us, on the piano."

"Oh, of course," Sylvia said, trying to relax her face. The letter was still in her hands.

He gave another bow before leaving as quietly as he came.

"I should've said something," she mumbled.

"I should've told him everything was okay."

"What do we do now?"

"What's there to say, really? 'I'm sorry for your traumatizing past that's lingering over you'?"

"'Join the club'?"

Vincenzo, fretting through nervous tics, slowed to a stop as he looked up at her.

Sylvia waited for him to speak before saying, "Oh. I meant for me."

"Oh."

"I mean..."

"No, I know. We're...alike in that way." He smoothed down his hair. "I'll get everyone drinks."

She let him go and prepared herself to face her friends, but that look he'd just given her, it was the same look Dominic had given her before giving her his letter: something more needed to be said, but he was stopping himself from saying it.

Why were these gangster boys so secretive with their feelings? She knew why, what with their work practices and all, but she was going to tear her hair out. She was a bit of an open book, occasionally a blabbermouth when she got too excited. She only hoped her friends would be able to tell her everything without silencing themselves in fear of getting hurt. She discerned it was too difficult to describe.

Like something his father had done.

Or that he liked boys as well as girls.

That's what she always thought, that his preferences swayed both ways. She'd act surprised if he told her that.

She earned a hoot from Luis when she entered the room. He'd been the first one to pop open Vincenzo's liquor stash and had a half-finished bottle at his feet.

She took her seat at her piano. After a sip from Vincenzo's offered glass, she relaxed enough to make up delightful melodies. Soon, it began to snow, and up against the window with their bellies full of Christmas dinner, tree twinkling like the night sky, it made her soft. The ups and downs she'd been through this month leveled out into a peaceful flat she could rest on for a minute.

She wished people like her didn't have to extinguish their lights in order to live like everyone else. She wished she could've told Dominic that, but she now knew he didn't take well to confrontation. He was a reserved man for personal reasons, so she'd have to find new ways to show him how much she loved him.

Maybe she'd bake him cookies. She'd have to ask *Nonna* for a recipe.

Upon reaching the end of one song, she arched her stiff back and took a sip from her tequila cocktail. Vincenzo was talking with *Nonna*, who looked asleep on her rocking chair, and Luis was cuddling his wife and child while Bobbie was getting up for more dessert.

When Sylvia started a new piece from scratch, Dominic got up, walked around Laurence's couch, and let his fingers trail over his shoulder.

Only Sylvia saw it, and Vincenzo. They were keeping an eye on him in case he ran.

Laurence, unreactive, took a sip from his coffee mug, patted his lips with his napkin, then casually got up and followed Dominic into the kitchen.

Both Sylvia and Vincenzo looked at one another, wondering and waiting for if and when. None of it might've been their business, but that didn't stop them from being ever so curious about their friends becoming more than friends.

Sylvia slowed down her song, Vincenzo promised to get *Nonna's* some cookies, and, like Laurence tethered to Dominic, the two of them snuck down the hall after them.

They were down the hall in a niche that held a small table and a cross mounted to the wall. Dominic was sitting at the table while Laurence played with his hair.

"So, you told her?" Laurence asked.

"With the letter, yes." He took his hands. "I ran from them. I should've explained myself."

"No, you *told* them, that's all the matters. What you dealt with in your past was traumatizing and no human being should've gone through what you did. Having the strength to

tell others who'll understand will make you feel less alone."
He placed his lips against his head. "I'm proud of you."

Dominic turned his head but didn't make an effort to push
him back.

"Was that too much?" he then asked. "Nobody's here."

Sylvia took cover around the corner just before Laurence
noticed her. Vincenzo pressed his lips together, silent.

"Look. You're safe. And it's not like anyone here will perse-
cute you."

"That's what you think."

"Don't worry about that woman in there. She—"

"It's not just Ana. I have this paranoia that people are
always watching me, waiting for me to slip up. It's why I have
so many curtains and locks. It's why I don't speak up."

"Well, I better have the keys to some of those locks now."

A pause. Someone touched another's shirt, running their
hand down their back.

"Shouldn't I?" he asked.

"I'm not sure yet. Nobody's had my keys since college."

"I'll be different, you know that."

"I know. I'll...I'll think about it. Is that okay?"

"Take your time, baby. There's no rush."

Dominic snorted, and then, after the shuffling of feet,
Sylvia heard two pairs of lips smacking together, quietly, in
fear of someone listening.

Her heartbeat skipped. She should've left them be, but
hearing them from the shadows stirred something strange
inside of her.

Vincenzo had had enough, though. Getting up, he lifted her
up and stepped away. He went further down the hallway so

they were far enough away. Then, cupping his hand around his mouth, he called out, "Dominic, where'd you go?"

In seconds, both men came out of the kitchen, folding down their dress shirts with new flushes on their faces.

"Oh, there you two are. Did you want to open presents now?"

"Uh, sure," Laurence said, and Dominic nodded along with him.

Vincenzo, too ready to run away, got to the Christmas tree first and organized the presents, leaving Sylvia alone with Laurence and Dominic in the hall.

She folded the letter in her sweaty hand. She had to do it now. She needed to be there for him. She...

Stepping in front of him, Sylvia took Dominic into her arms and hugged him.

He tensed up for the briefest of moments before taking her back in his arms.

"I'm so sorry," she whispered.

"It's not your fault. I simply hope you can understand where I'm coming from."

"Oh, I do, I do. I'll be here for you, in whatever way you feel safest."

"Thank you. You've always been there, I was just scared of taking the next step."

"Oh, darling." She kissed his scratchy cheek. "You shouldn't have to be this afraid. You're a beautiful, talented young man, and true friends would never hurt you for being yourself. They should only want to see you shine."

He squeezed her tighter at that, conveying what needed to say through his body. "Thank you."

"Alright, alright." Laurence jokingly placed his hand between them. "Mitts off."

"Oh, are you already claiming him?" Sylvia teased.

He gasped and gently hit her. "Stop that! That doesn't leave this house, do you hear me?"

"So it's true? When did this develop?"

"It...still is, technically. It's a long story, Sylvia. Leave us be to sort it out. Quietly, I might add. No blabbing about it to the press."

"Of course, dear, but might we cut your cake to celebrate this coupling?"

"Spare me, please," Dominic said, and finally smiled.

They all migrated closer to the Christmas tree with their bowls of ice cream and brownie mixes. *Nonna* turned on the phonograph and played a lovely classical piece by her rocking chair. Sylvia tapped her heels to the song, her mood now lighter and happier than ever, now that all of her bridges had been rebuilt. Dominic and Laurence were now sitting side by side, fingers almost touching. She pictured flowers and ribbons on that bridge.

Vincenzo became their Santa while Dominic and Luis acted as his elves. They helped pass out presents and stockings full of candy and jewelry. They slowly discovered Mezzanotte hiding underneath the tinseled tree. She darted upstairs when she'd been discovered.

Crisp foil mountained around them. Boxes built up at the fireplace for Dominic to shovel into the fire. *Nonna*, who had no interest in her presents, rocked in her chair until she dozed off.

Luis and Laurence were the most expressive with what they received. Luis, ecstatic at his new watches, shoes, and books. Laurence, taken aback and almost insulted that he was given a fur jacket, beautiful golden jewelry, and a record with someone's signature on it.

"I-I didn't know if you liked him," Dominic sputtered. "I've had this one in my collection for a while, and I know you like singing his songs at the Kitten."

"I *like* him?" Laurence asked. "*Like* him? Are you—This's Earl Hines' signature! Is this real? Are you playing me?"

When he shook his head that no, it was real, Laurence squeaked and gave him a hug. "You're incredible! Earl Hines, really? Now my presents are mere pennies compared to yours."

"I wouldn't, uhm..." He couldn't form another cohesive word until Laurence let go, which took two more present openings and a sip of champagne.

"Look at that, you tongue-tied him," Mitsuko teased, and ripped open a box from Vincenzo. "What is this now? Some record signed by my favorite artist? I doubt you got Leyendecker's autograph."

"I think you'll like it," was all he said.

"Oh, will I now?" Taking out one of her blades, she tore open her gift and slid out the box.

It was a fancy box with swirly patterns around the edges and calligraphy describing a type of knife inside. The blade itself was bigger than her usual one, but the metal was wavy, the handle, a mix of wood and gold.

"It's an Italian brand I found in Manhattan," Vincenzo explained. "I thought you'd like it."

She tested the opening and closing mechanism of the blade, twirling it around her thumb like a professional. "Feels nice. Thanks."

"And you like that?" Ana asked, then added, "Not that I'm judging."

"Clearly," Mitsuko said. "What you find in cooking and Sylvia finds in playing piano, I find with knives. They feel safe."

"And that's fine by us," Luis said, and gifted Bobbie a bottle of alcohol from the 1840s. He marvelled at the date and kept spinning the bottle to read its ingredients.

Sylvia tried pacing herself with her presents. She knew she clearly had the most amongst the family. While Ana received baby clothes and Dominic received cash and suspenders, Sylvia found a necklace made of real Japanese pearls, three new dresses, a new fan, a set of heels, a journal, fountain pens...

She hid the pearls before anyone noticed them. She felt the weight of each bead against her thigh.

Vincenzo frowned at her reaction. "You don't like them."

"No, I do."

"Sorry. You don't have to open any more if you don't want to." He took away one of her bigger presents.

Sylvia scratched one of her ribbons until it spiraled into a curl. She couldn't imagine not being able to show someone how much she loved them. She wrote it down, she expressed it, hugged them, kissed them. But if she couldn't do any of that, and if she had the means to buy extravagant things...

She put on the necklace. "It's beautiful. I just didn't think it'd go with my outfit."

Vincenzo's smile was shinier than all of the diamonds he received, and Sylvia couldn't help herself any longer and kissed him. If they were alone, she would've kept going until her knees hit the floor.

"I'm glad I came," Dominic said. He was surrounded with records and suits and expensive shoes, and Laurence, who'd found a way to get closer to him without physically touching him. "Back at the Kitten, you know, I was worried something might've come up."

"Did something not *come up*?" Mitsuko said playfully, relaxing into her pile of boxes like a queen.

"Just with how the men came in, I mean. I don't know if they saw me. I was concerned that they might've found me out. I don't want people knowing."

"What men?" Vincenzo asked.

"The two shadow creatures," Mitsuko said. "You don't remember them?"

"Shadow..." He uncrossed his legs. His tone dropped. "What men?"

"I believe their names are Drago and Luca," Dominic said. "They're friends of your father. They were looking for you."

Sylvia remembered no such men at the Kitten, but whoever they were, they scared Vincenzo enough for him to go statue-like still.

"They tried getting at you," Mitsuko added. "They wanted to talk with you, but I shooed them away. They looked inhuman, the way they were sizing you up when you were drunk out of your mind, like dogs prowling for an easy kill. I tried telling you about them when I drove you home, but you weren't making sense. I thought you'd remember that."

"And I chased them out before they could do any harm," Bobbie said. "They were in and out like a flash. I didn't even see their car leave."

Vincenzo stared into the floor, trying to remember such an event but being unable to. Before any of them reminded him of more, he got up and started closing the blinds. A snap of his fingers and Luis and Dominic were up and tending to the doors, making sure they were locked tight.

"Vincenzo?" Sylvia asked.

"Those are the names of my father's henchmen," he said. "They do his dirty work when he doesn't want to get his hands dirty. What did they say they wanted?"

"You, I think," Mitsuko said.

Vincenzo clicked his tongue as he tested the locks on the front door. "I want all of you to stay here tonight. My father's not shitty enough to do anything dangerous this close to Christmas, but I'm not risking your lives on that gamble."

"Are you serious?" Mitsuko asked. "Is this turning into a sleepover at Vincenzo's house? Again?"

"That's right." Killing off the joyous mood, he ordered Dominic and Luis to shut the rest of the blinds and to make sure all the windows were locked upstairs.

"Where're we all to sleep?" Bobbie asked, trying to clean up the living room before *Nonna* did.

"Upstairs. I have four extra bedrooms you can use. Sylvia will stay with me, *Nonna* will stay in her room. Luis, you and Ana will stay together with Sophie. Mitsuko and…" He blinked once, processing. "Mitsuko and *Bobbie* can stay in one bedroom together, while Laurence and Dominic, if you don't mind sharing a bed, you can have a room to yourself. That, or one of you can take a couch."

"Thank you," Laurence said for both of them.

After that, barely anyone had enthusiasm to open the rest of their presents. Vincenzo left to make a phone call. Sylvia thanked Dominic for the perfume he'd bought her. Bobbie tried out his new cigars. When they all reached Sylvia's letters—many of them had saved them for last—they read through her love quickly and thanked her.

They each said goodnight and left for their separate rooms. Vincenzo put *Nonna* to bed before taking a head count of each of his friends. He kept staring down the stairs to the front windows, almost expecting someone to arrive late to the party.

Sensing someone was watching him, he turned and got snagged on Sylvia's eyes.

"You okay?" she asked.

"Do you remember the men who came to the Kitten?"

"I do not."

"I don't, either. I was so drunk, I don't remember almost..." He sighed. "I'm tired."

"Let's head off to bed. You've been working hard, planning all of this."

"I don't think I'll be getting any sleep tonight," he fore-warned.

Once they were locked in their room, Vincenzo pushed on his face and groaned in annoyance. "This's *aggravating*. My father, sending his lackeys to monitor me like I'm a child? I have to go to Campo about this. I can't keep putting it off. This week, without a doubt. He can't keep subtly threatening me like this."

"I'm sorry," Sylvia said on instinct.

Vincenzo held her cheeks. "It's not your fault. It's the reason why I'm not seeing them this Christmas. My father is so...*controlling* and *hates* everything I do. I can't stand knowing he's now trying to spy on me, like..." His touch fell. "You know, knowing the type of man he is, it'd be foolish to think he wasn't the man attacking our homes."

"You think he's the one who attacked me in my apartment?"

"And the one who tried breaking in here a few months ago." He dropped his forehead onto hers. "Dominic was right. It's like everyone's watching and waiting for us to slip up."

"I understand, but like Laurence said, we're alone now. Just the two of us." She traced up his arms. "We're okay."

The kiss he gave her sent her back into bed. Different from his shyer kisses, he kissed her like he'd never see her again. She hoped that wasn't the case, though it was nice to be kissed like you'd be missed.

Mezzanotte meowed at them, trying to secure her spot at the end of the bed. Vincenzo shooed her away.

Sylvia fell on her back, mind racing about what he wanted to do with her. Titillated, she gave up her vulnerability and let her arms go slack around her head.

His breathing tickled her lips. "I need to...relax. For two minutes. No more drama. No more prep or sudden circumstances. I just want to *be*."

Sylvia tapped her heels together, then kicked off her shoes and hoped this daft man would take a hint and tear off the rest of her clothes.

He didn't. "And now I'm in no mood to do anything. I'm too mad to play, too nervous to relax. I'm built up. I want to release."

Sylvia gulped.

"And," he said, "I think I can only do that with you."

She sighed into a heated moan, twisted her fingers deep into his thick hair, and yanked him down to claim his lips.

He braced atop her with both hands, keeping himself from falling on her. He smelled of sugar cookies and cologne and all she wanted to do was devour him and every bad feeling he was feeling. She had no memories of these men trying to capture him, but she saw how upset it was making him. If only she could use her talents to get his mind off of things for twenty minutes. If he'd only let her.

Vincenzo licked her upper lip to end the kiss. "Can you...go into my bathroom and wash up?"

She rubbed her thighs together. Did she have enough time to *fully* wash up? Wouldn't it have been obvious to the whole house if she took a bath before bed? Did he have any prophylactics, lube?

He seemed to catch himself and faltered. "I mean, your face, and your makeup."

"Oh. Yes." She walked a little awkwardly into his bathroom and almost shut the door on Mezzanotte's tail, who insisted on following her now that she liked her.

What was he planning to do? More than oral? With her? Would he really do that so close to Christmas? With the option so plainly presented to her, she didn't know what to do next.

She sat on the toilet seat, thinking it over. She did *want* to have sex with him. She'd wanted to ever since their first date, when he'd asked so many questions about *her*, none of which pertained to who she was before finding the Kitten. He'd simply wanted to know about her favorite flowers, her favorite jewels, favorite music, favorite drinks. She hadn't met a man like that before, someone so engrossed with pleasing her.

Mezzanotte sprang into her lap for pets. Why was she so nervous all of a sudden? He'd tasted her so many times already, surely *this* wouldn't be anything different. But maybe he didn't want to have sex with her. Maybe this was all a miscommunication. He was different, after all. He might never enjoy it as much as she did.

Turning on the sink, she peeled off her eyelashes, rinsed her face, and wiped down her heavy eyelids without reddening her skin. Not only was it too romantic, it felt too impossible. She thought what she had with him was enough. This felt like too much of a step forwards.

She pulled up. Some of the makeup was still underneath her eyes and in her brows, but she'd basically gone back to her base self. She debated whether or not to take off her necklace. She didn't want to insult him, and she couldn't deny its beauty.

Tugging on them, she stepped back, gave herself a twirl, and left.

Vincenzo's nose was pressed against the door. He took her hand before she dropped it from the golden handle.

"Hi," she said. "Eager, aren't we?"

"I'm not sure yet. Is it odd to be excited about it, even though I don't...actively search for it?"

"It depends on what you're talking about."

He licked his lips and gently pushed her down into bed.

He got to work with her, like always, quickly. Disrobing her, making her feel warm and melty with only his hands and mouth. He'd gotten better at it; he used less teeth when pleasing her, and he used his tongue more effectively around her sensitive areas. It almost negated his inability to look her in the eye whenever he sucked her off.

She was naked save for her black garter belt. Thank God she wore the pair without many runs or tears. It made her feel better about herself.

"This okay?" he asked.

"It is." She touched his shoulders. "If you're any bit nervous, I can wait."

"I don't want to wait anymore." It sounded like he was forcing the words out of his mouth, jaw clenching as he spoke. "I want to...*push* myself as far as I can go with you. I don't want to be scared any longer."

"You're scared?"

"I'm a gangster, Sylvia. We're all scared."

She played with his hair. "That's quite comforting to hear, actually. It almost makes us equals."

"Were we not equals before?"

She didn't want to put herself down any more than usual, so she said, "In certain cases."

"Certain cases..." He licked a line down her chest.

She covered her mouth with the back of her hand. She'd been right. He was getting better. He even flicked his tongue over her breast, latching onto it and melting her willpower into a puddle.

"Did Laurence tell you about me?"

She opened her eyes. "Huh?"

"Just tell me if he told you or not."

"Told me what?"

He looked up past his bangs, finally meeting her eyes.

She covered her crotch. Those dark eyes would make her do anything. "Laurence hasn't told me anything."

"We're equals now," he reminded her. "We don't keep secrets."

She wasn't familiar with this kind of ill-defined flirting, but he hadn't pulled away. He was waiting for an answer on information she didn't have.

She lifted herself up on her elbows. "I have no information on anything Laurence has told me about you. If I did, I'd tell you. But Vincenzo." She held him. "I'll support anything you do. I know your work profession and still love you. You might be upset and I'll love you, you might be happy and I'll love you. Whatever you want to tell me and whenever you want to do it, I'll be here to listen and I'll *still* love you all the same, because you love me and treat me well. That's all I can ask for from you."

He took her in sentence by sentence, mouth agape and chin tickling the hairs leading up to her belly button.

Sylvia stilled her breath. There was a conversation he was keeping from her, this secret he thought Laurence knew but she didn't. She wanted to know, of course, but she didn't believe that they weren't allowed to keep secrets. Just like with Dominic, she needed to show her comradery with his anxieties.

Vincenzo lifted himself up and touched her face, her lips. His thumb pressed into her mouth until he opened it for his liking. "I'm not going to undress for you tonight."

"Oh."

"But I am going to fuck you." He kissed her hard. "So get on your knees."

The raw bluntness of his words froze her. She knew he swore. She hadn't expected him to say *that* to her.

Fighting through whatever he was feeling, he took off his jacket and tie and rolled up his sleeves to his elbows.

Even knowing what she was about to get, Sylvia honed in on his arms above all else. She'd never seen them bare like this. He slept in long sleeves and only wore sweaters or coats. Seeing the dark hairs over his tan skin set off her primal instincts. Suddenly, tasting his fingers and wrists were more salacious than tasting his cock.

Doing as told, Sylvia got on her hands and knees and spread them out to give him the best view. She felt her stockings stretch over her ass and hoped it was everything he wanted.

"Wow." His hand rounded her bottom, ring finger tickling her inner thigh.

"Here." Hooking a blind finger around her stockings, she unhooked the garter belt and let her lower half hang free.

"Looks...different," he scrounged up, "from the rear."

"But good?" she asked. "Is it good?"

"Wonderfully so," he said, and his tongue lapped her up in a way she hadn't experienced before.

She moaned and dropped her head into the pillows. She heard him breathing and moaning wetly into her. She was tempted to push into him, to touch herself as he worked, but all she managed to do was keep conscious and savor in the feelings he was creating inside of her.

He pulled back and swallowed, then pushed his front against her.

Her eyes snapped open. What she felt and how warm his crotch was, it came and went but lasted lifetimes for her.

Three adventurous fingers pushed into her mouth, and a surprise moan escaped her throat.

"Shh," he purred, slicking his fingers with her tongue. "Someone's gonna hear you."

Her eyes rolled back as she tried keeping quiet. Scooping up her spit, he took away his fingers and pushed them deep inside a new hole.

Mezzanotte hopped into the bed to watch more closely. Sylvia didn't care. The room disappeared and was replaced with only him. His fingers burrowing inside. His lips kissing her upper back and neck. She rolled over for easier access. With a free hand, he played with her front while keeping his lips on her tender skin.

"*Fuck*," she moaned. "Oh, fuck me."

"You want more?" he asked. "I'm already trying so hard, and you want *more*?"

Her answer got eaten up by a kiss. If she revealed how much she wanted to destroy him, he wouldn't see her as such a good girl anymore.

The pit in-between her legs grew into a fever she could no longer ride out. She'd been teased for too long. Her back arched up without knowing, she pushed into Vincenzo's hand. Her mind went blank as she came over his fingers, fast and messily yet perfect in every way.

Her eyes fluttered closed. She could've fallen asleep here, the wet, feathery feelings submerging her into a drug-fuelled stupor. If Mezzanotte hadn't bopped her face, she would've dozed off in Vincenzo's dirty hands.

He rolled her sluggish body onto her back and kissed her. "How wonderful," he said. "That really calmed me down."

"Did it? If you want, we can do that every time you're stressed. Every day, preferably, or hour."

"Don't tempt me." He tugged his dress pants away from his crotch. "I'm gonna...I need to take care of this."

"Want me to do it?"

He stopped to think, then left for the bathroom. "Perhaps another time."

"That secret's under lock and key, isn't it?"

He turned to her with a warm smile, eyes half open. "Ten minutes. Be right back."

When the door locked, Sylvia sat up like she had two dumb-bells on her shoulders. She cleaned off her sticky thighs with the napkins Vincenzo kept by his bed.

She took in the stillness of his room, the night bugs singing, the world and their situation coming back to her.

She fell back and kicked her legs in the air, silently squealing her happiness into her hands.

Chapter 23: A Change of Scenery

Sometimes, because of himself, Vincenzo didn't go to church. He either had work to do or couldn't take two hours out of his day to sit in the silence that church evoked. The feeling of being trapped in such a crowded building didn't help, either. His nerves often led him out with a cigarette and the hum of the organ on his lips. *Nonna* never expressed her disappointment aloud, but he always saw it on her face when he declined to go.

That morning, he dressed up in his best suit and tie and drove *Nonna* to their church. *Nonna* had thought he was merely dropping her off, but when he didn't leave after helping her up the steps, she smiled and snuggled into his offered arm. *"Thank goodness,"* she said under her breath.

After church, he quickly drove her home and headed down Brooklyn's snowy coastline. He had to bring up these confrontations with Campo, there was no more time to dally. With his power, he could possibly stomp out this annoyance by himself, but he knew Campo could dismember and eviscerate every disgusting man involved with defacing his love life.

He just wished he could do that himself.

He parked close to the fountain and fixed himself up before walking down the path to Campo's front door. As he waited to be let in, he couldn't help but look up. Four stories, with balconies in every bedroom window. He dreamed of owning such a beautiful house, but he couldn't compete with what Campo had given him. After pleasuring Sylvia in a new way he thought he'd never reach, he was not only proud, he wanted a better house, more money to give her things.

So, going to his boss with his tail between his legs because he couldn't be a man, it was a bit humiliating. Sylvia had told him otherwise.

"You're a wonderful man," she'd said, *"and Campo cares for you, so you shouldn't be afraid of talking to him about this."*

It'd take some time for him to believe that.

"Vinny!"

Vincenzo turned to stone. What a hateful nickname, but what was more hateful was that voice. Growing up, he rarely heard happy children, just screaming or hateful ones. How rare to see a child so happy with being alive.

Gabriella bounded out of the house and wrapped her arms around Vincenzo's waist. He stumbled a bit. If she were any other child, or grandchild, in this case, he would've swatted them away, telling them to back off if they knew what was good for them. But little Gabriella d'Antonio, she was a special case, the pride of this house.

She beamed up at him. "Good morning, Vinny."

Not knowing how else to handle kids, he treated her as one would treat a cat and pet her head. "Good morning, *la mia stella*. Is your *nonno* home?"

She pouted against his thigh. "Are you just here to see him?"

"Is that a bad thing?"

"Yes! You never come to visit. You used to come over all the time when I was a baby. Now you don't even come to say hello. It's not fair."

"I do apologize. I don't do it on purpose."

Her pout remained. "Let me see your gun."

"I don't think so. Not again."

Campo's footman went to take his coat and hat, but he didn't need another set of hands on him. "I'll be right back, Gabriella. Go play with your cousins. I know they're here somewhere."

"They never want to play with me, Vinny, please."

He waved her off and ascended up the steps to Campo's study. Inside this house lived cousins, daughters, and grandchildren alike, dozens of bedrooms keeping his loved ones in arm's reach. Across the hall, he saw two of them running with a ribbon. They looked just like Campo.

Campo was sitting at his study's desk, organizing papers near his paperweights and lacy lamp. He had his phone in his hand and he was about to hang up when he looked up. "Oh, speak of the devil. I was just calling you."

Vincenzo withstood a kiss on each cheek. "I'm sorry for coming unannounced. I decided to go to church and didn't have the time to call ahead. Though, I suppose I came at a good time."

"Three times and I thought you might've been hurt. I was this close to calling your father again."

His mood soured. "Speaking of..."

Campo's smile faded. "What's wrong?"

He'd thought keeping Sylvia's break-in to himself was best, but now it was affecting him, his family. It'd come to the Black Kitten, his second home. Those crimes of hate weren't because of Sylvia anymore, they were intrinsically tied to each other, and he needed to put them to an end.

After explaining everything to Campo, Campo asked, "Are you positive the men were Drago and Luca?"

"I apologize, sir, I don't remember what occurred at the Kitten. Dominic told me what he saw. But the thing is, Hannigan has also cornered Sylvia and I twice when they shouldn't have known where we were. And I haven't received any information from my father about all this, so I can't imagine what they want with me, either. I hope you can see why I'm so agitated as of late."

Campo lit a cigarette. "You should've told me this sooner."

Vincenzo lowered his head. "I'm sorry, sir."

He pinched between his eyes, thinking over the situation now thrown onto his doorstep. "Look, I won't sit here and act like I know what you endure to be the way you are. Some people are appalling and unfair to those who challenge the norms that've been set in place for generations. Yet it happens every generation, and us old folk seem to be surprised when a catalyst ignites."

Vincenzo's cheeks went hot at what he assumed was a compliment. "My father never got that message."

"He didn't, no." He took out one of his fountain pens and wrote himself a note. "Is that all you have for me?"

"It is, sir."

"Okay. Vincenzo, my boy, how about you head out to the Viola Tavern for me? Some of their stock has been going missing. If you could check in on that for me. Then, after that, I need you to go down to Manhattan and talk with a man on my behalf. He has a debt he forgot was due yesterday. Here's the address."

He took the note. "Of course. I apologize for burdening you with my troubles. I hope we get this figured out soon."

He picked up his phone and dialed a number. "I'm sure we will."

—◇—

The next day, Vincenzo drove Sylvia to work and summoned up the courage to kiss her on the pavement. He would've stayed for her performance if not for Campo. He'd called him during breakfast that morning. By the sound of his tone, it didn't seem urgent, but that was Campo's charm. He could've massacred an entire family and would've been as composed as a saint in the same breath. All that he pressed was that he needed to meet with Vincenzo today when he was free.

He stayed quiet in Campo's house and tiptoed up the stairs. He saw little Gabriella sleeping in her princess room and Campo's adult children resting in the rooms across the hall. Their bedposts must've been faux gold. He'd believe nothing else.

Instead of being at his desk, Vincenzo found Campo standing by his windows, overlooking the water with his hands behind his back. Late gulls and egrets, startled by his stare, flapped their wings and began their flight to someplace new.

Campo nodded at Vincenzo. "Any new upsets with your villains?"

"Not that I'm aware of, sir, no."

"Good." He offered him a seat.

He sat. "Is everything okay?"

"Absolutely." He handed him a document. "I've been in touch with a few people in a place called the 7th arrondissement. I'm not sure how they go about naming their counties or suburbs in that part of Europe, mind you, but I know it's close to that Eiffel Tower that's in all the magazines. I've seen it once. Very wonderful."

"The Eiffel Tower?"

"Paris. France. There's a wealth of liquor and wine in Paris, you know. Their speakeasies and bars, while incomparable to what we've done—what *you've* done—are at the forefront in Europe. I've been in touch with folks who're doing real marvels there. I've been trying to get my foot into their ports for months."

"I don't follow."

Campo smirked. "I'd go myself, but I don't have the time to ship myself to Europe. Plus, I know your birthday is in January. I'd love for you to celebrate it in France."

Vincenzo forwent trying to speedread the letter and set it down. "Sir?"

"If you'd be so kind, of course. It'd be about a week's journey to and fro with a few days spent in the capital, and I'll take care of all your expenses. I have an apartment ready for you and any company you wish to bring with you as well." He winked as he said that. "I know you and Sylvia are becoming close. Are you planning on marrying her? What a turn to propose to her in Paris."

Vincenzo's head and heart twisted into a knot, the thought of marrying Sylvia almost tipping him over in his chair. "We can't. It'd be too complicated."

"Isn't every wedding? And you don't think I can pull some strings for you to tie the knot? Vincenzo, you're like my own son. Consider it taken care of. That is, unless you don't pluck up the nerve to propose to her. I'm holding my breath for that moment, Vincenzo. I mean it. I love weddings."

He wanted to stay on this topic—Would he pay for the wedding? Did he really see him as his own son?—but still, "Sir, you're sending me and her to Paris?"

"Actually, I booked an apartment, so if any of your friends from that bar wish to come, they're more than welcome to. Luis, Dominic, your grandmother. The more the merrier."

Vincenzo played with the edges of his document, making sure it was real. "I'm not sure what to say."

"Hopefully, 'Yes'. I'll need you to persuade those queer folk to let me into their excess of gold, and I think you'd do much better at it than I ever would. And with your father..."

At the mention of the man, Vincenzo asked, "What about him?"

He blinked, then smiled. "Forget it. He's been on my mind, is all. I plan to have a word with him on how he's been handling himself under my name."

"Do you mean with his men? With Drago and Luca?"

"Yes. And anyway, you've been working hard, and your birthday is in a few days. You deserve a break to *Paree*, as it were. So? Do I have your word, or do you need some time to think it over?"

"No, I mean..." His heart pushed out of his throat. "I'll do whatever you ask of me."

"Perfect!" He gathered together a heavy manila folder. "Your departure will be this Thursday at nine. I have the address labeled on this document, as well as the apartment you'll be living in and who you'll be working with. Her name is Émeline. She's a niece of mine."

Vincenzo ran his hand through his hair. He didn't know if he could label France on a map, and now, through Campo's powers, he was not only free from his father's harassment, he'd be going on vacation with Sylvia and his friends, to a place most people dreamed about. "Thank you. Really, this's...I haven't even left the continent before. In my adulthood, of course."

"Yes, yes, of course. It'd be my pleasure. Now, go off, be merry. Be merrier there than you would be here."

Vincenzo pulled himself together. "Would it be possible to make a phone call here before I leave?"

"Of course." He pushed his candlestick telephone over to him.

He didn't know who to call first. Sylvia? Luis and Dominic? Would they even want to go with him? What about Ana and her child, should they be invited? *Nonna*? Laurence? Hadn't Mitsuko served in France during the War?

He called what felt the most natural.

"Hello?" Bobbie asked over the shouts from the Black Kitten.

"Hello," he said too loudly. "It's Vincenzo. Is Mitsuko available?"

"Let me find her." He set down the phone, leaving Vincenzo to twirl the cord and hoping his boss didn't mind him calling a pansy bar from his personal line.

"So," Campo asked, whispering over his shoulder, "do you have the ring yet?"

"N-no, I don't, sorry."

"Do you need help paying for it? I can get you a nice Tiffany ring. Beautiful rings, they have."

"I have the means to buy it, sir."

"So when should I mark it on my calendar?"

"I..." He hadn't a date in mind. Preferably before his death, though he couldn't imagine people like him getting married, so it hadn't been a real focal point for him. Having Sylvia around seemed like enough at first, but with Campo's blessing...

Someone picked up. "Yeah?"

His thoughts scattered. "Oh, uh, hello. I apologize for calling so out of the blue."

"Oh, God, it is you. Am I in danger of being shot at right now? Should I take cover? Hide behind the bar?"

"On the contrary. I wanted to ask how good your French was."

"Like the language? Only vulgar sayings that shouldn't be uttered outside of the bedroom. Why? Do you need help translating something?"

"How do you say, 'I just got offered a vacation to France, so start packing, and I'll be there in two hours to talk it over'?"

"What?" She sounded less enthused than he'd expected.

"My boss is sending me to France to do business with an alcohol supplier. I don't know all the details, but he said I can bring my friends along. It'd be about a week"—he checked the paper—"yes, about a week in France, in a place called the 7th arrondissement. Are you interested in coming?"

She was quiet for a long time. Campo went back to work. The songs from the Kitten beat in Vincenzo's head.

Then, in a faint voice he barely heard over the static, Mitsuko said, *"Tu me brises le coeur."*

Chapter 24: Transatlantic

"If Campo sent me on a business trip to Paris, would you like to accompany me?"

Of course, Sylvia had said yes, a simple, "Sure," to a dream that'd never come true. And such a fantasy, too. To think she'd ever leave New York.

But after she'd agreed, Vincenzo had begun taking out all of these papers and folders and explaining which port they'd leave from, how furnished their apartment would be, and what a grand time they'd have with all of their friends.

When he gave her a paper to sign, she asked, "Are you serious?"

"About the cruise liner? Yeah, apparently the captain is Italian. We shouldn't have any problems with them, though I'll get there early and have a 'one-on-one talk' with the crew."

"No, I mean about the trip."

"Oh, yes. Do you not want to go?"

After that, she reminded herself to always affirm if and when this boy was joking with her. He couldn't joke; he had a terrible poker face. So all of this, from the cruise to the apartment to France, it sounded like a dream, but no. She was going to Paris. With her loved ones.

She'd heard of this foreign land as one heard of fairy tales. Somewhere, this world existed of lovely people doing lovely things, drizzled in chocolate and roses. They ate delicacies, dressed beautifully.

And she was going to be in the center of it all in a matter of days.

"Come on, Sylvia! Hurry up!"

Sylvia struggled with her shopping bag. "One moment!"

Laurence giggled and carried on down the road. They were walking down Fifth Avenue again, now buying for themselves rather than for other people. They'd been to seven different stores and she'd only managed to buy a single blue dress for a reasonable price. Laurence had four bags' worth of new outfits and was planning on buying more.

"Oh, Laurence," she sighed. "Why must we go all out and buy new wardrobes? Aren't we content with what we have?"

"He wants to dress up for strangers in a foreign country," Mitsuko said. She'd come as the moderator for Laurence and his shopping habits. "You shouldn't get too excited for France. It was fine, I suppose, but the culture there is different than it is here. There's not a lot of people who look like me or you or even Sylvia, and the rules for pansies are..."

"They are?" Sylvia prodded.

She kicked a lump of snow into the street. "It's different. It's not as strict as it is here, and it's certainly better than places like England, but it's not Heaven. You can't prance around the streets kissing whomever you desire. You have to keep that confined to the home."

"Mitsuko, do you have any reservations about going to France because of the War?"

She looked up at the blurry, white sky and breathed out as if she were smoking. Sylvia always tried to swing conversations away from the War in front of her, but she wasn't acting like her usual self. She wanted to know what she could do to help.

"I don't know what to expect," Mitsuko said, "so I'm expecting the worst."

"You are being such a *downer*," Laurence said. "Vincenzo's given us seven whole dollars to shop for ourselves and I am not putting that to waste. We will have a grand time. There'll be no Prohibition, bars the eye can see, and that wondrous Eiffel Tower. Oh, I'm so excited to see everything. I want to get my picture taken."

"About that." Mitsuko caught up with him before they entered a clothing store. "What's this about you and Dominic?"

"Whatever could you possibly mean?"

"You can't pull the wool over my eyes, you little shrew. You've been putting your mitts on Dominic for weeks, haven't you? I saw the way you acted at the Christmas party. You're smitten."

"Me? Never."

"Stop it. You are positively glowing."

"We don't need to know," Sylvia said, pretending she herself wasn't innately curious about the affair. "It's none of our business to know."

"She's right," Laurence said. "As if I'd have the time to tell you two."

"Liar, you want to spill everything to us, you're just keeping it to yourself because of him."

"And so what if I am? Is that a crime? He said not to mention anything we do to our friends unless he approves of it and

I am planning on keeping my word. Honestly, two months ago, you hated anything to do with gangster boys, and now you want to know everything about them? Leave him be."

"Hey, I can keep secrets, unlike Sylvia."

"Hey!"

"Enough," Laurence said. "Dominic is like no man I've dated before. He's a private person, so take this as the last piece of information you will ever receive on him and me, *Mitsy*."

Mitsuko faltered on the crosswalk and bumped her shoulder against the light post.

"Are you alright?" Sylvia asked.

"Yeah." She balled up her fists at the slip up. "Just...weird to hear my name said like that."

"Do you like nicknames?"

She shook her head and walked ahead of them for the rest of the trip.

——✧——

Two days didn't feel like enough time to pack. She battled between bringing her boyish clothes and her girly ones, she needed to choose between heels in order to pack light. During the morning of departure, she preened herself in the mirror for two whole hours, fixing her face and making faces at Mitsuko to keep her smiling.

Vincenzo had left early to secure everything on the ship. In reality, he was probably arguing with the men on board to make sure that he and his friends wouldn't be harassed while on the voyage. Sylvia let him go knowing that. Besides, Luis and Ana had offered to drive her and Mitsuko to Manhattan. Dominic had stayed over Laurence's the previous night, so they'd be arriving separately. She didn't know if they'd officially moved in together like she had with Vincenzo. It felt too soon, but she respected their wishes and kept her questions to herself.

"What do you think about them?" Mitsuko asked as Sylvia got ready. While Sylvia had four bags packed for the trip, Mitsuko had a single duffel bag along with one long scarf wrapped several times around her neck. Mezzanotte slept on her lap as they waited.

"Who?" she asked. "Laurence and Dominic?"

"Yes. Don't you think it's dangerous what they're doing, or life-threatening?"

"No. How morbid."

"But it's the truth. It's different with you and Vincenzo. If someone finds out that they're together, it might cost them their life."

Sylvia set aside her blush. "It's the price we take to keep our love going."

Mitsuko tapped her foot. "So, what if they didn't take that chance? They can be pansies without being together. They can love each other without being so forwards about it."

At this, Sylvia turned her chair to face her friend. "Mitsuko."

She tensed up. "Don't look at me like that. I'm just saying that they waltzed into this relationship too hastily without thinking over the consequences."

"I don't see it that way at all."

"That's because—"

"Because what?"

Mitsuko was now sitting up, ready to fight her on this, but as soon as Sylvia raised her voice a bit, she returned to her casual self. "Sorry. I don't mean to pick a fight right before the trip. I'm just worried. I don't want to see them hurt."

"I know, dear." She got up and hugged her. "Everything will be fine. Nothing bad will happen to us."

"You can't say that. That puts too much optimism in the air. It'll poison us."

"And is that so wrong?"

"Uh, to be poisoned? Yes. Can you imagine people like us being unshackled by their fear? We'd be unstoppable."

"That's a good thing, Mitsuko."

"Bah."

"'*Bah*'? Are you a sheep now, little Mitsuko Sheep?"

She smiled, and with that sudden dip into melancholy, Sylvia was determined to keep her happy throughout the whole vacation. Going back to the country she'd watched innocent men die in must've been taking its toll on her. She'd be sure to keep the mood lighter from now on.

Someone honked outside.

Sylvia left for the hallway and peeked outside. One of Luis' cars was parked near the tree line. He was hanging out of the window, waving and wearing a red beret.

Returning his wave, Sylvia cycloned through her bedroom and picked up her last-minute things. Mitsuko helped with her makeup, stuffing it into one compartment of her suitcase, before they closed her bedroom door and headed down the stairs. Mezzanotte meowed at them for safe travels.

Vincenzo had taken his and most of Sylvia's bags to the boat ahead of schedule, so Luis heaved their remaining bags into his car. Mitsuko insisted that she carry all of her one bag. Luis didn't complain.

"Have fun," *Nonna* said before they left.

Sylvia waved at her, but this little grandmother called her over specifically. When she came, *Nonna* wrapped her skinny arms around her and hugged her as if she were her own granddaughter.

She felt *Nonna's* love when she made her food and offered to do her laundry, but that was always with Vincenzo near, and Sylvia bleakly assumed that it was only Vincenzo's presence that made *Nonna* act so friendly. Without him here and her hugging just as softly, Sylvia felt like they were finally a family, that this was real.

She hugged her back. "Goodbye, *Nonna*. I'll miss you."

"Have fun, my little angel," she said. "Enjoy. Be safe. You write, yes? Please write of the adventures."

"Of course."

"And you have little Sophie on the weekdays, right, *Nonna*?" Luis asked, then asked in Italian for good measure. *Nonna* nodded both times, and they exchanged more information about Sophie's meal prep and nap times.

"Sorry for the tight squeeze," Luis said as they stuffed into his car. "I had trouble choosing between what suits to bring."

"It's not a problem," Sylvia lied as she was placed next to Ana in the car. The two of them nodded to one another. She sighed in relief that the hardest part was over.

"You, in a suit?" Mitsuko asked.

"Hey, I can be dapper! I have to be, Ana said." He smiled at her. *"So, are we ready for a trip to Paree?"*

He said that part in a terrible French accent. Mitsuko spoke back in real French, then smiled to herself. "I've been practicing. Still bad, but it's enough to insult a man."

"Woah, Mitsuko, I didn't know you spoke the language. You have to teach us while we're at sea."

"No."

"Why not? I want to use it to impress the foreigners."

"*We'll* be the foreigner, Luis," Ana said, and closed her eyes until they reached the docks.

——◇——

Sylvia saw the ship before they drove down the dock. Dozens of cars and carriages were pulled up to the harbor. Here, nearly a hundred people were huddled together, not quite ready to board. Families were packed in groups so nobody got lost, their suitcases and passports at their sides.

"Thing looks like the *Titanic*," Mitsuko said.

It did. The vessel went up and up, stretching out like a castle with hundreds of tiny windows from which to gaze out. Its hull and smokestacks were black and had barnacles growing where the boat met the waves. It all seemed too mighty for someone like Sylvia. She thought she'd faint from arching her neck up so high.

When she spotted Vincenzo waving at them from the ramp, she surely thought she was dreaming. He was wearing a black peacoat, a Burberry scarf, and a trilby hat. Out of breath, he took off his hat and waved to catch their attention, smiling brightly as if he were greeting them at the gates of Heaven.

Sylvia couldn't stop her legs. She jumped out of the car and around the stagnant crowds. There were police officers lining the dock, but maybe Vincenzo knew them, so they let her do what she wanted. None of them questioned her as she ran up the ramp and nobody cared when she jumped into his arms bubbling with laughter, especially not Vincenzo. He twirled her in one swing before dropping her down and kissing her.

She relished in who she was with him with a thousand eyes on them. Even if being together would one day cost them their lives, it was worth it, to her, to have what she wanted.

"Ready to go?" he asked her.

"Wherever you'll take me," she said. "Where's Laurence and Dominic? We can't leave without them."

"They're already on deck."

The floors on deck were polished. The air, crisp and windy, so salty that she didn't mind the cold. As the boat prepared to leave and spewed steam into the air, passengers leaned over the railing and waved to their loved ones. Sylvia almost went to join them to wave at strangers when two people caught her eye.

Dominic, leaning over the rail and searching the sea with an absent gaze, and Laurence, hand around his waist, enjoying the view with his person.

Sylvia went to call out to them, then retracted her hand and simply wished them a quiet time together.

---◇---

Staying sober on an Italian steam liner set for France was a challenge not many men or women could beat. As soon as they sunk into the depths of the boat, they, like vultures, hunted down the liquor from behind the bar. With Vincenzo's forcefulness and Ana's lack of charm (which the sailors ate up greedily), they entered their rooms with bottles upon bottles of hard liquor concoctions.

Six drinks in and they were arguing about which pronunciations of the Italian brands were correct. They had four rooms booked in the same hall, but that night, they all corralled into Sylvia's and Vincenzo's room and drank the night away.

"You're saying it *wrong*," Luis said. He was on the vanity desk, putting an obscene amount of powder on his face like an 18th-century French aristocrat. "It's a *Domaine Raveneau Chablis les Clos*. It says so right here."

"Don't argue with me about fuckin' *wine*," Vincenzo slurred. He politely walked over Sylvia, who was lying on the ground like a cat, but he almost tripped when she wrapped her arms around his legs. "This's a *Salon Champagne Brut Blanc de Blancs*. Its bottle's black. It tastes like Chardonnay. Don't argue with me."

"But—"

"I didn't fight to be Campo's right-hand man not to know my goddamn wines. I can do it drunk, I can do it better sober. Hell, I can get this right wit' me eyes closed."

"Are you a pirate now?" Sylvia asked, and Vincenzo moved his legs to properly see her.

Sensing he was in the mood, she played with his shoe, untying his shoelaces and massaging his heel. Smiling, he gave her more room to better explore his toes.

"You're all hideous when drunk," Mitsuko commented on. "The stars are projecting to send at least one of you to the hospital."

"It won't be this fellow," Laurence said, and ran his hand through Dominic's hair. He'd been the first to pass out and had his arms around Laurence as he slept on the bed. It'd been an hour since they lost him. Laurence wasn't eager to wake him.

"Poor soul's got it bad," Mitsuko said. "Let's draw on him."

"No, ma'am," Sylvia said, but Mitsuko already had her pen.

"Wait." Luis popped open a bottle and took a swig. "Whoever guesses this brand gets to draw on him. The closer you get, the longer you get with the quill. Ready, go."

Everyone but Sylvia reached for the bottle.

The days passed rather hazily and full of gaiety. Drunk gaiety. Screaming gaiety. Falling asleep in each other's rooms, eating at odd hours of the night just to erase everything they'd done with a bottle of brandy. At one point, Sylvia slept with Ana while Luis was somewhere on the first deck. She didn't feel well, poor thing, and stayed bedridden for most of the trip. Sylvia had given her hot rags to keep over her head.

"Thank you," Ana had finally said after hours of Sylvia taking care of her.

"Of course," she was obliged to say, and thanked God their conversation ended there.

On the last few days of the trip, Sylvia and Vincenzo lounged about in bed like adolescents with too much free time. Kicking off their shoes, they stumbled into the covers together and even lost their bottoms to feel more comfortable.

An arm wrapped around her. His nose poked between her neck and shoulder.

He said nothing, but his hands suggested that he wanted to do anything but sleep. Was he drunk enough to hold her like a wife? Tonight, would he take her like she wanted?

"I'm really excited to go on this trip with you," he whispered. "I'm glad you came."

"I am as well. I can't wait."

"Do you have anything you wish to see?"

"Oh, the world. It'd be interesting to see the Eiffel Tower, but I'm not too much into the idea of sightseeing. I would like to go on a walk one day, or a carriage ride. Maybe dine at a fancy restaurant. Anything with you."

He hummed into the back of her neck. His lips hadn't left her skin.

"Is everything alright?"

"I'm just thinking. Campo recently asked me something that's been on my mind."

"And what'd he ask?"

His lips left her. "If I was going to propose soon."

Sylvia's heart, so full with how much it'd dealt with this year, ballooned in her chest and hurt her ribs. She tried to hold it down with her hand, but she couldn't stop it from thumping.

"Is that...is that something you'd be interested in?" he asked, choking on the words. "In marrying me?"

She'd never heard of a man asking for a woman's permission to marry her before the proposal even happened.

It should've been a surprise, a life-changing treat for a woman to graciously fall into. She should've guessed that Vincenzo, a man not one for surprises, would've asked beforehand.

"If you asked me to marry you," she said, "I'd fall to my knees and weep out of uncontrollable happiness, and I don't think I'd ever be the same."

"Oh." He swallowed. "Oh. Okay. Then. Good to know."

"Did you think I'd object?"

"I don't know. I thought...I should've asked first."

"Have you been thinking about this for some time?"

"Since I've met you," he answered.

She waited for any sign of movement, for him to get up and get down on one knee right then and there. She hadn't snooped through his bag, she didn't know if a ring was awaiting her.

He kissed her neck a few times, then, after a soft, "Goodnight," he rested on his back, sleep taking him minutes later.

Sylvia agonized over that looming question for several more hours, listening to the boat sway back and forth.

On the final morning of their trip, Sylvia awoke to the sound of commotion outside. People were running about while others made early morning conversation.

Vincenzo was already up and dressed when she finally opened her eyes.

She yawned. "What's happening?"

"We've just docked," he said, and parted the curtain for her to see.

A port she'd never seen before welcomed her to land. Its layout contrasted what she knew of New York. The buildings were made of brown brick and had black roofs and stout chimneys. A garden there, a pavilion if she pressed her face to the frosty glass. Snow had coated the grounds the night prior. Horse-drawn carriages were cutting through the streets with places to be.

"Are we in Paris?" she asked.

"I don't believe so. Campo's notes said a woman named Émeline was supposed to pick us up in a place called Nantes, so I believe that's where we are now. We have a train to catch, so hurry up and get dressed."

Sylvia moaned and snuggled into bed.

"Hey, no, no, no." He shook her bottom. "Come on. Wake up."

"Must I? It's only seven."

"It's six."

"Oh, even worse."

"Come on now." Biting his lower lip, he straddled her through the bedsheets and pinned her arms around her head.

"Oh, my," she said. "Now, how is *this* supposed to get me up? I simply must go back to bed and dream about what you'll do to me."

"I won't be able to do this when we're out, so I'm getting it out now." He leaned into her ear. "And I'll promise even more if you get ready quickly."

Two minutes later and they were out in the hallway. Dominic's and Laurence's cabin had been cleared out. Luis had on another beret and was trying to lug all of his and Ana's luggage down the stairs by himself. Vincenzo and Mitsuko helped where they could.

Outside, down on the dock, waited Laurence and Dominic. While Laurence took in the France coastline with a map in hand, Dominic was staring down at his free hand, taking reaches for it only for him to be deterred.

"Hey, careful." Mitsuko jogged down the ramp and lightly slapped Dominic's hand. "Keep it together. You're in public."

"Be nice," Sylvia said.

"Yeah, no fighting on this side of the hemisphere," Luis said. "Hey, where's the Eiffel Tower? I can't see it."

"You won't see it for another few hours," Mitsuko said. She pulled her scarf over her scowl. "How're we getting to the capital, anyway? From what I can remember, it's about four or five hours to Paris by train from here, even longer by car."

"A woman's supposed to pick us up," Vincenzo said. "She'll be our chauffeur for the trip."

"Great. Not a very punctual woman, is she?"

"We should've made a sign," Laurence said, casually brushing his shoulder into Dominic. Dominic smiled, giving him the same look Sylvia often gave Vincenzo when they were alone.

"God, calm it," Mitsuko stressed. "Honestly, two seconds in and you're already acting like love-struck fools. I commend you for your bravery and condemn you for your stupidity."

"Hey, come on, leave them alone," Luis said. "This trip's meant to be fun. Let them flirt."

"W-we're not—that wasn't—" Laurence covered his face in embarrassment and made Luis laugh. "Never mind."

"Here I thought this trip was going to be peaceful," Mitsuko continued, "but Luis and I are going to end up watching over you lot like two old caregivers. What a vacation. It's going to be more stressful than—"

"I'm so sorry to have kept you waiting!"

Across the boardwalk, a young woman ran up to meet them.

She looked very similar to the woman in Campo's photo, though her hair had been cut shorter and she was wearing more beautiful makeup. She was a small girl not much older than Sylvia, with tight, blond curls that accentuated her soft, round face, and a briefcase that hit her thick thighs as she trotted along.

She caught her breath on a street pole before greeting them properly. "I'm so sorry for missing you. My watch is running a few minutes slow..."

At hearing her voice, which was tender and probably too adjusted to apologizing, Mitsuko looked up.

The wind caught on the coastline and shot a gust at their backs. Mitsuko's hair flared out around her hat, and Émeline's hat, white with a wide brim, sailed up and over the light posts, lost.

Mitsuko pulled down her scarf to get a better look at the girl.

Émeline dropped her briefcase as she covered her mouth with both hands. Icy tears formed in the corner of her blue eyes. "Mitsy?"

Mitsuko stepped back, back on Laurence's suitcase. Unable to flee by sea or air, she abandoned her bag, ran past the girl, and sprinted into the French town.

Chapter 25: Émeline

"Mitsuko!"

It was too late. Mitsuko ran down the dock and skidded into oncoming traffic. She was small enough to dart around the carriages and cars, and before any of them could stop her, she was gone.

Sylvia lifted up her dress and gave chase. Laurence followed right behind her. Dominic and Luis went to go after them before waiting on Vincenzo's orders.

Vincenzo's instincts pulled him in two different directions. One, to follow Mitsuko and Sylvia into uncharted territory, or two, to stay with Émeline, this girl who was now sobbing into her gloves so hard, she was falling over. Dominic caught and consoled her, placing a handkerchief to her face in hopes that she'd use it.

He didn't know if she was friend or foe, this Émeline. He'd never seen Mitsuko so distraught that she'd run away from her problems instead of face them head-on. The only person to evoke such a fight-or-flight response in him was his father.

He sighed and went with his gut. "You three stay here. I'll chase after them."

Mitsuko had a considerable lead on them. With a knowledge of the streets, she cut corners faster than them, hurdled over fences quicker than they could. Two streets in and Vincenzo lost the tail end of Sylvia's dress.

"Mitsuko!"

He took a turn too slowly, white breath collecting around him. The city reminded him of both New York and someplace abstract. For every traffic cop yelling at passing cars was a vintage bakery with an illustrated French menu. And nobody spoke any English. Almost nothing reached him. He knew Italian and French were Romance languages, but he hadn't thought he'd feel so lost in so much company. He thought he'd be with Sylvia so he didn't feel so alone, or at least have Mitsuko as his translator.

"Mitsuko, where are you?" He jogged down an open street where, despite the cold, couples were dining outside with tea and hot loaves of bread.

"Monsieur?"

From a bakery came out a portly man who reminded Vincenzo of Campo. He wore an apron covered in flour and held a rag that he kept cleaning his hands with.

"Excuse me, monsieur, but were you looking for someone named Mitsuko?"

Vincenzo almost snapped at him for calling him "miss," then controlled himself. Poor man had a burn on his hand that looked as old as he was, carved in and around his fingers like bark.

He fixed his jacket and hat to look more presentable. "I am."

"Mitsuko Matsuoka?"

He didn't know her surname, so he said, "Do you know her?"

"Yes, yes." He nodded to himself, searching through his own memories to find her. "She was one of those little Japanese girls that came over. Is she back?"

"I don't think I follow, sir."

"Oh, yes, monsieur. Back during the War, Japan sent us a dozen or so of their nurses as extra military aid. They were like superstars here. Everyone knew them by name."

Vincenzo knew he should've been running after Mitsuko, but perhaps this man would give him answers that neither girl would divulge. "Did you know her well?"

"Me? Oh, no, monsieur. I was but another foot soldier who tried saving too many of his friends. Got scraped up enough times to be a regular with the nurses at Merchant Hospital. Some of them said I was getting hurt on purpose to see their pretty faces." He laughed. "There, I met Mitsuko, and her friend."

"Émeline?"

"Ah, yes, yes! What a blast from the past. Yes, she and her were something else back then, a real couple of gals. Mitsuko, she was the bluntest woman I've ever met, and rowdy, too. Some said she was a boy dressed as a girl to evade the trenches, but I never thought that. She was kind to men who she knew didn't have much time left. And Émeline, oh, what an angel she was. Soft and caring. She was like the mother we all needed."

"I didn't know that."

"They were also secretive, those girls, always running off after work and doing who knows what with each other. I think they were very close friends."

"Possibly," Vincenzo said, lying because he knew better. "Do you know what happened to them after the War?"

"Mitsuko left before the War ended. I thought she got shipped back to Japan along with all the others. One day she and Émeline were together, the next..." He blinked rapidly, the memories fading. "My apologies. Did you say you were looking for her? Do you need help finding her? I'd love to see her again."

"...No," Vincenzo said. "She should be up ahead. Thank you, though, for telling me this." He tipped his hat and carried on.

"If you find her, bring her back! I'll treat you all to some French pastries."

Promising that he'd see what he could do, Vincenzo turned right and kept running. He hadn't fought in the War, and neither had his father nor most of their acquaintances, but he knew of some who had. You saw it in their hardened faces, the way they carried themselves. He could only assume how many French people had the War scarred into them like the baker, and how deeply it'd affected both Mitsuko and Émeline.

He dipped down a dark alleyway with a turn at the very end. There was a stairwell leading to someone's backdoor and a small stone bridge with some garbage underneath it.

Hiding within that garbage, he found Mitsuko being cared for by Laurence and Sylvia. She'd fallen to the ground and was tapping her foot into the snow.

"Mitsuko, talk to us," Sylvia begged. "Please."

"It'll be okay," Laurence added. "Just breathe."

She didn't do either. Holding her hands, she blocked out their advice and focused on a patch of dead grass visible beneath the snow.

Sylvia looked up at Vincenzo. "We can't get her to move. It's like she's turned to stone."

"And she won't talk to us. It's worrying me. *Mitsuko.*"

"We shouldn't move her. She could be remembering things about the War." He went to take off his jacket and lend it to her, then guessed she'd probably cut herself out of it. He squatted beside her instead.

Her dark eyes were glossy like she was freezing over. Her hands had gone red and shiny from the cold, and her ring, the one she always wore as a wedding ring, was cutting into her hand and causing her to bleed.

He thought back on all the times he'd seen girls swooning over her at the Black Kitten, how she danced for their eyes alone. He recalled how animated the baker was when he talked about her and Émeline.

"She and her were something else back then."

"That woman," he asked carefully, "is she someone you knew from the War?"

Mitsuko sniffled.

"Did she hurt you?" Sylvia asked quietly. "Do you want us to distance ourselves from her?"

She curled more inwards into herself. Her hand was clamped over her ring.

"Okay, honestly, none of this is good for her right now," Laurence decided. "She's gonna fall apart on us. Let's take her to this apartment where she won't catch a death of cold. We'll heat up some water, fetch her some sweets. We'll make her forget all about this woman."

"I don't think she'd like that right now." Vincenzo played with his own ringless hand, wondering how such a commitment would weigh on him. "You loved her."

She inhaled.

"You loved her, but then you had to leave, offsetting your relationship. Now you're with her again and don't know what to do, and all the emotions you've been suppressing are resurfacing."

"Shut up." A labored sob broke through her sore throat. She tried covering it with her scarf. "You don't know what you're talking about."

"I passed by a baker who claimed to know you. He said you two were a notable pair during the War." He moved up closer. "Did you give her the other ring?"

"Fuck *off*," she said. "God, suddenly you're this observant prick who can pick up on the most basic of social cues? When the hell did that happen?"

He bit his cheek at her insult.

"We just want to help you," Sylvia told her. "We don't want to see you like this."

"It's not like I can help it right now." She sniffed hard and wiped her face with her scarf. They all gave her a minute to let the cold air clear her head.

She dropped her shaking hand. It fell into Sylvia's. "Back when I was young, when I thought I was cut out to be a nurse, I was sent to Paris to volunteer for the war effort. I met a whole span of nurses there, but then I met her, a woman leagues past me in humanity and beauty, and I stupidly fell in love with her. Then I had the audacity to propose to her out of wistful desperation to never be alone again, and this bastard of a woman..."

She pressed the palms of her hands into her eye sockets. "Why did she say yes? Why was she so cruel to me?"

"Because she loved you back," Vincenzo explained. "What happened after that?"

"What do you think happened?" she asked. "What happens to all of us when we get too in over our heads? We fucked it up. I ruined everything I'd built up with her. I punched that stupid Nurse Clément in her stupid face, and then Ém—'ma chérie, s'il te plait'—didn't want to be with me anymore, even though I was *defending* her..." She kicked the ground, splattering the snow. "She told me to leave, so I did! I did for her! So, why now, after ten years of wanting to kill myself over this stupid mistake, am I thrust back into her arms, expected to act normal when every word of hers drives a stake through my heart? Why has fate done this to me?"

"C-Campo couldn't have known," Vincenzo said. "He said Émeline was his niece."

At that, Mitsuko scoffed. "Better send a telegram to your boss, then, Vincenzo, because Émeline isn't Italian. She was born and raised in Paris. Your boss lied to you."

The train took two hours to get to the heart of Paris. Good news for Mitsuko: The time she needed to spend in Émeline's presence was cut in half. Bad news: She still needed to spend two hours trapped in a moving train with her ex-lover.

It seemed. None of them dared to ask for more details. When they boarded, Mitsuko claimed a whole cabin to herself and kept her bag against the door in case anyone came in. She shut the blinds, curled up in her lonely seat. That was that for the next two hours.

The rest of them invited Émeline into their cabin, but she declined. She still had Dominic's handkerchief with which to dab her eyes. They gave her her own cabin as well.

With their entourage down two women, Vincenzo and his friends piled into their snug cabin and discussed.

"Who is this girl?"

"Émeline. Mitsuko said she knew her from the War."

"So she's a friend?"

"No, Ana. You saw how they reacted. I think they're wives."

"Wives?"

"But Mitsuko never talked about her at the Kitten."

"It must've been too painful to talk about."

"Wait," Luis said, "Sir, Campo said they were related. Did Campo lie to you?"

That pierced him like a bullet. Why would Campo lie? He'd entrusted Vincenzo with private information about mayors and governors, about police officers, about *him*. No one knew about his worsening knee condition or his tax evasions from 1921 onwards but him. Why lie about something so mundane? What was he trying to hide? Who was Émeline?

And Mitsuko. Two women, marrying each other? There was no way. And to think about marriage like that, it was torture. Nobody would approve of such a bond between a Japanese woman and a French woman. They were rules that needed to be followed.

But they'd done it, and now they were back together to either mend the bond or destroy it completely.

"We'll have to leave them be for the time being," Laurence said. "It's no good to corner either of them right now. That little blond thing will cry herself to death and Mitsuko will break and run off to England."

"Vincenzo, you said a baker said he knew them," Sylvia said. "Did he say anything about how their relationship ended?"

"No."

"It must have been excruciating," Ana said.

Everyone looked up.

"What?" she asked, clearly not used to being the center of attention. "I'm not daft when it comes to a woman's heart. One of my church friends, she was a volunteer nurse during the War. She said it was nightmarish, all those young boys dying in their hospital beds and her not being able to save them. I can't imagine what those two had to live through. And no girl would react that volatilely to seeing someone she loved," she added. "They must've had a divorce." She blushed. "I-if they could do such a thing," she added, "two women."

Vincenzo looked outside to a field of flowers. He'd ask Mitsuko about all of this in private. He had to. He couldn't let her self-destruct on their vacation. And he needed to know more about Émeline and why Campo had chosen her. To his knowledge, Campo hadn't made a stupid decision in his life. He hoped that hadn't ended with choosing Émeline as their guide.

A hand touched his knee.

"Everything okay?" Sylvia asked.

He nodded. Everyone had broken off into their own separate conversations, giving them a small bubble in which to talk privately. "Just thinking."

"I'm worried about Mitsuko. I always thought she was this indestructible force that couldn't be swayed by romance. To think she's been bottling this up for years without telling any of us, it makes me want to cry."

"I'll have a word with her later. I think I almost broke through to her in the alley."

"I've just never seen her so reactive. Émeline must mean a great deal to her." She nestled her head against his.

Feeling her hair tickle his cheek, he closed his eyes and tried memorizing the feeling for later.

——✧——

Three black cars were waiting for them at the Parisian train station. They were part of Émeline's tourism business, paid ahead of time by Campo to escort them to their new apartment.

When Vincenzo opened Mitsuko's cabin door and found her missing, panic set in. They checked the bathroom, the neighboring cabins, even Émeline's, though she was waiting for them at the end of the train.

"Did she jump out the window?" Luis asked, checking underneath her seat.

Fearing just that, Vincenzo opened the window and scanned the streets.

Mitsuko, much to the driver's dismay, was sitting on one of the hoods of the cars, wrapped up in a blanket she'd most definitely stolen from her cabin. It looked like she had red makeup around her eyes. Vincenzo knew it was from her scratching away her tears.

He applauded Émeline for controlling her emotions. Aside from her far-off gazes, she'd cleaned herself up and was all smiles for the departure.

"Are you alright, dear?" Sylvia asked.

"Of course. I do apologize for that dramatic performance on the docks. What a show. I promise I won't cause another disturbance like that on your trip from here on out."

"It wasn't a disturbance," Sylvia said, but Émeline was already heading off to her next assignment.

None of them spoke as they divided into the cars, not even Luis. He knew where his jokes were needed and it wasn't now. Émeline and Mitsuko rode in separate cars.

They drove for fifteen minutes down the Parisian streets. At first, Vincenzo couldn't tell they were in Europe. Then he noticed the buildings. They neither varied in size nor did they reach the heights that New York buildings could. But weren't they beautiful in their nineteenth-century charm. The streets were compact to fit their small cars and carriages, and some of them were even made of cobblestone, bringing back a nostalgic feeling he had from childhood. He didn't remember most of Italy, but when *Nonna* or his mother spoke about Europe, he saw cobblestone. He saw these old buildings and stone bridges retained from a different era. It truly felt like home and of an entirely new place.

Their "apartment" was actually a boarding house made of brick, with trellises stretching up the sides that might've grown flowers in a different season. It was built beside a small school and a church with stone so black, it appeared burned. Around the neighborhood, school children, both boys and girls, ran about in uniforms, freed from the confines of school.

Émeline showed the doorman their papers and led them in. "Your rooms will be on the fourth floor. You'll be living in the suites, so rather than a communal bath, each room will be furnished with a lovely, private bath and kitchen for your convenience. You might find them a little aberrant to the ones you're used to in America, but you'll find that they work all the same." She flipped through more papers as they waited for the elevator. "Monsieur d'Antonio booked four rooms for this trip, one bed per room. Is that adequate?"

"So, that would be Sylvia and myself," Vincenzo said. "Luis and Ana..." He looked to Dominic. He gave one assured nod. "And Dominic and Laurence."

"Oh, I did have a question about that arrangement," Émeline said. "Monsieur Douglas, Monsieur Scordato, if you'd like, I can ask for two separate beds. It's no trouble."

"That won't be necessary, thank you," Laurence said. "Mitsuko—"

"Émeline and I are rooming together."

Outside, a bell chimed for the hour. School children squealed as their school day officially ended.

Émeline's briefcase knocked into the wall as they entered the elevator. The mask she'd been wearing was slipping. "That would be...out of place."

"Would it?" Mitsuko asked. "You're already here. What if one of us decides she wants to run away to the fifteenth arrondissement without a moment's notice? Won't you be there to guide her back home?"

She stammered on some type of dissuasion, but the quietness of the elevator hushed her up.

"That's what I thought," Mitsuko muttered.

Vincenzo held his tongue. No matter how much he wanted to intervene, this wasn't his conversation to meddle in. This was and had to be between them.

The papers promised that all of their rooms were identical, but Luis insisted that he must take the room labeled "403." Mitsuko gravitated to Room 404, her shoulder scraping against the wallpaper, and Laurence chose the room next to Luis. This left Vincenzo and Sylvia with Room 406, the room next to Mitsuko and, consequently, Émeline.

Mitsuko unlocked her chosen door, then shot a cold, deadly look at Émeline.

Flinching as if she'd been yelled at, Émeline followed her wordless order and shuffled into the room.

"Mitsuko—"

Mitsuko slammed and locked the door behind her.

"Well, that's that for right now," Laurence finally said.

Vincenzo's and Sylvia's room welcomed them to a magnificent foyer and a floor-to-ceiling window adorned by heavy curtains. It had a full kitchen, a bath with its own clawfoot tub, a dining room, and a sitting room, and everything smelled of fresh linens straight from the laundry. Vincenzo would be sure to send something to Campo for his generosity, for when he thought it was done, he opened two double doors and found an entire second living space complete with sofas and a massive painting of a French landscape.

Sylvia abandoned their bags in the foyer and did a twirl near the windows. "How marvellous."

"Which part? This boarding house or that scene we just bore witness to?"

"Oh, both, but I'm pretending I didn't see the latter."

"Good tactic." He walked up beside her. "She followed her in without a word."

"Do you think there's bad blood between them?"

"I don't see it. I just think it's complicated."

"I hope it works out between them. Perhaps we take a trip to the Eiffel Tower. I hear it's romantic, it's one of the most romantic places on Earth."

"Is that a hint for me?"

She smirked and held out her hand.

Smirking back, he laced his fingers around hers, and she pulled him into a dance, waltzing him into their new space.

She nuzzled her head against his as they danced. "Seeing what Mitsuko and Émeline have has me both petrified and incredibly envious."

"Really?"

"Marriage is such a commitment. To dedicate your life to a person? Forever? This time last year, I couldn't have dreamt of saying yes to a man." Her hand found its way to his chest, caressing the area around his heart. "That answer changed with you."

His heart picked up, and he knew she felt it pounding against her soft fingers. With her hands so close to his vulnerable skin, he broke away and patted himself off. He prayed she didn't think ill of him.

"Was that too much just now?" she asked.

"No. Well, yes. A bit."

"Remember, we're three thousand miles away from home. The chances of anyone finding out what we do are slim."

"I know."

"It's still hard, though."

He nodded and dragged their bags into the bedroom. "Let me get these out of the way."

"Take your time."

With her momentarily out of sight, Vincenzo closed the bedroom door and took a deep breath. He hated how much he cared about how other people viewed him, but he couldn't help it. Feeling accepted was tied to his being. His work profession, his race, where he lived, what he liked. Even in a new country, the thought of anyone finding out that he'd been born a girl made him as miserable as Mitsuko was.

He stared into his pile of clothes. Why, though? Why did he have to be so careful around them? He'd been through so much with these people, and with Sylvia. The love of his life who made him feel safe. Like she'd ever mind that his body was different.

He scratched at his heart, through the corset he always wore to bind his chest. He wouldn't lose Sylvia to this secret.

On this trip, he'd tell her the truth.

Chapter 26: Paris Date

Her dreams floated her through so many delicious worlds that night. She tasted her ideal France, dining on wines while she frolicked through meadows. What she'd hoped to experience was experienced tenfold while she slept, and when she awoke, she wondered why she wasn't on an ocean liner, waiting to set foot in that idealized France.

Then she awoke in the warmest bed that smelled like neither her nor Vincenzo. She tossed and turned for several minutes, savoring in her lingering dreams, before opening her eyes to Vincenzo sleeping next to her in their suite. He was outdoing himself with his bedhead this morning. If he wasn't a light sleeper, she would've slipped under the covers and given him a special good-morning kiss.

But she couldn't disturb such a beautiful face, so instead of getting up, she picked up the pen and paper she'd left on the desk the night prior and hiked up her legs to write.

Liberation swelled inside her when she started her note with, *"Dear Nonna,"* instead of penning Clara's name. The woman didn't even know that she was in France, thousands of miles away from her, and she never needed to know. Never again would Sylvia have to tell her anything about her life.

When she was to marry, she, the person who'd given birth to her, was not obligated to attend the wedding.

Her cheeks went warm. "When *she was to marry.*" No more what-ifs, though she had to be realistic. Vincenzo was here on business, how could he possibly ask for her hand now? And with Mitsuko's and Émeline's debacle? Completely out of the question.

"Is that something you'd be interested in? In marrying me?"

She stopped writing. He'd sounded so auspicious on the boat, so hopeful that she'd say yes.

She covered her face with the pad of paper, overthinking the possibilities. Perhaps she should've avoided the Eiffel Tower and any fields of flowers. She didn't trust Vincenzo to fully stick to his business trip.

The bed shifted on Vincenzo's side, and she turned to see him looking up at her, his smile peeking out from underneath the blankets.

She laughed nervously and flipped over her writing. "Good morning. Did I wake you?"

"Don't know. I've been watching you. What were you thinking about? You were blushing."

"Just thinking about you."

"May I know the details?"

"I don't think so." She kissed his forehead.

"What do you want to do today?" he asked.

"I don't know. Don't you have work to do? I don't want to step on your toes."

"Well, we can always hang out together on the side."

"When?" She went through the days in her head, how long they had here. "By the way, when's your birthday? It's early January, isn't it?"

To answer her, he smiled wider until he showed a bit of teeth, a shy smile she could devour.

"No." She put away her writing supplies. "Vincenzo DiFiore."

"That's my name."

"Vincenzo, is today your birthday?"

His smile somehow brightened more, and Sylvia squeaked and leaned down to kiss him. "Happy birthday! Why didn't you tell me?"

"I don't celebrate it too grandly."

"That doesn't count when you have a sweetheart." She maneuvered her way on top of him and, with his permission, pinned his wrists down into the plump pillows, straddling him like he'd done with her.

He kicked out his legs to give her room. "I definitely enjoy this view better."

"Do you now?" She kissed him again. "I love you."

"Love you, too."

She leaned down and kissed him once more, and this one stuck, deepening into quite a sultry kiss that had her tasting his inner mouth. She got to ruffle up his bedhead more to her liking. You had power, being the one on top. She so rarely had this type of dominance in her life, and hearing Vincenzo's breathing pick up because of her, admitting that he enjoyed her this way, she didn't know what to think.

He finally pulled back. "Now, then. We can't spend all day in bed."

"I can think of a few ways we can."

"Don't tempt me." He tapped her rear a little harder than she expected. "Come on, we need breakfast."

"Oh, what's there to eat?"

Nothing, apparently. When they finally peeled themselves out of bed and entered the kitchen, they found it stocked with bread, coffee, crackers, fresh fruit, eggs, and milk. They opened the cabinets to even more food ready to be cooked, then stared at the stove for thirty or so seconds.

"I don't want to cook," Vincenzo said flatly.

"Nor do I."

"Let's eat out."

"Agreed."

She didn't know how far she could go dressing as she liked in Paris. She hadn't been harassed on the steam liner because of Vincenzo, but she'd felt uneasy when she'd run after Mitsuko in the streets. Ultimately, she chose a rather masculine look, wearing pants and sweaters without makeup or jewelry on. She did button on her beige trench coat, which went to her ankles and gave her a slim waist and a nice bust. It was the most she could do for now.

Vincenzo, who'd given her the bedroom to dress up, was in the living room, examining his fingers or fingernails to kill time. When he saw her, his lips parted and he dropped his hands.

"This okay?" she asked.

He nodded once. "I...didn't know you brought those clothes."

"Should I change?"

"No." He covered his eyes with his hat. "You're very brave."

"Am I, though?"

"More than you know. I wish..." He cleared his throat. "Well, uh, nevertheless." He grasped for her hand like a child in need of someone's help. "Ready to go?"

She held him with her self-esteem teetering on the edge of appropriately high and devastatingly low. What did that mean? What did he wish? Did he like when she dressed like this, or should she have changed? It was too early in the day for mind games.

They paused. In the hallway, slumped on her side and wrapped in a comforter, was Mitsuko. It looked like she hadn't slept, with her watery eyes and eye bags. Dominic was crouched beside her with a plate of pancakes.

"What's wrong with her?" Vincenzo asked.

"I came out at around six to buy some breakfast and found her like this. She's been out here all night. I tried feeding her."

"You make it sound like I'm some animal hours from starvation," Mitsuko said through her blanket. "I came out here willingly. She"—she nodded at the door—"was upset last night. She didn't want to talk because, 'Seeing me after all these years is too much'. So I let her keep the bed and I came out here."

"And you slept out here?" Vincenzo asked. "Doesn't your suite have a couch?"

"It has two. What's your point?"

He backed off. "Understandable. I suppose."

"Did you eat?" Dominic asked them. "Laurence's inside making breakfast. I told him not to overdo it, but he insisted that he'd be cooking breakfast for everyone today."

"Neither of us fancied to cook," Sylvia explained.

"That's good. I thought I was going to have to eat all of this myself."

Apart from the paintings and wallpaper, their suite mirrored Sylvia's and Vincenzo's, though they kept theirs a little messier. Bowls were soaking in the sink and articles of clothing were resting over their couches and tables, making their living space feel well lived-in.

Luis and Ana were sitting in the kitchen. Luis was on his third plate while Ana grazed on cut fruit. Laurence, wearing a frilly, white apron, was cooking pancakes, eggs, bacon, sausage. All the fryers were live as he made sure his friends were fed.

"Good morning," Laurence said. "Sylvia, I already know your order: fruit oatmeal with a glass of fresh orange juice. We didn't have everything here, so Dominic was kind enough to pick up what I needed."

"We also have bagels," Dominic said, placing two slices in the toaster and readying them with strawberry cream cheese.

"He was very excited about the bagels," Laurence said. "Vincenzo, what would you like?"

He reviewed the options with a hand to his chin. "I'll...take bacon, and eggs. Please."

"Done. Sit. Dominic, where's Mitsuko?"

He sat across from Vincenzo. "I tried doing what you said, but she's persistent. She wants to stay out there."

Laurence groaned. "She isn't persistent, she's depressed. She probably killed off the idea of Émeline when she left for America, and now she's right in front of her and she's spinning in circles. We need to get her back on her feet."

"Why don't they go on a date?" Luis asked, mouth full of pancakes. "That's what I do with Ana when I mess up. What about here?" Tipping in his chair, he leaned to the window and pulled back the curtains.

Laurence and Dominic had struck gold with their room choice. Right outside their kitchen were beautiful houses outlined in gold, then in the corner, that children's school next to the church.

But then, behind the winter trees, the Eiffel Tower touched the sky. It was smaller than Sylvia had imagined, but she would've given anything to see this romantic sight right outside her window.

"How *beautiful*," she said. "Laurence, Dominic, how lucky you are."

"We're both more interested in the *Loov*, the *Louvre*. However it's pronounced. That famous art museum across the river. We're planning on going today."

Dominic choked on his bagel. "We don't have to do that just because *I* want to go. I can go by myself, you don't have to come."

"What else am I gonna do when I want to be with you? We're on vacation, I'd be happy enough lounging in bed with you. And you said there was some dinosaur something or other you wanted to see, and I want to see them, too, so there."

Dominic napkined his lips, his decision made.

Ana crossed her fork and knife on her finished plate. "I wish to go shopping. There're shopping strips around the Eiffel Tower that I wanted to visit. There's Chanel and Vuitton and...Vionnet, and Lanvin, if I can make it. I want to take a proper tour of their shops."

"That means I'll be sticking with her," Luis said, "but I'll be sure to buy everyone souvenirs. Gotta stock up on some European designers like Channel."

"*Chanel*," Ana corrected. "Then we can go to this bakery I saw for lunch."

"What do you want to do?" Laurence asked Sylvia.

She looked outside to the Tower, then gulped at the anticipation of what could be. If he asked her at the top of the Eiffel Tower...

No. He wouldn't. She didn't even know if you could climb up the Eiffel Tower, and it'd be too cold. Another day, another year. "What we need to do, I believe, is help Mitsuko. We can't have her like this."

"I agree, but we shouldn't dogpile her right now. We should try to get at her in waves. Why not you and Vincenzo go out and do whatever you're planning on doing and take her and Émeline with you, because we all know that you're planning to do something cute today."

"Says the man who's planning a day at an art museum," Sylvia teased.

Laurence stuck out his tongue. "Then that's that. Take them to the Eiffel Tower and make it romantic. Let us commence: Operation: Save Mitsuko's Marriage."

"Save Mitsuko's marriage!" Luis echoed encouragingly.

The front door rattled, startling Dominic to his feet. He'd left it ajar for Mitsuko, but he must've thought she wouldn't have come in.

She had, but not alone. Lost of her blanket, she entered in begrudgingly with a frown on her face, and behind her, not one hair out of place, smile faker than yesterday, was Émeline.

She held up a map of Paris. "Are we ready to depart?"

——✧——

Émeline still had her cars and drivers ready to drive them wherever they wanted, so Luis and Ana left in one while Laurence and Dominic left with two large maps of the *Louvre*. Dominic had stars in his eyes, eager to see his art and dinosaur bones.

Their drive from the hotel to the Eiffel Tower was like one of Sylvia's dreams. The houses, you could tell their owners lived well, every white building identically perfect. She thought they were types of apartments and went to ask to make conversation, but then, as they drove around yet another beautiful building, she was met with an unobstructed view of the tower.

She couldn't help herself. She gasped. The park was relatively crowded, but not enough to make Vincenzo nervous. The pathways had been cleared for couples to take morning strolls with their parasols and babies. The trees and statues of men on horses decorating the park were coated with a fresh layer of snow and made everything appear fresh despite the cold. When she left the car, she took a breath of air and grinned up at the massively tall tower disappearing into the fog. It was perfect, for her.

"I can give everyone a tour of the Tower," Émeline said. "There're many statues and historic sites in and around the *Champ de Mars*, this green surrounding the Tower. There's also the, uh, École Militaire, a military training facility founded in 1750 by King Louis XV." She cleared her throat. "I can give you a tour of that as well, if you wish."

Mitsuko closed her car door, staring at Émeline with concern.

Émeline caught her eyes. She put on that fake smile and gestured to the tower. "There're also a few lakes around the

Tower where you can feed the ducks and geese, but I'm not sure if any of them are still with us. They might've, uhm, left us for the season."

"Can we skate it?" Vincenzo asked.

"Skate it?" she asked. "Well, at times. Sometimes, there're people around from which you can rent skates."

"Then let's try that. Sylvia, do you know how to skate? Mitsuko? Émeline?"

"Oh, I couldn't," Émeline said. "I'll just watch."

"You should try. It'll be fun. Sylvia, have you ever skated before?"

"I haven't, no."

"Then I'll teach you."

Sylvia tried reading Vincenzo without asking him outright. Teach her? Did he know how to skate? Surely not, and why would he want to go ice skating, anyway? It wasn't like him.

Then she looked at Émeline and Mitsuko pretending the other didn't exist, and she understood. This was Operation: Save Mitsuko's Marriage. Save her love life. Save her happiness. Today wasn't about her vacation or Vincenzo's birthday. They only had a week to repair their hearts, otherwise they might find Mitsuko drinking herself away in darker, less familiar bars, wanting to die but being unable to do anything about it. Sylvia had been in those situations before with the wrong loves, but from the looks in their eyes, she could tell what they had was worth saving.

The frozen lake was right underneath the skirt of the Eiffel Tower, letting them study the hundreds of metal pipes and beams curving to its shape. And the lake itself was more of a pond underneath a large willow tree frozen with icicles. Next to it was a small shack to rent their skates.

Vincenzo paid for everyone's skates. Émeline tried to decline her pair and then insisted that she pay for her own, but Vincenzo wouldn't take either bargain.

"I really shouldn't be doing this," Émeline said as she tied them on. "I'm supposed to be your guide."

"You are, you're *guiding* us on how to skate."

"But I'm not very good at it. I've only done it a few times."

"With Mitsuko?"

Sylvia inhaled. So sudden. Didn't he know how a girl's heart worked?

"Uh, let's try to test the ice," Sylvia said, quickly taking Vincenzo away from Émeline. "Mitsuko—"

Mitsuko stepped onto the ice, hands out to level herself, and drifted onto the pond.

"We, uh, should be a bit careful," Émeline said, eyes glued on Mitsuko's back. "We don't want anyone to fall."

"Sylvia can hold on to me," Vincenzo said. "Émeline, do you need help?"

"...No. I'm okay."

"Do *you* know how to skate?" Sylvia asked him.

"A bit." He stepped backwards onto the ice.

"*Careful—!*"

He glided effortlessly onto the slate of white, his hands fitted casually in his pockets. He even stopped himself by cutting his back foot into the ice behind him, creating a perfect circle.

Sylvia clapped her hands together. "Vincenzo, you never told me you knew how to *ice skate* like some champion in the art."

"My parents took me to a rink in Brooklyn that's since been shut down. My father bullied my way in so I could have an hour or so on the rink a week." He gave her a perfect figure eight and settled naturally beside her, hands resting on her hips and guiding her onto the ice.

Gravity brought her closer to him. She held onto him for balance, ankles concaving.

"Careful."

"Not very natural, is it? These skates."

"If you have a stable foundation, it's easier to stay up." He led her halfway around the rink to where Mitsuko and Émeline were still getting their bearings. Both of them were close, but neither of them were looking at each other.

"We need to help them," Sylvia whispered.

"I'll try again in a moment. Let's just see what happens."

"You were quite bold, asking if she'd ever skated before with Mitsuko."

"I thought she'd respond best to boldness. Guess it's the other way around."

The four of them skated as professionally or as poorly as was expected of them. Vincenzo bested all of them with his curves and turns, and spins, too, if he was feeling cheeky. Émeline knew how to keep herself up for the most part, and Mitsuko could take turns better than Sylvia could.

Vincenzo held her out as one did for a baby taking its first steps. "You got it."

"I most certainly do not—" One of her skates skidded out from underneath her and she yelped.

Mitsuko, either prepared for her or just that stable, caught her and helped her upright. "What a natural."

"That easy to tell?" Sylvia asked, panting. "This is too hard. Curse Vincenzo for suggesting this."

"Hey, don't curse me." Free from Sylvia, Vincenzo skated across the rink towards Émeline, who was skating back to the benches, done for the day. "Mitsuko, could you watch Sylvia for a moment?"

"Will do," she said, and watched him plod over the snow to meet with Émeline.

"He's good, isn't he?" Sylvia asked. "You are, too. You all are."

"I'd hardly call myself good. I've only done this a handful of times." She watched as Émeline and Vincenzo sat next to one another. "I know what you two are doing. You're not very good at whispering."

"We weren't trying to hide it. Mitsuko, darling, tell me what's wrong. Why haven't you tried talking to her?"

"I have. She said she didn't want to talk."

"You know what I mean."

"No, I don't. I tried talking to her. She started crying. What more can I do?"

"You need to fight for her. You need to be there for her and show that you're willing to listen and talk to her about whatever happened between you two in the past. What happened, sweetheart? What made the two of you have a falling out?"

Mitsuko turned away, but her gaze brought her to Émeline now speaking secretly with Vincenzo. She now had a handkerchief in her hand, the one Dominic had given her yesterday.

Mitsuko clicked her tongue, then brought Sylvia off the ice behind the willow tree.

"You see, all this secrecy isn't good," Sylvia explained. "You must be upfront with your emotions if you plan on being with her again..."

Mitsuko's back grated the back of the tree, and she slid down again into the dirty snow, giving up before even starting her fight. Either she was crying, or...

Sylvia squatted beside her once more.

"I can't do this," Mitsuko cried. "I ruin everything, that's what I do."

"No, you don't. You love her so much, Mitsuko. I can see it. And she loves you, too."

"No, she doesn't. She hates me."

Sylvia pulled her into a hug, which she thankfully accepted. "That's not true."

"You weren't there. You don't know."

"What don't I know?"

She shoved her head into the tree bark. Sylvia wiped off her wet cheeks so they didn't freeze.

"When we were...together," she started, "we were *so* close. We told each other everything, we confided in one another. One night—she was a nurse, Sylvia, who was afraid of blood, couldn't stand the sight of it—she came into our room crying, and I told her what an amazing nurse she was. She was so much more caring than I was, she knew how to talk to people who weren't going to make it. But it tore her up inside. She thought she was spoiling herself by saving others. So that night, I...I kissed her. I couldn't help it. I didn't want to see her cry anymore. And at first, I thought she was going to turn me away."

"But she didn't. She loved you back."

She blew her nose into her scarf. "We went steady. We went out on our days off and played at the beach. We drove all throughout the countryside and had picnics together. When I was ready, when I thought she was ready, I proposed to her.

Now, we knew it wasn't going to work, but we didn't care. We wanted that for us. We were happy. But then that bastard of a woman, Nurse Clément, came into the picture."

"What did she do?"

"I think she knew about us. We kept everything under wraps, we were careful. Hell, we didn't even wear our rings when we worked as nurses. But Nurse Clément must've known. She tried making us move rooms, she gave me the shoddiest jobs to work. And then she wanted to send Émeline to the trenches, to be more involved with on-site injuries." She bared her teeth at the thought. "She wasn't meant for that. She was supposed to stay at Merchant Hospital with me and all the other nurses stationed there. There were dozens of others ready to go—I *demanded* to take her place, even though I knew it meant we wouldn't see each other for a while—but she forced Émeline to go. She knew she was overwhelmed and she still forced her to go."

Sylvia heard someone walk up behind them.

"I don't remember what I did to her exactly. I was blinded by anger. I remember going to her office. I remember her calling me a harlot and how I was poisoning the women around me, and I just...lost it. I punched her in her stupid, wrinkled face and tossed her desk against the window. I was a wreck, Sylvia. I wasn't myself, but I wouldn't let her hurt Émeline like that. It took Ém coming in and putting herself between us for me to finally calm down.

"After that and a rather well-earned punishment from Nurse Clément, Émeline took me aside and said that we shouldn't be together. She thought she was making my life miserable. She said she wanted to stay safe. With my name swimming through the ranks, the rumors spread, and she was getting worried we'd be found out, so to make her feel safer, I...left."

She slumped into her knees. "What do I do, Sylvia? How do I fix what I ruined?"

She peered around the tree, then covered her mouth and got up. "Maybe you should ask her yourself."

Mitsuko looked up to make sure Vincenzo and Émeline were actually this close to her, watching her wipe snot and tears off her face in the middle of the snow. Too afraid to make another move, she covered her lower face with her scarf.

Émeline, almost in tears herself, knelt down and gave her her handkerchief. "You came at her with a knife."

"Huh?"

"You didn't punch Nurse Clément. You came at her with a knife. It's why you were suspended for thirty days. It was my way of gauging how long I had to be in the trenches, for when I'd come back, I'd yell at you for getting yourself into so much trouble."

"Oh." She sniffled. "Don't remember much. Blocked out a lot of memories."

"You shouldn't. You cried in my arms when I came back. It was the first time I'd ever seen you cry."

"...Again, blocked most of that out."

"I haven't. It's one of the strongest memories I have of you."

Sylvia slowly got up and gave Émeline a bow to leave. She didn't know if she caught it in her peripheral vision; her eyes were now locked on Mitsuko.

Taking Vincenzo's hand, she left the two of them to talk underneath the willow tree.

Chapter 27: Bakery Decision

After three days of living in France, Vincenzo determined that he was deathly afraid of Émeline DuPont.

Afraid as one feared wolves or sickness or outstanding goals expected of you. Not only did she have their entire week mapped out—he was to speak with Campo's people tomorrow about opening up the potential trade route from Canada to Brooklyn—she also kept cheerful, even after speaking with Mitsuko beneath the willow tree.

She'd shed tears with her fiancée, made a truce only the two of them knew, then fixed herself up and continued on as if nothing had changed. But something had; they were holding hands now, and Mitsuko had stopped sleeping in the hallway of their boarding home.

But what Émeline had said to Vincenzo on the park bench had left him rethinking everything he thought he'd once known.

"I'm sorry about this."

Those four little words had broken through to her and finally worn her down. Crying into Dominic's handkerchief, she'd disclosed the story of how she met Mitsuko, her "Mitsy."

The way she'd explained how she'd clumsily fallen in love reminded Vincenzo of how he'd fallen for Sylvia. How she grew up with a strong-willed mother and an easy-going father—Mr. DuPont, the man who'd been his chauffeur in Canada. Because of this, she'd grown up to be this sweet girl who let anything happen to her, someone who'd exchange her own happiness for the best of others.

She'd stayed with the War for four whole years and had thought about deserting before she met Mitsuko halfway. The light of her life, this headstrong girl who blew her out of the water with decisiveness and power. He found himself falling in love with her as well, or the idea of their haphazard love.

And to accept the proposal of your best friend whom you treasured, during the time when you were the most vulnerable, and to say *yes*. How happy she'd looked then, reminiscing about an agreement she was so sure had died off when in reality it'd been growing, manifesting into something even stronger.

He feared the strength of their bond. This woman was absolutely in love with her friend and had decided to take that plunge with her despite who they were. He praised her for being strong enough to console Mitsuko at the Eiffel Tower. They'd kissed after that, in public, and held hands in a way that might've suggested they were friends when they were so much more.

After she'd recounted her tale, Vincenzo asked if she remembered where Mitsuko had bought her ring. A simple question, to add to her story. That was the only reason he'd asked.

She'd sniffed and pulled out a necklace from inside of her coat. On the end of it dangled a beautiful ring encrusted with diamonds.

"Le Bijou de Fleur."

The Flower Jewel.

Surely, he'd imagined marrying Sylvia. It was a fairytale, but a fairytale he often fell asleep to. He'd wake up to her making him breakfast with their child playing in their front yard. He'd go to his office job, Sylvia would be cooking and cleaning for him when he returned, and at night, they'd make love with the hope of bearing a new child.

But they couldn't have that fantasy. Not yet. Maybe not ever.

Yet Émeline, Mitsuko, *they* had it. *They'd* been brave enough to join their lives together and were now happier than before. And he and Sylvia, they *could* have that, but it wouldn't happen unless he became as brave as Mitsuko had been and currently was. And what a better place to buy a ring than France? He knew she was expecting it, and if he had the rings, if he wasn't meant to ask for her hand on this trip, he'd have the chance to ask her in the future.

About telling Sylvia about his past, well, that was put on the back burners for now. Propose to her first. Then dismantle it with the truth about his sex. He hoped Laurence had kept his promise and kept his truth to himself.

"Vincenzo."

He inhaled. Luckily he hadn't been driving, otherwise he might've crashed the car.

They were in Émeline's company cars, being driven around to find a place to eat. He'd foolishly lost the address of that veteran's bakery but rediscovered it on Émeline's maps.

"Sylvia, my love, I love you more than I love myself."

No, that was too self-deprecating, and *'love'*? He'd never said that before.

"Sylvia, would you be interested in marrying me?"

Again, the self-hatred was too obvious. Had he always been like this?

"I love you, Sylvia. Please, please *marry me."*

He wanted to die.

"Vincenzo, hello," Mitsuko said. "Is this the place or isn't it?"

"Oh." He refocused on the street. "It is."

"Finally, it only took ten minutes." She ordered the driver to park close.

The bakery didn't look like a bakery owned by a war veteran. The walls were pearly white with pastel pink swirls painted near the ceiling. The lights gave off a melty gold hue, making it feel warm, and the *pastries*. The fine breads and cupcakes in the storefront, the cakes behind the counter glass that looked so beautiful, they looked fake. The chairs were petite and the signs and illustrations were written in curvy French, giving the place an air of sophistication and, dare he say, cuteness.

He immediately turned to Sylvia, who had her hands clasped together in joy.

His heart skipped. He'd buy this place, he swore to God, if it meant seeing her this in love with life. Since they'd left America, he hadn't seen her dip into her darkness. Her Moon hadn't waned. She was, to his knowledge, *happy*.

"Mitsuko! And is that Émeline?"

The man Vincenzo had encountered in the street came out. He was still covered in flour and patted himself off before greeting his former friends.

Mitsuko squinted at him. "Lieutenant Jean?"

"I'm no longer a Lieutenant, *Nurse Matsuoka*, please." He kissed Émeline on both of her cheeks. "My, it's been forever. Émeline, you're still in France?"

"I am, yes," she said. "My apologies, I have a horrible memory. It's been so long."

"Yeah, without your arm bleeding out on my work table, you…" Mitsuko stole a glance at Émeline's squeamish face, then said, "Anyway, glad to see you again."

"Thanks to you, my hand's still in working order. Two hours she worked on me." He flexed his burnt fingers. "Come, have a seat. I'll treat you. Are these your friends? Are they American? How'd you find them?"

He sat them at a long table near the front windows. On the tablecloth waited a plate of bread, cut cheese, and dipping oil, to which Vincenzo, Dominic, Luis, and Ana gobbled down without question. They were comfort food for them, but Vincenzo ate more vigorously than they did due to his nerves.

"Sylvia, I love you so very much."

No, not *"very much."* Maybe *"dearly."* No, who was he to say that?

When Jean gave them their menus, everyone looked to Émeline and Mitsuko.

"Hey, I have the literacy of a toddler," Mitsuko said, and handed their attention to Émeline.

Sylvia ordered light, but too accustomed to Vincenzo's house life, every sandwich, cookie, and bowl of ice cream got mixed into the table's community pot until everyone was sharing everyone else's meal.

They split into their own conversations. Luis and Ana talked about what they'd bought, Sylvia and Laurence spoke about the food and a bit about Laurence's relationship flourishing into something concrete, and Mitsuko and Émeline caught up with their soldier friend. Dominic stared out the window, quiet yet looking strangely optimistic.

Vincenzo swirled his olive oil with his serving spoon. He couldn't focus, but he couldn't fall into his head either. All of his thoughts were now hyperfocused on Sylvia. Should he? Shouldn't he? Should he have just dropped the subject and waited? He was twenty-four now. He didn't have much time before society considered him "undesirable" for marriage, as if such a state existed due to age.

"Vincenzo."

He jolted. "Yes?"

"Is everything okay?" Sylvia asked. "You seem distracted."

"I'm fine. Thinking. Did you need anything?"

She split one of her bread loaves. It looked like a cookie but pulled apart like warm dough. "Taste this. It's divine."

"Alright." He held out his hand.

She smiled as she held it back, squishing it between her thumb and forefinger.

He returned her smile. "Devilish."

"No, I said it was divine. Didn't you hear me?"

"I did." Scooting in his chair, he leaned over and let her hand-feed him. She was right. It tasted as nice as she made him feel.

"Get a room," Mitsuko drawled out.

Vincenzo pulled back as he worked the piece into the corner of his mouth. "Look who's talking."

Mitsuko, being the hypocrite that she was, was holding Émeline's hand, stroking it, even, on top of the table. "And? We're two friendly girls holding hands as good friends do."

"Is that what you are now?" Jean asked. "You could've fooled me. Word around the barracks was that you and this one were—"

"Just friends," Mitsuko pressed. "I'm not getting put on probation for kissing her again."

"*Again?*"

"N-not too loudly, remember," Émeline said.

"Right. Sorry."

"You're keeping it quiet," Jean surmised.

"For her sake, yes."

"I don't blame you. Here, let me treat you to a free dessert. It's the least I can do for you saving my life. You know, it's not fair, the way you all..." He held back. "It's not my place, but if I can make your lives easier, I'll do my best. Girls and boys come here, and I don't know if it's because of my demeanor or my establishment, but they enjoy this place." He motioned to two men sharing a plate of cookies together. "It's nice, helping those who have it harder than you do."

"That's the only reason I saved you," Mitsuko said, "because you were a decent human being."

"Is that all? You haven't changed!" He laughed at her, then left to whip up their free dessert.

With him gone and everyone returning to their individual conversations, Vincenzo followed Dominic's lead and day-dreamed out the window.

His jaw went slack. Across the street was a hair salon and a type of general store, neither of which he could name in English, but between the two, adorned by artificial flowers, was an old-fashioned jewelry store with a wooden sign.

Le Bijou de Fleur.

His insides went cold while his heart went warm. Not that he had to copy Mitsuko and buy his rings here, but Émeline's happiness, he *wanted* that. He wanted Sylvia to know that, if she were to have him, she'd be protected, taken care of, and happy for the rest of her long, beautiful life.

Shoving a whole loaf of bread in his mouth, Vincenzo excused himself to the bathroom, slipped into the kitchen instead, and escaped into the alley for the jewelry store.

Chapter 28: Nighttime Refresher

Three reasons why Sylvia was suspicious of Vincenzo:

1. He was spacing out. Sylvia, *she* spaced out. Mitsuko had spaced out when she'd thought she lost Émeline when Émeline had actually been lost without her. Vincenzo, Vincenzo didn't space out.

2. He wasn't eating well. He stuffed his face with bread so quickly, she worried he was going to choke.

3. He left for the bathroom wearing his coat and hat.

She drank her leftover soup that'd come with somebody's meal. He'd been acting strange this whole trip, touching her and being more flirtatious than usual, taking her ice skating when they both knew they weren't the couple to do that. He was acting like a whole other person she didn't know how to act around.

Mitsuko said something that made Émeline laugh. Ana, who was sitting across from them, turned away and muttered to Luis. Sylvia didn't know if Vincenzo had noticed, but she and Luis had been buzzing like bees beside them. When Dominic brushed Laurence's shoulder, Ana had something to say. When Émeline played with the tips of Mitsuko's fingers, she'd bite her inner cheek and take a sip from her drink.

Sylvia thought about confronting her about her passive-aggressiveness but refrained from doing so. She had to take Mitsuko's advice and only focus on what *she* could change.

She turned back to her friends, to Mitsuko. "I assume everything has gone steady between you and Émeline?"

"Not too fast. We've been working out what to do now that we're back together."

"And what are you planning to do? Are you going to take vacations to see her?"

"That's the thing." Mitsuko played with her cake, fork scraping through the icing. "Don't be cross if I don't get on the boat with you."

"What?" both Sylvia and Laurence asked.

"It's...We're still deciding," Mitsuko explained. "We're here for, what, another four days, yeah? We have time to figure out what we're really doing."

"So you're thinking about living here, forever?" Laurence asked, voice pitching like he was in the Kitten. "You're not gonna get back on the boat?"

She lowered her eyes, in shame for considering it. "I love you all, and the Black Kitten means everything to me. It saved me after the War. It got me to where I am now." She took Émeline's hand. "But now I'm back where I feel the most like myself, where I left so many of my memories. I don't know if I can just *leave*. Plus, you know, I have someone tethering me down now."

"We still need to talk about it," Émeline said.

"A-and I don't want to ruin the trip with the news," Mitsuko added frantically, "but...it's okay, isn't it? If I stayed?"

'Absolutely not,' Sylvia wanted to shout. *You mustn't. Think about how sad Bobby would be if you were to leave.*

We're your family, we need you, you can't just up and leave us."

But she couldn't be so selfish. If Émeline was truly Mitsuko's partner, she deserved to be happy with her. If it'd been Vincenzo living in a little villa in Sicily and Sylvia had to choose with whom to stay, she, while it would hurt immensely, would have only one choice to choose from.

Laurence sipped his coffee. "I had the feeling this was gonna happen. I knew right when you saw this little girl that you weren't coming back with us. And because of, what, love? Gag."

Despite the bitterness in his tone, both Sylvia and Mitsuko smiled, for if Mitsuko were to follow through with the move, all of them seemed to be on the same page with where they stood.

"Whatever you choose, darling," Sylvia said. "We know you love us, and you know we love you. Whatever you do and wherever you go, we'll always support you."

Mitsuko smiled. "Thank you."

"Thank you for understanding, Sylvia, Laurence." Émeline bowed her head. "Thank you for being so kind to her. I know I haven't known many of you for very long, but I'm glad she has such good friends."

"Of course," Sylvia said.

"But you *must* write," Laurence said.

"Oh, yes," Sylvia agreed. "Write, and make calls."

"I don't think that exists," Mitsuko said.

"No, they do," Luis said. "They invented it last year. Transatlantic phone calls. I read about it in the paper."

"How do they invent a call?" Ana asked.

As Luis tried explaining it to her, Émeline whispered to Mitsuko, and Mitsuko promptly spat out a mouthful of milk.

"What's wrong?" Sylvia looked behind her, but all she saw was a food store, a hair salon that reminded her of Clara, and a store she couldn't name.

"Uh, nothing," she said. "Just...remembered a joke." She whispered more to Émeline. Émeline nodded apologetically.

"Course he would've," she said.

Five minutes later, Vincenzo came back, out of breath and pulling off his jacket and hat. "Sorry about that. Couldn't find the damn bathroom. Waiter sent me around the building to find it."

He sat roughly next to Sylvia and started eating like everything was normal, but Sylvia knew. She knew something was upsetting him.

She kept her eyes on him for the rest of dinner. His hand never left his coat pocket.

——◇——

It'd begun to snow, lessening both Sylvia and Vincenzo's need to see every shop and attraction France had to offer, but her friends still wanted that vacation experience. Laurence and Dominic, they continued their tour of French museums, and Ana had yet to finish shopping, so she and Luis meandered through the streets hand in hand.

Mitsuko and Émeline retired to their room, as did Sylvia and Vincenzo. Sylvia was tired, or her brain was, and Vincenzo recognized that and retired with her at six.

He paced in the living room, then caught movement out of the window before pacing once again.

"You're okay, aren't you?" Sylvia asked.

He nodded too heavily. "Are you hungry?"

"Well, since we just ate…"

"Oh. Right."

She played with the buttons of her button-down. She had no idea how men wore these without suffocating. "I'm going to take a bath."

"Okay. Have fun." He looked up. "I mean—"

She smiled teasingly. "I'll be sure to do so."

She loved their bathroom. Wide, with translucent windows, marble walls, and ivory tiles. The towels stayed warm by these fantastic little towel radiators, a concept that was common in Europe, according to Émeline. They kept your towels warm all day long and wrapped you in a hug when you exited the bath.

She sighed in relief as she disrobed from her starchy boy clothes and slipped into the tub. She drew lazy circles in the sudsy water with one finger, trying to catch her reflection between the bubbles.

A knock rapped on the door.

She tightened her knees together. She saw a wisp of Vincenzo's hair behind the door.

"I'm naked," she warned him.

The hair disappeared.

"But you can come in," she added.

He came back, hands still in his pockets, shoulders high like he was hiding from her.

"How bashful," she said. "What happened to all that confidence you had when you were ice skating?"

"Waxes and wanes, I suppose." He took out the step stool in the corner of the room and sat it beside the tub.

Sylvia brought her knees up to her chin. "Wanna come in?"

"Perhaps tomorrow," he said, then, "or tonight."

"You usually get cleaned up in the morning. Why the sudden change?"

His hand ran up the nape of her neck. "Maybe I'm planning on doing something to you tonight that'll require you to take a second bath."

Her mouth popped open, and his reddening face made her laugh into her bubbles. "I've never heard you propose it so explicitly before."

"You're aware that I'm running a bit in circles at the moment."

"Why? Why're you so nervous? You know you don't have to do anything with me tonight." She twiddled her fingers through the bubbles. "I have my hand."

Vincenzo smiled forlornly and took her hand, playing with her palm and the inner parts of her fingers until he was giving her a massage. She noticed the faint scars broken into his skin from strikes of rage. They looked so old compared to when she'd first met him. Even then, they felt nice to the touch.

His lips felt different with her in a bath. The heat from the steam clouded her thoughts until they mixed into a batch of nothing but warm, wet sensations.

He kissed her several times, each peck quicker than the last. She leaned up to elongate his kisses, but he wouldn't let her. A tease, even when drowning in unexplained anxiety.

"I love you," she whispered into him.

He pecked her once more before getting up. She waited for him to say it back, but he stared at her like she had something on her face. She rubbed her cheek just in case.

"I love you, too." He said it so slowly that she had to focus on every single word. She hid her mouth underneath the bubbles.

"Take your time," he then said, then folded her towel out of the way and departed into the bedroom.

Waiting for him to be out of earshot, Sylvia plunged her face underneath the bubbles and moaned. She felt his hands on her like he was still there. Would it be rude to ask for more touches like that? Elsewhere, perhaps? Hopefully, soon, he'd be comfortable enough for her to do the same to *him*, touching him for long periods of time, running her hands down the muscles of his back, down that chest always hidden from her...

She submerged her whole head into the water. First fantasizing about marriage, now wondering how his naked body felt? She needed to calm down before she got too ahead of herself.

It wasn't wise to keep your expectations high.

Chapter 29: Vincenzo's Question

He wanted his cat.

He wanted to snuggle against her black, furry neck and give her kisses, reminding himself to breathe, breathe, fucking *breathe.* Everything would be alright.

He'd trapped himself in the bedroom, pacing more erratically than ever. He even started rearranging furniture like some nesting bird. He made the bed, adjusted the flowers in their vase. The rug wasn't centered, so he needed to fix that, and the sunset was hurting his eyes, so he played with the curtains until he got frustrated and collapsed into bed.

He pushed his hair back, staring up at the ceiling. He hated how unworthy he felt. Back home, to sort out his feelings, he'd confide in *Nonna* or Campo and discuss the proposal in detail. He'd show them the ring and they'd tell him there was nothing wrong with proposing now.

He fished out the velvet box. He didn't know if he'd chosen right, he'd been so nervous. The jeweler hadn't spoken any English and he was second-guessing this silver ring as opposed to the many gold ones she'd shown him. While Sylvia mostly wore pearls and silver jewelry, what woman didn't want a gold engagement ring?

That was a whole other disaster. Did engagement rings count as wedding rings? Would he have to buy another one? It hadn't crossed his mind until after he sat back down at the bakery, but at that point, he'd been too focused on not crushing the box in his hand.

He'd return it. He'd throw it into the Seine or sell it to another man more put together than himself. Sylvia was ready for marriage, he knew that, but was he? He was a gangster. He'd be lucky to survive into his thirties.

He thought about his mother and father and how much they fought behind closed doors. His father would hit her during arguments and play it off like it was normal. Then he thought about his grandmother. He didn't remember much about his grandfather because the man had never spoken to or acknowledged him apart from birthdays. *Nonna* had taken care of everything back then, even his funeral.

He held the box to his heart. If she were here, he'd ask to go through the photographs of his parents' and grandparents' weddings back in Sicily. The grainy texture of the yellowed photos, the faded family trees written on the back of group pictures. They were such big events, bringing in dozens of aunts and uncles living on the island. Now, if he and Sylvia were to marry back in New York, how would his parents handle it? Would they even know?

His nose itched. The ties he had with his mother and father were frayed—at times, they felt completely torn—but despite everything, he still wanted them at his wedding.

And this was all if Sylvia said yes.

"Of course she'll say yes," someone in his brain said. *"She loves us, she's been with us for almost a year. How could she say no?"*

"Well, what if she hates us?" another someone said quite coldly. *"We've kept our sex from her for so long, both literally and figuratively. How hurt she might feel."*

"Throw the ring away," a third someone said.

He hid the box and shut away the voices.

"Sylvia, I have something to tell you."

"Sylvia, you know…"

The door opened, and he sprang up, folding down his sweater that'd rolled up his stomach.

Sylvia came in wearing only a towel. "Hi."

He nodded. He should've said, *'Hi,'* back. What was he doing? "Let me, uh, give you some privacy."

"You can stay. If you want," she added, and showed him the door, slightly ajar but not closed.

He thought about it, then sat back down.

She smiled brighter and closed the door. He'd chosen right.

He watched, feeling guilty for feeling envious that she could do this in front of him and he couldn't. Her movements were slow and seductive, letting her hands fall through her lace and silk. She crossed one ankle over the other as she took her time picking out her nightwear.

He couldn't take it anymore. He needed something to give. "S-Sylvia."

She turned, nightgown chosen.

"Did you want to go anywhere tonight?"

"I don't think so." She slipped into the white slip and a lavender night robe that felt nice in his hands. Her bath had curled her hair like she'd put hot curlers in. Her skin looked as soft and pink as a baby.

"Sylvia."

She turned again.

"Come here. Please."

She did, and when she went to kiss him or sit on his lap, he leaned back and patted the space next to him. "Sit."

She did, her weight gravitating him into her.

The shivers came back. Why couldn't he control this? Why couldn't he make it go away? This was like Campo's mansion all over again, locked in a room at fourteen and forced to...

No. He wasn't being forced to do anything tonight. Tonight, he had a choice of letting someone know.

He took her hand. "I want to tell you something."

"What is it?"

He faced her properly and tried not breaking eye contact with her. "I want you to know that I cannot describe how much I'm in love with you. Ever since we met, you've changed my world. You've changed *me*. I never want you to meet the man I was two years ago. I was ruthless and unforgiving. I did anything to make sure I stayed afloat. Meeting you has made me tempered, and kind, and...*loving*. You've given me my firsts in love, and I can't repay you for that."

Sylvia tilted her head to one side. She gripped his hand harder. "Thank you. I'm glad I'm with you, too. I'm glad I saved you as much as you saved me. I don't know if I'd still be here if it weren't for you. Rather than being angry, last year I was so miserable that...I won't go into it, but know those feelings faded the more time I spent with you."

Which way to go now? He had two impossible questions to ask. "So," he started, "uhm, I wanted to tell you, and you need to promise me that, whether you hate me or are disgusted by me, I need you to promise that you'll never, ever tell anyone, okay? This'll be just between us."

That smile he loved so much disappeared. She'd heard something she didn't want to hear. "I promise," she said.

He closed his eyes. Could he do this with his eyes closed?

He said, "You know how, when you were born, you were considered a man. You were treated as a man, and expected to do as one expects of a man, like all the men in your family."

She nodded thoughtfully.

"But you never felt like being a man, or a boy, even when you were small, so you decided to drift. You started dressing differently and talking differently. You took on the role you saw in your dreams, and that confused a lot of people. It broke them away from you. It hurt."

"It did."

"I didn't know that when I met you, but when I did, when you told me, I didn't see you any differently. You were still Sylvia Belmonte, the girl who played the piano at the Black Kitten, the girl I fell in love with."

She moved in even closer. He did, too.

"So, with all that out of the way, I need to tell you. That I. I understand."

"I'm glad you do."

"No, I—" He clenched his jaw. It'd been going so well, too. Why had he screwed up the most crucial part? "I mean, that's to say, I didn't take the job at the Black Kitten because nobody wanted to. I mean, it's true, not many men wanted to take the position. But I…*relate*…very strongly to what you and the performers stand for. I'm…"

He shuddered. What the hell was he trying to say?

He just needed to say it.

Just say it to her.

Say it.

Tell her.

"Sylvia, when I was born, I was born a girl."

Her head lifted, eyes widening. In betrayal, likely. In pain. Distrust.

He could no longer endure it and looked away. The blood began draining from his head to his ears, his brain detaching from his body and floating away. "Y-you're the only person I've ever told. My family knows, and Campo, he knew. My father told him, even when I begged him not to tell anyone. He knew how it made me feel and used it as leverage against me. But Campo, you know, Campo knows how to act. He treated me right. He let me dress the way I wanted and switched from my old name to my new one *instantly*. He accepted me into the Family as Vincenzo and nothing else, and I was able to live out my life the way I wanted to."

His head felt too light, so he took his hand off of her and leveled himself on the bed. "I wanted to tell you, for so long. I'm sorry I kept it from you until now."

Only when he stopped rambling did Sylvia finally take her eyes off of him. She stared down at the floor, thinking.

He left her to her thoughts. He'd told someone. He'd done it.

"So," she said, "so, you're like me, but the opposite."

"Yeah," he said, "I am."

And she hugged him. A full embrace, hands rubbing over his back and shoulders, their beating chests becoming one.

The weight he'd been carrying since walking into the Black Kitten and thinking, *I don't belong here,* disintegrated from her touch.

She sniffled into him. "It's okay," she told him.

He squeezed her harder. "I'm sorry."

"Why're you sorry?"

"I was a coward. I never told you or let you touch me."

"That's okay, baby. You were protecting yourself. You didn't know. *I* didn't know."

"Still, I'm sorry."

"Don't be. I understand." She touched his lips. "No wonder we haven't had sex yet, huh?"

He nervous-laughed. "Right? I mean, did you ever suspect anything? Anything at all?"

"No, never. Maybe only that you liked men as well as women, being that you went to the Black Kitten so often."

That really got him to laugh. "Honestly, that's what I thought before all this happened. Turns out I just wanted to *be* like them."

"Oh, Vincenzo." She sighed audibly. "You scared me, goodness! I thought you were breaking things off with me."

"What? Really?"

"Yes! *'Oh, I love you, and I'll always love you'*. But this, sweetheart, I—" She fell back into bed, one hand over her forehead. "Can I ask you a few questions?"

He fell beside her. "Go ahead."

"Well, I never suspected anything. How did it come about? With your work profession, you'd think it'd be impossible."

"It felt like that for some time. Before I grew into this body, I used to steal my neighbors' clothes. We'd run through the streets like dirty vagabonds, me and the neighborhood boys. None of us understood it back then. Then I started growing. I lashed out, got angry at my parents for things I couldn't voice. I didn't know what was wrong. Years went by and I accumulated this unnatural anger towards myself. I was growing into my father.

"Then Campo found him. He was tested and joined the Family quite suddenly. I was so envious that I ended up doing lackey work for some of the lower-class men. I did everything they asked of me. Soon Campo heard about me from both my father and the whispers around the docks. When I was fourteen or so, he took me aside and asked me questions."

His fingernails dug into his upper hand, and Sylvia took those hands in hers, calming him. "I was so scared. It was the first time I met him, so I couldn't *lie*. I thought he'd kill me. So, I told him everything. I told him how I was a girl but didn't want to be, that I was strong but only as a boy. And then, instead of casting me out, he gave me a job: Stalk this man who owed him money, find out where he lived, get the name of his wife, and report back. Truthfully, he probably knew all of this, it was just a test to prove my loyalty. When I completed it and reported back, he started treating me like one of his men, just like that. It wasn't a question for him to call me Vincenzo or treat me right. Everything was perfect."

He paused. The memories gnarled their way inside of his torn-apart chest.

"What happened then?" Sylvia asked.

"When I was eighteen, Campo offered to take me up to Canada to meet with a doctor he knew. The doctor was under the table—he'd lost his license after deserting in the War—but he did work for Campo when he needed to scar someone up or change the features of a man's face.

"When we got there, he..." He touched his upper chest. "He sort of...*cut* away my chest, draining and scooping out all the fat that was there. You've seen my mother and grandmother, you could imagine what I needed to hide. I'd worn corsets and sweater upon sweater to hide them, but after this procedure, when I woke up a few hours later, they were *gone*. It wasn't the best surgery and there're lumps and scars that won't go away, but the operation was like night and day.

"After that, it was like I'd been resurrected. Our men suddenly thought I'd fully transitioned into a man. The new recruits weren't told as per Campo's orders. I rose in rank. I became respected, and feared. I became Vincenzo DiFiore, and then I met you."

Sylvia closed her eyes, imagining it. "How harrowing. Do Luis and Dominic know?"

"No."

"Does the state?"

"Campo altered my birth certificate on my eighteenth birthday. Not even my mother knows about that."

"How wonderful, to change that part of yourself."

"If I asked, he could do the same for you."

"I couldn't."

"I could."

A beat. "Would it be expensive, or dangerous?"

"The least expensive and dangerous thing we do."

"Then I wouldn't mind if it was altered. That would make things a lot easier. We'd be seen as a real couple by the state."

Right. He'd gotten one speech out of the way and had just barely survived. Now the final part. "Speaking of." He sat up and controlled the wobble in his arms. "If I could jump in here. As you're processing this, may I ask *you* a question?"

"You may."

He shoved his hands back into his pockets until the stitching popped. After pushing through one of the most heart-wrenching reveals he had, this question had become world's easier. "Can you sit up for me?"

She did, with his help.

He wiped his palms of sweat. He wondered if he'd ever not feel nervous around her when he was exposing his heart. "I should've prepared more for this, but I'm afraid if I don't do it now, I won't find the resolve to ask you again."

"What is it?"

He braced himself, tried to come up with something better than what he'd been rehearsing all day, then threw it all away and knelt down on one knee.

She covered her mouth.

"Sylvia, you're so lovely, and wonderful, and patient with me, and I can't imagine going on without you. You accept even the worst parts of me, something that still eludes me to this day, because you somehow see the best in me every single day we're together. You're perfect, wholly and truly, and I want to keep that love with me forever." He shakily took out the velvet box. "I know this's rash and that we're too much of misfits and rule-breakers to have this go smoothly. And I know our parents won't ever approve, but—"

"Yes."

He looked up.

She touched him, touched the box. "Yes, please," she said. "Don't finish. I already know that it's yes."

The setting sun caught on her watering eyes, making them shine like the jewels in his hand. "It'll always be yes," she promised.

He choked on his breath, on his gasp, and he fell forwards and hugged her, making that final connection with the person he trusted and loved most.

"Oh, Vincenzo," she said, crying now. "I love you."

"I love you, too. I love you so much." He held her tighter, affirming the belief that they could fall and love and get married and have every opportunity anyone else had.

"I can't believe it," she cried. "I won't."

"Please believe it. I may or may not want to hear you brag about this to your friends later." He helped place the ring on her ring finger.

She ran her thumb around the diamonds. "Why?"

"Pardon?"

"I've been trying to be more confident with myself, but I never thought this would ever happen to me. It's hard to process the reason why."

"Because this's been real ever since I met you. Since our first date, I knew I wanted to dedicate my life to you. You've brightened me up in ways I didn't know was possible. You've given me back my happiness." He kissed her ringed hand. "You deserve this. You deserve happiness."

She covered her mouth to cry quietly to herself, but Vincenzo left kisses all over her to show it was okay to cry in front of him. Soon she did, and he held her until she poured out every tear she had.

She lay down beside him, exhausted and with a delirious smile on her face.

He dabbed her face with the back of his fingers. "You okay?"

"Ask me in a few years when we're married with our baby."

"Just one? I pictured at least two."

"Two, huh? I don't think my belly could take that." She rubbed her stomach. "Before I met you, I would've...I don't know if I'd be here. It's a morbid thought, but with how I've been treated, I didn't think I was worthy of this. Paris, your parties, these friendships. It's like a dream. How I feel about myself is going to be a hardship I'll need to work through, but I'm glad I have you with me. Forever?" she then asked. "Do I have you forever?"

"If you'll have me."

"Oh, Vincenzo." She kissed him. "Thank you."

He gave her his thanks by dragging his lips down her chin and exposed collarbone, tasting the hint of strawberry on her skin.

"*Vincenzo*," she suddenly moaned, and he pulled back, realizing he'd gone too far.

For him. Not for her. Staring up at him with lust-filled eyes, she scrunched up her toes, waiting for him to act on what he'd been teasing her with.

"I guess I don't have any more excuses," he said.

"You still don't have to, though. You're not obligated to do anything. I just didn't want you to go any further than I can take. I'm very sensitive right now."

He pulled on his turtleneck. He shouldn't have still disliked sex after telling her his secret, but he did. Or he didn't get it, not as well as she did. But he also didn't want this fear controlling every decision he made and haunting him with his inadequacy.

"I want to try," he said. "I want to experiment again."

"That's all I can ask for."

"I should be able to do more."

"No, this amount is perfect." She sat upright and placed her ringed hand over his chest. "Lay down for me?"

Like he could say no.

She straddled him, putting as little pressure on his crotch as she could. Her hand was like a feather over the folds of his sweater, tracing the outline of him before retracing up to his cheek. The cold ring kissed his jawline.

"This feel good?" she asked him.

He nodded and fell into her touch. He wished that sex could only be about touching, not so much inserting or penetrating. How content he felt with just her hands feeling him up and igniting the belief that he was alive.

"Then, may I?" Her hand went to the end of his sweater.

He helped her get himself out of his first layer.

"Oh," she said, "you wear a corset?"

"As a safety precaution, to make sure everything stays flat."

"How smart."

"I try." He'd chosen one of his dark corsets that evening that helped suck everything in, even his hips. It was worn from use, loose around the edges.

Steeling himself, he undid the laces down his last piece of armor and exposed his bare chest to her.

She gasped.

Honestly, he expected a more horrified reaction. Two thick lines of melded skin crossed his chest, taking away most of the fat along with his nipples. He'd wanted to keep them so he could feign a fighting injury, but the doctor had needed to work fast. He'd used illegal anesthesia in an abandoned warehouse that didn't belong to him. Now, Vincenzo was left with an uneven, lumpy, nipple-less chest.

He wouldn't have traded it for all the money to his name.

"I expected so much more," she said, regaining her voice. "It looks so much better than I imagined. Vincenzo, it looks like *my* chest."

"That was kind of the goal."

She stared for a few more seconds, mouth quirked in a curious smile. She took in the tiny hairs leading up to his belly button, the bareness of his arms. "You're quite handsome," she ended up saying.

"Thank you."

She touched his hips. "Do you..." She gave a quick glance down. "Want me to? Down there?"

He gulped again, mouth watering too much for someone whose throat had been too dry to speak.

Then, with a need to have her, he nodded.

"Okay." She slipped off the bed to her knees. "Tell me if I go too far. I know how it feels when someone touches you in a way you're not comfortable with. I don't want you to experience that."

"I trust you," he promised.

"Thank you," she said, and began undoing his pants.

Alarm bells in his brain rang off, but he manually shut them down. She wasn't an intruder seeking to hurt or embarrass him. He had to keep telling himself that.

But by the time he kicked off his shoes and trousers, he had to close his eyes. He was naked, he didn't have to face the body that made him feel so outcast yet. That was only for her, her treat.

What hit him first was the airy openness between his legs. Her breath made his hairs stand on end.

Then the sounds.

And her *tongue*.

The indecent slurping and moaning she made set him off. She opened him up and dug her nose into him. With both arms over his head, he panted and tried to conceal the noises coming from his own mouth, but she was so *good* at it, so talented at cracking him open and spilling out his inner heat.

And what shocked him the most was that he wasn't minding this as much as his brain was telling him to. His stress melted into her tongue like sugar as she licked and sucked away his doubts.

He spread open his legs a bit more. The sensations were rising. She continued at a different pace. Her tongue, licking just the tip, before her fingers fondled their way inside of him.

He threw back his head. His mind went blank. Her fingers thrust in a motion so fast it was like torture. His knees trembled. He swallowed back a lustful moan. A release was coming.

Pulling back, Sylvia kissed his navel as her fingers worked faster in and out of him.

He grasped at the sheets and bit down a loud moan.

"It's okay," she told him.

It was, wasn't it? His body was telling him it wasn't, but he couldn't go against her soundproof logic.

So, letting himself experience what everyone was allowed to feel, he closed his eyes, tightened his knees around her, and came.

His brain fuzzed up like radio static, the connection momentarily lost. He hadn't done this many times, touching himself with the intent to cum, but never had it felt so right. His body wasn't seizing in disgust. It simply felt *good*.

Sylvia kept inside of him until his senses returned and he needed to push away.

She licked up the leftover cum from her fingers. "You okay?"

"Yeah," he said, surprising himself.

"Feel good?"

"Yeah. It's intense, you know? I don't know if I can do that as often as you'd like."

"You don't have to do anything." She rested her head against his thigh. "I'm happy it felt good."

"Well, it was done by you."

"What a compliment." She touched herself. "Should I say anything?"

"No, just...hold on." He pulled on his discarded sweater. "Too exposing."

"That's alright."

He hid his remaining half beneath the covers. "Okay."

"Okay. If you want." She shook her rear like a puppy. "If not, I do have my hand."

"Well, when you ask that nicely." He kissed her hand. "Get ready."

She almost jogged for the bathroom and came back with a bottle of lotion and a hand towel. He remembered that this was a step in the process, but when she started coating her fingers, he took the bottle himself and did it for her.

He kept his face relaxed as he played inside of her. Finally back in control, he satiated her need for him. He fingered her, sucked her off, then tried doing both at the same time. When she started grinding against him in a desperate need to release, he found himself watching her, intrigued by her reaction. He hoped he hadn't looked this desperate when she was playing with him.

"Oh, *Vincenzo*."

"I know," he moaned.

"I love you. You're so good to me."

This time, he didn't hesitate on reciprocating her feelings.

———◇———

He awoke with his heart pounding. It was pitch black outside. An owl hooted in a nearby tree.

He tried to return to his dreams when he heard what'd likely woken him up: a knocking. Someone was waiting for them out in the hall.

Both he and Sylvia had gone to bed nude, so he had to redress and slip out of their bedroom without waking her. His memories from last night smeared with a new fear that something was wrong. Not even the street lights were lit outside.

As he walked to the door, he realized he didn't have a weapon on him and grabbed a knife from the kitchen sink. "Who's there?" he called out.

Behind the front door, a woman sniffled.

"It's us," Mitsuko said. "Open up, if you're decent."

He dropped the knife and unlocked the door.

Standing before him was a composed Mitsuko and a crying Émeline. They were ready for bed but had on matching bathrobes and slippers for their midnight walk.

"What's wrong?" he asked.

"A lot," Mitsuko said. "Émeline has something important to tell you."

Chapter 30: Émeline's Secret

Sylvia awoke to the sound of heels tapping in circles, then people whispering in secret.

She was alone in bed, and the bedroom door was cracked open. A stream of light not from the Sun or any of the lamps was hitting her cheek.

She got dressed in her slippers and bathrobe and peeked around the door.

She must've missed something. A letter, a meeting. All of her friends—Laurence, Dominic, Mitsuko, Émeline, Luis, even Ana—were in their living room. Laurence and Dominic were standing near the fire. Ana was sitting on the rocking chair while Luis paced in the kitchen. Vincenzo had just handed Émeline a cup of tea. She looked grief-stricken, like she'd been wailing for hours. Mitsuko had an arm around her back.

Sylvia let the door creak to announce herself. "What's going on?"

Whatever she'd said sent Émeline back into tears. Vincenzo sighed and went to tend to the fire. "I was just about to come get you."

Sylvia took the poor girl's hands in support of whatever she was going through. "Hush, dear. It's alright."

"It's…Well, I don't think I can say it's not bad," Mitsuko said. "Ém and I were talking."

"I'm so sorry," Émeline blubbered.

"It's alright," Sylvia said, not knowing what else to say.

"But now that we're all here, now's a good time to explain things," Vincenzo said. "Émeline, what is it that you wanted to tell us?"

She blew her nose. "I've been trying to find a way to explain it. It was all so sudden and I was too afraid to speak up, but after eating with everyone today, I…"

Sensing that Vincenzo wanted answers by whatever means necessary, Sylvia beckoned for him to sit. He did and took her free hand, rubbing the ring still on her finger.

Goodness, she'd almost forgotten about that. Everything he'd told her, the promises he'd sworn to keep. She sucked in her lips, hoping her friends' sharp eyes hadn't noticed the diamond band.

"Want me to explain?" Mitsuko asked.

"No, I…I'll try." She wiped her eyes. "About three weeks ago, I received a telegram from a Mr. Campo d'Antonio asking me about my escort services. He wanted me to lead a group of his acquaintances around Paris for seven-hundred dollars. I thought the proposal was…off, and a bit perplexing. My services weren't worth that much, so I thought it was a trick and declined the generous offer. Then, the next day, I received another telegram mentioning Mitsuko's name."

At the sound of her name, Mitsuko shivered. "I never told anyone about her. There's no way he could've known about our relationship."

"And I never referred to you after the War ended," Émeline said. "Not even my parents knew, so it frightened me that this strange, wealthy man from America knew about us.

"I was afraid he was going to expose my past and wrote back inquiring about the offer. He said he was going to send over a boy he saw as his own son and many of his acquaintances from New York. He said he was afraid for your well-being, especially you." She looked up at Vincenzo. "He seemed to think you were in serious danger."

Vincenzo leaned in to better see her. His expression was incalculable, eyes unblinking. "Why did he tell you this?"

"He said you were, I don't remember the word, but he explained your profession and your lover, *you*," she said to Sylvia. "He explained that someone was targeting you and that you needed to leave the country."

"But why?"

The question tensed her up. "I-I don't know. Something about a talk with Sev...Sevi—"

"Severo," Vincenzo answered.

She nodded. "I believe Campo told you that this was a vacation meant to celebrate your birthday with a small job to accomplish on his behalf."

"He did."

She dabbed her eyes. "He said that was a lie. He told me not to tell you until you got suspicious, but I can't do it anymore. He said you're not to come back to America. You're all to live here now."

Vincenzo's hand slipped away from Sylvia's as he stood, knees locked as he processed the news.

"He said *what*?" Ana asked. "That's preposterous! I have a child back home. He can't do this!"

"And I have my family," Laurence said. "How could he do this?"

"*Why* would he do this?" Sylvia added. "I thought..." She looked up to Vincenzo. "I thought he liked us."

Vincenzo walked to the windows. His vacant eyes stared out to the street beneath him. He slowly closed the curtains.

"I'm sorry," Émeline said. "Mitsuko told me you're in those gangs I've heard about in the newspapers, so I was scared to speak up until now. And it's been so hard, keeping this from you, and seeing Mitsuko after so many years..." She started crying again.

"That's about it," Mitsuko concluded, "so we're absolutely fucked."

"But he can't keep us here, can he?" Luis asked. "I mean, Ana and I, we're not part of this. We have our baby back home. We have a house. We can't leave all that behind just because Campo and Severo are fighting."

Vincenzo pulled back his hair as if to tie it up. He let his face breathe, took in a harsh breath. Then he stormed into their bedroom.

"Vincenzo?"

He came back with a bundle of papers. He sorted through them as he walked. "There's no return date. He hasn't given us a ship to return home on. There's nothing scheduled." He slapped the end of the couch. "Fuck!"

"I'm sorry," Émeline said. "He told me to tell you at the end of your trip, but I couldn't withhold it any longer. I didn't think it was fair."

"This isn't your fault, dear," Laurence said. "You were caught up in something much bigger than yourself."

Vincenzo searched through his papers once more for any answers to Campo's decisions. When he couldn't find any, he then tossed all of them into the fire. He, Luis, and Dominic watched them crinkled into themselves and burn.

"We have enough money to get back, right?" Luis asked.

"I have some," Dominic said.

"Please, use what he sent me," Émeline said. "Seeing all that money in my bank account makes me sick."

Vincenzo stuffed his hands in his pockets, watching the fire burn until a log broke in two. Sylvia saw him clenching them, giving himself more scars. "We'll figure this out in the morning," he said. "You can all leave now. Dominic, Luis, we'll leave at six. I need to send a telegram to Campo, then find...fuck, *seven* tickets back to America all on the same boat as soon as possible."

Luis and Dominic agreed dutifully and left with their lovers in tow. Mitsuko helped Émeline out, but before leaving, she caught Sylvia's eyes and grabbed Laurence's sleeve. She pointed at the ring on her own hand, then at Sylvia.

Sylvia should've known she couldn't hide this from them. They cared too much for her. Giving in, she showed them the ring.

Laurence covered his mouth and ran back to give her a hug. Mitsuko joined in but kept an eye on Vincenzo. His shoulders were heaving now.

"Congratulations," Laurence whispered.

"I can't believe he really did it," Mitsuko said. "Ém told me he'd asked her where I'd bought her ring. Didn't know the stick in the mud could pull it off."

"I can't believe it, either. I wish I could've announced it under better circumstances."

"It must be a Kitten tradition, to propose at the worst possible time." Mitsuko nudged Laurence. "You're next."

"Not on your life," he said, and gave Sylvia another hug. "We'll talk about this tomorrow."

"Of course. Goodnight."

"Goodnight."

When they were alone, Sylvia walked up to Vincenzo by the fire and held his hand. She'd only met Campo twice, but even though he was a gangster, and a powerful one at that, with how highly Vincenzo talked about him, she didn't *mistrust* him. He had their best interests at heart. He protected them. He *loved* Vincenzo.

"I don't know what to say," Vincenzo whispered. "I'm...angry. I'm confused. I'm pissed."

"Émeline said he was worried about us. He must only be doing this for your safety. *Our* safety."

"But to never *speak* to me about it. I thought I was his right-hand man. I thought..." He sighed. "I guess I thought wrong."

"I'm sorry." She helped bring him to bed. She didn't want to leave him alone as his world was falling apart and find him hitting the couch or ambling the streets at three in the morning.

"I've never lied to him," he vented as he tucked himself in, "not once. I've always been upfront with him, I did everything he asked. To endanger and inconvenience us like this, to send us away without explanation. Luis has a *child*, for God's sake. If he's so worried about my father, he should've talked to him, not sent *me* away."

"I agree. It'll be okay. We'll go back home and you'll be able to sort everything out."

"Yeah," he said unconvincingly, "if I'm even welcomed back into the Family."

To make him feel better, she let her hand fall over his upper chest, tickling him.

He took her fingers and brought each one of them to his lips. His mouth lingered over her ring.

"Mitsuko saw," Sylvia said.

"I heard." He looked away. "I'm scared of you wearing this when we go back home."

Her full heart panged only for it to swell back with his love and concern. "We'll be okay."

"But what if we aren't? I don't want my father hurting you."

"He won't. Campo probably panicked from all those attacks and didn't know what else to do. You'll talk with him and smooth things over, then we'll go back to the Kitten and everything will be normal."

He sighed, so Sylvia kept repeating her lies until she believed them herself.

Chapter 31: Returning Home

Before the Sun rose, Vincenzo, Luis, Dominic, and Émeline left for the nearest telegram office.

He'd assured Émeline that she didn't have to come—their force and presence would get the job done—but she insisted. She, like Vincenzo, hadn't slept after hearing Campo had abandoned them.

He'd betrayed him, there was no point in arguing that. He'd stranded them on a deserted island without so much as a wave goodbye. Vincenzo had *Nonna* to take care of, his family, his *cat*. He couldn't believe Campo had cut all that away from him without a break in character.

He wondered if he should've taken this as an order, but he hadn't been "ordered" to do anything. This was his vacation and he deserved to come back home when he felt like it.

At six that morning, he sent the telegram.

FOUND OUT THE TRUTH.
WE REQUEST TO RETURN HOME.
WE WISH TO SEE OUR FAMILIES.
WHAT IS YOUR STANCE ON THE MATTER.
-VINCENZO DIFIORE

He hadn't delivered a telegram like this before, having to wait so long for it to reach the receiver. The officer owner said it would've only taken a few minutes for a telegram to reach America. They insisted that Campo must've been thinking long and hard about what to say, or that he might've been out of the house.

Two hours passed. Vincenzo sent Émeline away to spend what little time she had left with Mitsuko and Luis to buy their tickets home. He didn't want to waste any more time. He almost left with them to clear his head before the machine spat out Campo's response.

STAY THERE.
IF MONEY IS AN ISSUE, I'LL SEND MORE.
DON'T WORRY ABOUT FAMILY. I'LL TAKE CARE OF THEM.
-C. D'ANTONIO.

Vincenzo clenched his fists so hard, he heard something crack.

"Don't worry about family."

"Fuck him!" He slammed the door to the telegram office. "*Fuck* him. He can't keep us from coming back. We're leaving. This week." He huffed. "Don't tell him I said that."

"I'd never." Dominic folded the telegram in his pocket, knowing that if Vincenzo touched it again, he'd shred it. "Vincenzo, may I speak openly with you?"

Vincenzo pulled a face at him. Since when did Dominic ask to speak? Since when *did* he speak? Normally, it was Luis or Vincenzo who decided those types of things for him. "...You may," he said.

They started walking back to their boarding house, Dominic's feet dragging to elongate the time he had to talk. "As you might be aware, I haven't always been...upfront about my personal life. I try and keep my thoughts to myself, as I don't think it's helpful to mix the pot with my input, but I wanted to tell you that I..." He scratched his nose. "Laurence and I have become very close this past month, close enough that I do consider him my...partner." He said the last word in a whisper.

Vincenzo waited for more information before he spoke. He was scared of where this was going.

Dominic continued. "I say this because I don't want you to feel like this only affects you and Sylvia. You've been the target of most of these attacks, but when we go back to the states, *all* of us will be in danger, so don't take on all the burdens by yourself. Don't feel so alone, I guess is what I'm trying to say." He cleared his throat, the embarrassment burning him red. "I don't know what I'm saying. Laurence told me to say something to you, but I'm not good at this."

Vincenzo stared up at the man's profile. He couldn't remember the last time he'd spoken up when he hadn't been asked a question, and to flip it into such a personal declaration, too.

He smiled for the first time that day. "I didn't know you were official with Laurence."

"Ah." He hid his mouth. "Well, you know how it is."

"Are you happy?"

The smile peeked from behind his fingers. "The happiest I've been in years."

"Then I'm glad it worked out. And it still will, when we get home. I promise you that."

"Thank you. Congratulations, by the way. About the proposal. Laurence told me last night."

"Better be careful. In a few months, it'll be you and him travelling to France and popping the question."

"Gracious, he said the same thing."

"'*Gracious*'? Are you picking up his mannerisms now?"

He laughed, and Vincenzo swore that was the first time he'd ever heard that kind of joy leak out of him. The tension he felt from Campo's harsh words lessened. "We should celebrate before going back. It'll probably take a few days before we can book passage back home."

"Do you have anything else you'd like to do here?" Dominic asked.

"It sounds like you have something in mind."

He pulled out a small brochure from his back pocket. "Laurence was telling me that France is known for these salons that cater to people like us. They're like pansy bars. They're all over. I don't know if they'd remind you of work, but to calm down from the news last night, I thought it'd be fun if we went to one."

Vincenzo considered it. While he'd visited many pansy bars across New York, he hadn't thought about going to one for pleasure. And certainly not to toast his engagement with his fiancée.

But then he thought back to all the times he'd gone to the Black Kitten without purpose. He'd sit and sulk in the corner of the bar, watching Sylvia like a bear in its cave, waiting for someone to badger him for taking up space in a place he thought he didn't belong.

He took the brochure. "Where's the nearest one?"

——◇——

Ana was not amused by how a French pansy bar operated. Luis had encouraged her to come in with them, but when she was greeted by a woman wearing nothing but feathers and heavy eye makeup, she ran out blabbering about "common decency."

"Oh, you drop that off at the doorway, sweetheart," Laurence yelled at her, and Sylvia laughed.

The smell of crisp alcohol in crystal glasses brought him back to semi-normalcy. The bar wasn't held in a dark basement, but the feeling, the freshness of the people dancing and having a good time, it was there and welcomed them.

The performers were, for lack of a better word, nude, albeit for the perfectly placed pearls and skimpy dresses hugging their bodies. Vincenzo covered his eyes as their waiter, a woman showing full knee, took their orders. Luis shamefully watched between his fingers. Mitsuko and Émeline took long gazes. Sylvia complimented them on how beautiful they looked.

It amused him how Dominic and Laurence paid the women no mind and laughed when they tried to flirt with them. But when the men came in wearing cherry-red lipstick and high heels, the whole table laughed at Laurence's open-mouthed reaction. One server, a built man with a curly mustache, even sat on Dominic's lap for a fraction of a second before dancing off. *That* didn't please Laurence. He chugged the remainder of his champagne with a scowl.

"Sit on his lap, then," Luis teased. "You'll lose that frown quick enough."

"Not interested," he grumbled. "We're not like you lot. Dominic doesn't like public—" He caught himself too late. Dominic had hidden his face, his ears a hot pink.

Vincenzo didn't know what he was laughing at. He'd only drunk one glass. For once, the atmosphere was more intoxicating than the drink in his hand, and when he saw his friends together like this, with Sylvia laughing and enjoying herself in the most pleasing way, he realized he was happy. The thought of Campo imprisoning them in Europe left with his sobriety.

A song started up, an English one he and the rest of the table knew. With drinks in hand, they volunteered to provide the needed vocals. They raised their glasses—Luis stood on his chair to get a better vocal range. Émeline wrapped her arms around Mitsuko's neck as she rocked to the beat. Sylvia took up Luis' offer and sat on Vincenzo's lap, the weight of her bottom pressing down on his crotch. The Frenchmen and women stomped their feet to their lewd performances.

When the songs reverted back to French, Laurence had lost his shirt, Dominic's was unbuttoned, Mitsuko and Émeline had excused themselves to the bathroom for a full hour, and Luis had somehow held an entire conversation with a French man drunker than he was.

Vincenzo and Sylvia had found their way on stage. There was no microphone or piano for them to hog, but that didn't stop them. Vincenzo sang. Sylvia kicked out her heels as she danced. Nobody minded except the performers whose performances they were ruining. By the time Vincenzo was dueting with Laurence and Sylvia had found her dance partner with

Mitsuko, the French people were laughing at their attempts to be engaging.

Hours drained into the night, and by midnight, Vincenzo had lost both his drink and voice, turning into "a little mouse," according to Sylvia. He didn't mind the pet name, and neither did the French pansies. They'd all become friends. Vincenzo was going to invite them to his birthday party.

Ana, the parent that she was, was waiting outside for them. She had a mug of hot cocoa in her mittens as she dined with two women of the night. When they ambled out, she bid her company goodnight and wrangled in her husband.

"Who're they?" Luis slurred.

"Two girls from America. We got to...talking, and I was watching you all make fools of yourself in there. Even though I don't approve of letting oneself go so extravagantly, I suppose...I understand this livelihood a bit more. I can see how it's comforting to be with people you see yourself in."

"Ah, Ana likes pansies!" Vincenzo said, which erupted into a chorus of "*Ana likes pansies*" that continued throughout the car ride home.

They all somehow slept in Vincenzo's suite that night. He'd woken up hurting all over and feeling sick, and as he blindly made his way to the bathroom, he found Luis using the curtains as a blanket and Ana on the couch. Laurence was using Dominic as a pillow, Émeline was nuzzled up against Mitsuko in the bed. Sylvia had strangely passed out in the bathtub. She was cradling a bottle of tequila and a blanket stolen from Mitsuko's room. He kept quiet as he relieved himself across the room.

His eyes had adjusted to the dark, and as he trekked back to bed, he found Mitsuko sitting upright, petting Émeline's hair as she slept on her lap. The softness of her eyes showed Vincenzo a different side of her. If he hadn't been so tired, he would've sworn she'd been crying.

——◇——

He didn't know what Luis had done, but he'd booked their voyage for that morning. Ana had refused to be without her child for a second longer, and he knew he himself was feeling homesick. He missed the smell of his bed and the taste of *Nonna's* home-cooked food. He felt like Dominic and Laurence could've spent another week here and Mitsuko would've spent the rest of her days by Émeline's side, but the urgency to get back home was weighing down on everyone's minds.

He thought.

They got to the docks as the Sun was coming up. Their hangovers were working against them—Sylvia hadn't budged until ten minutes before they needed to check out—but they were on a time crunch. They could no longer bask in France's delights. They needed to return home.

As usual, they took their three cars to get there, but once they got their bags and filed onto the boat, they misplaced Mitsuko and Émeline.

"Where could they have gone?" Sylvia asked, turning in circles. "Weren't they just behind us?"

Luis ran back up the ramp. "All their stuff's out of the car."

They scanned the top deck, then the stairwells and first floors. Dominic and Laurence waited by the boarding dock in case they crossed paths.

The officers and sailors called for everyone to board. The horn wailed out across the docks and echoed into the city.

"We can't leave without them," Sylvia said.

"Did she say she was coming?" Vincenzo asked.

"No, she hasn't," Laurence said, and looked over the railing once more.

He gasped. "There!"

Down beneath a metal awning, Mitsuko and Émeline were standing hand in hand, ready together.

"Is she getting on?" Sylvia asked.

"Which one?" Vincenzo questioned.

Mitsuko looked up at the boat, scanning it from bow to stern, shaking her head. She said something to Émeline and squeezed her hand. They exchanged a muted conversation that Vincenzo didn't strain to lip read.

Mitsuko turned Émeline's face so they were looking at one another. She caressed her soft cheek, took it in one hand, then stood on her tiptoes and kissed her right in front of a police- man.

People stared. The policeman stumbled back, aghast. They didn't care. Mitsuko took in all that she loved about her wife with her lips. She held her in one last hug and whispered a secret in her ear. When the boat signalled for its final passen- gers, she kissed her cheek tenderly and boarded alone with her satchel.

Émeline touched her cheek, then waved until the ship sailed out.

Luis, Ana, and Dominic left to find their rooms. Vincenzo, Sylvia, and Laurence stayed for Mitsuko's sake. Even though she could no longer see the coastline, she still had her hand up.

Vincenzo went to touch her, but she swung around and exhaled into a loud groan. "I need a drink."

"But you're sober."

"Drink. Of milk. A gallon of it. If I puke, don't stop me. Any of you."

"You made a hard decision," Sylvia said.

"Damn right, I did. *'Long distance'.* I've been pining for that woman for a goddamn decade. I can take another year. Can you imagine how many letters I'm going to send her? If I didn't love the Black Kitten so much, I would've given her a quicker answer than I did. At least I know her address now. And her parent's house. And her cousin's place. And her place of work." She wiped her eyes, then shouted at a sailor, "Where's the bar?"

"Let's go, darling," Laurence said, and escorted her down into the ship.

———✧———

The trip back home was clearer, mostly because they drank a third of the alcohol and split up into their respective couples, Mitsuko's couple being her and her bottles of milk. When they reached Liberty Island and stepped onto American soil again,

390

they got into their parked cars with their brains fried. They didn't talk much, but they knew who was leaving with whom. Dominic would sleep over Laurence's, Mitsuko would drive Laurence home. Luis and Ana followed Vincenzo in his car, and Sylvia sat next to him, her hand over his thigh.

"Do you know when you're going to meet Campo?" she asked as they entered Brooklyn.

"I was planning on dropping you off and saying hello to *Nonna*, then I was going to phone him. We left early, so he won't be expecting us."

"I hope everything goes well. I'd hate for you and him to have a disagreement. He must've known that you would've found this out sooner or later."

"That's what I was having trouble figuring out. It doesn't make sense. He should've known better."

He pulled up to his house and saw Mezzanotte waiting for him in the window. She poofed up with her hackles raised. He almost waved to her when he noticed a car parked out on the curb.

He slowed to a stop in his parking space.

"Who's that?" Sylvia asked.

He reached underneath his seat and pulled out a pistol.

Sylvia stayed close to him as he carefully made his way up the steps. Mezzanotte would've run if there'd been a commotion, but none of *Nonna's* friends drove those types of Fords. Only Campo's people did, and his father's henchmen.

He unlocked the door.

A man was sitting in his living room with a hat clutched in his hands. Vincenzo knew him as Sylvester, a worker who helped Campo with measly tasks.

"Oh, sir." Sylvester stood up and bowed. "I was just looking for you. Your father said you'd be home by now."

"What?" Vincenzo asked. How had his father known? He'd been in Paris the whole time.

Sylvester squeezed his hat like he was wringing out a rag. "Have you heard the news, sir?"

"What news?"

"It's Campo, sir. He..." He gulped. "He's dead, sir. His whole family was shot and killed last night. He's gone."

Chapter 32: Visiting Campo

"I heard it from Severo, sir," Sylvester had said. *"He told everyone about it."*

Vincenzo didn't speak as Sylvester drove him and Sylvia to Campo's house. He couldn't. He couldn't think. He couldn't think of a life without Campo.

Campo, his mentor, the provider and father figure he thought he hadn't deserved. The man who cared about his men, who helped them with the struggles they faced outside of the business, all of that was gone. *He* was gone.

His knee hopped uncontrollably. So many times he'd fallen apart, and before Sylvia, he had Campo to lean on, to fix him. Without Campo, the Black Kitten would be no more. He'd lose his right in the Family, he'd lose Sylvia. Everything he loved would be stripped away from him until he was left raw and bleeding on the pavement.

His nails tore into the top of his knuckles. If Campo was really gone, then Vincenzo had no choice but to believe that God had died with him.

Sylvia placed her hand over his. "I'm sorry."

He shook his head. He felt so much sorrier for her.

Campo's house, if it could even be called a home anymore, lay in destitute. His private property had been set ablaze. His lawn was etched with tire marks and the police had barricaded the driveway with police cars. Like that would stop Campo's associates from mourning.

At the sight of an officer carrying out a piece of charred evidence, Sylvia inhaled.

"You don't have to come in with me," Vincenzo said as he helped her out of the car.

She nodded but stayed with him.

"Hey, you can't come in here," one officer said.

Vincenzo kept walking.

"Hey—"

"Tell me I can't!"

Sylvia, as well as the officer, jumped.

"Tell me," he said quieter, voice quivering. "Tell me I can't."

The officer, who was reaching behind him for a weapon, dropped it and let him pass.

In the front entrance was a mass covered by a white tarp. By the size, it must've been a child, running for the front door but being unable to escape. Sylvia choked on a sob. Vincenzo continued on in respect.

The carnage worsened the deeper they went into the house. Tables were flipped over, portraits were torn. The kitchen had the worst burns and must've been where the fire originated. All of Campo's riches—the golden curtains, the art—were either charred black or gone completely.

Three tarps lay on the ground: one woman, one young boy, and one older man, whose hair was beginning to thin from age, whose kind smile could brighten the most hopeless situation.

Vincenzo shook. He tried to blink back the tears but they were already there. Campo's skin had gone white. His lips were blue. Three bullet holes had turned his tan suit a deep maroon.

He growled through a shout and kicked the edge of Campo's counter. It wouldn't matter; he wouldn't be using it again. None of his family would. It'd been tainted. It'd been taken.

"That's enough."

Vincenzo bared his teeth at the voice behind him.

Severo, wearing an evening coat and bored expression, watched Vincenzo mourn with dead eyes.

That nonchalance, the act of thinking himself greater than anyone in the room. Sylvia had earned a fucking better rank in life than this coward.

Vincenzo reached for his knife in his back pocket. "What did you do to him?"

Severo scoffed and looked to a burned painting of Campo and his family. "I got here before it happened."

"Oh, you lying, sack of dog shit—"

A firm hand pulled Vincenzo back. Sylvia almost put herself between them before she realized how much hatred was in the air and just brought Vincenzo back.

"What did you do to him?" Vincenzo demanded. "What did you do?"

"I did nothing. I was home with your mother. I have witnesses. Where were *you*?"

Vincenzo had told neither his mother nor father about the trip. It would've caused more problems, one of them might've talked him out of it. "I was doing business for Campo. I just came back."

"Where?" his father demanded. "*Nonna* was senile when I asked her. She said she couldn't remember. Were you in Canada?"

A lie. *Nonna* was smart and knew what kind of man Severo was. She wouldn't have told him his location if she were on her deathbed.

But that must've meant *he* didn't know. He only knew Vincenzo would've come back from wherever he'd been if this news had reached him, which of course it would've. He was, in every way, Campo's adoptive son.

Vincenzo's eyes went wide. Severo had lost track of him.

Taking Sylvia's hand, he stepped back.

Severo stepped forwards. "Where were you?"

He walked around the kitchen island.

Severo followed. "I went to the Black Kitten, you know. Lovely folk you've been fucking with. That bar owner, Bobbie, was it?"

Sylvia gasped.

"It took a few beatings to get him to talk, but he finally fessed up. You went to Paris, didn't you? A little honeymoon, was it? Why would Campo send you so far away? He must've paid for everything. Why?"

"It's none of your business," Vincenzo mustered up. "It was between him and me."

"It was between you and your *boss*," Severo said, "which, under the line of succession, now falls to me."

The thought made him physically sick. He stopped backing up, trying to imagine that kind of life. He couldn't. Not without Campo.

An officer came up to Severo and asked him questions from his notepad. Severo turned to him, but his eyes stayed on Vincenzo.

Vincenzo could no longer stand it and ran when he had the chance. Two officers were examining the body of Gabriella near the front door. To keep from throwing up, he took to the stairs. They were intact, but the walls, the blood and tears Campo had shed into this house, all of that was gone and replaced with the smell of ash.

His feet walked him into Campo's study. Something had to be here. Clues, photos, letters. Campo would've left him one last note explaining himself.

"We're looking for...something," he said to Sylvia. "Something to help us summate what happened."

"Clues."

"Or the intentions of what my fucking father did to him. I know he had a hand in it. I know he did." He touched the top of his writing desk. His paperweights had survived the fire.

Not only his paperweights, but his papers, which had been strewn about in a windstorm, were here. The desk drawers had been thrown out, their contents thoroughly scavenged through.

"He's already been here," Sylvia said, taking the words out of Vincenzo's mouth.

He pulled out the drawer someone had cracked open. Inside were papers ripped, envelopes torn without a care for who'd sent them.

They searched carefully so as not to disintegrate any evidence with their touch. What had his father wanted that he couldn't already obtain? He had money and power. He had a home, two, in fact, with a wife and child he should've loved.

He had everything he'd ever wanted after travelling to America. What else could he have wanted?

"What did he take?" Vincenzo asked, mostly to himself because he didn't think either of them would find an answer. Why ransack his study if only to kill him and take his title as boss? Unless it hadn't been him, but...

He reopened a drawer and reached in. There had to be something, something to key him in on what really happened.

His fingers grazed a ruffle of papers.

He pulled it back. A handful of letters had been saved. They were wrapped in twine. The name on the top would've made his father suspect nothing.

'Émeline DuPont' told Vincenzo everything.

He tore it open. His father wouldn't have known about her. He wasn't a sleuth like Campo, he just tortured and murdered without care. He wouldn't have done extensive research to find out why she mattered.

He flipped through the documents. His photo. Sylvia's. Her friends. *Their* friends. They were birth certificates forged with a masterful hand that would've fooled every police officer downstairs. Instead of their addresses and names, Campo had fabricated new Parisian lives for them. Vincenzo was now Jeremy Costa. Sylvia was Emilia Neuville. Even their pictures had been altered with new hairstyles and smiles that didn't suit them.

"What *is* this?" He handed Sylvia her pages.

She flipped it over. Attached underneath was a booklet stamped with an eagle. "A passport."

Vincenzo checked his own passport. And Mitsuko's. And Laurence's. Dominic. Sylvia. Everyone but Luis and Ana was here.

"He wanted us to start new lives," Sylvia said. "He wanted us to stay there."

"Because he was scared of my father."

"He'd wanted to protect us."

"But to send us away."

"It's extravagant, ludicrous, even."

Vincenzo smiled darkly, tears stinging his eyes. "That's so much like him."

A pair of boots stomped down the hall.

Vincenzo wedged the drawer back into place while Sylvia stuffed the documents into her coat.

Severo came in as Vincenzo stood back up. "I wasn't done talking to you."

Vincenzo said nothing. His father had his dominant hand behind his back, hiding whatever gun he was ready to pull on his own son.

Vincenzo glared him down. Sylvia's unwavering stare kept him from saying the wrong insult, any insult at all. His father was developing that animalistic snarl.

"Mr. DiFiore?" someone called from downstairs. "Vincenzo DiFiore, I need you down here for a second."

Vincenzo kept Sylvia back as they passed his father. His father didn't take his eyes off of them, slowly turning his head like a hungry wolf. Vincenzo wanted to say so much to him about what he'd done, but he knew what his power of silence could do to him.

"Whatever you found," he said, "won't leave this house. What's in this room is for me and me alone."

Vincenzo and Sylvia kept walking forwards.

His father swore every insult he knew at them, trying to diminish their love and their chosen lives.

They, holding hands, never looked back.

Chapter 33: Cheap Shot

Vincenzo didn't attend Campo's funeral. He didn't go outside at all, really. For the next three days, he stayed at home with Sylvia, *Nonna*, and his cat, sleeping on the couch and staring into the fireplace until he passed out from anxiety around noon.

Dominic, Luis, and Ana went to the funeral. His friends tried to lighten the mood, but Sylvia didn't know if anyone could help him. He'd been sitting in the same position for hours now, watching the snow fall from the locked window.

As their cars drove off, the grandfather clock chimed three. Its haunting tolls sent Mezzanotte into Vincenzo's lap and Vincenzo into a surprised, gasping fit.

"Hey, it's okay." Sylvia held him. What more was there to do? She needed to be there for him, but she didn't know how to respond to loss. When she'd lost her father, she'd broken. Mentally, emotionally. She stopped pretending to smile, stopped going to school. Her mother had become ruthless and she'd become a shell of her former self. She couldn't let that befall Vincenzo. But she knew she couldn't simply tell him to be happier or to look on the bright side of things. Right now, there wasn't any. She just had to be there for him.

After sitting in silence for a few songs on the record player, Vincenzo whispered, "I should've gone."

"Oh, honey." She kissed his temple. "He was such a kind man to you. He would've understood."

"It's disrespectful."

"Your father would've been there…" She trailed off, unsure of what needed to be said to someone thrust into grieving. She said honestly, "I don't know what to say, sweetheart. I'm sorry."

He rested his cheek on her shoulder. She brushed back his hair to reveal his face. Stress pimples were budding near his hairline. "We'll be okay," she landed on.

"How, though? Campo was the only reason we could be together. Without him, we're doomed."

"We aren't doomed. There're many, many people like us. Think about it."

"But they don't have my status."

"Sure they do," she lied. "There were probably many kings and queens who loved people just like them. Mayors and presidents, poets and artists. You have to suppose *some* of them were able to live out their love happily. We might have to be more secretive and lie, maybe run away for a while and leave the people we love, but nothing for us is doomed. Not yet."

"'*Not yet*'," he said, laughing. "Not yet."

Nonna came in with a plate of chocolates, and they ate quietly around the fireplace, letting Vincenzo grieve in peace. It surprised Sylvia how easily she believed herself and her lies. Of course this life was burdensome. It was stressful and painful and almost never worked out in anyone's favor. Her usual doubts settled quickly into her stomach, but that hope she'd spoken aloud kept her from plunging into that normal bout of fear. Two years ago and she would've laughed at herself for thinking she'd be okay. Now, while faint, her mood felt different. Lighter. More optimistic.

She called Laurence and Mitsuko while holding Vincenzo's hand. She updated them on Campo's death and the ripple effects it would have in the Family. They updated her on the Black Kitten and Bobbie. Severo had roughed him up while they were in France and had given him a black eye and a broken tooth. He promised that he had no ill-will towards Vincenzo.

"Just be careful from now on," he said. "I think this nonsense is only going to get worse."

After the funeral, everyone convened at Vincenzo's place. Despite eating what must've been delectable Italian meals and wine, Dominic, Luis, and Ana came back sober and dreary-looking. All the pep Luis usually had had seeped from his face, leaving him looking older.

"I saved this for you," he said, and gave Vincenzo a red rose from the casket. "I tried sneaking out more, but your father was watching us."

Vincenzo opened his mouth to speak, then placed the rose on the fireplace mantel next to a picture of *Nonna*.

"It was peaceful," Luis said, cutting through the silence. "Everyone had nothing but nice things to say."

"There were more than a hundred people," Dominic added. "Friends and distant relatives from Chicago."

"They said they're looking into who did it," Ana said, holding her baby tightly. "The murder."

"And that there'll be repercussions," Luis said. "That's what your dad said, anyway. Your mother said hi, by the way. She said she wants to meet with you."

Vincenzo looked away. To Sylvia's knowledge, he didn't have a relationship with his mother but not in the way Sylvia had with Clara. Instead of hating her, because of her involvement with his father, she seemed untouchable. He had more pictures of her in his home than of his father.

Dominic folded his hands. "He was too good for this world. Even though he was lenient on a lot of rules, he and his family were going to do good things for the world."

They all lowered their heads in respect. The crime scene Sylvia had walked through disfigured that beautiful smile Campo always wore. She closed her eyes, trying to picture happier moments.

Then her eyelids snapped open. Outside, a car rolled by. She'd tapped into Vincenzo's worry about ominous cars lurking in this street and looked out the window to find something bad.

An expensive-looking car drove to a stop outside. She couldn't see the men's faces, as they had scarves pulled over their faces to hide their identities, but she did recognize them as men she should've been wary about. She saw Hannigan's men. She saw Severo's men.

It was the first time she saw a Tommy gun in broad daylight, and her first thought was how unnecessarily scary they looked. The large circle that contained all those bullets, how bulky they appeared in their small hands. Why would a man need such a dangerous weapon to kill so many people?

Keeping their car doors open, the men stepped out and aimed their guns at Vincenzo's home.

"Vincenzo—"

The rest of her warning was drowned out by a flurry of gunfire that blew out her eardrums. It went off in waves, shattering window glass and shooting the front door off of its hinges. She fell to the ground, not knowing what else to do, and hid behind the coffee table. *Nonna* wailed brokenly, hauntingly. Ana screamed and ducked beside Sylvia, hiding Sophie underneath her own body.

Seconds passed, and the gunfire continued. More people yelled, ran around her, but she didn't dare open her eyes. Luis choked on Ana's name. Someone shot from inside the house. Vincenzo's condition was absent between the rounds.

After what felt like minutes, the gunfire ceased, and the car skidded against the pavement and down the cul-de-sac. Someone ran for the door and shouted: Luis, furious at those who'd almost murdered his family.

Ana clung to Sylvia as she cried into her chest. "Thank you. Oh, God, thank you." Sylvia didn't know if she was addressing her or the Man in question.

The air was smoky and hard to take in. New bullet holes littered their home like spiders on the wall. The paintings and trinkets *Nonna* had up around the house had fallen to the ground, cracked. Dominic was splayed out across the staircase holding his bloody shoulder. Luis was tending to him frantically.

"Who the fuck shot at us?" he asked.

Vincenzo was pressed against *Nonna*, slumped on the ground, still acting as her shield. Poor *Nonna's* face was white in shock as she stared up at Sylvia.

Helping Ana to the couch, Sylvia, shaking, went to Vincenzo.

Both of their chests were splattered with blood. A bullet had ripped one of them open and was creating a dark pool of blood on the floor. It smelled of metal, scorched and hot.

"Vincenzo—"

Vincenzo coughed up blood and fell against the mantle, dropping Campo's rose into the flames.

Chapter 34: One Last Harbor Meeting

Vincenzo remembered trying to drive himself to the hospital. He'd said he didn't want to get any more blood on *Nonna's* floor. According to Sylvia, he'd made it to the door before the pain made him pass out into her ready arms.

He assumed they'd followed him to the hospital. When he was out, high on either morphine or opium, he'd heard Sylvia talking him through the pain. She'd assured him that he was going to be okay and that she loved him. Or maybe he'd dreamt that. It was getting harder to keep his eyes open. Honestly, if she'd been whispering her love into his ear, he wouldn't have wanted to wake up.

But then he heard another's voice. It was softer than Sylvia's but deeper, yet somehow even more familiar than hers. The only other woman with that sweet of a voice was *Nonna*. Had Sylvia brought her along?

He opened his eyes. They felt swollen and he wanted to fall back asleep, but this person, whoever they were, was too close for his comfort.

He'd snagged one of the nicer hospital rooms. It was a private room, furnished like a bedroom with lacy curtains, a comfy bed, and an armchair to his right. In the armchair was someone he hadn't seen in months. It made sense why her voice had brought him out of his dreams.

His mother held a handkerchief to her lips as she looked down at Vincenzo. She'd been crying, her makeup black and blotchy around her caramel-colored eyes. It looked like she'd dressed for a party before coming here, as she wore her black gloves and real Japanese pearls she must've bought for herself.

"Mom?" he asked, coughing from how dry his throat was. The cough awoke the dormant pain in his side.

"Oh, dear." She held his non-IV hand, trying to keep from sobbing over him.

He stared at her, baffled. He couldn't remember the last time he'd talked with her alone like this. He searched the room, anticipating his father.

"He's downstairs," she said. "He's only allowing me a few minutes to see you."

"Who? Dad?"

She nodded and started playing with his hair.

If he hadn't been so high, he would've felt some type of way. In his head, *Nonna* had become his mother, and Sylvia had alleviated his need to be held and cherished. After years of her existence melting away from memory, who was she now?

His mother. He knew that. But her touch had lost that meaning.

"I don't have much time, and I know I haven't told you this enough times this year, but I do love you, Vincenzo. I love you so much more than I can put into words, in however you choose to dress, in however you choose to live. You've become your own man and I'm so incredibly proud of you. Remember that, okay? I've always loved you."

Delayed emotions flowed into his head. He must've really been dreaming. She never used his name when speaking to him. She called him "him," she abided by those rules, but it was always "son," "he," and he'd thought that was all he'd ever receive.

Hearing the name he'd chosen for himself, it made his nose tingle. But why? Why was she telling him this? Because she'd almost lost him? Did that make things more real for her?

He didn't have the chance to ask. The opium had awakened in his veins, and he fell back asleep.

He lay awake early the next morning alone, that addictive taste still in his veins. He was more aware of his injury today, which, after carefully lifting his arm, he found as a scar the length of his pointer finger above his hip. He sighed; yet another mark he'd have to make up an excuse for having. At least it looked more believable as a bullet wound, but getting it from his father—his new boss—was a detail he'd have to change in his story.

With his mind clear and his hospital room empty, Vincenzo finally filtered through the memories of that night.

His father had shot at his own mother's house. He knew it. How inhuman could a man be? It'd been so easy when Vincenzo had joined, when Prohibition had begun and the money was coming in stacks. He'd recently gotten his surgery, he had Campo as a new father, and he'd been introduced to the concept of pansy bars, a safe haven he hadn't known he needed. He'd never felt more comfortable living as himself.

And his father had fucked it all up.

Could he do the impossible? He had to run away, but could he leave everyone behind? For good? Run to Canada, or even back to Paris? He'd have to cease communication with *Nonna*. The Black Kitten would be a dream too good to dream about. Would Campo's spirit think ill of him for returning back overseas on his own accord?

He tapped his foot underneath the covers. The drugs were wearing off and he needed to leave. He needed to see his friends and family and decide where to go from here.

When he was able to sit up and take more medication, he asked his nurse for a phone.

Sylvia picked up after the first ring. "Hello? Vincenzo?"

"Hi, baby."

He didn't know why he'd chosen that pet name, but upon hearing it or his voice, Sylvia bawled. "Oh, Vincenzo, darling, you sound so much better. Can I visit you? They wouldn't let me into your room because we aren't family. I've been so worried, I haven't slept."

"Don't come now. Whatever they gave me is making me thick. Really, all crossed-eyed and everything. You'd think they've given me a bottle of rum to dull the pain."

She giggled through her tears. "Are you being discharged today?"

"I should be. I'll call back when I meet with the doctor. I just didn't want you fretting about it all morning."

"Oh, I have been, don't worry. Are you feeling any better?"

"A hundred percent," he lied. "I'm sure I'll be back this afternoon. Wait for me, okay? Tell *Nonna* I'll be home soon, and pet Mezzanotte for me."

"I will. Dominic and Luis are here, too. They're protecting me. Do you want to talk to them?"

Hearing how stupid he was sounding, he said, "No. Just tell Dominic that he'll probably have to pick me up sometime today."

"Of course. Listen, go back to bed and rest. Make sure to take your medicine and relax, and don't sit up unless you need to."

"I will, I will." He shut his eyes, already heeding her advice. "I love you."

"I love you, too," she said sweetly. "Heal up well."

An hour later, his doctor came in with a clipboard and a smile. "Good morning, Mr. DiFiore."

"Good morning. May I leave?"

"Careful now. I have to check your wound before you get up and walk around. Your party is waiting downstairs for you, you know. You must be popular."

"They are?" he asked. Why were they already here? He hadn't yet called.

"They are. Now, may I?"

Grimacing, Vincenzo obliged and helped him get access to the scar. They must've undressed him to tend to the bullet sound. He'd never live that down.

"How fortunate," the doctor said as he probed the wound, "that God allowed you a second chance."

"Yes, He's very considerate of me."

When the doctor pressed on the scar and Vincenzo bit down the pain, he nodded to himself. "It seems alright. Are you having trouble breathing or eating? Does it hurt when you lay down?"

"I'm fine, it's just a graze. May I please leave now? I have someone important waiting for me."

"Of course. You and your...business seem to attract immediate attention." He helped him to the door, then gave him a bottle of cocaine for the road. "Take care now, Mr. DiFiore."

Dominic wasn't in the foyer, so Vincenzo checked the bathroom, then went outside, bracing for both the cold and the pain. It'd felt so much warmer in France.

One of the cars parked outside opened its doors.

Three men in black suits came out.

Vincenzo froze and went back for the hospital.

Two new men came out and blocked his path.

He ran through all of his options to defend himself, but his mind was numb from the medication. He couldn't run. He couldn't fight.

He'd been set up.

"Come with us," one of the men said, and threw Vincenzo into the back of the car.

His father's docks were uncommonly empty that afternoon. Only a few boats were tied up, covered in a foot of snow, abandoned for the winter.

The driver stopped at the longest dock. "Get out."

Vincenzo controlled his breathing and got out by himself. He didn't know any of these men. He tried to, God, he tried to recognize anything. A scar, a hairline, but nothing came. He was lost at sea against an unnamed foe.

"Unnamed." Like he hadn't known the man he was meeting his whole life.

His father was standing at the end of the dock, coat flapping in the wind. Whether he was facing him or not, Vincenzo couldn't tell, and he knew he didn't care either way. This was just a business meeting for him. Or something worse.

Vincenzo lowered his head as he stepped onto the dock. The sloshing, murky water made his footing uneven until he stopped at the start of his father's shadow.

The two of them were silent. The waves carried on. Snow continued to fall.

"Dad."

He punched him in the stomach.

Bile rose to his throat. He choked on the air in his lungs as he shielded his scar, but Severo kept hitting him until he fell and rolled into a ball to keep himself from coming apart.

Severo knew where he'd been shot. He kicked and struck at his sore side, breaking Vincenzo into begging that he stop. He didn't. His boot crushed his body and face until a protective numbness spread over him. It did little to mask the real pain of the assault.

After Vincenzo swore he'd die, Severo stepped on him. *"You have been a* fucking *sore on my side since the day you were born. Year after year, you've disgraced me and your mother's name with your fucking habits in a back alley. Now, though, now that Campo's out of the picture, I don't have to sit back and let you sully the Family name any longer."*

Vincenzo spat out blood. He'd been kicked too hard in the mouth. His jaw couldn't close all the way. *"You killed him."*

"He was ruining the Italian name by being so lenient with you people. I put a stop to it." He grabbed Vincenzo by the hair and made him look at him. *"You have one last job to do, understand? One last job, then you're done."*

Vincenzo didn't ask for elaboration. He knew what that meant. Every gangster knew what that meant.

A piece of paper fluttered between Vincenzo and Severo. It fell face-first. He flipped it over.

"I want him dead by nightfall. If I don't see a burial mound behind your house by midnight, you and everyone in that bar is dead."

Vincenzo burned a hole into the picture with how hard he stared at it. He'd never seen this photo of Sylvia before. She was sitting on a chair, posing with the sweetest smile towards the camera. She was so beautiful, even then. Now, forever, she'd always be beautiful.

Satisfied with his work, Severo buttoned up his coat and left Vincenzo to his final job.

Chapter 35: Adrift

"He was *shot*?"

Sylvia pulled the phone away from her ear. "Yes, but he's alright now. Vincenzo was hit on his side, so he's still at the hospital—"

"But what about Dominic?" Laurence asked. "Dear God, why didn't he tell me? Where was he shot? How is he? Is he there? Slap him for me, Sylvia, right where the bullet hit."

She was thankful for Laurence's mood. It'd been more than twenty-four hours since the shooting and nobody in the house had tried to lighten the mood. She'd been in bed for most of the day, with blankets wrapped around her and every pillow barricading her. She was still shivering. Mezzanotte, who was sitting in her lap, helped to warm her up.

"This's unbelievable," Laurence said. "Mitsuko, my boy's been shot. It wasn't just Vincenzo."

"Wow," Sylvia heard Mitsuko say in the background. Both were at the Black Kitten performing tonight. "It's almost like that's their job and that we should expect them to be peppered with bullets. Did we not have this conversation a few months ago with Sylvia? Weren't we all against this?"

"Oh, hush," Laurence said. "But damn him all the same. Him *and* his work. This's all too much to risk one's life over. This Severo man, he's a...he's a big..."

"*Akuma*," Mitsuko said.

"Yes, that. And a bastard. Cripes, what if they're monitoring this call? That's a thing those men can do, isn't it?"

"If they are," Mitsuko said, "then let them know this." And she spoke in Japanese that, while Sylvia couldn't translate, sounded incredibly unladylike even for Mitsuko. Her ending it with a raspberry noise, though, hopefully deterred anyone who was truly listening.

"Anyway, Sylvia, all these men aside, I'm glad you're alright. You're always welcome to my house anytime. That goes for Vincenzo and his grandmother, too."

"Thank you." She bundled up her blankets. "So, how do you two feel about this? About the passports and the move? Would you come back to Paris with us?"

She'd presented this option to them after they'd found out Campo's intent about keeping them in Paris for their protection. It was a big decision on everyone's part, but unlike Campo, Sylvia wanted to make sure they had a choice to move.

Before they answered, Dominic creaked open the door with a heated bag of rice and soup. He offered them to Sylvia and went to escape, but she held up a finger, making him wait.

"I...don't know," Laurence finally said. "It's a life-changing offer. You said he'd prepared altered passports?"

"Yes, and the papers say we'd be in that boarding house until July. That gives us six months to get new jobs, readjust, and begin anew."

Dominic crossed his arms and looked away.

"Well, if we can get there without being shot at," Mitsuko said. "I don't have any complaints about going."

"You'd get to see Émeline again," Sylvia said. "You could start a life with her."

Mitsuko didn't reply.

"Well, for me, I'm still thinking about it," Laurence said. "I have family here. It'd be hard for me to leave them."

"I understand." She lent Dominic the receiver. "Would you like to speak to him?"

"What?" Laurence asked.

"Dominic's in the room with me. I asked if he'd like to speak to you."

"Oh."

"Would *you* like to speak to him?"

"Please."

Hearing Laurence's desperation made Dominic hesitantly take the receiver. He crossed his ankles as he twirled the cord around his fingers. "Hey. No, no, I'm fine. Don't worry. Yeah, just a scrape." Sylvia heard what must've been a snort. "That's what I call a bullet wound, yes."

Leaving them to their conversation, Sylvia left downstairs to help *Nonna* with the dishes. Throughout this affair, *Nonna* hadn't stopped tending to the house. She made sure the laundry was done and that the dishes were put away. Sylvia helped to reach the higher shelves for *Nonna* to either piece together her heirlooms or throw them away. Many were pictures that could be saved. Sylvia discarded the broken glass.

"Frames can be thrown away," *Nonna* said. "Pictures cannot."

Sylvia was especially careful about these memories.

After heavily cleaning the first floor, a knock came from the front door.

Nonna dropped what she was doing and hid behind Sylvia. Sylvia protected her and waited to hear Dominic come back down, but he must've still been on the phone with Laurence and hadn't heard the visitor.

"I got it," Sylvia said.

"Be careful," Nonna warned in Italian.

She made her footfall steady as she peeled back the curtains farthest away from the door. She didn't know if she'd ever feel safe opening a front door again.

She breathed a sigh of relief and quickly unlocked the door.

"Hey," Luis said. He air-kissed both of her cheeks. "Has Vincenzo called yet?"

"I don't believe so. Dominic's been upstairs talking on the phone with Laurence."

"What, is he some heartthrob now? Some lovebird, talking on the phone like that." He whined. "I can't stand Vincenzo being so far away. I feel like there's so much that needs to be said, but I don't feel comfortable doing it without him." He felt up one of the bullet holes they hadn't yet sanded down in the main wall. "It's scary to be up in the air like this, like our world is suddenly changing without our say so."

"I know. Do you have any interest in coming with us?"

He turned to her. "So, you're really leaving?"

"I think it's a good idea."

He sighed and placed his hands on his hips. "What a day. What a week, a year. To think my boys would be in danger like this. You know, here I thought I was gonna be the one to get everyone in trouble with the way I act. Vincenzo was so serious, Dominic so level-headed. Now look at us. I feel like a buoy adrift on a misty shore, I do.”

“It’s a lot to take in. I’m scared of separating from everyone, but I don’t think any of us are safe here.”

“I don’t blame you. What we really need is Vincenzo. There’s a phone down here, right? We’ll call him and see how he’s doing. Where’s Dominic? Hey, Dom!”

He came down a minute later, fixing his trousers and reparting his hair.

“Welcome back,” Luis said as he dialed for the hospital. “Have a nice time upstairs?”

“...Didn’t hear you come in,” was all he said.

“No, no, I heard you were oh so busy, yeah?” He winked, then hung up after receiving a dial tone. He redialed. “So, what’s your decision, then? About the move?”

“I mean, what’s there to say?” He cast a longing look upstairs. “What’s there to do?”

“Think about what we should do next,” Sylvia said.

“I shouldn’t be the one to make that decision.”

Luis got in contact with the hospital and began talking to the receptionist in the kitchen.

Dominic lowered his voice. “What I think about shouldn’t matter. Severo might not even be after me. You two should go. I’ll be fine by myself. If things turn for the worst, I can hide.”

“But what about Laurence, and Mitsuko?” She took a different approach. “Dominic, I know you love Laurence.”

He stepped back, still afraid of that word.

“And I—everyone—love you, too. Think about what you want and how you want to live now. Severo’s your boss who will hate and criticize everything you stand for as a person.

"I know leaving this line of business is meant to be impossible, and France might not be the safest place to live, but we'll be far, *far* away from that man and the people who wish to harm us. Please consider that when you make your decision. I don't want to see you hurt, but I don't want to see you kill off the special part of yourself just to benefit a man who wants you dead."

The last part, as she expected, cut deep into him, but before he could say what he wanted, Luis interrupted him.

"Okay, okay, thanks so much," he said, and he hung up. "Okay, so good news and bad news. Good news: Vincenzo's operation went well and there were no complications with his hip or intestines or anything like that. Bad news: he's not at the hospital."

"What?"

"The doctor said he was discharged four hours ago."

"I thought he was gonna call when he was ready," Dominic said. "He doesn't have a car, he can't drive himself home."

"Perhaps another man picked him up?" Sylvia said.

"I don't think so," Luis said. "That's not like him. He would've called to reassure us, especially you."

"Then let's go find him," she said. "He's in no place to be walking around or working when he's injured and his father has his eyes on him. Where could he have gone?"

"He could've gone to the pier," Dominic said, "one of his bars in Manhattan, the Kitten, or he could be walking back home."

"In four hours, he should've been here by now," Luis pointed out. "It'd barely take him two hours at most, and I'm giving him an extra half hour for his injury. Hell, where is he?"

Sylvia already had her coat on and was putting on her shoes. Luis was right, this wasn't like Vincenzo. Something had gone wrong, but she wouldn't let herself think of the worst. She just needed to think of a way to get to her husband before his demons did. "Let's go."

They combed through the streets of New York all night. The night air kept her awake, as did every dead-end they came across. He wasn't at the docks—nobody was; everyone had gone home for the night—and he wasn't at any of his Manhattan bars. In a desperate attempt, they began checking alleyways to find him crumpled up behind a dumpster or calling for a ride home. Maybe he'd gone out to eat. Maybe he'd slept over a friend's house.

Those worst-case scenarios she'd been shoving into the back of her head were coming to fruition. A kidnapping, a murder. He was hurt or he'd left for a different country without telling her.

She kept telling herself that she'd find him, and if they didn't, well, she'd keep searching. Abandoning him wasn't an option. The ring on her finger kept that promise.

"We should head back home to see if he made it back," Luis said.

"I want to keep searching," Sylvia said. "Are there any other places he could be? Anywhere in Brooklyn either of you can think of?"

"Ah, I don't know," Luis said. "Dominic?"

Dominic bit his lip and looked outside.

"What?" Sylvia asked.

"Well, would it be foolish to think he's at his parents' house?"

"Parents'—Like Severo's house?" Luis asked. "No way."

"Not so much his house, but he might be confiding in his mother. I'm not too sure how close he is with her, but since he's so close with his grandmother and he just got hurt, along with this decision about leaving everything behind, I can see him going there. If my mother hadn't disowned me, I'd go to her about all this first. Well, maybe other people now, but she'd be an option."

"Where does she live?"

"That, I don't know. I'm sorry."

"Oh, jeez." Luis flexed his fingers over the steering wheel. "Well, I know what neighborhood he used to live near. Let's check there."

—◇—

Vincenzo's childhood neighborhood was comprised of parks and wide dirt roads meant to be pavement. Rusty construction equipment was parked off near the shoreline. Hardly any home had their lights on and the streets weren't lit. Luis relied on the moonlight and his car lights to guide their way.

Sylvia craned her neck to read the tenant housing numbers. She couldn't imagine Vincenzo living here, but she could

422

see him *growing up* here. She pictured a little Vincenzo gathering the neighborhood kids in gangs, causing mischief while their parents worked hard to provide for them.

She wiped her eyes at the thought. She needed to find him.

They drove past a playground connected to a play area of slides, unsafe jungle gyms, and park benches covered in snow. Not a soul had crossed through the snow, none that she saw, until they circled to leave and she spotted a single line of downtrodden footprints.

"Wait!"

There, sitting—slouching—in a swing, a hunched-over man was thinking to himself.

She jumped out of the car before Luis stopped the engine.

"Woah, watch it!" he said. "Is that him? Can you tell?"

"I can!" she said. "Vincenzo!"

He didn't move. He didn't look up or even breathe. Thinking he had some sort of earmuffs on, Sylvia physically turned him around. "Vincenzo."

His face was barely recognizable. His right eye was swollen shut and the whole left side of his cheek was red and purple. One of his fingers looked broken, but he was still holding onto a photograph. It was one Bobbie had taken of her the first month she'd come to the Kitten. He'd designed a whole set for her to encapsulate her beauty.

And he was crying. *Her* Vincenzo, crying in the middle of a children's park over a picture of her as a suicidal youth. He wasn't sniffling or trying to hide it. The tears simply flowed down his beaten face.

Sylvia took a knee. "What happened to you? I thought you were going to call us before you left the hospital. Why're you here?"

He blinked twice, focusing on her eyes.

She wiped away one of his tears. "Baby, what's wrong?"

"...Everything," he whispered, then wiped his eyes himself, wincing at the pain. "How're you here?"

"Never mind that. Why're you crying?"

He glanced down at the photograph. "My father gave me this. His men kidnapped me from the hospital and brought me to the docks. He said..." His lower lip quivered. "He said I have to kill you, and then he's going to kill me. He said I have until tonight, and if I don't do it, he's going to kill everyone, and I can't...I—"

He fell into her to hide his tears, and she allowed him that. He sounded so defeated.

Like he'd already given up before the fight.

She held him. "We'll fight it."

"What?"

"We'll fight back," she said, because she hadn't survived a horrific decade of anguish just to keel over like she would've done in that photograph. She had a family to protect now. She had herself to fight for.

"But we can't," he said. "It's impossible."

"What's impossible? You're Vincenzo DiFiore. You're one of the best gangsters there is. And what were you going to do? Sit here and let these people kill us? That's not the Vincenzo I know. The Vincenzo I know would fight and snarl and claw his way back to the top. He thinks you're going to go through with this, right?"

"He probably has eyes on me right now. Sylvia, please, just come with me. Stay with me until the end."

“I plan on living several more decades with you before we meet the end.” She kissed him, and he kissed her back like it was the last kiss they’d share.

“Do you have a gun on you?” she asked.

“No.”

“Then let’s go home first. We need to arm ourselves before we do the impossible.”

Chapter 36: Run Away

She was an angel. In no way could she have found him so quickly right when he'd lost the will to fight. She had a kindness to her that most people would never have, a love that made God proud.

She sat there with him, in the car with Luis and Dominic, her hand in his. Some of the anxiety remained—he didn't know where his father was or who could've been following him—but at that moment, he could finally breathe without hiccupping.

"So, this changes things," Luis said. "I thought we'd have more time to figure this out, but now that's shortened to...now. Like, within the hour. When we get out of this car, you need to know if you're skipping town on that boat or not."

"Are you coming?" Vincenzo asked. In the documents, Campo had given neither him nor his wife new lives.

"Nah," he said. "Somebody's gotta take care of the Black Kitten while you're gone. Can't have it falling to shambles when half of its family has to leave it." He laughed at nothing, a shake in his voice. "So, uh, anyone gonna say anything?"

"I think everything's been said," Sylvia said. "You're a good man for doing this, Luis."

He wiped something from his eyes. "Fuck," he whispered. "This isn't fair."

"I know, sweetheart. I know."

When they reached Vincenzo's driveway, every whisper of noise set Vincenzo off. It was almost midnight, his deadline to erase everyone who mattered to him.

Nonna seemed to be asleep. The kitchen was deserted. The living room, lifeless.

"Go, go," Luis whispered, instructing them upstairs. "The quicker we do this, the better."

Vincenzo threw open his closet and took out two duffel bags and a large suitcase. Two were already filled with the essentials—clothes, shoes, socks, a blanket, his Bible, a gun.

"When did you make this?" Sylvia asked.

"The day before I got shot. I'd already known what I wanted to do, I just didn't think we had this short a time limit to decide."

"Oh. Good." Reaching underneath the bed, Sylvia took out her own hidden, packed bag. "I started this afternoon."

He tried figuring out how to pack the rest of his life in two bags. He loaded in his less formal attire, his corsets, an abundance of socks and undergarments, the remainder of his gun collection. In his pants pockets, jacket, and suitcase, he hid around $1,225 and about fifteen ounces of cocaine in a tight bag. Sylvia marvelled at the hundred-dollar bills and packet of white powder.

He then turned to his bedside drawer. Paper wouldn't weigh down his bags, right? Talking himself into it, he opened the first drawer and stuffed all of Sylvia's letters into his suitcase.

"You've kept those," Sylvia said.

"Every last one."

That made her smile, but she lost it as she helped finish wrecking his room. She knelt down on his bags so they could seal it up properly, they cleaned out the rest of his closet. They packed more of their sentimental belongings—a hand-sized picture of *Nonna*, Sylvia's pearls, Vincenzo's signed Dodgers baseball. They made sure each of them had everything they needed and then some. The last piece came as their altered passports.

"We have to go to the Black Kitten," Sylvia said, keeping the documents safe in her bosom. "Mitsuko and Laurence are working until two. If we can catch them, they can start packing at home and be ready before we—"

Someone opened the front door.

Sylvia covered her mouth. Vincenzo crept to the door and listened. He couldn't hear either of them breathe.

"I don't know, I don't know."

"This isn't happening. Fuck!"

Vincenzo went for his gun, but *Nonna* pushed herself into his room carrying Mezzanotte in her arms.

"*Nonna?*"

Luis and Dominic came up behind her.

"There're two cars waiting outside," Luis said.

"We can go out through the back, but we have to go now," Dominic urged, and started taking their bags in both arms.

Vincenzo held his hip, the pain radiating to his heart. He couldn't come up with a solid plan. His feet wouldn't move. Sylvia, his friends, they were waiting for him to act and he couldn't.

Nonna took his face in one hand. Her fingertips were ice cold. *"I knew this would happen sooner or later,"* she said. *"I knew that you'd have to leave me one day because of this."*

"I'm sorry," he said. *"I should've protected you."*

"You shouldn't have been in the position to protect me as much as you have already. Your father shouldn't have done this to you. He called me about an hour ago. He was...different. He sounded like the Devil, the way he spoke about you. And I've seen the way you look at her. I used to be scared of it, but now, I can't see you with any other girl. This love is one of the best things that's ever happened to you, and I want to see that love protected."

She kissed both of his sore cheeks. *"I love you so much, Vincenzo. Your father is a damned soul, but you have created a very pure, very loving heart, and you should be proud of that. Now."* She tugged Sylvia down and kissed her, then handed Mezzanotte to Vincenzo.

He cradled her warmth into his chest, this little stray he'd taken off the streets. She'd grown so much. With so many people in the room, she hadn't even made a run for it yet.

He kissed her head before handing her back to *Nonna*. *"Thank you for everything, Nonna. I love you."*

"I love you, too, my loving boy."

Giving his room one last look, Vincenzo bit down his tongue and followed *Nonna's* orders. "Let's go."

Floodlights shined through the living room windows. At least two or three cars had skidded to a stop right outside, their motors running.

"We'll go out through the back," he whispered. "Sylvia, stay behind—"

The first *bang* of gunfire sent them to the ground. The second blew out the newly installed windows and covered the ground with glass.

Luis knocked Vincenzo to the floor. Dominic and Sylvia hid around the door. Vincenzo gagged from the wealth of pain erupting from his side, but the pain was drowned out by Luis scooping him up and thrusting him out the back door. "Go, go!"

In a scramble to stay up, Vincenzo reached out and found Sylvia's hand. "Our cars."

"We'll take one of mine," Luis said.

Vincenzo looked back into his home. "*Nonna—*"

"Be careful!" Sylvia tucked down her head just as two police officers barreled into Vincenzo's own home.

He went for his gun to kill them right there, but they aimed their weapons into the home, saving them from the real threat.

"Get down!" they ordered. "Get down, take cover! Outside, now!"

"Will do," Luis said under his breath.

"What're they doing?" Sylvia asked as they passed another officer. "How'd they get here so fast?"

"Don't know, but we should count our blessings while we have them."

Ignoring the officers' orders, their group crossed the street to Luis' house. Severo's cars were parked against the sidewalk. Two bodies were on the ground. Three men were being led into a wagon. Vincenzo's father and the bowler-hat men were missing.

Luis led them through his gardens to his cars untouched by gunfire. His bedroom light was off, but as they came around, the window opened to Ana holding her child. "I saw the cars circling around here fifteen minutes ago," she said. "I knew it'd be bad, so I called the police ahead of time."

"That's my girl," Luis said. "Baby, I need to drive this lot someplace safe, then I'll be right back. Don't worry about a thing, okay?"

She smiled. "I'm a moll, darling. All I do is worry." She dropped something heavy out of the window for Luis to catch. It was a handgun. "Be safe, everyone."

They crammed into Luis' car. Vincenzo was sitting on Dominic's hand. Sylvia was somehow in the passenger seat and Luis was driving. He felt like baggage, being thrown around like this, but he also felt like an important guest being led someplace safer.

They peeled out of his backyard gardens over the curb and sped through the parked cop cars. Vincenzo caught sight of one of his father's unmanned cars and looked back at his cul-de-sac. *Nonna.* Her Christmas decorations. Her food. Their *love.* Had he chosen too abruptly? Had he even said goodbye to her? He had one picture of her in his wallet. Was that all he had now?

They drove northeast and crossed Queensboro Bridge, skipping over the lower east-side traffic to put as much distance between them and Brooklyn as possible. When they pushed through the west side of the borough, Luis finally sighed and drove in a steadier line. "Jeez."

That one word breathed life back into the rest of the car. Dominic took out a handkerchief and wiped the sweat from his brow. Sylvia swore and fanned herself with her shirt. Vincenzo kept looking back for something. A car, *Nonna.* They passed his father's docks without a word.

"When did you say Laurence and Mitsuko leave the Black Kitten?" Dominic asked Sylvia.

"They leave at two."

"Then we have to drive faster. If they're gone, you can drop me off. I can run to Laurence's. It's only five or six blocks away from the bar. If he's there, I can bring him back."

"Should we separate? I don't know if it's safe with so many people after us right now."

"I'm separating if it means keeping him safe."

Vincenzo eyed him. Not that his request was unreasonable, he'd just never heard him declare anything so powerfully before.

"We'll swing by the Kitten first," Luis said. "Stopping by their houses might lose us some time. If they're both there, we'll be golden. If that's okay with you, sir."

Vincenzo was already nodding along with them. "That's good."

Dominic covered his eyes with one hand. His knee started jumping and didn't stop until they passed the bridge.

"It'll be okay," Sylvia told him. "We'll save him. We'll save all of them."

"Damn right," Luis said, and pressed his foot on the gas.

Dominic had one hand on the car door, the other on the gun in his pants, when Luis turned into the Kitten's lot. As the car slowed down, he heaved himself out and ran for the front door.

"Let's go get our darlings," Luis said.

Somehow, being back in the Kitten's smoky basement made Vincenzo want to cry. If he could, he'd crawl back into his little niche with Sylvia, listening to Mitsuko and Laurence perform while Dominic and Luis shared drinks at the bar. How he wanted that simplicity again.

But Dominic wasn't at the bar. He wasn't hiding or keeping himself isolated. He was on the stage, interrupting a jazz quartet while he searched the crowds for his lover.

Men came here too often incognito, hiding their faces and creeping in the shadows so nobody knew about their needs. Tonight, the Black Kitten was pretty packed, and he saw at least twenty men hiding their faces in scarves or underneath hats. If he called out Laurence's name in front of everyone, if he caught the interest of one bowler-hat man…

The back door leading to the dressing room opened and, with a glass in each hand, Mitsuko and Laurence came out to the main floor. They weren't dressed up, not yet. Laurence had yet to put on his wig while Mitsuko had started with her makeup.

"Lau—" Dominic choked on his name and jumped off the stage.

Laurence was able to pass his drink to Mitsuko before Dominic pressed him against the wall and hugged him like he'd lose him. Laurence, lost for words, mouthed a question to Sylvia before taking him in his arms. "What's going on?"

"Vincenzo's father just shot up his house. Again. Now he's coming after us. He wants both Vincenzo and me dead, and we don't know if any of you are at equal risk."

Mitsuko stared at her glass of milk before chugging it and dumping Laurence's drink on the floor. "So, we leave."

"What?" Laurence asked. "Right now?"

"Unless the last impression you want to leave on this Earth is a bloodstain on the pavement, we have no choice. We have five free tickets across the world where murderous, Italian gangsters have a lower chance of killing us for sport. I'm leaving. Whatever you choose is your decision."

Laurence looked away, trying to decide what to do with the rest of his life in thirty seconds. He looked to the left, then the right, then his fingers curled around Dominic's. "Okay," he said. "I'm in."

Bobbie hooked around the corner with a gun in his hand. "I was just upstairs. Three cars pulled up. They have Tommy guns."

Vincenzo calculated their odds. He had two guns on his person. Luis and Dominic had one each. Bobbie had at least two on the property, and Mitsuko had her knife.

"Well," Mitsuko said, "are we busting out now, or are we waiting for them to corner us?"

"We need to get everyone out," Vincenzo said. "It won't be easy, or quick."

"Sure it'll be. Excuse me." She climbed up on stage and took the mic from one of the performers. "Everyone!" she yelled. "Drop your glasses and the hands you're holding. Everyone needs to evacuate immediately. There're men upstairs ready to raid this bar with Tommy guns and a need to see people like us dead. Don't give them that primal satisfaction of seeing our bodies drop. Now get out!" She almost screamed the last part, and dropped the microphone on the floor to make her impact more meaningful.

"Let's go, everyone!" Bobbie said in a deeper tone. "Now. Kitten's closed. Let's go!"

With Dominic's, Laurence's, and Luis' help, they got almost all of the patrons into the back room. Questions and nervous glances swam through the drunken crowd about whether this was real or not. Vincenzo readied his gun to make sure they knew.

He and his men aimed at the door. Sylvia kept back with a hand hovering over his back, Dominic was holding Laurence's wrist.

Mitsuko had a deadly, homicidal look in her eyes. "They're not taking this place from us," she promised. Spinning her knife into her fist, she kicked the door open and went to cut the first person in front of her.

The lot was empty. No gunfire, no cars skidding to claim their first victim. Luis' car was parked against the entrance, giving them a proper cover, but Vincenzo had been anticipating more than nothing.

Then the first man jumped from the roof.

Dozens of armed men in black rained down on them. They jumped and skidded over the hoods of their cars. A few were cheeky enough to fire through Luis' car only to hit the brick and scatter the less prepared.

As Vincenzo should've expected, his father had planned a final sneak attack.

He only fired when he had a clear shot to the chest. He ended the lives of men he never saw the faces of, he shoved them to the ground before shooting them in the back of the head. One man got on top of him, gunless, and began strangling him with his ugly hands. Vincenzo went to kick him off when Luis collided into him and buried him in a pile of snow.

Vincenzo went to thank him, but he hadn't the time. People were running now, screaming. He couldn't tell who was who.

Between the fighting, Laurence had fallen to the ground, defenseless, and called for somebody's help.

"Fucker—"

Circling one another like dogs, Severo and Mitsuko were locked in a spiraling knife match. Mitsuko was crouched, Severo was standing at an angle due to an injury to his leg. He'd somehow retrieved a butcher knife from inside the Kitten, but he wasn't holding it right. The skill and precision came from Mitsuko, who was slashing the knife Vincenzo had given her for Christmas in the air, inching closer to Severo.

Severo jumped. Mitsuko side-stepped, tripped. She pushed herself up from the concrete before Severo struck her. Then she kicked his bad leg and sliced into the air he was breathing. Around them were both Severo's and Hannigan's men shouting at them, trying to grab Mitsuko but missing.

So, Severo had been working *with* Hannigan's men all this time, fighting a common enemy: Campo's ideal world. And who'd been the Family traitor?

Vincenzo met his father's eyes. Mitsuko had ripped open his shirt and left a line of blood across his skin.

The look in his eyes was that of a stranger, and now, that's who he was. In the end, Vincenzo didn't know his father any more than his father knew him, and he was alright with closing that chapter to his life in order to start a new one.

Coughing, Severo picked himself up and came after his son.

"No!" Mitsuko darted between them and expertly disarmed him, sending the blade spinning into the air. Then she pushed him off of his feet and defended Vincenzo with her life, her eyes darting around for her next challenger.

Vincenzo looked for help and saw Dominic close, but as he yelled his name, he, for the first time ever, ignored him, and he ran back to the Black Kitten.

Laurence had cornered himself against a man with a Tommy gun. He'd fallen to the doorsteps with his hands covering his head, unable to protect himself against the automatic weapon. He was lucky, in that sense, when Dominic rammed his shoulder into the man and knocked him out against the wall. He twisted the gun from his grip, used it to slap him across the face, and dropped him on the ground, unconscious.

He wiped his sweaty brow and helped Laurence up. Laurence looked like he tried to thank him, but a sob caught in his throat and he just hugged him.

"Keep still, you piece of shit." Mitsuko switched her blade to her non-dominant hand and slashed a red line down Severo's arm, but with now three visible injuries from this fight, Severo hadn't lost any steam. Grabbing a fistful of her hair, he brought Mitsuko down and went for her eyes.

Sylvia, quiet like the modest girl she was, stood up behind him with her arms raised. In both hands, she held a heavy brick from near the Black Kitten's wall. It made her top-heavy, but it didn't stop her from bringing it down hard atop Severo's head and cracking his skull wide open.

Someone hit Vincenzo, but he couldn't be bothered to see who. The impossible had happened, breaking his perception of everything he'd once known, and left him in shock and so incredibly terrified of and in love with Sylvia Belmonte.

His father went down hard. He hit the ground headfirst. He didn't get up. Some of the men stopped to take in the scene, but the customers from the Black Kitten had started fighting back, giving them an earnest row.

Sylvia dropped the bloody stone and backed away. Mitsuko didn't let her waste her shot and turned her towards the car. "Can you please move and stop giving us more to work with?" she yelled at Vincenzo. "On your feet!"

He tried and went for Luis' car. His father hadn't gotten up.

"I tried calling for you," Sylvia told him as they ran. "Were you hurt?"

"No." He checked his side. His stitches were holding up. "Just seeing my father like that, I don't know. I tuned everything out."

"Which one was your father?" Mitsuko asked.

"The man you were fighting with, the one Sylvia bludgeoned."

She chuffed out a humorless laugh and wiped her blade on her shirt. "Damn. I guess you're welcome."

He wanted to look back again to see what'd become of his father, but he forced himself to keep moving forwards. He'd chosen which direction he wanted his life to go, and nothing about that man should've meant anything to him.

What hurt the most was that Severo *did* still matter to him, a lot, but Vincenzo kept running. That was all he could do now.

"Come on!" Luis skirted his car in front of them. "Let's go!"

"Be careful."

Vincenzo turned to Bobbie. He was bleeding from his upper brow, ready to defend his bar until the end.

"All of you," he added. "Wherever you're going, stay safe, and stay together. Keep your community strong."

"We will," Sylvia said. "Thank you, Bobbie. Thank you for everything."

He nodded once, then heard someone shout and ran. "Go!"

Vincenzo helped Sylvia into the backseat. From the other side of the car, Laurence and Dominic got in. Mitsuko took the front seat, doors closed, and Luis pressed his foot on the pedal and drove out of the parking lot. A few brazen men shot at their car, but after only cracking the back window, their group escaped alive.

Mitsuko pushed back her hair, revealing a shakiness she was trying to hide. Laurence was stifling back tears as Dominic consoled him in the back seats. Because of the tight squeeze, Sylvia was sitting partly on Vincenzo's lap. His hand found its way into her sleeve, feeling like it was the safest place to be.

"We're all okay, yeah?" Luis asked. "Dom? Sylvia?"

"I'm okay," Laurence said, controlling himself. "My knees are scraped, but that's it."

"And I'm okay," Dominic said.

"Ask me again when we're on this fucking boat," Mitsuko said. "Where're we leaving from? Manhattan?"

"What about my things?" Laurence asked. "When's our departure?"

"Tomorrow morning," Vincenzo said. "I'll make sure we leave by then. I'll...persuade them, do something."

Sylvia rubbed the top of his hand. "We can drive back to their homes, have them pack like we did."

"It's too risky."

"I need to get my things, Vincenzo," Laurence said. "You have your bags. It's cramped. At least let me get a picture of my family, honestly."

Sensing the boiling hostility, Vincenzo keeled over. "Fine, but give it a few hours, let them think we've gone. Then we'll come back."

"Thank you," he said, then hid his face in his hands. "This's awful. I can't stomach it. I saw people die right in front of me. I don't know what to do."

Sylvia went to open her mouth to encourage everyone that it'd be alright, but Dominic spoke first. "We'll...be okay." He said it carefully, like he was trying to make himself believe it. "Yes, things are bad. They're about as terrible as they can be right now, but we made it. Right now, we're all alive and ready to start anew." He looked to Sylvia. "Right?"

She nodded enthusiastically. "Yes. You're absolutely right."

"And can we talk about your finishing blow?" Luis asked. "Just *wham*! You knocked Severo out good."

"She did?" Dominic asked.

"He was going after Vincenzo," she explained. "I just...acted as one would."

"Well, I'm glad you did," Luis said, "otherwise we might've lost a member of the pack, or I guess it's a litter, and we can't have that happening, can we?"

"No, we can't," she agreed.

——◇——

Luis pulled into a snow-covered alley and parked behind a dumpster. It was close enough to the start of the street to escape, but they were out of sight from the main road.

They sat with the engine running. Luis chatted about who'd thrown the best punches and who'd gotten whom exceptionally well. Laurence went off about how Dominic had taken on

440

three men at once for his honor. Mitsuko polished her blade of Severo's blood.

Vincenzo rested his head against Sylvia's shoulder. Not that he was tired; he was so awake and alert with the world that he needed to cut off and think about nothing but her continued breathing.

At two-thirty, they inconspicuously drove up to Laurence's house. There weren't any cars around, all the neighbors had their lights out for the night. Dominic still went in with Laurence.

"Your own bodyguard," Mitsuko said. "Vincenzo, you'll need to hire a new guard in France."

"We'll be quick," Laurence told them, and glided his hand over Dominic's back. At this angle, Vincenzo couldn't tell who was whose bodyguard.

"What about you?" Sylvia asked.

Mitsuko leaned back in the passenger seat. She pointed at the Moon. "Everything I'll ever need is three thousand miles away across the ocean."

"But don't you want your things? Don't you want anything?"

She shrugged. "I'm not one to keep hold of junk. If we can't show our faces here again, I'd like to start fresh."

"We can make the stop, ma'am," Luis offered.

"I'm good, and don't call me *'ma'am'*." She smiled to herself. "Only certain girls can call me that."

In total, it took Laurence fifteen minutes to pack away his life. They'd left with three bags, all of which Dominic was carrying, and a new change of clothes for the ride. Vincenzo saw books and journals and even two records tucked underneath

Laurence's arm, one of which was his Christmas present from Dominic.

"That was quicker than expected," Mitsuko said.

"It's hard to pack your entire life at a moment's notice," Laurence said, "and I was so worried about someone sneaking in on us. It helped that Dominic had a few things over my house. We got them packed here."

"You had things over his house?" Luis asked.

"J-just within the past few days, yes," he said.

"I'll just sit in my sweaters and knickerbockers, then," Mitsuko said, "or I'll steal some from Vincenzo, huh?"

Vincenzo didn't even recognize she was playing with him until Sylvia giggled. He knew what they were doing, trying to change the subject for their sanity's sake, but he couldn't play along. He wanted to disappear.

The drive through Harlem into Manhattan took almost an hour. Their departure was near Battery Park, just across the river from his father's docks. He saw them through the night fog, some distant world he couldn't return to. Even if his father died from his injuries. Even if every man who worked for him dispersed to Chicago or across the border. He couldn't come back, and neither could Dominic. Maybe Sylvia could, and Mitsuko and Laurence, but he prayed to God that they wouldn't, that they'd stay together forever. He'd never had childhood friends. He wondered if he could have some in his twenties.

Campo hadn't fucked them over. All of their documents got them aboard without much difficulty. Gone was their anticipation and joy about going on a new adventure. Now all Vincenzo wanted was to fall asleep and dream of better days.

Luis watched them board with a fake smile. "Hey, you know, you might be back in a few months. Things might calm down. Your dad might forgive a brick to the head. Eye for an eye, right?"

Vincenzo, halfway aboard, stepped up to Luis. He was taller at this angle. To fix that, he walked down so they were at equal height.

He opened up his arms.

Luis' fake smile cracked, and he lifted Vincenzo to his tiptoes in a hug. Vincenzo gladly hugged back, taking in that cologne he always thought was too strong.

"Thank you," Vincenzo said, "for everything. You didn't need to risk your life for us tonight."

"Oh, shucks, sir. Don't say it like that." He sniffed. "You're such a class act, Vincenzo. You've taught me so much that I'm going to take into my adulthood. And Dominic, man." He took him in and slapped his back. "You're such a good guy. I know you've told me differently. I know you're still going through the worst of it with how you think about yourself. But I'm gonna miss you so much." He kissed both of his cheeks. "I'll take care of *Nonna*, I'll take care of everything."

Laurence called for Dominic to help with their bags. He gave them all a nod before departing.

Luis chewed on his lower lip. "You all deserve so much better than what the world gives you. You should be able to live the way you choose. You and Sylvia, and how you were born to be."

Vincenzo looked up at him. The way he said that...

Luis shrugged. "Two years back, back before we were properly introduced, I guess your dad heard that I was going to be working underneath you. He took me aside and told me about...certain things." He glanced over at Sylvia. "In case it's still all private information, I won't say what he told me, but not once did I ever let that color my perception of you, sir. It did put a lot of things in perspective for me, things I hadn't thought about until then. But now I know why the Kitten meant so much to you and why you have to leave. Oh, I never told anyone," he added as Vincenzo continued gaping at him. "Not one soul."

You knew?" Sylvia asked for Vincenzo.

"Uh, if we're all talking about the same thing, yeah. Between this secret and Dominic's, I've been the harborer of a lot of my friend's confidence over the years. It was hard, it was, but I would've expected the same from my friends."

Vincenzo was lost for words. A year ago, if he'd heard this from Luis, he would've screamed at him and thrown chairs to keep him away. A breach of secrecy, a chink in his armor. Now, though, seeing him battered and exhausted, all for his sake...

He took him in for another hug, clutching him as if he was scared of losing him as a friend. "Thank you," he said again. "I won't forget what you've done for us."

"Don't make me cry, man, come on." He nodded to Sylvia and the rest of them waiting on the boat. "Ya'll better write home, you hear! I want essays and books written about your adventures! I mean it!"

—✧—

The moment the boat departed, Laurence began to cry, and Dominic took him into their room to comfort him. Mitsuko stayed up on the main deck for so long, she needed her coat and scarf to keep warm. Sylvia stayed close to Vincenzo as he would've liked her to, but after last night, he needed to be alone.

"I'll be inside," she said as he left. "Whenever you're ready."

He slouched against the port railing. His breath left him in puffs of white, drifting back towards New York City. He expected to see his father standing at the passing docks, waiting for the Sun to rise before continuing his chase.

Water splashed against the boat's hull. It was so loud, drowning out the city and leaving him on this floating island to a new home to which he was being forced to relocate.

Taking in a deep breath, he leaned his stomach against the coldness of the rail, raised his shoulders, and screamed. All the energy he'd accumulated seeped out from his strained voice. He couldn't remember a time he'd ever screamed, not even when he'd gotten his surgery. When his voice cracked and it dwindled to a soft cry, he felt embarrassed, and silly, and felt like he should've gotten off the boat to find and kill his father and all of his men for what they'd done to him and his loved ones.

Then he caught the Sun rising over the buildings in a soft hue of orange and gold. The city warmed up. It awoke for a new day. Just like it did every day. Just like it'd continue to do forever.

Feeling the energy of New York still inside of him, he wiped his eyes and walked back to his room.

Chapter 37: Runaways

Sylvia concluded that most people probably didn't enjoy travelling. The destination could've been grand, with wondrous opportunities awaiting you on the other side, but getting there, especially in cramped living, proved burdensome on even the mildest of people.

Vincenzo didn't sleep for most of the trip. He kept reading through Campo's letters, making sure he knew everything about their new lives. He'd tried to give everyone their documents to memorize, but Mitsuko had no interest in lying and Dominic and Laurence hadn't picked theirs up from their bedside table. At night, Sylvia heard them arguing across the hall, then at breakfast, they'd be holding one another, comforting each other in their own special way.

Mitsuko seemed the most put together out of the bunch. She was used to packing up everything and skipping town because of her time in the War. And, as Sylvia had guessed, she wasn't too sad about revisiting her wife. She heard her practicing French after every meal.

Sylvia left Vincenzo alone for the first few days. He worked, she didn't want to smother him. To her surprise, she was taking the trip well—she hadn't gone into a panic, she hadn't burst into tears—so she used this tranquility to her advantage.

For one, she wanted to buy everyone gifts. The main level of the boat—she didn't know the word for it—had many places to purchase trinkets. Men were offering prized paintings, gold silverware, and jewelry that caught her eye first. They handled them with white gloves and closed eyes, letting the rich passengers place their prices.

Vincenzo had given her twenty dollars to humor herself on the week-long boat ride, which she hadn't refused. He'd given them to her with glazed-over eyes. The bruise on his cheek had yet to heal, and he deserved something from her that wasn't affectionate touches.

Wiggling herself through the crowd, she examined the jewelry side of the auction, her fingers rubbing apart her dollar bills.

Vincenzo was right where she'd left him, sitting cross-legged on their bed, surrounded by papers weighed down by bundles of cash. He had a hand over his mouth in thought.

"Hello," she said, shutting the cabin door behind her.

"I should've brought more," he muttered without looking up. "Even if we don't split this with everyone, it still won't be enough, and we'll need to convert it, which might look suspicious to the banks. And I can't rope Luis into wiring us money from America. My father's ghouls will be monitoring everything that comes over." He sighed. "We can't even call them."

Sylvia sat beside him and pushed back the curls from his eyes.

"We're screwed," he said. "We're dead and we're screwed."

"No, we're not. Not yet."

"We'll be running for the rest of our lives. You can't just *leave* a gang. What was I thinking? Dominic and I will have targets on our backs until the day we die."

"Surely they have a clause that states a man is warranted to leave the country with his wife and friends if his father ruins everything he holds dear."

She felt his cheeks tighten in a smile. "If such a clause were to exist, I'm guessing most men would pack up their lives and move to, God, Morocco. Or England. Or Brazil." He shut his eyes. "I wasn't meant to do this. I should've never joined."

"If you hadn't, you wouldn't have met me."

"You are, and perhaps will only be, the best woman I've ever had in my life."

"What a thing to say. Imagine how upset *Nonna* would be if she heard you say that."

"You know what I mean." He kissed her hand. His nose brushed against her ring. "I love you."

"I love you, too. I bought you something, you know."

"Bought me something? What did you buy?"

"Since you've always been insistent on buying me things, I felt it was appropriate to repay the favor, now that that part of our life is over." She positioned herself in front of him. "To be honest, I don't know how this works. I've imagined it countless times, but it's different when it's happening to you. Still, I wanted to give you those feelings you gave me."

Before he could question her vagueness, she took out her velvet box and showed him his new engagement ring.

He breathed in like he was afraid it might attack him. It was a simple piece, a silver band with the tiniest diamond in the center. She thought it was elegant, subdued.

"You never bought yourself a ring. I heard some men don't buy one for themselves until the wedding, but I thought it was important for you to have this. I hope you like it."

He looked off to the side, then down at his argyle socks. She couldn't tell at first, as his whole face was red from exhaustion, but as he took in her offer, his face burned with embarrassment until he was noticeably sweating.

She couldn't stop herself in time and laughed. "I didn't mean to embarrass you."

"You...haven't." As he spoke, he covered his face with both hands.

"Your look says otherwise." She tried to pry off his fingers from his face, but he held firm. "Hey!"

"I'm a fool," he confessed. "I should've bought one for myself. Who forgets something so important?"

"We're still learning." Helping him fall back to Earth, she tackled him backwards into bed. "We'll learn how to work normal jobs and be a normal couple. With our new passports and everything, I wonder what we can do?"

He settled beside her. "Buy a house together without strife."

"Adopt children together."

"Get married. Officially. To see you in a wedding veil is all I want."

She smiled. "I'd say that I'd want to see you in a beautiful three-piece suit, but that's already happened."

"I suppose I'll have to find a new way to amaze you."

"I'll await it." She slid the ring onto his finger.

He admired it between them, then against Sylvia's matching one. "Thank you."

"You're welcome."

He interlaced his fingers with hers. Even while he dreamt, his smile never left his face.

———◇———

On their final night together, after Vincenzo made love to her for a sloppy three hours, Sylvia awoke with her thoughts running. Vincenzo had finally fallen asleep on her hand, cuddling it like he would his cat. She didn't mind. With him being so out of it, she was able to pet his face without waking him. If she had, he was doing a marvellous job at keeping still.

Out of all the thoughts chasing each other in her mind, she kept landing on her mother and how she would disapprove of all of this. She couldn't rationalize that her ties had officially been cut. She wouldn't have to deal with her or her cruelty again.

She was officially Sylvia Belmonte, or whatever silly name Campo had chosen for them. Whatever it might've been, she would forever be herself, a frazzled girl who loved to make music and write out her feelings, who ate ice cream when she was feeling down, who was married to one of the most caring men who had the softest of spots for cats and people's feelings.

She leaned over and kissed Vincenzo's lips, to which he generously reciprocated with a smile.

—◇—

When they docked, the clouds had settled low over the port, making the city grey and the air stiff and cold. A glaze of ice had overtaken the outside of the ship. Sylvia bundled up in her mittens and scarf before departing.

Laurence and Dominic were in worse shape than when she'd left them. Laurence's hair was unkempt, Dominic's mustache had grown into a stubbly beard. While Mitsuko came out teething on a toothpick, her other friends looked like they had a longer way to go before they were at peace.

Luckily, Vincenzo had gained a boldness to him. As they gathered on the curb, he came up to Laurence and asked, "What happened?"

Neither of them spoke. Laurence used his turtleneck to cover his mouth.

"It'll help to talk out your feelings," Sylvia encouraged, "but if you don't want to talk about it right now, it can wait."

"Or we don't have to know," Mitsuko said. "Sometimes business is business."

The two men looked at one another for a brief moment before tearing apart. Sylvia noticed that their hands kept reaching out for something they didn't feel right taking.

Laurence licked his lips. "We were talking last night about the future—our future—and what we're going to do next. We have different...not ideas, but different ways we were thinking about moving on. And, in a fit of anger, he..."

He walked off with his arms raised. "Ugh, never mind! I can't handle it!"

Sylvia waited until he was out of earshot before asking Dominic, "What happened, darling?"

"I said...the 'L' word."

"L word?" Vincenzo asked.

"The forbidden L word," Mitsuko surmised. "The word Laurence has never said to any man, the word he refuses to utter."

"Wait, I'm confused. What did he say? Lady? Language? Like..."

Sylvia laughed at Vincenzo's guesses, and he dropped his shoulders as he waited for the punchline. "Wait—*Wait*. Guys, come on, what did he say?"

"I said—" Dominic lowered his voice. "I told him that I love him, and that I'm not going to apologize for it because I've just been run out of my own home with nothing but the clothes on my back and I'm done feeling ashamed for how I feel." He fixed his hat over his eyes. "That's all," he said, his ears turning a new shade of pink.

Laurence flung up his hands again. "Stop it! You can't say that. It'll undo me."

"I think we've all been undone," Sylvia said. "Now we need to weave ourselves into a new tapestry."

"How about new clothes?" Mitsuko said. "I've been wearing the same thing for almost a week. We need new outfits stat."

Mitsuko called for a taxi. Instead of bringing them to their apartments, she, in broken French, sent them to Émeline's house. They needed to reconnect, and Sylvia knew Mitsuko needed to see her and touch her and find herself back with her again before they planned anything. She saw it in her hands, clenching and unclenching on her thighs. She was ready.

Vincenzo was doing the same, but digging his nails into his knuckles. Not wanting him to make any more scars, Sylvia pulled his hands into hers.

"Sleep," she told him. "We'll be there soon."

He ran a tired hand over his eyes. They swarmed with the possibility of everything failing. Then, slipping away from his anxiety, he dropped his head onto her shoulder and fell asleep minutes later.

Sylvia looked out the window. The clouds were parting. Up above, a promising blue sky was welcoming them to their new home.

Acknowledgements

Firstly, thank you to everyone who's supported BLACK KITTEN! Whether it was through reading the weekly updates, posting about it online, sending me messages about the story, or just by word of mouth, I cannot thank you enough for helping me create Sylvia's and Vincenzo's story.

This idea came to me in November of 2017 when I was writing THE CAVES OF ARKEH:NA. I was taking an LGBTQ+ History class in college and we'd just come to the 1920s section of the class. I wanted to expand upon this important history marker that so often comes to us as an elective rather than a critical part in our academia, and breathe new life into it through Sylvia, Vincenzo, and all of their friends' lives. Thank you for letting me achieve that.

Thank you to my family for taking me on many haphazard adventures across New York for fun location scouting, and thank you to all of my generous Kickstarter backers for pledging to make this book a reality. Without your help, I wouldn't have been able to print this little piece of my heart.

Thank you for being a patron of the Black Kitten.

Thank you to all my wonderful Kickstarter backers!

A Pale Lily
Aerylaance.Starlight
akimika
Alana M T
Alex Carpenter
Alexandra G
Alexis Paperman
Alistar Sarkany
Alix Zeligman
Ally P
Alynne
Amber
Amber Killoran
& Maria Castro-Jacobo
Anaxphone
Andromeda Taylor-Wallace
Anon H
Arianne B.
Arnela Bektas
August Quinn
Ava Dickerson
Bracken
Briar Elian
Briseis
Brittany S.
Caitlyn Dean
Chelsey
Chris
Connor Cassie Thomas-son
cym70
D. Kleymeyer

Daisy J. Gallegos
Daniel Clark
Daniel Lin
Derek Frerichs
Dira
Dre Lasana
Echo
Elizabeth Sargent
Ellie Dimopoulos
Emily P.
Ergane
Erik Nieto
Eva H.
Evalyn Roberts
Finn!
G Murray
Gavin Gonya
GeekFeminist
Gilbert Zenner
Gizmo Martin
Hikaru_wins
Hoss Keen
I McClure
Ink Lowrey
J.H. Rose
J.J. Vargas
James Lucas
Jez Gleeson
Jonathan Adam R.
Jorge Oviedo
Kara
Kathryn Coker
Kayla D.

Kimberly Lucia
Kopycat
Kyla
L Wang
Laura CM Morrow
Lauren Geier
Leah Cruz Art
Lenny
Liliana Peixoto
Mahan Harirsaz
Makaylah Hughes
Malena Jensen
Mariah Griffin
Marissa Quinn
Marren MacAdam
Marten van der Leij
Mary Beth Case
Mary Crauderueff
Matt Knepper
Matthew Beckham
McGarrigle
Megan Morrison
Megan Noone
Meyari McFarland
Mochi
Morgan Tupper
Morgane Bellon
Morrigan Proude
Nanija
NoteNatural
Oliver Scholes
Olivia Montoya
Olivia S.
Phillip A
Pixie
Rhiannon Raphael
Rose Chord
Rosyabomination
Ryan Nelson
S. L. Puma
Sal Manzo
Sam
Sapphire
Sara-Maude B.
Sarah Kingdred
Scarlet
Shana Jean Hausman
Shay Holley
Skywings14
Spencer Fournier
Spirit Healer Mage
Stuart Chaplin
Susan S.
Sven "DrMcCoy" Hesse
Syd Hale
Tora
Void Crittenden
William C. Tracy
Zeb Berryman

Melissa Sweeney grew up in a small farm town in Connecticut and got her B.A. in English at Central Connecticut State University in 2017. Before, during, and after that time, she drew and wrote about her characters as a dubious coping mechanism for her anxiety. She currently lives with her cat Gizmo and continues battling on which story to write next. You can follow her on Instagram (@makoninah) or on her blog melissanovels.com.

The duplicate grinned ear to ear, the same grin that so many of Heater Kay's enemies saw just before they died. "My friend, we're gonna get along even better than we thought. Now c'mon, let's get you on your feet."